A KILLER'S CALLING CARD

The entertainment center opposite the bed was closed. The TV dialogue was coming from the bathroom. Fantastic, Amy thought. The lawyer and her husband would arrive just in time to join the home's owner in the master bath.

"Meredith?" she called, expecting the woman to step out the door screaming about invasion of privacy. Only she didn't. "Meredith," she called loudly, one last time before pushing open the bathroom door.

RED. This was the first thing she registered followed immediately by BODY, then BLOOD. The words screamed through her head as she stared at what had been Meredith Chomsky. She was hanging by her hands and her hair from the back wall. Her lower body was sprawled, legs akimbo, in the water, which was red.

It looked as if nails had been driven through her palms, which were shredding from the weight of her body. Her long blonde hair had been yanked up and also nailed, holding her head forward so that Amy could see the sightless red sockets where her eyes had been. . . .

DON'T
BE
AFRAID

REBECCA
DRAKE

PINNACLE BOOKS
Kensington Publishing Corp.
www.kensingtonbooks.com

To Joe
F + 1

PINNACLE BOOKS are published by

Kensington Publishing Corp.
850 Third Avenue
New York, NY 10022

All Kensington titles, imprints, and distributed lines are available at special quantity discounts for bulk purchases for sales promotions, premiums, fund-raising, educational, or institutional use.

Special book excerpts or customized printings can also be created to fit specific needs. For details, write or phone the office of the Kensington special sales manager: Kensington Publishing Corp., 850 Third Avenue, New York, NY 10022, attn: Special Sales Department; phone 1-800-221-2647.

ISBN 0-7860-1805-4

First printing: September 2006

10 9 8 7 6 5 4 3 2 1

Printed in the United States of America

Prologue

She would be dead in less than a day. This knowledge gave him power and he was content to watch her, as he'd watched her for weeks, knowing that everything she did that day would be her last. Like most pleasures, the joy in killing was heightened by the delay.

He followed her as she wound her way to the office down tree-lined streets and through the center of town. An artists' seaside refuge growing mainstream. A Starbucks next to the old gallery, a Talbots edging out the dusty five-and-dime. Old money rubbing shoulders with new. He wedged his forgettable sedan between a boxy Volvo and a new Mercedes and watched her laughing with a friend over lunch at the newest little bistro on main street. She shook her head at the metal dessert cart, smiling regretfully at the young waiter, fighting the eternal battle to lose weight. It was her last chance for the chocolate cheesecake. She should have said yes.

She didn't notice him when she strolled back to the office, pausing to chat with people she passed on the way. Everyone *noticed her. Kisses exchanged in the air, flirty little waves. Nobody noticed him.*

If anyone saw him walking half a block behind her, they wouldn't remember. He had a gift for becoming invisible. Later, after he'd killed her, the town would ask who had done it and why, but no one would remember the man trailing behind.

Even if they did, he'd mastered the art of appearing harmless. A handsome face. A charming manner. No threat to anyone. Don't be afraid.

Chapter 1

Empty houses scared Amy Moran. They seemed to hold the lives and secrets in their walls of all the families who'd ever lived in them and there was something otherworldly, almost ghostly about that. Houses needed people in them to come alive. They needed voices and laughter and light, otherwise they were a shell of something and that something wasn't pleasant.

It was ironic that she'd become a real estate agent, spending her workdays traipsing through the echoing hallways of vacant homes. Sometimes she wondered if their very walls could sense her desperation.

The farmhouse sat back from the road, hidden from the probing eyes of motorists by a grove of hemlocks. Amy turned into the gravel drive and sped up the wide lane, her Camry crunching along beneath the trees, until the house came into view. A classic New England colonial, originally as plain and spare on the outside as its Congregationalist builders. The years and increasingly affluent owners had not been kind. It was now a mishmash of architectural styles. Federalist fanlights, Greek Revival columns, and Victorian gingerbread, all unified by sunflower yellow paint and black trim, gave it the appearance of a giant bumblebee. Strangely enough, it was always featured on design shows about the area.

The buyer, a hale-and-hearty banker with too much money and far too little time to enjoy any of it, hadn't wanted to do the walk-through. "That's what I'm paying you for," he'd told Amy and Sheila. His third wife enjoyed it, though. She wanted the house for weekend parties, though she complained about the location as if Sheila and Amy had done wrong by her.

"I really wanted something on the water," she'd remind them every chance she got. She conveniently forgot that she hadn't wanted the half-a-billion-dollar price tag that went along with property fronting Long Island Sound.

Sheila's large, silver Range Rover wasn't on the drive. Had she gone on to the closing? Why hadn't she called?

Amy picked her cell phone off the passenger seat where she'd tossed it after trying Sheila at the last traffic light. At the same time she had been applying makeup and attempting to get her hair to stay in a hastily formed French twist.

She'd formed the apology in her mind, trying to reduce a chaotic morning and the demands of an asthmatic five-year-old into a simple explanation of how she could possibly be late for this, her first big closing. Not that she'd anticipated any sympathy. Sheila was a single mother, too, though her boys were older now.

Four rings, five, and still there'd been no answer. The light turned green and Amy had tossed the lipstick aside and accelerated with the phone still to her ear.

Seven rings, eight. Finally she'd hung up. Maybe Sheila had her phone off. Maybe she'd be waiting outside the house for Amy.

Only she wasn't.

Amy put the car in park and ran as quickly as her heels allowed up the short flight of wide steps to the large black door. The lock box was still attached to the brass knob, but it was open and the door stood slightly ajar.

Amy pushed it open and stepped inside calling, "Sheila? Are you here?"

There was no answering shout. Amy's shoes clicked loudly on the vast flagstone floor. The curtains were drawn in the large barren rooms adjoining the front hall and the foyer itself was gloomy. She turned on the light switch for the chandelier overhead, but nothing happened.

Swallowing hard, Amy moved forward, trying not to think about how dark it was, taking deep breaths to calm nerves already frazzled by being late.

"Sheila?"

Her voice seemed to echo in the empty hall and then it was swallowed up as she sank into the plush carpeting of the family room that adjoined the kitchen. The rooms were empty of furniture, devoid of everything but the sheer draperies blanketing the windows left by the soon-to-be previous owners.

There were tracks in the carpeting from the vacuuming done by the professional cleaning service, but a thin film of dust had already settled on the bare mantel sunk in the fieldstone fireplace.

The lights were on in the kitchen, a blazing swath across black granite countertops and a gleaming Viking range. Sheila must have been here, Amy thought, looking around for some sign of the older woman. Only there wasn't one. A single drip of water came from the tap and splashed far below in the old-fashioned soapstone sink. The repetitive *plink* was the only sound.

She must have given up on Amy and headed for the office, but would she really have forgotten to close the door on her way out? That wasn't like her. Amy pulled out her cell phone again and dialed Sheila's number, walking out of the kitchen as she did so and back toward the front of the house.

She checked the front door and the floor, looking for a

note, but didn't find one. There was a short gap between punching in the number and the dull ring as it connected. A split second later, a muffled ringing echoed within the house.

Startled, Amy almost dropped the phone. It rang again and again and the ringing echoed back. Only it wasn't the same ring at all. Amy moved toward the sound. It was coming from upstairs.

"Sheila?" she called again, mounting the carpeted steps. The ringing was louder once she was on the second floor. She tried to follow the sound, peering into open bedrooms. From one of the windows she caught a glimpse of something silver. It was Sheila's Range Rover parked behind the house.

Amy stared down at it in shock for a moment while the phone continued its shrill beckoning. Then she tore herself away, following the sound. Not the next bedroom nor the one after that. It was coming from the room at the end of the hall. The one with the closed door.

The knob slipped in her palm, which was suddenly clammy, but the door swung open and there was the phone, practically vibrating on the windowsill. But Sheila hadn't left it behind, because Sheila hadn't left.

She was lying in the center of the floor where a bed had been, her arms stretched out to the sides, with her palms facing the ceiling as if they were catching the small pools of blood they held. Her legs were bound with what looked like her own nylons. Her eyes, or what had been her eyes, stared blankly at the ceiling as if looking for answers.

Amy stumbled backward, her mouth opening in a scream that came out like a siren, gathering momentum. She tripped in the doorway, struggled up and ran, hurling down the stairs and across the hallway, racing from the house as if she were being chased, the ringing of the phone echoing behind her. She didn't stop running until she'd gotten out the front door and made it across the driveway and then she fell to her knees in the clean, sweet grass and threw up her breakfast.

Chapter 2

Detective Mark Juarez was getting his second cup of coffee in the squad room when the call came. The throbbing in his head had reduced itself to a dull roar and with this cup, he hoped to banish it at least until the afternoon.

If anyone had asked him if he'd had too much to drink the night before, he would have answered honestly: yes. Nobody did ask him, though, and nobody would because he was clean-shaven, his shirt was pressed and none of these officers knew the difference between this man and his less hungover self.

"Hey, Juarez," his partner called to him, drawing the name out as if it was unfamiliar to him, and hadn't been the name of the desk sergeant, Mark's father, who'd sat downstairs for more than twenty years running the front show.

Mark turned to look inquiringly at Detective Emmett Black, stirring the coffee with a calmness that he knew irritated the older man. They looked like a study in contrasts, or as another detective had commented, like the before and after on one of those extreme makeover shows. Emmett Black was forty-two and five feet, nine inches, if he stood up straight. Paunchy around the middle and jowly around the face, he tried to comb the remaining strands of his thin blond hair to cover as much of his dome-shaped head as he could. His surname belied the color of his skin, which was a pasty white, and he hid his small, watery-blue eyes behind glasses frames that had gone out of style ten years before.

Mark was twenty-six and six foot, three inches, and hard-muscled from hitting the department gym at the end of every shift. His skin was olive-colored, his jaw was firm, his eyes were a large, dark brown and he was convinced that he could have earned his partner's animosity solely because of his full head of dark brown hair.

"We've got a call, let's go." Black didn't give him any information, as usual treating Juarez like he was a raw recruit. And Juarez responded as he usually did, purposely taking an extra sip of coffee, slowing down just to aggravate the older man. Each knew what the other was doing; it was an unspoken standoff they'd been engaged in since Juarez transferred from the NYPD six months ago.

He grabbed his jacket and followed Black out of the station at a sedate pace, taking the passenger seat in the unmarked because Black needed the testosterone boost that came with being behind the wheel.

"What's the call?"

"Homicide. Out off Tepley Road."

"Victim?"

"White female."

"Domestic?"

"Probably."

They drove in silence for several miles, leaving Steerforth's town center behind them and heading out past the clusters of older frame houses into the Connecticut countryside.

It was a gray, damp morning and Mark couldn't help but contrast the rain-soaked rolling lawns and low stone walls with the city neighborhoods he used to travel. He knew that most people would say that this was prettier, but he missed the encompassing feeling of all those tall buildings of concrete and brick and limestone and the way the streetlights would be reflected in puddles on rain-slicked streets.

Not that there wasn't a city center in Steerforth. There was, after a fashion. Converted colonial boxes turned into high-end office space sitting next to modern corporate headquarters of brick and steel and a state-of-the-art courthouse. It was a small area. The rest of it was residential housing and countryside swiftly being converted into bigger residential housing.

"Shit, that's it." Black passed a driveway occluded by trees and screeched to a halt, backing up and turning into it. At first there was nothing but a long canopy of green, but then Juarez could see an updated farmhouse ahead. One of the properties that the wealthy seemed to cherish for its historical value, paying fortunes to preserve rotting frames and sinking extra money into securing the foundation so it could hold their whirlpool tubs. A real estate sign was leaning askew on the front lawn, a little swinging SOLD sign attached to it. They parked behind two black-and-whites that were blocking in a small blue Toyota Camry.

An ashen-faced woman in a black skirt and white blouse was huddled on the front steps talking to one of the uniforms. October wind was whipping strands of her long, black hair around her face. As Juarez and Black approached, she moved one trembling hand from its grip on her waist to push it back.

Another uniform stopped wrapping yellow tape around the front of the house and intercepted them. He was young, probably no more than twenty, moon-faced and acne-scarred, his gray eyes alight with excitement under the brim of his cap.

"Body's on the second floor. Shot. No sign of the weapon or the perp. Victim's friend found her." He jerked a thumb in the direction of the witness.

"Her name, Officer Feeney?" Black asked.

Feeney took a notebook out of his back pocket. "Moran," he recited. "Amy Moran."

"I'll go on up, you talk to the woman," Black said, moving up the steps without waiting for an answer. He gave the woman an appraising look as he passed her. Mark introduced himself and she extended a trembling hand to shake and he saw that she was very pretty, even sick to her stomach as she clearly was.

"You knew the victim, Ms. Moran?"

The woman nodded, opened her mouth to speak and closed it again, struggling for composure. "Sheila Sylvester," she managed after a minute. "She's a real estate agent. Was a real estate agent." The past tense made tears well in the already red-rimmed blue eyes. "We were supposed to meet here to do a walk-through and I was late—" She stopped and blinked rapidly to hold back the tears.

Juarez asked if she'd go through the house with him, and show him exactly what had happened. They started with the door and she showed him how it was open, the lock box still there but not closed.

She walked him through the house, trying to remember what she'd done. But when she got to the part where she described how she'd found her friend by following the ringing of her phone, she hesitated halfway up the stairs and settled for pointing in the direction he should go.

Every homicide scene required a few seconds for Mark to adjust. Always, there were warring emotions coursing through him of revulsion and excitement. Here was a dead body, someone's sibling, spouse or child. But here, also, was a puzzle, a set of clues that he had to connect to find the bad guy.

A woman's body was lying in the center of an empty bedroom, her skirt hitched up, her panties ripped off and left on one thigh. She'd been arranged face up, her arms carefully out to the sides, her legs tight together, ankles bound by nylons. Her clothes were on, but everything was in disarray: the blouse ripped open, the bra cut open, the breasts spilling out, and the nipples strangely red at the tips.

Juarez pulled on a pair of latex gloves, took a few deep breaths, and joined Black, squatting on the far side of the body near the woman's head. The older cop waited until the crime photographer had taken his pictures and then he used one gloved hand and the tip of a capped pen to gently turn the victim's head to the side.

"Does this look like a gunshot entry to you?" he asked, nodding at a small dark hole with dark red blood surrounding it.

Juarez squatted next to him and peered at the wound. "No. Edges aren't frayed. Ice pick?"

"Maybe, but you'd think there'd be more blood."

Sheila Sylvester had been in her late thirties or early forties, a woman struggling with her weight, Juarez thought, noticing the tight fit of the gray suit she wore. Making good money, or just liked to spend it if the designer label in the jacket flap was anything to go by. Expensive shoes, too, and a nice collection of jewelry—several gold rings with precious stones, large gold hoops in the ears, a chain of some sort just visible around the neck.

"None of the jewelry's been taken," he said. Black grunted.

"Purse is here, too." Black pointed and Juarez saw a black handbag underneath the window. A cell phone was resting on the sill above it and Juarez made a mental note to make sure that it got checked for recent calls. He looked back down at the victim and saw something else. The ring finger of the left hand was missing. The only sign that it had been there was the bloody hole left behind. That was weird. That didn't fit with a typical domestic.

"Did you see this?" Mark pointed at the hand.

Black groaned as he stood up just as the crime scene investigators walked in with their cases. "Getting too old for

this, Black?" one of them said as he set his case on the floor
and knelt to open it. He had hair plugs and a lime-green shirt
and had fashion victim written all over him. Black just gave
him a sharklike grin.

"You dress up for your date, Dubow?" he said, nodding at
the woman's body.

"No, that's for later when he meets your old lady," one of
the other guys said.

They continued the banter, rude jokes about each other
and the victim. From the outside it looked insensitive, unkind. Some of it *was* unkind, certainly disrespectful of the
dead. But they had to do something to deal with what was in
front of them. It wasn't so much the body that they had to
distance themselves from, it was the voices inside that compared this victim to their wives, sisters, daughters, mothers.
The fear that came with the job was what had to be kept at
bay.

It shocked outsiders if they heard it, which they were
never supposed to. But there was the woman in the doorway,
still looking green around the gills, her lips pressed tightly
together as if she was willing herself to be there.

"Shut up," Black barked at the other men. He walked over
to her, took her arm. "You don't need to be here, ma'am."

She resisted being turned away. "I-I need to see her. I
need to say goodbye."

"Not now, not like this," Black said with uncharacteristic
gentleness.

"But I have to." She pulled out of his grasp, moving
across the room, her eyes on the victim. "I was afraid," she
said in a whisper, voice apologetic. "I'm so sorry, Sheila."

Juarez stepped in before Black could react, stopping her
forward progress, but not impeding her view. "How did you
know Ms. Sylvester?"

"She was my friend. I mean, we worked together. We're
both agents with Braxton Realty, but we were friends first."

Her gaze kept stealing from Juarez's face to the body and then jumping back again.

"Do you know of anybody who wanted to harm Ms. Sylvester?"

"No, nobody." She shook her head, hair falling forward again and tucked it back. "Everybody loves Sheila."

This was a standard answer, but Juarez had been a cop long enough to know that nobody is universally loved. "What about her husband?"

"Ex-husband." Recognition dawned; he could see it in her blue eyes. "Okay, I'll grant you that Trevor didn't love her. He was abusive, but that was a long time ago. She doesn't have dealings with him anymore, not since she gave up all claims for child support."

"She had children?"

"Two boys. They're teenagers. Oh, God, what are Michael and Jason going to do?"

The coroner's arrival interrupted them. Rail-thin, with aristocratic features and a manner to match, Dr. Wallace Crane strode into the room clearly fresh from the links, sparing barely a glance at Juarez and Ms. Moran, his interest solely on the body. Juarez turned his own attention toward the coroner long enough to see Black puff up like an angry cock at Crane's arrival. Their mutual antipathy began years before when Black was a rookie and had inadvertently disturbed a body at a crime scene. Crane had treated him like a rank amateur ever since, according to Juarez's father.

"Do you know Trevor's address?" Juarez turned his attention back to the victim's friend.

"No. I know he lives in a nearby town. Lewiston?"

Juarez jotted that down in a small notebook. "What about Ms. Sylvester's address?"

She rattled it off and gave him the address of the realty office as well. Her face was still pale and she was crying again, swiping at the tears in an impatient way. Juarez thought she should be treated for shock, and over her protests had one of the paramedics take her pulse.

"Is there someone I can call? A spouse?"

"No, I'm separated." A blush stained her face as she said it. "I'll be okay."

"We'll get an officer to escort you home," he said. "You've had a shock and probably aren't safe to drive."

At last he got her to concede to having one of the uniforms drive her car home while a black-and-white followed. He walked her to the door and handed her over to the uniforms. Officer Janice Kingston was warm, putting an arm around her, walking to the patrol car slowly. Feeney was clearly disappointed to be given the job of driving the witness's car, but he left his post without arguing.

Juarez looked at the front door. There was no sign of forced entry, no sign that anyone but Sheila Sylvester had been in the house, which didn't mean much. If it was the ex, then she might have let him in, or he might have forced his way in as she was getting the key from the lock box.

He thought about that for a few minutes and spent some time studying the front door, but there were no scuffmarks, no impressions in the wood frame, nothing that gave any indication that a struggle had taken place. He traced what could have been her journey through the house and back upstairs.

"Missing ring finger," Crane intoned in his microcassette recorder. "Signs of vaginal penetration. Bruising." He moved through the stages of his preliminary examination.

Juarez plucked the leather handbag from the wall and began going through its contents, bagging each item separately. Most of it was standard stuff—wallet, keys, Kleenex, breath mints, a train pass, reading glasses and hand lotion. There was a PDA, too, and to this he gave particular attention.

It took only a few seconds to find the address book and then a quick scroll through the listings to reveal that there was no Trevor Sylvester. Of course there wasn't. Did he really expect to see the ex's name in here? He scrolled back up, pausing when he saw Amy Moran's name, and noting her address before he continued.

It was likely to be the ex, despite what Ms. Moran said. It usually was the spouse or the ex-spouse or a neighbor or friend who'd been jilted. Much of police work was paint-by-the-numbers: predictable domestic situations, known-to-victim homicides, break-ins prompted by drug habits, shoplifting, car heists and the occasional ill-conceived bank robbery.

It was the same here as in the city. Oh, the domestic situations were a bit different, say, from what he'd witnessed in housing projects in the city. More muted, sometimes, but otherwise virtually identical. Alcoholic husbands who beat their wives looked pretty much the same everywhere, even if the assailants wore hand-tailored suits and drove BMWs instead of riding the city bus to low-paying jobs.

Most police work involved getting enough evidence to arrest and convict the sons-of-bitches who committed these crimes. It wasn't particularly glamorous, but it sure was satisfying to lock up some of these excuses for human beings.

Still, there was something niggling him about this killing. Something that didn't fit with the usual sort of homicide. That snipped-off finger kept coming to mind.

"Entry point at the base of the head centered near the spinal column," Crane intoned. "Entry wound not consistent with a gunshot. Wound approximately one-eighth in diameter. Perfectly cylindrical suggesting a single thrust that must have impacted with the brain stem. Death probably instantaneous. Limited discharge from the wound, also inconsistent with gunshot."

Black held up a hand to interrupt and Crane switched off his machine. "What about an unusual gun—Japanese model or something high-powered?"

Crane shook his head. "It's just not consistent."

"Ice pick?"

"Possibly. I won't rule that out at this stage."

"Well, what else could it be? It's pretty damn round."

"I'm assuming you'll keep looking for a murder weapon, detective," Crane said. "Now let me do my job."

Black stepped back, arms folded. Juarez moved beside him. "What about the finger?"

Black turned his glare on him. "What *about* the finger?" His voice was heavy with sarcasm.

"Doesn't fit the angry ex-spouse."

"Why? He's pissed, he wants the ring back, and he cuts it off. It's a show of power."

"Then why not leave it. And why so clean? It doesn't look bitten off or hacked off. It looks snipped off. Too neat."

Black grunted. "Well, you can ask this bastard Sylvester that when we catch him. You get the number?"

Juarez shook his head. "General idea of where he lives, though. And that's another thing. Why here, in this house? Wouldn't he confront her in her own house?"

"Christ, Juarez, I'm not this poor woman's drunken ex, how the hell should I know? People do stupid things all the time. It's the reason you and I have a job."

Crane finished describing what he could about the injuries to the victim's hands and shut off the recorder for a moment, stepping to one side to allow Black to bag them.

"Be careful not to lose the blood," he said to Black, who growled in response. Juarez hid a smile.

"Yeah, be careful," he said under his breath, but loud enough for Black to hear him. The older detective shot him the finger and Juarez laughed.

Lab technicians moved in to help. Black attempted to pick up one hand and immediately stopped. "What the hell?" he muttered. Dubow tried to lift the other hand and also stopped.

"What's the matter?" Crane said.

"We can't move her," Black said with astonishment in his voice. "She's nailed to the fucking floor."

Chapter 3

The finger was a beauty. Guy smiled at the cleanly severed bone and removed the ring, careful not to damage the skin around it. The jewelry interested him less, but he polished the band nonetheless, admiring the cut of the marquis diamond before setting it aside.

He attached the finger, nail up, to a small padded clamp, suspending it so that any blood that hadn't been soaked up by the white cheesecloth would spill into a glass bowl. The skin was already changing color and becoming waxy.

He pulled out a small tin box he kept in a drawer and carefully arranged the seven colors of nail polish it held on the desk's surface. The newest, an orangey shade called "Tangerine Mist" was still unopened. He didn't know why Violet had never worn it. Perhaps she'd regretted the purchase, but he opened it now before adjusting the clamp so the nail was horizontal.

Applying the polish evenly took a steady hand and he hummed a little Mozart under his breath. While he waited for the first coat to dry, he fixed a drink.

He tended to follow a very similar routine when he got

home: take care of souvenirs, have a drink, shower, change and eat something light that wouldn't upset his stomach before going to bed. Sometimes he was so excited that he skipped the eating, but he always had the drink.

He fixed a vodka tonic and took a couple of sips before sitting back down to finish his work. A second coat of varnish and the nail was a lovely shimmery orange. As soon as it was dry, he carefully undid the clamps and laid the finger on a bed of cotton in a small cardboard box. He sealed the box and marked it with the name and date and then he opened the small freezer and moved it in next to the others. Things were getting crowded. He might have to invest in bigger storage.

The ring went in a separate box, large, flat and velvet-lined, that he kept in the bottom drawer in his desk. He took a moment to play with the other pieces he'd collected, trying to conjure up tangible memories as he held them in his hands, but there was nothing beyond a pleasant sensation. It had been this way for several years now. He needed to touch flesh to relive those glorious moments.

When everything was away and his drink finished, he retired to the bathroom and took a long, leisurely shower. Violet hated that. She used to hammer on the door to hurry him along. As always when he thought of her, there was a dull pain, like his stomach was being pinched from the inside out. He took a casual measure of it as he toweled off and realized that the ache of that loss was still there, but not nearly as strong as it had been even a week ago.

There was still a picture of her on the nightstand, one of the few things she'd left behind. She was smiling in it, open-mouthed, as if she'd been laughing at something funny, just as she'd been when he first met her. He first spotted her at the movies, caught by the sound of laughter as the lights came up, turning to see hair like a cascade of rippling black water, eyes a shade of blue that made him think of violets and a smile of welcome that seemed brighter when she talked to him.

He called her "Violet" and she called him "Guy." These were their private names for each other. From the beginning he knew that she was his destiny and he proposed on their third date.

She laughed. Afterwards, he would think about that laugh and wonder what it meant, whether it was a warning he should have heeded. At the time he was mesmerized by her and incapable of doing anything but begging for her response. "Yes, Guy," she said finally with a deliberation that told him she was careful. Later he would think she was calculating. "Yes, I'll marry you."

When he got his next paycheck, he spent it all on a spectacular diamond engagement ring. He planned the wedding with her down to every detail, including what sort of flowers they should have: cascades of violets.

He didn't share his avocation with her. Not initially. Like any artist, he was sensitive about opening himself to the public's criticism. Plus, he knew that it would frighten her. Someday, she would be ready, but until then he would practice his skills in private so that it wouldn't disturb her, waiting until she'd gone to sleep before slipping out of their bed to watch the neighbors.

Except she caught him at it. Surprising him one night when he was fingering the jewelry he'd taken, misinterpreting this and his obvious absence from their bed. She thought he was cheating on her and resisted his efforts to explain, albeit obliquely.

She didn't understand, didn't want to understand. Was this the moment he knew it wouldn't work? Certainly, it was a moment of great disappointment. He'd anticipated being able to share the experience with her, but she wasn't open to it. He began thinking of her less as a flower and more as a closed bud.

The dream of the house tied them together. Ultimately, it was the only thing they had left, but that bitch of a realtor intervened at every step. There was always something else to consider, some other expense they hadn't foreseen. Violet thought he wasn't working hard enough, but she didn't know that he worked double the hours of most men. She closed her eyes to the evidence that he was gone at night. She refused to discuss the special room he wanted in the basement. She told Sheila about it, though. He'd overheard her on the phone laughing about "Guy's fantasies."

After it was over, after she'd left him, after he'd finished crying over what he couldn't make work, he realized that this was the cost of his gift. He couldn't have the life of other men because fate had seen to it that he didn't live like other men.

In this realization came strength. If he couldn't be like other men, he'd be stronger. How many athletes over time had eschewed sex because it drained them? He would be like that. He would be stronger without her.

Taking down Sheila had been a pleasure. She was so oblivious to his planning, the selfish bitch. He'd followed her several times in his car and she'd never been aware of him. Getting her schedule had been trivial—a simple phone call. Breaking into the house was only slightly more of a challenge. In disguise at an open house, he'd discovered that the security system was disabled while the house was on the market. All he had to do that morning was pick the lock and that was a skill he'd perfected over the years. It took him barely five minutes.

He'd been waiting for her in the master bedroom, knowing that her own compulsive behavior would ensure that she'd check every room in the house. He'd picked the master bedroom because it was a statement about what she'd destroyed in his own life, though he doubted that she or anyone else understood the symbolism.

He'd stepped out of the shadows in the closet and softly called her name and she'd screamed, just as he'd thought she would. But then she'd laughed, trying hard to be brave, acting as if his being there made some sort of sense and asking what he needed, as if it had been just yesterday that she'd seen him and not months before.

Justice was meted out with careful deliberation, just as it should be. He'd shown her the nail gun and told her how he'd found it at the abandoned building site. He'd silenced her skillfully, holding her trembling head still with one hand wrapped tightly around her blond hair. She'd been scared when she felt the pressure at the base of her neck and he'd relished that fear, pressing his erection against her. He took his time, running the nail gun along her spine, whispering about the damage it could do to her body, letting her believe that maybe he'd let her live.

She begged him. She would have done anything he asked if only he'd let her go, but he didn't. Once he'd shot her, staggering under the sudden weight as her body sagged in his arms, he laid her carefully on the floor. He arranged her to his liking, pinning her to the floor and plugging out her eyes, her breasts. It was all very simple.

Only then suddenly it wasn't. He heard a car door slam and then the other woman was in the house. There'd been no time to leave, no time to do more then step back into the closet.

The shock when he saw her. A complete shock because it was Violet he saw when she came into the room. The same cascade of dark hair, the same oval face, the same dark-blue eyes that seemed to spot him when she scanned the room. He'd almost called out to her, so eager was his mind to make it her, but then she'd stepped closer to Sheila's body, and he'd realized that it wasn't her after all. The eyes were a different shade of blue and this woman was taller, and her gait was different. Still, they could have been sisters, and he couldn't take his eyes off her. He wanted to touch her, to stroke her hair, but she moved too swiftly for him, running from the room when she realized Sheila was dead.

He didn't pursue her through the dark hallways of that house, knowing that she wouldn't welcome his embrace, not there, not like that. She'd be afraid of him and he didn't want that.

He knew she'd phone the police, so he'd left, slipping out the same back door he'd come in, pulling it locked behind him and crossing the barren grass into the patch of woodland that bordered the property. His car wasn't far away and he was a fit man. The nail gun was warm and heavy against his side and he stuck his cold hands into his pockets, whistling in the cold, brisk air.

Lying alone in the large carved bed that had been his and Violet's, he stroked himself as he thought of the dark-haired woman, coming when he relived her cry on discovering Sheila's body. He slept more soundly that night than any other night since his Violet had gone and he woke with a clear sense of what he had to do.

Chapter 4

On the night her marriage ended, Amy had come home from her first solo show to find her husband in bed with another woman.

He was supposed to be working late; that had been his explanation for missing the highlight of his artist wife's professional life. Big case, sorry, honey, but it can't be helped. An explanation she'd accepted because that's the way it was when you were an up-and-coming lawyer who wanted to make partner at a big firm.

Everything else about that evening—the gallery in Soho, the glamorous feel of the red velvet dress she'd worn, the pleasurable sensation of seeing her photography being admired, the glittery lights, the buzz of champagne—all of it had faded in her memory.

Only one image stuck out: Chris tight in the embrace of another woman.

Amy had dropped into an armchair, too stunned to support her own weight. She was sitting in the same chair now, having made it home and in the door, thanks to the Steerforth police. She'd called Braxton Realty on the ride in the squad car, managing to tell the office manager about Sheila and having them postpone the closing. It couldn't happen now anyway, not until the police were done with their investigation. Once the buyers found out what had happened in their brand-new master bedroom, they might very well back out of the deal.

She'd made it as far as her own bedroom before collapsing. Strewn across the bed were the various skirts and blouses she'd pulled from her wardrobe only to discard. It had started as such a promising morning—her first big sale, the beginning of financial freedom for her and Emma. It seemed inconceivable that so much could change in just a few hours.

Amy's whole body was trembling and she kept seeing Sheila lying on the floor. But just as when things with Chris had blown apart, she couldn't quite wrap her mind around what had happened. That couldn't have been Sheila. Sheila couldn't be dead. She couldn't be, but she was.

The ticking of the clock on the wall reminded her that she had to go soon, had to pick up Emma at kindergarten. Today was a half day and Emma looked forward to spending the afternoon with Mommy. Sometimes they walked into town and had lunch at Joe's Diner, a converted train car on the edge of the shopping district, all shiny chrome and red leatherette seats. Or Emma had lunch while Amy nursed a glass of iced tea because she had the money to buy Emma the mac-and-cheese off the kiddie menu, but didn't dare spend the money on lunch for herself.

Today, though, with the closing fresh in her mind, she'd been going to treat them both. Lunch for both of them at Joe's and ice cream to follow.

Not anymore, not now. Amy didn't think she could manage it. She wasn't sure she could manage anything. She pressed a hand against her mouth as a fresh wave of grief washed over her and saw through a blur of tears the smears of dirt and grass stains on the cuff of her blouse.

Change clothes. That's what she should do. She had to do something; she couldn't sit here like this. She had a sudden memory of Sheila talking to her about that, eight months before when she first met her.

"You've got to get up and get dressed every single day," Sheila had preached. "Even if you feel like shit. Even if you feel like it's going to take all your energy just to get vertical, you've got to do it."

She'd followed that advice because it was hard not to follow Sheila, a five-foot, four-inch buxom blond dynamo who loved spike heels, big sunglasses and the color hot pink.

She'd been something of a surprise that first meeting at the Single Parent Support Group. Amy had seen the notice posted at the library and held out for at least two weeks before the desperate urge to have a childfree evening and some adult conversation overcame her fear of attending some weirdo self-help group at St. Andrew's Catholic Church.

For the first few minutes after arriving she wished she hadn't bothered. The meeting was in the basement, a low-ceilinged, poorly lit room with leftover Christmas decorations piled in a corner next to a blue felt banner on a pole that said PREPARE THE WAY OF THE LORD. Milling around the coffee urn and store-bought cookies or sitting in one of the folding chairs set up in a semicircle were some of the most desperate-looking adults Amy had ever seen.

Then she'd met Sheila. Or rather, Sheila had met her. Striding over to say hello, she'd offered Amy her first piece of advice: "Honey, I can tell you feel like crap, but that doesn't mean you have to look like it."

It hardly seemed like an opening that would form a friendship, but the truth was that Amy was looking as miserable as she felt and everybody who knew about her split with

Chris was treating her like she'd crack if they did anything
but congratulate her for the little bit of grooming she managed to do. "You've combed your hair—good job!" So she'd
been stunned into laughing at Sheila's remark and then pouring out her troubles to this little woman in a pink wool suit.

And before long the rest of the group had gathered in the
semicircle to "share," as the facilitator had said, making
Amy cringe. Only it turned out that talking about what had
happened with her marriage had been cathartic. In some
weird way, admitting to a group of strangers that it hadn't
been the first time her husband had cheated on her, that she'd
stayed with him through multiple affairs, provided her with a
feeling of release. They applauded when she talked about
the moment she realized she was finally ready to leave him
and afterwards several people came up to welcome her to
Steerforth.

It was the first time that she'd felt that leaving Chris, leaving the city and trying to start over again in Steerforth, might
actually work.

Of course, she'd been lucky to have the house. On better
days, on days when she thought things might just work out
and she'd be able to support herself and her child, she was
grateful for the house.

It had been a wedding gift to both her and Chris from his
wealthy and eccentric great-aunt. The late Louisa Moran had
been especially fond of her great-nephew and she'd extended
this fondness to his fiancée, though she'd only met Amy a
handful of times. Once, at a family reunion, she'd pulled
Amy close with one arthritic hand and said that she was far
"too good for the likes of this family." A smile and a wink,
the rheumy blue eyes twinkling, but Amy sometimes wondered if she'd known what Chris was really like and had
somehow foreseen the future.

When the shock had worn off that awful night, Amy realized that the house offered an escape. She knew she had to

leave. She'd reached the breaking point in her marriage, but she also knew that she had no money to rent a place of her own in the city. She'd thought of the house and it seemed like the perfect solution.

What she'd quickly learned, of course, was that the charm of an old cottage paled when you had to deal daily with its quirks.

It was two story, but had its own quirky footprint. A gray-blue frame outside that matched the color of the Sound, which could be seen off in the distance from a second-floor window. It had an old stove, radiators that rumbled when the heat came on and the original windows that rattled in their frames.

Slowly, ever so slowly, they made it home. Emma slept through the night in her own room now, instead of dashing into her mother's bed, frightened by unfamiliar creaks and groans. Amy put a welcome mat at the front door and hung curtains from the windows.

Once she'd made some more money, she planned to make real improvements. First, she'd found work photographing houses for Braxton's website. When it became clear that even with this work and other freelance photography Amy couldn't afford to start her own business, much less drag enough clientele away from the local studio to make a steady income, Sheila suggested that she become an agent.

Amy stripped off the soiled clothes and left them on the floor of the closet. She didn't know if she could bear to wear them again. She changed into jeans and a long-sleeved T-shirt and tried to scrub her face clear of tears. She tried to stay focused on the present, on Emma, on moving forward, even though she felt like curling up in the fetal position.

It was Sheila who'd always preached perseverance. Sheila knew when people needed a helping hand, but also believed strongly that sometimes the biggest help was a kick in the pants.

She always told her own story, managing to make a bad

marriage to a meth-using drunkard sound vaguely comical. She even managed to find humor in the horror of fleeing with her two young sons while "the bastard," as she'd dubbed him, was sleeping off another binge after giving her a ritual beating.

"You get through it, sweetie. No man is worth throwing your life away, but I didn't know that for so long."

She'd point to a small, jagged line of white, a faint scar marring the line of her perfectly tweezed eyebrow. "His wedding ring did this to me. The ring I put on his finger, even though he'd hit me the day before our wedding. Chalked it up to pre-wedding jitters, said I was making him feel pressured. When I look at that scar, I remind myself never to be that dumb again."

And she hadn't been. She was the farthest thing from dumb that Amy could imagine, so how had she ended up dead? Had she actually opened the door to Trevor? And why on earth would he have followed her?

None of it made sense, least of all that Sheila, so vibrant, so successful, so kind under that hard-talking exterior, was gone.

It was late and Emma hated it when she was late. Amy didn't trust herself behind the wheel. Her whole body was still shaking and she suddenly wished that she'd taken up the detective's offer of a ride to the hospital. If only there was someone to watch Emma. If only she had someone else to share the burden.

And the thought that she tried to push out, but came at least once a day, reared its ugly head, tearing through her with a pang of hurt that never seemed to go away: *If only Chris were here.*

Emma was standing alone with the young kindergarten aide when Amy arrived. The five-year-old hurled herself at her mother, yelling, "You're late!" The fierceness of her hug was an accusation.

"I know, I'm sorry," Amy apologized, holding her daughter close and looking up to include the young woman in her apology. The aide was already walking back into the building.

Amy took Emma's Disney Princess backpack and listened to her chatter about what letters they were working on and how badly behaved the boys were in class. Her little hand felt warm and comforting. Alive. Amy clutched it, until Emma pulled away.

"Mommy, you're hurting me." She skipped out of reach, small ponytail bobbing, and threw a smile back over her shoulder at her mother.

"Emmy," Amy called, using a nickname she knew her daughter was particularly fond of, "slow down and walk with me."

She needed to hold her daughter's hand; she needed the weight of it to ground her. It would be okay, things would be okay. With every step she repeated this mantra, but another one repeated itself: *Sheila is dead, Sheila is dead, Sheila is dead.*

There was a hush when Amy walked into Braxton Realty the next morning. Agents paused in their morning rituals to stare, their faces a mixture of sympathy and interest.

"I didn't think you'd be in today," Douglas Myers said, sidling over to her with his usual proprietary air. "Are you sure you're up to this?"

"Yes, thanks." She managed a brittle smile. "The houses won't sell themselves."

He laughed. "How true. But surely you can spare a moment to talk about Sheila. Did you see her? How was she killed?"

"I've got work to do, Douglas." Amy pushed on toward her desk and thanked God he didn't follow. She had to swallow a few times to keep her stomach down, anger and bile rising in equal amounts.

The office strove for elegance with its reproduction Georgian furniture and faux dynasty vases, complete with miniature orange trees.

The trees were dusty though, and the striped silk of the small sofa in the entryway bore the outline of a soda stain. The potpourri couldn't quite overtake the faint odors of microwave popcorn and takeout Chinese.

The closing had been postponed indefinitely, a note on her desk informed her. "In light of what happened," the buyers wanted to renegotiate price. Amy had never smoked a cigarette in her life, but felt desperately like starting. Rummaging in her desk, she found a stick of gum and popped it into her mouth.

"Amy, we're so sorry." Amy looked up to see Claire Rubinstein, the office manager, standing at the edge of her cubicle. Her angular, immaculately powdered face wore an expression of mourning and determination, gray eyes shrewd behind the small reading glasses.

"We were horrified by the news, just horrified."

Claire had a bad habit of talking in the royal "we," although Amy suspected that she truly believed it was her duty to speak for the entire office.

"I see you got the info about the closing," she said. "The Towles weren't pleased, of course, but who can blame them? None of us were expecting this, I told Mr. Towle."

"Least of all Sheila," Amy said dryly and Claire blinked at her and gave a nervous laugh, hands rising to fiddle with her glasses.

"Of course," she said, regaining her composure. "Do the police have any idea who did it?"

"Maybe her ex. That's all I know."

"Trevor? I thought he'd stopped bothering Sheila years ago. Were they having any issues with the boys?"

"I don't think so."

But she didn't know. Had Sheila been struggling with Trevor over something new? What issues had Sheila been dealing with that Amy didn't know anything about?

Suddenly Amy wanted to know. The shock and sorrow she'd been experiencing gave way to a fierce determination to find out who had killed Sheila and why.

Sheila practically lived at the office when she wasn't home with her kids. Amy hurried over to the empty cubicle across the room.

There was nothing immediately obvious. Framed photos of Michael and Jason sat in one corner, next to a large pink African violet and a mug that said WORLD'S GREATEST MOM.

"Such a lie," Sheila had declared once while she was sipping coffee from it. "I'm hardly the world's greatest mom. Who is? They should make real ones like, 'Hanging on to Sanity Mom,' or 'Only Screamed Once Today Mom.' "

Amy smiled, remembering, but tears filled her eyes. She sat down at Sheila's desk and opened the center drawer, looking for an address book or anything that might have Trevor's number.

There was nothing other than notes on Sheila's listings and a record of conversations with possible clients. That was it, aside from a pack of breath mints, engraved stationery, pink paper clips and a small sheaf of thank-you notes from happy homeowners.

In the left-hand top drawer was a padded manila envelope hand addressed to Sheila. There was no return address. It had been opened but put back in the drawer. Amy pulled out a smaller, flat manila envelope she found inside, fastened only by a copper butterfly clip. Flipping it over in her hands, she recoiled from the single word written in red ink on the other side: BITCH.

Chapter 5

Mark Juarez woke confused and hungover, stunned for a moment to find himself in his childhood bedroom, feeling as if he'd somehow gone back in time, until he remembered where he was and why.

The insistent *tap*, *tap*, *tap* of his father's cane was what had woken him and he struggled out of bed and down the hall to the master bedroom. Oscar Juarez was lying against a few rumpled pillows, looking as large, strong and crotchety as ever, despite the stroke that had left him incapacitated.

"Hey, Dad, I'm up. Need to use the bathroom?"

His father opened his mouth to speak, but the sound that issued forth was garbled at best. The single nod was clear enough and Mark moved to his left side, the side that he couldn't move, and helped to shift him to a sitting position. Then began the slow, agonizing step-drag that led to the bathroom. His father leaned on his cane with his good right arm and allowed his son to support him on the other side, taking one good step before dragging his useless left leg and foot into position with the other. He was sweating with the effort. Mark could feel it through the thin cotton of the pajamas, and see it in a sheen across his father's unshaven face, but Oscar didn't make a sound. Once a Marine always a Marine, Mark thought as he helped his father into the small bathroom, lifted the seat of the toilet and averted his eyes.

A faint blush spread across Oscar's face while he fumbled to free himself and pee. He'd always been a proud man and having to rely on his youngest child and only son was hard.

When he was safely back on the side of the bed, Mark got together the shaving cream, basin of water, mirror and razor that his father needed and sat watching his father shave just like he had when Mark was a boy. Oscar's right hand moved swiftly and surely over his face and Mark wondered if he found pleasure in still being able to perform that small task.

It was the sort of thing he didn't talk about with his father, though, because Oscar wouldn't discuss the stroke except in terms of his recovery. He didn't discuss emotions, he didn't discuss what having been forced to take early retirement from the police force felt like or the double humiliation of watching his wife pick up longer hours at her nursing job.

He had, however, scolded his son for leaving a good job with the NYPD to come home and take care of him. He'd written a terse note in the hospital ordering his son to return to Manhattan and his job, but Mark had politely ignored it. He'd made his decision and he'd severed his ties with the city. It was too late to return.

He brewed a strong pot of coffee while making his father breakfast and after bringing it to him, he took a cup with him into the bathroom. He gulped it down while he raced through his own shave and shower, hurrying so he could be at his desk by eight-fifteen. The deep gray circles under his eyes weren't going away. Too many late nights in Steerforth bars. He hadn't returned home last night until after one and then only to lie awake, trying not to think about exactly what he'd left behind in New York, while staring at the border of cowboys on horseback that circled his room.

His mother arrived home as he was knotting his tie.

"I'm here!" Elena Juarez called up the stairs, just as she did every morning, as if they couldn't hear her unlocking the back door of the small house. She hurried up the stairs to see them, though Mark knew that she was tired from her long shift at the hospital.

She checked his father first. Mark heard the murmur of conversation before she appeared in the doorway. He was combing his hair in the mirror above the dresser, having to stoop a little to see the top of his head.

She stood on tiptoe to kiss his cheek. "Did you have breakfast?"

"I'll get something on the way in."

She frowned and her hands moved to her hips. "Breakfast is the most important meal of the day."

Mark grinned. "Thank you, Surgeon General. Any other advice?"

"Fine, don't listen to your mother," she said, but she smiled, too. He leaned down to give her a hug.

"Dad's had his breakfast," he said as she walked him to the door. He put on his holster and slipped his jacket over it. "You get some rest, too, okay?"

"Sure, sure," she said, waving him off. "Be careful."

Detective Black was already at his desk, wearing his usual cheap suit and loud tie, looking as rumpled as if he'd slept there, though Mark knew that he had a wife and two kids he went home to every night. He grunted at Mark in greeting and said, "Crane called. Confirmed cause of death."

"Nail gun?"

"Rapid discharge, fired at close range. Apparently it punctured the brain stem."

"Well, there's a first."

"That's why so little blood, too. Crane says the nail acts as a dike, holding back the blood. That's what's saved some construction guys who've shot themselves by accident."

"This wasn't an accident."

"No shit, Sherlock. Just saying that she might have lived if he'd fired even slightly to the left. According to the genius, that is. But the perp fired more than once and he was determined to kill her. I don't think she had a chance."

Black picked up a slip of paper from his desk and waved it at Mark, his smile wider. "Oh, and your lady friend called."

Mark felt his face flush with color. "What lady friend?"

"Victim's friend. Pretty chick with the dark hair. She called and asked for you. Specifically."

"What does she want?"

Black shrugged. "Call her and find out. Probably a date. She goes for that Latino charm." He faked a Spanish accent and a few of the other cops milling about laughed.

Mark gave him the finger and dialed the number, turning his back on Black and the room. He stared out the windows at the parking lot, watching the chief pulling up in his Jaguar.

The voice that answered was nervous, but determined. "Is this Detective Juarez?"

"Yes, ma'am. What can I do for you?"

"Service me, please," Black hissed in a falsetto behind him. Mark resisted the urge to deck him and waited for Amy Moran to get to the point.

"I found something. In Sheila's desk. I think you need to see it."

The word BITCH on the envelope had stunned her, but it was nothing compared to the shock Amy felt when she saw the photos inside.

They were all of Sheila, six black-and-white shots ascending from partial to full nudity. It wasn't clear if she knew she was being photographed, but how could she not have known? They were taken in her bedroom. Amy recognized the bed, the dresser.

Were these taken by some disgruntled lover? By Trevor? There was a coldness to the photos, a starkness that made the hair on Amy's neck prickle.

She checked the envelope, but there was no letter or note, no explanation of any kind beyond that one awful word in red.

She shuffled through the photos a second, then a third time, forcing herself to look with a dispassionate eye, trying to figure out who had taken them and why.

At first she thought that they'd all been taken at one time. Looking closer, she realized that Sheila's clothes and hair were different in the two where she was partially dressed and that the nude shots had been taken from different angles.

"I think whoever took them was in her house," Amy told Detective Juarez when he laid the photos out on a table at the police station. She'd brought both envelopes in at his request, telling only the receptionist at Braxton that she was leaving, and not specifying where. She didn't want to reveal the photos to anyone else. It seemed like a violation of Sheila to have them displayed at all.

The detective didn't seem disturbed by them. He'd ushered her into a room that had only a plain industrial table and chairs as furnishing. It was a sharp contrast to the room at the realty office where she'd carried the photos after taking a quick glance at them. She didn't want anyone else to see them and she'd locked herself in one of the conference rooms. It was designed to give clients an impression of wealth and luxury, with a mahogany table and chairs, plush carpet and some nouveau impressionist paintings in gilt frames on the wall. It was quite a contrast to this room, where there was nothing on the walls except a large industrial clock, which ticked the seconds loudly as the detective silently examined both envelopes before carefully laying the photos out.

He'd donned latex gloves before accepting the envelope from her and Amy realized belatedly that she'd touched all of the pictures without thinking of them as evidence.

"It's okay, we'll just take your prints to eliminate them," the detective said. "Why do you think the photographer was in her house? Couldn't these have been taken with a tele-photo lens?"

Amy let go of the strand of hair she was nervously twist-ing and leaned across the table. "These, yes," she said, point-ing to the two shots where Sheila was partially clothed. In one, she was obviously about to unhook her bra, and in the other she was free of a bra and pulling down her panties. "These could probably have been taken outside a window. But not these." She indicated the other photos, where Sheila was lying on a bed, doing some sort of exercise or stretching. In all of these she was naked. "I think these are in her bed-room and I think they were taken there."

"So she was posing?"

"I don't think so. These don't look posed to me."

"Really?" The detective tapped the one where Sheila looked like she was posturing in front of a mirror. "What about this one?"

"Well, she was posing in that, but I don't think she knew her picture was being taken. If she was posing for someone, she wouldn't have sat like this." Amy pointed to the one where Sheila was lying on the bed. "Or done this stretch." She indicated another one where Sheila's legs were spread at an unflattering angle. "This isn't the way people pose, not even for erotica."

Amy looked up to find the detective appraising her. "How do you know so much about this?" he said.

"I'm a photographer," she said, then realized he knew her

only as an agent. "I mean, that's my real career. Not that real estate isn't a real career." She stopped talking, feeling idiotic.

Juarez nodded. "It's what you do to pay the bills."

"Exactly."

"I have friends who do that. Musicians and actors, but they take dozens of other jobs—waiter, file clerk, telemarketer."

"Yeah, that's it exactly. It's hard to make a living in the arts." She was surprised and then embarrassed that she'd assumed that a police officer wouldn't be cultured. "Are your friends working in Steerforth?"

"No, Manhattan." He turned abruptly back to the photos. "Any idea when these were taken?"

Amy shook her head.

They were interrupted by a knock on the door. The other detective who had been there yesterday stuck his head around the door.

"Crane wants to see us."

"Can you handle it? Tell him I'm with a witness?"

"I'm not your errand boy, Juarez." The other man cackled, flashing his teeth at both Juarez and Amy in what could be construed as a smile, though it looked more like a sneer.

Detective Juarez's jaw twitched, but he said nothing, gathering up the photos quickly but carefully and sliding them back into the envelope. "Thank you for bringing these in," he said to Amy, forcing a smile and she understood that she was being dismissed.

He handed her over to an older, burly cop at the front desk who looked like he could crush her, but whose pudgy hands gently cradled hers as he took her fingerprints.

When Amy left the station, she hesitated before driving back to the Braxton office and instead took a detour.

The noon Mass was almost over at St. Andrew's Church and Amy slipped into a pew in the back. She wasn't Catholic, hadn't been to a church service in years, but she knew this building well, at least its basement, and the small, white-haired priest who was leading his congregation in prayer.

She closed her eyes and let the words and the music rush over her, thinking of Sheila and of what she'd suffered. It wasn't fair. She'd worked so hard to get beyond her past, to become more than just another single mom, just another victim of domestic violence. Sheila didn't like labels or pity. She used humor to block emotion, sure, but she'd also used it as a defense against the very real temptation of self-pity.

Amy felt her throat tighten and tears gathering behind her eyelids. At that moment she would have given almost anything to hear Sheila's big, brassy laugh. What was she going to do without her? It was strange that there could be people you knew for such a short time who could have such a tremendous impact on your life. She'd known Sheila for less than a year, but meeting her had been like meeting a long-lost friend or relative, someone you'd always had with you.

Suddenly the church felt too close. Amy had to get away. She slipped out a side door and into sunshine, tilting her head back to feel the warmth on her face as she blinked back fresh tears. An accented voice called her name and she turned to see Father Michael pulling away from the small crowd of people filing out of the building.

"I heard about Sheila," he said when he reached her, breathing heavily from his hurry. His vestments billowed about from the wind and his cheeks were ruddy. He looked like central casting's version of the Irish parish priest and had a good sense of humor about this. There wasn't a hint of humor in his voice when he said, "May she rest in peace. She was a good woman."

"I'm sorry I didn't call and tell you myself. I was too upset yesterday to phone everybody."

He waved her apology aside. "Of course you were. It's quite a shock. I'm so sad for her boys."

"Yes. Did she ever talk to you about their father?"

"Her ex-husband?" He sounded surprised.

Amy nodded and Father Michael pondered this for a moment. "Not that I recall. No more than she ever said about him at meetings. I know about the domestic violence, of course. I think she was open with everybody about that, wasn't she? But I never counseled her about her dealings with him. Except, maybe once—"

"When was that? Recently? What about?"

"I take it the police are interested in talking to Mr. Sylvester?"

"Absolutely."

"Horrible. It's a terrible thing for a man to beat his wife. But to kill the mother of his children—may God have mercy on his soul."

Amy nodded, urging him mentally to get to the point, feeling a sick eagerness to hear something that would bring Trevor Sylvester to justice.

"He wanted the boys to spend Christmas with him and she wasn't sure. They wanted to go, I gather, but she didn't want them around his drinking and she didn't want to be around him and I gather that was the time of year when he made his pleas that she come back."

"So what happened? Did she let them go?"

He crossed his arms over his chest to pin his vestments down and thought for a moment. "No, I don't think she did. I'm not entirely sure, but I do know that I counseled her not to give in to him. That it was a risk to the boys and to herself and she shouldn't allow herself to be persuaded by the sentiments of the holiday."

And Sheila would have listened to this, Amy thought. She wouldn't have been swayed by Trevor's sweet talk and pleas. She was tough, she was strong. But she hadn't been strong enough.

"Well, I'd better get back to work, Father. I just wanted

you to know that the police will probably be contacting you. They asked me for a list of everybody that Sheila knew and I had to give them the names from our group."

"I'd have done the same," he said, as reassuring as ever. Then he did something uncharacteristic and reached forward, capturing her in a brief hug. "Take care of yourself, my dear, and Emma."

She was startled for a second and then returned it, clasping him briefly before both of them withdrew. He was quite red in the face and she wondered how often he had any physical contact with anyone whatsoever.

"Is there still a meeting tomorrow?" she asked, moving them back to comfortable ground.

"Yes, yes, I thought everyone needed to meet. I saw no reason to cancel."

She said her goodbye and walked back to her car. Halfway there, it occurred to her to ask whether Sheila had ever mentioned anybody else bothering her, and she retraced her steps to the side of the church but stopped short when she saw that Father Michael was in conversation with someone else. The man was wearing a dark blue windbreaker, though it didn't look as if it was protecting him from the cold. His shoulders were hunched and he didn't appear to be listening to whatever Father Michael was telling him. Then the priest put a hand on his arm and Amy was startled by the other man's sudden move to knock it off. He said something, scowling as he looked the priest in the face before turning abruptly and stalking off.

Father Michael looked after him and then turned and walked rapidly back toward the rectory. The moment to catch his attention was gone and Amy walked back to her car, wondering what that had been about. The other man had seemed genuinely angry about something and it was hard to imagine benign Father Michael inspiring that sort of emotion in anyone.

She returned to Braxton Realty to find the office in an uproar. Apparently she'd missed the police visit and the two less-than-polite uniform cops who'd insisted on accessing Sheila's computer files.

"I tried several times, very patiently, to explain to these—these lug heads that I couldn't just unplug the central computer and give it to them, that disconnecting it meant shutting down the entire system, but they were too stupid to understand." Alison Paddington, the IT manager, ran one hand repeatedly through her short red hair as she explained to Amy what had happened.

"We were down for over two hours and we're still offline. I don't know how those idiots managed to screw up our Internet connectivity, but they managed it."

"Did they take anything else?"

Alison raised her eyebrows in a look clearly meant to imply that what else could possibly be worse than the computer system crashing, but she managed to summon a reply. "All Sheila's files. All the office files on her clients. They went through everybody's files, for that matter, and then they insisted on personally interviewing everybody here. Do you know that they actually expected Bev to phone all the agents who weren't here and bring them in to be interviewed?"

"What were they asking?"

"How well did we know Sheila? Did we know who might have wanted to hurt her, did we have an office photographer, etc. . ."

"Did they single out anybody?" She tried to sound casual, but it hadn't occurred to her that it might have been someone other than Trevor. She thought of smarmy Douglas, trying to picture him being angered enough by Sheila's behavior toward him to kill her.

"Actually, they were asking a lot of questions about you." Alison looked faintly apologetic. "I told them you often took photos of the houses."

"That's what they were interested in?" Anxiety uncurled in her like a small, new leaf. "They can't possibly think that I took those photos."

"What photos?"

Amy caught herself. "Did they want anything else?"

The other woman shook her head. "I think they were just trying to find out as much about Sheila as they could. I heard she was stabbed multiple times. Is that true?"

"No."

Alison waited for her to say more, an expectant look on her face that sickened Amy. Was this what it was like to be the friend of someone who'd been murdered? Had she been this insensitive at one time? Only she couldn't think of a single time before now when she'd even been an acquaintance of someone who'd been murdered.

She was spared from saying more by Beverly, the middle-aged receptionist waving frantically. "Your school's nurse just called. Emma's having an asthma attack!"

Chapter 6

The Steerforth coroner's office looked from the outside like a fairly nice hotel. The flowerbeds flanking the concrete walkway were overflowing with mums in autumnal colors. Probably the only living thing in the place, Juarez thought as he followed Black in through the front doors.

There all resemblance to a hotel abruptly faded as one's nostrils were assaulted by the smell of cleaning fluids and formaldehyde.

"He's waiting for you downstairs, boys." The paunchy security guard sitting at the front desk barely glanced up from his *People* magazine. He took another bite of an enormous meatball hoagie, apparently impervious to the odors that made Juarez's appetite curl up and die.

They took the elevator down to the basement and came out into a dimly lit hallway slightly warmer than a freezer. Wallace Crane poked his head out of an open doorway and beckoned to them.

"Like we haven't been here enough times to figure out which room he's in," Black muttered. "Pompous jackass."

What was left of Sheila Sylvester was lying on a stainless-steel examining table illuminated by powerfully bright dangling lights. The coroner was wearing a lab coat, which was immaculately white except for a small constellation of rust-colored spots just above the waist. Juarez, who was used to seeing victims of gunshot wounds and visiting crime scenes splattered with blood, nonetheless felt squeamish and looked instead at Crane's face.

There were two bright spots of pink on the coroner's pale cheeks and a small smile played on his thin lips. "I've got something very interesting—very interesting indeed—to show you, gentlemen," he said with the air of a magician about to perform a spectacular trick. Juarez half expected him to rub his hands together with glee, and perhaps he would if it weren't for the gloves encasing them.

"What?" Black's bluntness was deliberate, but Crane seemed to take no notice.

"I told you that the murder weapon was a high-speed, rapid-fire nail gun—have you found it yet?"

"Yeah, it was delivered this morning with a big bow on top and a note from the murderer thanking you for figuring it out."

Crane narrowed his eyes at the older detective for a long moment as if he were a specimen he longed to be able to cut open on one of his tables. Then he gave a dry laugh. "Crudely amusing, detective. No doubt you missed your true calling on the comedy circuit."

"You found something else?" Juarez asked, stepping casually in front of Black to prevent a possible lunge at the coroner.

"Yes, and I thought it best that you see it for yourselves." He stepped closer to the examination table and removed a metal basin from one of the equipment tables nearby.

"While examining the deceased's internal organs I found this." He reached into the basin and held up a tiny brown figurine.

"What the hell is that?" Black said, but he, like Juarez, was already reaching for gloves from the box on a counter. They took turns examining it. It was a crudely formed plastic statue.

"It's St. Joseph," Juarez said, noticing the faint hammer and carpenter's square the robed and bearded figure was holding in his folded arms.

"I believe realtors use these as some sort of good-luck totem to help them sell homes," Crane said.

"Where was it?" Juarez asked.

"In the vaginal cavity very close to her uterus."

"He'd shoved it in her twat?" Black said, oblivious to Crane's wince. "That is one angry son-of-a-bitch. Before or after?"

"Excuse me?" Crane looked puzzled.

"Before or after he killed her?"

"I can't be entirely sure, but I believe it was placed there postmortem."

Juarez felt his body prickling with the tension that always seemed to precede major cases. "Was there anything else?"

"No more statues, if that's what you mean." Crane chuckled at his own humor.

"I mean anything else out of the ordinary."

"No, not especially. She didn't appear to fight whoever attacked her. There's no skin under the nails and all the nails are intact. Minimal bruising, mainly of her wrists. I think he surprised her and it was done very rapidly."

"What about the missing ring finger?"

"Snipped off, not cut. It's a clean cut, not jagged. Probably pruning shears." He bagged the small statue and handed it over to them. "Oh, and there's one more thing, gentlemen. There were traces of dirt on the statue."

"Anything unusual?"

Crane shook his head. "Trace amounts of fertilizer, but it looks like what the average homeowner would use on their lawn."

Juarez took large gulps of fresh air when they exited the building a few minutes later. "I don't think it's Trevor."

"Because of the statue? I think that fits him to a T."

Black pulled out a cigarette and put it in his mouth, taking imaginary puffs. His own personal nicorette system to force himself to quit.

"The nail gun, the finger, the statue—this has the earmarks of a skillful killer," Juarez said.

"Maybe. Or maybe it's just a pissed-off, drunken ex."

"What about the statue? What message is he sending with that?"

"That he's angry and he wants to hurt her."

"Then why do it postmortem—"

"Crane wasn't sure about that—"

"—and why kill her with a nail gun? She was killed pretty quickly, Crane said. That doesn't sound like an angry ex to me."

"Which is why he used the statue. He wanted to kill her fast and he needed the satisfaction of hurting her." Black sounded pleased with his theory. He eyed his partner knowingly. "Missing the excitement of the big city? Looking for some big-time killer? You hoping to find out that she was some mafia bigwig's mistress?"

"I think we need to keep an open mind and consider the possibility of other suspects."

"What we need," Black said grinding the unlit cigarette out under his foot, "is to find our boy Trevor."

As soon as Amy pushed through the doors into the school, she saw the school secretary waiting for her.

"She's in the nurse's office, Mrs. Moran," the older woman said, hustling her down the hall to another door.

Emma was lying on a leather chaise with an oxygen mask being held to her face by a uniformed paramedic. Another paramedic was kneeling next to an equipment case. Emma's eyes were huge, her face pale, and she looked very, very small.

"Mommy's here," Amy said, pushing through the small crowd of adults clustered around the couch and dropping to her knees so she was eye level with her daughter. She took one of Emma's tiny hands and pressed kisses on it. "How are you doing, sweetie?"

" 'Kay, Mommy." The sound was muffled but clear.

"She's stabilized," the paramedic sitting next to her said. "It was fairly mild. Levels at eighty percent but she's had oxygen for ten minutes and I think the levels will rise even further."

"Thank you," Amy said, never taking her eyes off Emma.

"I don't know what happened, Mrs. Moran." The kindergarten teacher sounded flustered. "She was fine at lunch, maybe a little wheezy, but nothing out of the ordinary. During quiet time it just suddenly got a lot worse and she couldn't seem to get anything from the inhaler—"

"Mrs. Strohmeyer got Emma straight to Nurse Hannigan who immediately called the office and we called 911," the principal's gravelly voice interrupted. "Thanks to their quick action, help got here right away."

Clear in her tone was that the school had done nothing but help Emma and they weren't responsible for her state.

"Thank you," Amy said, turning to acknowledge all of the women, "but why wasn't my cell phone called? You have that number in the file, right?"

"I did call that number," the secretary said, "but it put me through to your voice mail. I left a message there, too."

Amy suddenly remembered that she'd switched it off instead of turning it to vibrate when she stopped off at St. Andrew's. Stupid, she thought, mentally berating that thoughtless action. She was usually so careful with her cell phone— she had to be. Sheila's death had thrown her off balance.

What if she hadn't been at the realty office when the school called? The thought made her stomach lurch.

"This was a pretty severe attack," the paramedic handling the equipment said. "But Ryan's great with kids."

"Thank you," Amy said, lifting her head to look at both paramedics. The sandy-haired woman loading the equipment acknowledged her with a smile and after a moment so did the dark-haired man named Ryan. He smiled at her, and a small scar above one of his eyebrows quirked along with his mouth.

"Let's see how you're doing now, cutie," he said to Emma, gently pulling the mask off her face. He gave her the peak flow test again and carefully watched the dial, calling the numbers out to his partner.

"That's well within the normal range," he said to Amy, "but I'd monitor her for the rest of the day and have her take it easy." He ruffled Emma's hair. "No trapeze practice today, okay?"

"Trapeze?!" Emma giggled. "I'm not in the circus."

"You're not? I thought you were a trapeze artist. I must have you confused with someone else. Are you the ring leader?"

"No!"

"Lion tamer?"

"I'm not in the circus!"

"Oooh. You're not a clown, are you? Because you can't do any clowning today either."

Emma was convulsed by giggles and Amy tensed for a moment before realizing that Emma was breathing easily. She also realized that Ryan was watching her closely and that making her laugh hard had been his intention so he could see just where she was post-attack.

"You seem to know a lot about asthma," she said while he was packing up. The nurse was busy recording the incident for her files, while the principal and her secretary had returned to their offices. Mrs. Strohmeyer had gone with Emma to fetch her backpack and coat so Amy could take her home.

"One of my cousins had asthma," the paramedic said. "I learned a lot about it."

"Well, thank you so much. I was terrified when I got the call."

"She's a strong little girl. She might grow out of it."

"Do you really think so?" It was Amy's secret desire, but one that she was afraid to give voice to with the doctors, terrified that they'd tell her that there wasn't a chance.

"She might. It happens."

Emma came back, hand tightly clutched in Mrs. Strohmeyer's. Now that the danger had passed, Amy could appreciate just how flustered the unflappable teacher had been. Under other circumstances, Amy would have been more amused, but she did take a small amount of pleasure in having the upper hand for once. Until Mrs. Strohmeyer and the school nurse pulled her aside.

"Maybe Emma needs a little break from school," the kindergarten teacher said, while the whey-faced Nurse Hannigan nodded enthusiastically.

"A break?" Amy looked from one woman to the other, not immediately understanding.

"Kindergarten is optional, you know. Emma might do better at home."

Amy's own chest tightened. "At home," she repeated.

"Yes. That way she could have the one-on-one attention she needs."

"I think Emma needs kindergarten and she definitely likes it." Amy struggled to keep her voice level, but she could feel her face coloring with anger.

"There are other schools that might be better," the nurse said.

"What other schools?" Amy snapped. "Schools for asthmatic children? I didn't realize Steerforth had an Academy for Asthma Sufferers."

"We're only trying to help, Mrs. Moran," Mrs. Strohmeyer said, in a voice at once placating and condescending.

"Emma is just fine and she's staying right here," Amy said. "She has a treatable medical condition and if she needs help, like today, I expect you to help her."

She grabbed her daughter's backpack and pulled Emma away from the glass unicorn on the nurse's desk. The paramedics were loading equipment back into their van and Ryan paused as Amy walked stiffly to her own car and ushered Emma into her booster seat.

"Everything okay?"

No, she wanted to tell him. No, everything is most definitely not okay. My best friend's just been murdered, my husband is soon to be my ex, I'm not sure I have enough money to pay my mortgage and my daughter has been in and out of the hospital since she was born. Everything is most definitely not okay.

Instead she said, "Just ignorance. Teachers who are afraid and don't want to have to deal with an attack again. It happens."

"That sucks. I'm sorry."

She shrugged, trying to appear casual, but the day was getting to her and she could feel tears rising yet again.

"Some days you just wish you'd pulled the covers back up and waited for the next one," he said with a sympathetic smile and she laughed, a little shakily.

Emma seemed her usual self on the ride home, chattering about what she'd done in school and what some stupid boy had said at recess. Amy half listened while she drove, checking her often in the rearview mirror. She struggled to put the teacher's words out of her mind, but they'd nurtured the anxiety inside her and she could feel it blossoming.

They pulled into their driveway and Emma announced that she was going to play outside.

"No, Em, no playing outside this afternoon."

"But I want to play on the swings!"

"You can play something quiet inside."

"Outside!" She hopped out of the car and slammed the door to emphasize her displeasure.

"That's enough, young lady. You have to take it easy today—that's what the nice paramedic said. How about watching a movie?"

"*Little Mermaid*?"

Amy sighed. Her daughter was going through a Disney phase and there was nothing she could do to dissuade her. She'd watched *Little Mermaid*—the current favorite—more than fifty times and still wasn't tired of it.

"Okay, *Little Mermaid*."

"And chocolate milk?" Emma smiled her super-sweet, manipulating-Mommy smile.

"And chocolate milk," Amy capitulated.

Soon the sounds of "Under the Sea" were echoing through the house for the umpteenth time. Emma was happily singing along off-key between loud, slurping sips of chocolate milk.

Amy collapsed on the living room sofa and closed her eyes, just for a moment. A loud bang startled her awake.

Emma!

Amy sprang up and ran toward the kitchen, expecting to hear an answering wail, but there was no other sound. The kitchen was empty, the chair where Emma had been sitting still upright. The only thing left of her presence was the smudged glass with remnants of chocolate milk.

The back door was ajar. Amy stepped out on the back porch and looked around the yard. "Emma?"

The only answer was the wind rustling the leaves in the trees and the faint creaking from the playset where an empty swing rocked slowly back and forth. Amy turned to go back in the house when a scrap of bright pink caught her eye.

It was Emma's stuffed bunny. Amy plucked it off the lawn

and looked around again. What was it doing out here? This was a toy that rarely left Emma's bed.

"Emma? Emma, come out this minute! This isn't funny, Emma!"

Trees bordered the back of the property. Not enough to be considered a real forest, surely, but that's how Amy thought of them, as their woods. She'd embraced the privacy at one point. Now the dark stretch of trunks seemed menacing. She blinked in the sun, shading her eyes to see any movement. Everything was in shadows. What if Emma had wandered off, or worse, been taken?

Amy ran back in the house clutching the stuffed bunny. "Emma!" she screamed as she barged through the back door. "Emma, where are you?"

She searched the house, bargaining with God. *If she's all right, I'll never fall asleep again. I'll keep her safe. Please let her be all right.*

She was turning away from her bedroom when she heard a faint giggle. Amy whirled around. "Emma?"

Silence. She slid back the closet door. Nothing. Then she saw the smallest movement of the embroidered bedskirt. Amy knelt down and lifted it. Emma's small face grinned at her. "Boo!"

Relief mixed in equal parts with anger. Amy pulled her out from under the bed and crushed her against her chest.

"Don't ever do that again," she said in her fiercest voice.

"It was hide-and-seek, Mommy."

"I don't like that game, Emma. That game scares Mommy."

"Didn't I pick a good place to hide?"

She sounded unsure and her fingers slipped into her mouth. Amy relented. "Yes, you picked a good place. That's the problem—you're too good at that game."

"Sorry I scared you," Emma said, but she smiled as she said it and her small fingers left her mouth to pluck at the bunny in Amy's hand.

"What are you doing with Hoppy?"

"I found her outside. Were you outside playing when Mommy was asleep?" Amy said, holding her still so she could look into her daughter's eyes.

"You said not to," Emma said patiently, as if that explained it all.

"But did you anyway, Emma? Did you take Hoppy and go outside?"

Emma looked solemn. "No, Mommy."

"Then how did your bunny end up outside? Did you leave it outside yesterday?" But even as she asked, Amy could remember tucking Emma in with it last night. Or had she? She'd been so distracted yesterday because of Sheila's death, maybe she'd overlooked it.

Emma twisted in her grasp. "Let go, Mommy. You're hurting me."

Amy loosened her grip, but didn't release her. "Mommy won't be mad, Emma, but I need to know the truth. Did you go outside just now?"

"No! I already told you! No, no, no!" She stamped a small foot for emphasis and then her face lit up. "She must have hopped away herself, Mommy!"

She looked so excited that Amy couldn't help smiling. She released her and Emma carried the bunny off down the hall, scolding her in a tone that was an obvious imitation of her mother.

Amy went back downstairs and carefully closed and locked the back door. She was sure it had been locked when she left that morning and she hadn't touched it when they came home. Could Emma be lying? She seemed like she was telling the truth, but how else to explain the door standing ajar like that and the toy left on the lawn?

All at once, Amy was aware of just how isolated they were. In the city she could have knocked on the next apartment for help. Here her closest neighbors were farther away and elderly. Would they have even heard her if she'd shouted for help?

She checked all the windows on the first floor and carried on to the second, all the while telling herself that it was ridiculous to feel this afraid on a clear, sunny day. It was Sheila's murder. That had made her anxious, maybe even paranoid.

"Nothing important," she said when Emma asked what she was doing. "But it's time for you to rest." And against her daughter's wishes, she put her down for a nap, listening to Emma's breathing for a few minutes to be sure that she wasn't about to have another attack.

Once she was asleep, Amy went into her own room and sank into the big armchair, allowing herself a few moments of grief. She felt more alone than she had at any other time in her life. She wanted Sheila's company so badly that she ached with it, feeling the grief building like an enormous wave inside her. She needed to talk with another adult, to have an adult conversation about what had happened, to be held by another adult and comforted.

At that moment she realized that she wanted Chris. No matter what he'd done, what he'd said, he was still the man who'd held her for the six years they'd been together and she wanted his arms around her. Without stopping to think, afraid that if she thought about it for a moment more she'd lose her nerve, she grabbed a phone and rapidly dialed his cell.

The number was busy. Amy hit redial and this time it went straight to voice mail. She waited out his message and hesitated after the beep, unsure of what to say, but not wanting to disconnect. After a long moment of dead air, she came to her senses and hung up without leaving a message.

She dialed a New York exchange again, but it went straight to Perry's machine. This time she left a message, asking her old friend to call when she got a chance, trying to instill a peppiness that matched Perry's bright voice on the recording.

The doorbell rang as she hung up, startling her. The only thing she could think was that it was Chris, that somehow he'd heard about Sheila and knew that she needed him. She was so convinced that she forgot all about personal security and ran to the door, opening it without checking to see who was on the other side.

It wasn't Chris. That disappointment registered first, followed quickly by the shock of seeing the last person she really wanted to see at that moment: her mother.

Chapter 7

Finding Trevor Sylvester wasn't proving easy, though that was hardly surprising. He'd have to be a total moron to stick around after killing his ex. He'd be found and when he was, they'd get the truth from him, even if they had to beat it out of him. None of that civil rights violations crap was going to come back and haunt them either. Closed doors and closed lips from all involved and the perp could squeal to the DA all he wanted, but nothing would come of it because that's how the job got done.

This was Detective Black's stream-of-consciousness banter on the forty-minute drive to Lewiston, the town next to Steerforth that Trevor Sylvester called home.

Sometimes Mark thought that Black spent too much time watching cop shows on TV. This was the first homicide in Steerforth in a year, if you didn't count the knifing in a bar. That was hardly a homicide since the victim was so damn drunk that he'd died of alcohol poisoning as much as from the slice another former mill worker had left in his gullet.

That crime had been solved before it even started and Black was looking forward to having someone to rake over the coals. Probably thought of himself as a Sipowicz, Juarez thought, tearing his gaze from the view of pumpkin fields out the window to glance at his partner's face.

His slight smile at his own humor was obviously interpreted as support of whatever Black was ranting about, because his partner grinned back at him.

Lewiston was to Steerforth as pizza was to gourmet Italian cuisine. Instead of high-end boutiques, its main street had a dollar store, a sub shop, a Payless Shoes and a dusty bridal boutique that looked like it hadn't sold a dress since the seventies. There wasn't much traffic either in car or on foot in town, but once they'd reached the outer edges of the business district, they saw the reason why. A big Wal-Mart with a choked parking lot loomed into view.

The Steerforth police contacted the Lewiston police, who had attempted to pick up Trevor Sylvester at his house. Only he'd left Tuesday morning, according to his second wife, and she didn't know where. The police searched his home and determined he truly wasn't there and promised to keep looking for him. Black and Juarez had come with a warrant to search again and talk to the second wife. They hoped Trevor had managed to sneak back home.

With this in mind, they approached the Riverview Estates town-house complex from the opposite end, parking outside the perimeter and entering the development on foot. It was probably pointless, Mark thought, since people would realize they were cops the minute they walked in. The residents of Riverview Estates looked as if they were very familiar with the police. The name was far grander than the place itself. The only river in view was a shallow, muddy creek that ran through the middle of the development and had graffiti-laden footbridges across it. The town houses, alternating white and blue frame in clusters of three, looked like they'd blow over in a heavy nor'easter. The little bit of lawn available around most properties was overgrown with dandelions and other weeds.

Trevor's home was a dirty white center town house with a bedraggled awning over the front window above a connect-a-brick patio. A mobile made of Budweiser cans hung from the awning, clacking unpleasantly in the wind.

They split their approach, Juarez waiting until Black had snuck around the rear of the property before he stealthily approached the front. They had their guns drawn, pointing down.

Once Black radioed that he was in back, Juarez kicked the door and hollered, "Police! Open up!"

There was a sound of scuffling from inside the house and Juarez kicked the door again. "Open up!"

"Hold your damn horses!" a muffled female voice said.

"I'm going in," Juarez radioed to Black. He tried the knob first and the door opened. He stepped inside and came face-to-face with an enormous pale women clad only in a large purple towel.

"Can't you even give people one goddamned minute?" she said. "I was in the shower." Her face was flushed, but he wasn't sure whether it had more to do with anger or embarrassment. "I already told you people that Trevor's not here."

"Why don't you let us determine that."

Black's voice behind her made her shriek. She whirled around, giving Juarez a brief yet memorable glimpse of an enormous white derriere before the towel flapped closed. "You can't just walk in my house like that!"

"We can if your husband's wanted for murder, Mrs. Sylvester." Black waved the warrant at her.

"I told those other cops that Trevor wouldn't touch that bitch. He's not like that."

There was a fading purple bruise high on her right cheekbone that made a liar out of her, but Juarez wasn't interested in arguing the point.

They heard a small scuffling noise from upstairs and Black demanded to know if she was hiding Trevor. She let out a stream of obscenities at this, demanding to know why they weren't finding Trevor for her since something had obviously happened to him. Why weren't they looking into that crime?

Ignoring her, Juarez started up the stairs with Black backing him up. "Come out, Trevor! You're outnumbered."

"That isn't Trevor!"

"Then come out whoever it is!" Juarez had his gun up and ready. To his right was an open door through which he could see a sagging mattress and a tangle of sheets. In front of him was a small bathroom, shower curtain pulled back, crusted tiles beyond it. To his left was a closed door. He silently signaled to Black and, on the count of three, he turned the knob and kicked the door open, his gun moving ahead of him. A wide-eyed toddler in a soggy diaper was standing in a crib staring at them. As if on cue, he started to wail.

Juarez immediately lowered his gun and Black turned on the woman who'd followed them. "What the hell were you thinking, lady! Why didn't you tell us you had a baby in here!"

"You didn't give me half a chance!"

"We could have shot him," Juarez said, feeling a tremor shake through him as he holstered his gun. For a split second he was back in Manhattan, the darkened hallway, the figure raising his hand.

He blinked hard, relentlessly pushing the images away. The baby was crying and the woman plucked him out of the crib and straddled him on her hip.

"Quit your crying, Dylan," she said, jogging the baby up and down. "I told you that Trevor's gone, so get out."

"We can't do that, Mrs. Sylvester," Juarez said. "Not until we talk to you."

The song and dance went on for another two minutes

until she lumbered off to get some clothes on, the baby in tow. She took her time about it, but they made good use of theirs, heading back downstairs to have a thorough look to see if there was any indication of where Trevor Sylvester might be.

There were no recent phone calls from him and no messages on the answering machine. The overflowing ashtray on the coffee table held lipstick-tainted butts and there was only one glass in the sink. If Trevor had been here recently, he and the missus had done a pretty good job of hiding it.

When Mrs. Sylvester came back into the living room, she was wearing jeans and a too-tight tank top, her breasts swelling like two small hams. She'd changed the baby's diaper, but hadn't otherwise dressed him, and she took a seat on the sagging couch and plunked the little boy down on the stained carpet at her feet. He promptly picked up the TV remote that had been left on the floor and began gumming it.

"All right, you can ask a couple of questions—again—but I've got better things to do with my time," she said, folding her doughy arms across her mammoth chest. She'd pulled her hair back in a tight ponytail and put on makeup. The metallic purple color of her lips matched her nail polish.

"Mrs. Sylvester," Black began, only to be interrupted immediately.

"It's Mandi. Nobody calls me Mrs. Sylvester. Reminds me of my mother-in-law."

"Mandi, you know why we're looking for Trevor, don't you?"

"Because that bitch of an ex-wife of his got killed."

"Yes, and we think that Trevor is the one that killed her."

Mandi shook a cigarette out of the pack on the battered coffee table and placed it to her lips. She fished around in the couch cushions and came up with a lighter. "That's not Trevor," she said, lighting up. "He's not like that. He wouldn't harm a flea."

"How did you get that bruise on your cheek, Mandi?" Juarez asked.

"And that one on your arm?" Black added, pointing to a greenish spot near her right wrist.

Her eyes narrowed. "I fell," she said, blowing smoke up at the ceiling. The baby gummed the power button and the large TV in the corner came on. Mandi yanked the remote out of his mouth, shut off the TV and slammed the remote down on the coffee table.

"Look, Mandi, we know that Trevor gave you those, just like he knocked Sheila around. You can deny it all you want, but we both know it's true," Juarez said.

"He only does that when he's been drinking," Mandi said defensively, her opposite hand moving to cover the bruise on her arm.

"Maybe that's why he killed Sheila. Maybe he was drinking that day."

"He didn't kill her! He didn't have anything to do with that bitch!"

"When was the last time he saw Sheila?"

"In May. At Mike's graduation."

"Did you go, too?"

"Sort of. I waited in the parking lot."

"Were Trevor and Sheila getting along?"

"As much as they ever did."

"Does that mean they were fighting?"

"No, just bickering. Same old, same old. They didn't like each other, but he wouldn't kill her. He had no reason to kill her."

"Did he get to see the boys as often as he wanted?" Black asked.

"No."

"Then he must have felt some anger toward her?"

"Not enough to kill her." She stubbed the cigarette out in the overflowing ashtray and immediately reached for another.

"Was he drinking on Tuesday?"

"He wasn't home on Tuesday. I've told you that. He's been gone since Tuesday."

Juarez thought of the photos postmarked a week before. Had Trevor been planning this killing a long time? He couldn't reconcile that very meticulous crime scene with this scruffy town house and this stupid woman. None of it fit.

"Where does he go when he's not at home?" he said, trying another tack.

"I don't know. The Oak Barrel bar, I guess. Work."

"Does he visit any friends? Do you have relatives out of town?"

"Yes, we've got friends and relatives, same as you!" She scowled at him. "But he's not with any of them. I've already called them all."

"We'll need their names and addresses anyway, ma'am."

This elicited another stream of curses, but eventually she got to her feet and fetched a surprisingly well-organized address book from another room. She jotted down a series of names and phone numbers on a scrap of paper, glaring as she did so, but Juarez knew it was a futile exercise. If he had killed his first wife, Trevor Sylvester had already proved that he wasn't an idiot and only an idiot would flee to a relative's house. Still, maybe he'd called one of them. It was the pedestrian side to police work, the endless paperwork and phone calls, dotting the "i's" and crossing the "t's."

They also took a recent picture of a grinning Trevor standing in front of a race car, over Mandi's objections, assuring her that they'd return it once they'd made copies.

"It's important that Trevor turn himself in, Mandi," Black said as they were leaving. "You understand that, don't you? The longer he's running, the more dangerous it gets. You don't want him getting shot running from the law."

Mandi glowered more deeply at this, but the cigarette trembled as she brought it to her lips.

"If he calls here, you call us," Juarez said, giving her a card. "Do the same if he comes here in person. We need to talk to him."

They stepped out of the town house with Mandi on their heels, the baby back on her hip.

"It's her own fault that bitch got killed," she said in a resentful tone. "She kept his boys from him with all that screaming about abuse. Keeping kids from seeing their own father—now that's abuse."

Next door, a large-muscled man straightened up from the Harley he was working on and surveyed Black and Juarez with a wrench in hand. "These guys hassling you, Mandi?" he said, looking from her to them.

"They're cops." She spat the word. "They're looking for Trevor. Think he murdered his ex."

The man spat on the ground. "Trevor ain't here," he said, "and she don't know where he is."

"Do you?" Black jumped in.

"If I did I wouldn't tell you," the man said and that was all it took. In a split second, Black had him up against the side of his own house, one arm bent high against his back.

"Let go of me, man, you're hurting me!" the man cried while Mandi shouted at them from her front door. Juarez put his hand out to stop Mandi from thinking of interfering as a dog started howling in the man's townhome and scratching at the door.

"Where's Trevor?" Black demanded, pulling upward on the man's trapped hand. He groaned.

"I don't know," he said. "I ain't seen him in days."

Other dogs had taken up the howl. At any moment they'd probably have a pack of dogs down on them. Mark shouted above the howling, "He doesn't know anything, let's go." If his partner heard him, he gave no sign of it.

Mandi was screaming "police brutality" and the baby on her hip was crying so loudly that neighbors had probably called child welfare. Even now they were probably being caught on someone's video camera.

Keeping a close eye on Mandi, Mark moved over to Black and laid a restraining arm on his partner's shoulder. "This punk isn't worth it," he said. "We've got other things to do."

Black snarled in response, but after a final hard tug at the neighbor's arm, he let him go.

"I can sue you, man," the man said. "You can't put your hands on me!"

"I already did," Black called over his shoulder. Juarez mentally shook his head, but waited until they were safely out of the town-house complex and back at the car.

"What the hell was that about?" he demanded as Black moved automatically to the driver's side.

"We don't have to take that shit from people," Black said nonchalantly.

"Yeah, well, we also don't have to create an unnecessary scene and risk getting cited for something stupid."

"Are you afraid of standing up for the job?" Black said.

Juarez's temper, carefully held in check, finally snapped. "Is that some line from *Dirty Harry*?" he demanded. "Because this isn't some movie or TV, this is real life and if you play it like that, things can get fucked up fast."

"Are you lecturing me, Juarez?" Black stormed back. "I've got more than twenty years on the job, kid, so don't you tell me what this job is and isn't."

"I'm not your kid and I've had plenty of experience—"

"You were NYPD. God forbid we forget that for even a minute. Well, you didn't last long, did you, big shot?"

"Fuck you!"

They glared at each other over the roof of the car and then Black jerked his door open. Juarez did the same and both got in and slammed the doors.

Silence reigned for a full five minutes, though Black

made his feelings pretty clear with a squealing exit from the parking spot and a lead foot on the road. They got caught in heavy traffic heading back toward Steerforth. The funeral for Sheila Sylvester was due to start at two P.M. Black moved to put the magnetized light on their roof.

"This doesn't violate your ethical code, does it?" he said, his voice laced with sarcasm. "Do you object to using the siren?"

Juarez shook his head. "Try not to hit any civilians," he said. "I wouldn't want to have to explain the body in the trunk to the boss."

A few minutes later, Black said in a gruff voice, "How's your dad?"

"He's okay. They've got him doing speech therapy now, in addition to the physical."

"Shame what happened to him. He's a good cop."

Which was as close to an apology as Black could get, Juarez knew. "You really think Trevor's our guy?"

Black nodded. "He took off after he killed her and he's not coming back."

"Just seems like a pretty organized killing for a man who lives like that. Trevor's got two-time loser written all over him, yet he somehow managed to pull it together to leave a crime scene that clean?"

"He wore gloves. Big deal."

"Okay, maybe the gloves explain why there are no prints. But they don't explain why a man who uses his fists to communicate suddenly develops more finesse."

"Look, you're thinking too hard about this. So he decided to use a nail gun. Maybe he had it in his car. Maybe he was going to knock the crap out of her after he'd wounded her, but he killed her instead and then he has to get out of there because that other realtor shows up."

"And the missing finger?"

Black laughed. "Hey, you're the one telling me this isn't

the movies or TV. If it wasn't Trevor, who was it? He fits the profile—he's got means and motivation. Stop trying to find drama where none exists."

It was something his father would have said. Most homicides were committed by family members or friends. Sheila had gotten away from an abusive marriage, but she hadn't been able to escape the man himself. He'd probably been resentful of how well she did after she left him. It probably was enough motivation to kill her.

So why was it that some instinct was pricking Juarez, telling him that the crime scene they'd looked at was far more sinister and the man they were looking for was far more dangerous?

"Aren't you going to let me in? These are very heavy." With a bright smile on her face, Dorothy Busby hefted the two big bags she was carrying and waited for her daughter to hold the door open for her.

"Mom, you should have called," Amy said, even as she moved aside so her mother could enter the house and offered her cheek for a glancing kiss. "Emma's taking a nap and she needs to rest."

"A nap? Oh, shoot, I brought some clothes for her to try on."

As if on cue, Amy heard a door creak open, the soft slap of small bare feet running on tile and then Emma launched herself into Dorothy Busby's arms.

"Nana!"

"Emma!"

Amy stifled a groan and took the bags her mother had brought. "Mom, you don't need to keep bringing us things, we're doing okay."

"Who said you weren't?" Dorothy planted another loud smooch on her granddaughter's cheek as the little girl squirmed and giggled. "There's the cutest children's boutique in Westport and I just had to buy some clothes for Emma. Wait until you see the jacket I found."

Amy held up containers of what looked like chicken soup and gave her mother a mute inquiring look.

"Now don't start, Amy."

"We're not starving, Mother—"

"Well, of course you aren't—"

"And I can cook—"

"Of course you can—"

"So why do you keep bringing us food?"

Dorothy ignored her, reaching for the other bag and unpacking brightly colored clothes, but Amy saw spots of pink appear on her mother's cheekbones.

"Look, Em, isn't this dress adorable?" Dorothy pulled out a blue smocked dress and held it up against her granddaughter.

"Mother," Amy repeated, giving the word its full weight as she pulled out boxes of cereal and jars of expensive-looking jam.

"Cereal's expensive, Amy, and I know you like that apricot jam. You said so when you had it at my house—"

"We're doing okay, Mom. We don't need you to do this."

"Do you really think I'm going to let my daughter and my granddaughter fend for themselves?"

"We're doing fine."

Dorothy piled some clothes into her granddaughter's welcoming arms. "Go and try those on in your room, honey. Then come on out and give Nana a fashion show."

As soon as Emma was gone, Dorothy looked directly at her daughter and let the smile drop from her face. "You are not doing fine, honey. You look tired, you're working too hard and just look at your house. When was the last time someone dusted in here?"

Amy gave a short laugh. "Bringing me chicken soup is not going to get the house cleaner, Mom."

"I know, but it might just wake you up and make you realize that being stubborn is not helping either you or Emma."

"Oh, not this again." Amy stood up and carried the food into the kitchen. Dorothy followed.

"When was the last time you talked to Chris?"

"The last time he called here, which was about a month ago." Amy put the soup in the fridge, the jam in the cupboard.

"And? How did it go? Did you talk?"

"Yes, Mother, we talked."

Dorothy sighed. "You know what I mean. Did you tell him you're coming home?"

"No." Amy's answer was flat and final. "And I'm not going to tell him, so you can drop that right now."

"You've always been stubborn and it's not an attractive quality in a woman, Amy."

"Neither is infidelity in a man."

This time Dorothy's sigh was softer. "I know he hurt you—"

"And Emma."

"And Emma," her mother conceded. "But men are always going to do stupid things. You can hold on to foolish pride or you can fix your marriage. Doesn't Emma deserve a father?"

"I didn't take away her father—he did."

Dorothy stood up, shaking her head. "Fine. Have it your way. But did it ever occur to you that maybe you're asking for a perfect life that just doesn't exist?"

Chapter 8

Guy was looking forward to attending the funeral. Sheila Sylvester would be buried, he'd read that in the paper, and though he would have preferred cremation—such a lovely, clean thing to reduce all that useless flesh and bone to ash— it would still be satisfying to see her lowered into a hole in the ground.

There was a little coverage of the impending event on TV and he watched it over lunch, nursing his sandwich while he stared at the screen. He was mesmerized by the numbers the newscasters were talking about, the crowds of mourners who would gather to say goodbye to a woman most of them had never known. Vultures. Lured there by all the reporting. It was the biggest crime to hit Steerforth in years.

The reporters were invariably standing in front of St. Andrew's Church. He didn't like churches like that. Modern and angular, all big airy spaces and comfortable seats. That wasn't church. Where was the structure? Where was the focus? It was all feel-good religion now and Jesus as some big psychotherapist. He was surprised they didn't depict Him wearing a cardigan.

Not like the religion he grew up with. At St. Joe's religion had been hard work. Hard on the knees, hard on the back—proper behavior drummed in through physical pain. A church with uncomfortable pews but glorious stained glass windows to look up at as reminders of all the wonders that awaited those willing to make the effort.

His mother wasn't willing. She'd drop him off at St. Joe's and pay the tuition, but she didn't attend Mass. She was too busy fucking to focus on that. He'd seen her once when he was very young. That's how he knew what she was doing, how she was supplementing her secretary's salary and making sure the rent got paid and they ate. He was playing with his Matchbox cars and one of them ran under the closed bedroom door. He heard the strange creaking noises and the grunt, grunt, grunt before he opened the door and saw them on the bed like two pigs rutting.

After that she'd locked him in the cellar when the men came or when she went out at night to find them.

"Now you be a good boy and stay here and be very quiet. Do you think you can do that? Can you be my big brave boy and be very quiet? Mama will bring you a present."

He was scared of the cellar. Scared of the shadows and the dusty jars of pickled things left by the old lady who rented them the house. There was mold and damp and spiderwebs and only a little light from a single incandescent bulb. He didn't want to stay down there. No, Mama, he didn't want to stay. And he'd clung to her until she'd pulled him off and slapped him.

"Stop that! You should be ashamed, a big boy like you!" And he held himself while she disappeared into the gloom, listening to the *click, click, click* of her heels on the stairs, listening to the key turning, locking him in. He needed to pee that first time. He needed to pee so bad and Mama hadn't thought of that. He was a bad boy not to hold it, she said later. Bad boy! Bad! She shoved his nose in the wet underpants, made him wear nothing the rest of the day so he stood around trying to cover himself with his shirt. One of the men saw him like that and laughed.

"You trying to compare dicks with me, kid? You want to see a dick, I'll show you a dick." He pulled his out of his pants and waggled it at the boy while his mother laughed.

"Put that away, Mike. Stop it."

The next time she left him in the cellar, she left a jar with him. "You pee in that."

There were two windows in the cellar, covered with grime. One looked out of the west side to a stretch of barren lawn and a cracked sidewalk and the street. The east-side window looked out on the apartment building next door, so close that he could see into the first-floor windows where the woman with yellow hair lived.

She seemed unaware of him. She probably couldn't see him at all. He'd dragged an old chair over to the window and opened it a fraction in order to see out and with the gloom in the basement she'd have seen nothing but shadows. He liked that. He liked watching her without her knowing he was watching.

One day it occurred to him that he could probably squeeze through the window if he opened it farther. He tried it at the other window, so he'd crawl out near the sidewalk and not risk having the yellow-haired woman see him. Only he couldn't boost himself up to get through the window. It took a strength he didn't have. So he worked at it, pushing himself, trying every time he was down there and in the moments when he wasn't, focusing his attention.

On a hot summer day, he made it up and slipped through the glass into the heat outside. He could still remember that rush of late-afternoon heat, the dizzying sensation as he'd stood up in the sparse grass, freed by his own hands from the prison his mother had made.

His freedom was short-lived. He went to the playground

and stayed there until all the other children left. He didn't notice the looks some of the kids' mothers cast his way. It got dark, but the basement had trained him. He'd learned not to mind the dark, and besides, there was a streetlight at the playground, so he could still see the silver of the slide and the rungs of the jungle gym.

The cop surprised him. "It's late, little boy. Does your mother know you're out here?"

And when the cop took him home, there was his mother, frantic. She hugged him to her, digging her nails into his arms where the cop wouldn't see, and repeatedly thanked the policeman for bringing him home, blaming his disappearance on a teenage babysitter, not mentioning the basement.

When the cop was gone, she hit him, with her hands, with a belt, again and again, while he wrapped himself up tight in a ball on the floor, trying to play dead. Accompanying her blows was a litany of reasons why he couldn't go out: It was dangerous, there were dangerous men, they'd hurt him, and they'd touch him where no one should touch him.

When she got tired, she left him there, sobbing on the floor, and the next morning she took him down to the basement and made him watch as she nailed the windows shut.

This was when he became Houdini. He'd read about him in a book at the school library. He used an old wire hanger and a screwdriver to pick the lock. It took him many tries before he got it. He learned to listen to the scrape of metal against metal and the click as the pins moved into place. The final click, when he turned the knob and the door opened, gave him a sense of pleasure that never left.

By the time he was ten, she'd stopped locking him in the basement, but by then he'd graduated to picking other locks. He visited the home of the yellow-haired woman and learned her name was Pamela. He visited the other apartments as well, getting to know the lives of all the different residents of the building.

The first time he killed a person—the moment of his second birth—it was an accident. He was a teenager then, the size of a man and getting attention from girls. He'd graduated from his own neighborhood to others, driving around in the secondhand car he'd purchased with money from his job as a florist's delivery boy—a job that gave him the chance to check out other houses, other people. He could tell pretty quickly if it was a house he'd revisit. Picking locks was easy. Slipping in and out undetected was easy. He'd joined the drama club at school, becoming a backstage presence, using his strength to lift the curtains and man the lights, staying in the shadows though he was urged to reconsider.

"You've got a classic profile—the face of a Caesar or Hamlet!" the drama teacher wailed, wringing his hands at the waste of it. But it wasn't wasted. Guy had free access to the costume room and he borrowed wigs and mustaches, learning how to apply them by watching the student actors. From then on, he'd go into houses in disguise.

He was visiting what he thought was an empty house and sorting through the contents of a lingerie drawer when someone walked into the bedroom. She was an older woman, probably in her seventies, and she must have been sleeping in another room, for she was wearing a nightdress and carrying a lamp without the shade as a weapon.

She lunged at him, but he easily sidestepped her and she fell hard against the far corner of the dresser and then she started screaming. Neighbors would be alerted, police would be called. She'd probably remember him as the florist's delivery boy and then he'd be caught and sent away to prison because the one thing he knew for sure was that nobody in society appreciated his type of talent. It was impulse to grab the stockings lying right there in the drawer. He pulled them taut around her neck until the only sound she could make was a faint gargling and her eyes protruded from their sockets and her face turned purple.

When she was finally dead, he removed the stockings and wiped off her body and left her tucked in a corner near the dresser. He scattered a few pieces of paste jewelry about the floor and wrapped the more valuable stuff in a pillowcase. Then he broke one of the small panes of glass in the kitchen door downstairs, because otherwise the police would wonder how he'd gotten into the house.

That drive home, with the pillowcase stuffed inside his jacket, was the longest of his life. He cut the pillowcase into little pieces and burned it. The jewelry he sealed in an envelope and locked it away in the bottom of a small fireproof safe, underneath his birth certificate and Social Security card and the passport he'd recently gotten because he wanted to travel.

It was more than a week before her body was discovered. The mail carrier noticed that her papers were piling up and called the police after she failed to come to the door. In the paper it said she had surprised a burglar. He was satisfied, then, that they'd never catch him. And they never did.

Power could be addictive and addicts spiraled out of control. He made sure to keep his life in balance. He studied hard and made good grades. The college of his choice offered him a scholarship and he studied hard there, too, rarely going to bars or partying with other students.

"You never relax, man," his hard-drinking roommate complained his freshman year. "You've got to just chill out sometimes."

He did chill out, just not with others, and not in the same way. His methods of relaxing were different. While others spent their weekends lost in the smoky, pulse-throbbing and beery haze of the local bars, Guy spent his alone. In good weather he went on foot. If it was raining he preferred his car. He cruised the streets at an unhurried pace, looking for women.

How to choose? This was the delightful dilemma he faced

each and every time. It could be a smile given him in passing, the fullness of a lip, the roundness of an eye. It could be the sway of the hips as a young woman teetered on high heels or a sudden spicy breath of perfume.

He liked to know those he chose, but not in the standard way. It was a different, more intimate kind of knowing. Instead of approaching and conversing he watched them. He followed them on the journey from class to sorority house or bar to dorm. He knew how to blend in with a crowd and how to follow several feet behind. In an inside pocket of his jacket he carried a few carefully chosen lock picks and a length of thin, strong rope.

Who were the chosen? There was the pretty co-ed who smiled drunkenly at him when he offered her an arm as she tripped out of a bar one evening. Then there was Tania, a student cashier at the campus bookstore. There was an older professor, Dr. Susan Burke, who taught in the English department and spent her nights drinking and flirting with students half her age. There was the plump freshman who did her laundry alone on Saturday nights. He chose them for their looks or their attitude. He chose them because they wore a certain dress or smiled a certain way. He chose them because they were available.

It was a cold night in February when he killed Karen Chang. She sat in the row in front of him in biology class, tossing her long, black hair in a distracting way. He'd watched her for weeks, visiting her apartment when she was out, getting to know her. He passed her as they exited the movie theater, their breath mingling in the cold air. She walked ahead of him down the sidewalk and he followed after half a block, moving stealthily, hands in the pockets of his black jacket, a dark knit hat covering his head.

Five blocks later she approached a dilapidated row of duplexes. Student rentals. He watched her fumble for a key in the flimsy macramé bag slung on her shoulder. He waited until she was in a shadow between streetlights and then he moved swiftly, one hand covering her mouth, the other holding a knife to her back.

He dragged her around the back of the building while she struggled, the heels of her boots dragging. She clawed at his arms, at his hands. She tried to bite him, but his leather gloves were too thick and the pressure on her mouth too tight.

Forcing her into a dark corner between two teeming dumpsters, he shoved her hard against the brick building and pressed his lips against her ear. "Don't be afraid," he whispered. "Just do what I want and you won't get hurt."

She nodded earnestly, her eyes wide with fear. He turned her to face the wall and ran his free hand along her body, feeling it tremble under his touch. "I don't want to hurt you."

He reached his hand under her wool skirt and stroked along the inside length of her leg, traveling past her high boots and up to the cotton tight–covered thighs. Her tremors increased as he tickled along the edge of her crotch. When he moved his hand away she sagged slightly in obvious relief, and in that moment he reached swiftly into his pocket and pulled out a ball of socks and a length of rope.

It was simple really. Shoving the sock ball into her mouth as a gag, he used his weight to keep her pinned to the wall and circled her neck with the rope. Then he used both hands to pull it tight.

She struggled like a fish on a line, tearing at the rope, gagging, begging him with her eyes to release her. He panted along with her, tightening the rope and rubbing his body against hers until her fingers faltered and the muffled exclamations died away.

When she'd stopped struggling he eased her body onto the ground and arranged it to his liking. He took a small camera from his coat pocket and snapped two pictures of her, one a close-up of her face frozen in fear, the other of her entire body, clothes carefully peeled back to expose her.

When that was done, he took a piece of her jewelry as a remembrance of their time together. Karen Chang always wore a gold ring shaped like a flower with a small ruby at its center. He slipped it off the stiffening finger of her right hand.

For many years the photos and mementos had been enough to relive the experience. Recently, though, he'd needed more. He chose the left ring finger for all its ancient significance. The Romans thought a vein from that finger ran straight to the heart. It was a tangible sign of his love to take that finger.

Of course, after Violet things changed. Now taking that finger symbolized the severing of any connection. These women were heartless, adulterous, whoring bitches. He removed their wedding bands and their rings so the world would know what sort of women they were.

When Guy was finished with lunch he carefully cleaned up his mess before putting on a Mozart CD and taking the newest box from the freezer.

The soprano's voice soared in the aria and he opened the box slowly, as if it were a present he wanted to savor. He stroked the finger lightly and was transported back to the bedroom and how he'd stepped from the shadows to confront Sheila. He could see her face, hear her scream, relive the panicked begging and the feel of her body sagging in his arms. He closed his eyes and rocked with the memory, enveloped in the swell of music and the sweet scent of dead skin.

All too soon it was time to put the box away. Already the sensations were fading. Soon the finger wouldn't be enough to hold him. He could feel the dull ache in his head that signaled the need for more. Soon, very soon. It was coming. He just had to be patient. He didn't know who and he didn't know when. The only thing he could be sure of was that he'd need to kill again.

Chapter 9

Sheila's funeral was well attended. Amy wanted to believe it was because of Sheila's success in real estate and because of the good work she'd done for the battered women's shelter, but she knew the crime had also brought them here.

The funeral was being held at St. Andrew's, which surprised Amy because she knew that Sheila hadn't been a practicing Catholic for years. She wondered whether Sheila had wanted this because of her relationship with the single-parent support group, or whether this was the work of Sheila's mother, who sat stoically in the front row, comforting her grandsons.

Amy was in the pew behind Sheila's surviving family, sitting between star realtors Hope Chiswell and Poppy Braxton. She'd been afforded this place of honor because she'd been such a close friend of Sheila's. Hope focused on what the other mourners were wearing, leaning past Amy to hiss in Poppy's ear that "lavender is so passé," an apparent reference to the suit worn by some hapless mourner.

Father Michael presided at the altar and Amy tried to focus on what he was saying, but her eyes invariably strayed to the walnut coffin standing in the center aisle. Sheila was in there, or what was left of Sheila's body. Amy would never hear that laugh again or catch her eye across a room, knowing that they were sharing the same joke.

The whole event felt like a monstrous joke. Amy half expected Sheila to sit up in her coffin and wink. How could it be that one day there was Sheila and then she was completely and utterly gone?

The lilies piled high on the coffin filled the church with their cloying scent. Father Michael came down from the pulpit waving a metal orb on a chain and incense swirled around the coffin. It competed with the flowers and this pungent perfume filled the church, leaving Amy nauseous and lightheaded.

When the service ended, she stepped out into the sunlight, blinking and shivering in her thin black suit. Poppy, the de facto head of Braxton Realty now that her father was approaching eighty, knew the press and how to use them. She and Hope welcomed the swarm of reporters and Amy slipped into the crowd.

She spotted Detective Juarez and he nodded at her, but before she'd made it past the crush to ask if he had any leads, Douglas Myers caught her.

"There you are!" he said loudly, as if she were a child who'd escaped a nanny's care. "Why aren't you standing with the illuminati?" He nodded in the direction of Poppy and Hope. "You're one of them now, at least for the day. Celeb du jour, that's you."

She shook her head, trying to move past him, but he took her arm and came in close. "You should take advantage of it," he hissed uncomfortably close to her ear. "A little media exposure is good for sales."

Mercifully, someone called his name, and he disappeared into the throngs of mourners. The detective had also disappeared. Damn. Amy stretched up on her toes to see above the crowd, but she couldn't find him.

"Amy, sweetie, I'm so, so, sorry."

She turned to find Audrey, another member of the single-parent support group, standing with opened arms. Amy couldn't refuse her sticklike embrace. Fortunately, it didn't last long. Sheila had once compared Audrey to a praying mantis, tall and pencil thin with large eyes and arms constantly sawing the air. They were moving now, as Audrey described how she'd learned of Sheila's death and how horrified she'd been and continued to be and who could do such a thing and wasn't it so, so sad?

Amy nodded, but she could barely comprehend what Audrey was saying, so acute was her pain at Sheila's absence. In June, the oldest realtor at Braxton had died and Sheila dragged Amy with her to the funeral.

"I hate funerals," Sheila had confided as they were walking out afterwards. "All those platitudes about what a great person the deceased was and how much she'll be missed. Everyone knows that Edie was a first-class bitch and all the realtors are glad she's out of the business for good. When I die, I hope they'll be honest—here lies Sheila who sold more properties than I did and thank God she's gone."

"Don't you agree, Amy?" Audrey patted her arm, calling her attention back.

"Agree?"

Audrey laughed, a nervous trill. "I said don't you agree that Richard would look hot wrapped in nothing but a palm leaf." She nodded her head and Amy turned to see the best-looking member of the support group standing alone, leaning against a pillar.

"I think I'd like to see him without the palm leaf," Amy said, feeling as if she were channeling Sheila, and Audrey offered her nervous trill again.

Once she started looking around, Amy realized that everyone from the support group was there: Penelope, who didn't need a funeral to look depressed; Jackson, wearing a suit jacket as if he were a bear who'd been stuffed into unaccustomed clothing; Bridget, in vaguely funereal-looking earth mother garb, complete with Birkenstocks; and Charlie, who looked suspiciously red-eyed and kept swiping his nose with a Kleenex.

"Allergies," he explained when he made his way through the crowd to Amy's side. "Not that I didn't care for Sheila, but it's the changing season that's causing this reaction."

"So who did it?" Richard said in his typical blunt fashion when he deigned to join them. Amy had seen him in conversation with a good-looking blond woman, but then he'd caught her eye and made his way over to them. She tried to suppress the little flutter of excitement she always felt in Richard's presence. "Pure sex appeal," Sheila had declared. "They should bottle him."

"They don't know who killed her," Amy answered him. "But they think it might be her ex."

"Ultimately, she couldn't escape him," Penelope said in a mournful voice. She wore a voluminous purple dress that covered her billowing figure and ended somewhere around her ankles. "Men are such shits."

Charlie sniffed loudly, looking offended, but Richard gave her a short, hard smile. "I don't think the shit factor is limited to the male species, Penny."

"It's Penelope," the woman said. "I don't like Penny, I never have."

"Too small a name?" Richard said.

Penelope sniffed. "I'll see you tonight," she said and stalked away, her dress gently swaying against her large hips.

Audrey tittered and slapped at Richard's arm. "Oh, that was cruel."

"Only if you think there's something wrong with being

large," Richard said. He managed, as always, Amy thought, to keep everyone at a distance, maintaining the illusion that his interest in everything extended only as far as his own amusement.

Amy spotted Detective Juarez talking to Douglas. She wanted to move closer, hoping she could overhear that conversation, but Jackson blocked her view.

"You gave my name to the police?" he demanded.

"They asked me for the names of Sheila's friends," Amy said, but he cut her off.

"You should have asked me first," he said, scowling. "I don't need police calling and asking me questions."

"I'm sorry," Amy said, "but they asked me for names."

"So you served all of us up as suspects?" Charlie said. "Thanks a bunch."

"I'm sure you're not suspects," Amy protested, but she knew it wasn't true. They were all suspects until Sheila's killer was caught. She wondered again about Trevor. Could he really have taken those photos? It seemed so unlike the man that her friend had described.

"I thought you said they were looking for Trevor?" Audrey said. "I don't want them asking me questions. I'm no good with that sort of thing. I feel guilty when I haven't even done anything. This is all so, so strange."

Poppy Braxton hailed Amy with a fluttery wave and she excused herself and fended her way through the crowd to the older woman's side. There was no small talk or cheek bussing with Poppy, no matter how sweetly Waspy she might look. "Meredith Chomsky just called me," she said without preamble. "I don't have to tell you what that means, do I?"

"I talked to her yesterday."

"Well, she says you're not doing enough. She says you promised to have the fliers for the open house done three days ago."

"I was a little distracted by Sheila's murder," Amy said, making sure the irony was in her voice.

"I know, I know," Poppy said. "I'm just telling you what she told me. Oh, and she says there's still no sign on her lawn."

"I'll take care of it."

"Today, okay?" Poppy gave her the winning smile of a skilled businesswoman. "I really don't want to get another call from her." She paused. "If you can't handle it, Amy, you could turn this one over to another realtor. Everybody would understand."

"I can handle it." Amy needed this commission. With the Towle sale in question, she couldn't lose this one.

"I hope so, Amy, because Meredith is a big client and we don't want to lose her to another company. If you fail to make this sale, it reflects on all of us at Braxton."

Meredith Chomsky, née Rubin Maxwell Sloane, took another sip of her mocha latte and contemplated the list she'd made of other realtors. She was tied to Braxton for two more weeks, but if things didn't start moving that was definitely the end of that relationship. How much crap was she expected to put up with?

"Gloria, the flowers in the foyer need to be replaced," she said to her housekeeper, who slowly polished the granite countertops with a dishcloth.

"Yes, ma'am."

"And check the flowers in the bedrooms before you order the new ones. They might need to be replaced, too."

Gloria nodded, moving with a slowness that Meredith found irritating. It was a mystery how the little Puerto Rican ever managed to get anything done, but she did, so Meredith didn't complain. Out loud.

"I'll be at the gym for a few hours and then I'm getting

my hair done, so I won't be back for lunch. Oh, and could you call Phyllis Simon and tell her I won't be able to make it to her party. The invitation's on the board."

Gloria continued down the long row of granite, her eyes focused on the honey-colored stone. Meredith wished she'd pause and make eye contact, but the last time she'd mentioned that, the look in Gloria's eyes had scared her.

"Did you get my clothes from the dry cleaner yesterday?"

Gloria shook her head. "No, ma'am."

"I told you I needed that dress today, Gloria."

"Yes, ma'am."

"Maybe you need to keep a list of things that need to get done, Gloria."

There was no response.

"Don't you think that would be a good idea, Gloria?"

"I didn't forget, ma'am."

"But you didn't pick up the dry cleaning."

"The dry cleaner was closed yesterday, ma'am."

Was it Meredith's imagination or did she see a hint of amusement in Gloria's eyes? The housekeeper seemed to relish these exchanges. The problem was that Henry had hired Gloria and she'd worked for him for a year before Meredith accepted his proposal of marriage. It didn't help that he was still visiting at least once a week, ostensibly to pick up things he'd left behind, but Meredith knew it was mainly to piss her off. Gloria seemed to enjoy that almost as much as he did. She'd fire her, but then she'd have to find and train another reliable housekeeper. Better to put up with the crap you know, especially if it was just for a while.

As soon as the house sold, she could rid herself of Gloria, of Henry, of Steerforth and its boring residents, and start a new life where people understood the meaning of the word "fun."

She took a last sip of mocha latte and carried the open

Starbucks cup over to the counter, deliberately slopping it so the liquid spilled over the edges and spread onto the freshly cleaned granite. "Oops," she said with a little laugh. Two could play at this game. Gloria showed no reaction, but moved slowly over to mop up the spill.

Meredith took the front stairs to the second floor, her bare feet sinking into the plush carpeting, trying to survey the house with fresh eyes. Why was it taking so long to sell? It wasn't priced too high; the people in Steerforth were just Yankee cheapskates. She'd done everything she could to make sure the place was spotless whenever there was a showing, even hiring an extra cleaning service to keep up with the demand. It was exhausting and it was taking a toll on her physically.

The lights surrounding the vanity in the master bath were shockingly bright. Meredith traced the lines at the corners of her eyes and turned sideways to survey the cellulite on her outer thighs. She hadn't had time for a full spa treatment in months, and with the divorce she'd had to cut down on facials. The biggest asset she'd gotten was this house, which had seemed like a great thing at the time. But if it didn't sell soon she wouldn't be able to keep the gym membership, much less have the money to quit this town.

She'd met Sheila at a spin class and she'd been confident that the bubbly, effervescent, and hardworking real estate agent would be able to sell her house. And it had almost sold in the first week. Sheila had a buyer in from Texas and he'd been to see the house twice, even bringing his wife in to approve his choice. But then they'd brought in a home inspector. Five thousand dollars for French drains later, the buyers had found someplace else they liked better and Meredith still had to pay a small fortune for a landscape crew to come and prettify the mud piles left behind.

Sheila called it a "small setback," but that was before the neighbor next door decided to contest the survey she'd done to sell the house. Another couple of thou to have the survey redone, plus the lawyer's fees for battling the neighbor. It just went on and on. This house was sucking her dry and wasn't it just her luck to have her realtor get murdered? Nobody believed her when she told them.

Of course, the powers-that-be at Braxton had been apologetic and assured her that this would not slow down the sale and that Sheila's close friend and fellow realtor would make it her highest priority. They kept reminding her how "shocking" Sheila's death was and how "devastated" everybody was at the office. As if they needed to remind her that Sheila had been killed. Like she wasn't well aware of that. She didn't lack sympathy, but for God's sake, this was business.

Well, she knew how to make them pay attention. It hadn't been just a threat to take her business elsewhere, either. Meredith was just about convinced that it was the realty office itself that was bringing her all this bad luck. Probably bad feng shui.

She dialed Amy Moran's number. Again. It was easily the fourth time today that she'd gotten the woman's voice mail. Was this woman ever working?

She heard the faint ring of the doorbell as she fought her way into a blush-pink lycra-and-spandex ensemble that made her look ten pounds thinner. She had the shirt over her head when a sudden voice made her jump.

"Amy Moran is here, ma'am."

"Jesus, Gloria!"

The woman didn't hear her. She was already making the bed, moving with the same slow efficiency with which she did everything else.

Amy Moran stood in the foyer examining a framed black-and-white photo of mountains, looking far more cool and collected than she had a right to with an unhappy client.

"Is this an Ansel Adams?" she said, looking up when she heard Meredith's footsteps on the stairs.

"I have no idea," Meredith said crisply. "Is the sign up in my yard?"

"It'll be up later today. Four at the latest."

"I want it up now."

The realtor nodded. "I know, I'm sorry, but it's been a very bad week—"

"Ms. Moran, I'm not interested in hearing another sob story—I want the FOR SALE sign in my yard and I want it now."

"I'm afraid I can't put it in for you. You need a hole digger to sink the wooden pole. I don't carry a hole digger around in my trunk."

Meredith thought she might truly choke with rage. "Is that what you came here to tell me?"

"No, I came to tell you that I've got two more showings arranged."

"It's about damn time. Who are they?"

"Um, I'm not sure . . ." the woman faltered, struggling to open her leather purse as if the answer was somehow mysteriously contained inside. Meredith didn't bother to hide her annoyance.

"You're not sure? Look, I don't want my time wasted with people who aren't serious buyers. Don't you vet any of these people before showing them better properties? Why on earth should I put myself through so much for people who can't even afford my house?"

Amy extracted a notebook and flipped through its pages. "One's a neurosurgeon. He's relocating with his family from Atlanta. Does he meet your criteria?"

The sarcasm was hidden. Just. Meredith longed to yank out the chignon, rip the wool suit and reduce this woman to tears. She had to settle for looking unimpressed.

"And the other one?"

"A lawyer."

"Just a lawyer? What kind of law?"

"I don't know, I didn't ask her," Amy snapped. "I do know that she works for one of the biggest firms in New York."

"Oh. Well, that sounds good." Things were definitely looking up. "When are the showings?"

"Friday."

"And is the open house being advertised for tomorrow?"

"You're not on the open house schedule for Sunday—"

"Oh, yes, I am. I made it very clear when I talked to Poppy that I expect another open house this Sunday." Meredith tried to do the deep breathing she'd learned in her yoga class, massaging her temples to stave off the migraine she could feel beginning to pulse.

"Poppy didn't mention that—"

"Then talk to Poppy. But I expect you here on Sunday and I expect to see it advertised, unlike last time." Meredith checked her watch and saw that she now had all of five minutes to get to her spin class. Was it any wonder that she needed another Botox treatment only four months after the last one?

"I'll try, Mrs. Chomsky, but—"

"Don't try," Meredith said, ushering the realtor ahead of her out the door. "Just do it."

Chapter 10

In his sleep, Mark returned to the same place over and over. One A.M., near an intersection on the Lower East Side. There's a call on the radio but it goes to static. Domestic dispute in an apartment building near the corner they're staking out. Neighbors complaining about two men fighting.

"Probably some faggots," Mark's partner says and his laugh seems to echo, going on for a long time in the silence of the night.

"We're on it," Mark radios in. They step out of the Taurus, regulation unmarked, and scan the corner one more time. There are supposed to be some heroin sales going on here, but narcotics can't be bothered with some penny-ante single sales. They sure as hell aren't going to take one of their men off the smuggling case they're about to crack to pull in homicide's low-level drug dealer suspect in last week's no-name, pull-from-the-river gangland killing.

So Mark and Tyson have been here for three nights waiting for action that never happens, the Taurus getting full of wrappers from Mickey D's because Tyson has this thing for Quarter Pounders and he's a big man with a big appetite.

The apartment's a walk-up, naturally. They can hear the fighting before they get to the fifth floor. Loud shouting, male voices and the occasional sound of something shattering. They're both sweating in the stifling heat of the stairwell and Tyson's cursing as they take the last flight 'cause his knees haven't been good since he played high school ball.

He pounds on the door when they get there, using his best Black Panther don't-take-no-shit voice to tell the noisy fools that the police are there and they'd better open the fuck up. Dead silence. Tyson grins over his shoulder at Mark. They hear whispering and Tyson pounds again, demanding that they open up and open up now.

When the door opens, and it seems to open in slow motion, Mark is behind Tyson, backing him up. The door swings open and there's that unmistakable *pop*, Mark swears he hears that *pop*, and Tyson clutches his chest and drops, all in one motion. Mark shouts his name and then the figure in the doorway swings his way, arm rising in his direction, something dark in the hand—

Mark woke with a gasp, ambulance sirens ringing in his head. Only they were real and he stumbled out of bed and was halfway to the door when the sirens faded into the distance.

He was sweating, even though the temperature had dropped to freezing, and he stripped off his T-shirt and mopped his face with it before heading out to the bathroom across the hall. It was dark, but there in the light socket next to the mirrored cabinet was the same night-light he'd grown up with, a small plastic crucifix, the Jesus figure glowing. His mother had brought it home from a retreat years before and it had been in this small bathroom ever since. Unless it broke, it would probably stay here forever because his parents seemed to think that you needed divine intervention in every single room in the house.

He pissed and washed his hands and then splashed cool

water over his face, trying not to think about the dream, not to see Tyson falling, that arm raised in his direction.

A small tap at the door startled him. Mark hastily turned off the water. His mother stood outside the bathroom, huddled in a red fleece robe that he'd given her for Christmas the year before.

"I heard the water," she whispered. "Are you okay?"

"Yeah, I'm fine. Sorry, I woke you—especially on your night off."

He found it hard to meet her eyes when she looked at him with such a knowing expression.

"Are you hungry? Come on in the kitchen and I can make you something to eat."

"No. Thanks, Mom, but I think I'll just head back to bed."

But she tugged his arm with her small hand, ushering him along to the kitchen. "I've got just the thing to help you sleep."

She switched on the light in the small kitchen and pushed him toward the table. "Sit. I'll do this."

"Mom, I've got to be up in a few hours."

"Yes, yes." She had her back to him, fussing at the stove and opening the fridge to fetch something she poured into a saucepan.

"Tell me that's not warm milk."

"It always helped you fall back to sleep after nightmares. Do you remember?"

"I'm not sure you've noticed, but I'm not ten anymore."

"So? You still have nightmares, don't you?" She shot another knowing look over her shoulder.

"I didn't mean to wake you."

"We've covered that," she said in a deep growl that was such a perfect imitation of his pre-stroke father that Mark burst out laughing.

His mother smiled. "Hush, you'll wake your dad." She brought two mugs of milk to the table and then fetched the bear-shaped bottle of honey.

"I'd prefer a shot of whiskey," he said, reaching for the honey and drizzling it into his mug.

"The last thing you need is more liquor."

Mark blushed. "I haven't been drinking that much."

"Oh? Is this what you did in the city? Every night out to the bars?"

His blush deepened and he avoided her gaze, relentlessly stirring the milk. "I'm a grown man."

"Who's still my son. I want to know what's going on with you."

"Nothing's going on with me."

"You're out until all hours drinking. I heard you crying out in your sleep. You look tired and run-down."

Mark scowled at the milk and took a small sip.

"I'm fine, Mom."

"You're so far from fine that I'm not sure you even remember what the word means."

"Don't you have enough to deal with? I'm not one of your patients."

The smack of his mother's hand on the table startled him. "Jesus, you made me burn my mouth."

"Do you need some ice?"

"No, it's okay."

"How about some water?"

"No, I'm fine. I mean, I think I'm fine, but I'm not sure I remember what that word even means."

"Smart mouth."

They smiled at each other and for a few minutes there was just companionable silence. Why it happened in that silence, Mark didn't know, but all at once his eyes filled and spilled over and he was crying. It wasn't a few dignified tears either, but real crying with long, ragged-sounding sobs.

Mark turned in his seat, swiping at his eyes and struggling to contain himself. Then he felt her hand on his head, softly stroking. When she pressed gently, he let his head fall forward against her and allowed himself to be held.

The clock said four A.M. Amy was wide awake, lying alone in the dark in the spacious cavern of the bed they'd once shared together, thinking of Chris. Out of habit, out of desire for what wasn't, she still slept on what had always been her side of the bed, though lately she'd begun creeping toward the middle. It was here, in the quiet of the night, that she missed him the most. The irony was that sex, which had been at the heart of her troubles with Chris, was also the only thing that had worked perfectly for them.

She'd been angrier with him than with any person she'd ever known and still, even at the height of whatever fight they'd been having, she could fall into bed with him. Of course, that was exactly what he was doing with everybody else, and that was the problem.

"He chases anything in a skirt." She'd heard an adult use that expression when she was growing up and thought they were talking about a neighbor's German shepherd. She'd always been naïve.

When she looked back at her first meeting with Chris, all the signs had been there. They met at a frat party she'd been dragged to by a friend and he'd been attending with another girl.

"Don't you like parties?" he'd asked, finding her nursing a beer in the kitchen and examining the photos someone had stuck to the dirty fridge with alphabet magnets. He'd smiled at her, his trademark boyish grin, the charm kicking in automatically because she was a girl, because she was there, because he could never resist the challenge of having a female focus her attention on him.

Amy sighed and rolled to her other side, trying to forget the way it felt when he'd moved toward her, extending one arm to rest on the fridge so that he was almost touching her shoulder, his head ducking down, ostensibly looking at the photos. She could smell the citrus shampoo he used on his sunshine hair and see the tiny freckle on one earlobe.

The other girl, his date, found them like that, announcing her arrival with a fake cough and a pissed-off sounding, "Chris?"

She should have known then, watching him in action. Seeing how swiftly he moved, turning that smile on the other girl and taking her in his arms as if she were a meal he'd been waiting for. "Baby," he'd said, just loud enough for Amy to hear. "Baby, where've you been? I've been looking for you."

Warning bells should've sounded, but they didn't because she was naïve and because that was part of Chris's charm. Instead, she'd wished that she were that girl in his arms. She'd felt that desire flash through her, a tingling sensation that reached up inside her and shook her to her core. She thought it was the sign that she'd met her one true love and not that he had some unique ability to tickle a woman's G-spot without even touching her.

When Amy saw him on campus the next day, she thought it was a happy accident of fate. When she went to bed with him the following week, she thought they'd both been briefly overcome by passion. When she married him the summer after graduation, she thought it was funny when he stumbled over the word "fidelity."

She was six months pregnant with Emma when she got her wake-up call. Chris worked late nights, the golden boy of the Manhattan firm where his uncle was a senior partner. They lived in a small, but modernized apartment in Brooklyn in a good building. It was affordable only because it was rent-stabilized and they had help from their parents, and she was still working at the gallery in SoHo and spending evenings and weekends trying to work on her own portfolio.

It was summertime and they had a single air-conditioning

unit in their bedroom. She was trying to find a comfortable spot on the lumpy mattress, looking through some photos she'd taken of barges on the East River and trying to ignore the kickboxing going on in her stomach. When the phone rang, she had to waddle into the other room to answer it.

"Is Chris there?" A breathy, giggly, little-girl-in-a-big-girl's-body voice.

She was curious, but not alarmed. Not yet. "He's not here right now. May I take a message?"

"Oh. No, I'm sure he'll be here soon. Thanks!"

Click. She'd rung off before Amy could ask where "here" was. She paused, wondering if it was a wrong number, just a weird coincidence that the person calling had been looking for a Chris. Then she hit the redial.

"Hi!" Breathy voice again, sounding happy. Conversation in the background, the sound of glasses clinking.

"Hi, you just called my number? You were looking for Chris?"

"Yeah?"

"Chris Moran?"

"Yeah. Listen, is he coming or not?"

"Where?"

"What?"

"Where is he supposed to meet you?"

"Longfellow's on Ninth. Who is this?"

"Who are you?"

A pause and then she heard a whispered, "Oh, shit." The phone clicked quietly off.

She rang again and this time no one answered, not then and not the next two times she called. She took the phone with her back to bed and stared at the photos of barges until they blurred into black-and-white pixels. At two A.M. she heard Chris's key in the door. She didn't call out. She didn't say anything, listening to the sounds of him taking off his jacket, peeing, brushing his teeth and slowly undressing in the tiny hallway, leaving his clothes in a neat pile on a chair, something he always did so he wouldn't wake her up when he came home.

"Whoa, baby, you're up late." He looked startled, the self-assurance gone just for a split second, but then the smile was back. He sank down on the bed next to her, resting a hand on her belly. "What's wrong, is Sprout giving you trouble?"

"Sprout" was for the baby growing inside whose sex they'd been dying to find out but decided not to at the ultra-sound a week before. Amy had been ecstatic that day and un-able to sleep that night because her baby was healthy and whole and beautiful.

"Where were you?"

"Have you been missing me? I'm so sorry, baby, but it's this case. It's killer."

He'd stripped down to his boxers, but she found herself sniffing him anyway. Could she detect another scent? She leaned toward him and he laughed.

"Oh, I see." His hand snaked down and rubbed her mound through the thin nightgown. "Have I been neglecting you?"

There was shame at feeling herself aroused by him. "Did you make it to Longfellow's?"

The hand stilled, but just for a moment. He brought his mouth down to her thighs, licking up the insides, long, slow strokes of his tongue inching closer and closer to the part of her that always responded to his attention.

She arched toward him automatically, but realized it and stopped, filled with a sudden rage at him for being so manip-ulative, at her for being so easily manipulated.

Arching her right thigh, she caught him hard in the jaw. "Get off!"

"Ow! What the fuck?" He was stunned, kneeling there in bed beside her, holding his hand to his cheek with a wounded expression. She found she didn't care.

"I know you were at Longfellow's, Chris. What I'd like to know is who the woman is that you were meeting."

He was going to lie. She watched it on his face and wondered how she could have been fooled for so long. He must have seen her expression because he sighed, a long drawn-out sound of defeat.

"She's just a woman I met at a bar. A nobody."

The first thought she'd had was to wonder if that's how he'd referred to her back in college. Who was that girl in the kitchen? Oh, just a nobody.

"What's her name?"

"Amy, you don't need to know that—"

She'd pulled away from him, huddling against the headboard. "What's her name!"

"Tempo."

"Tempo? That's the name of a car, not a person."

"Well, that's her name."

"Did you have sex with her?"

"Jesus, Amy!" He pushed off the bed and stalked out the bedroom door and she followed after him, but he was only getting his clothes to hang up. He'd always cared for his clothes, buying the highest quality and taking care of it when he got it.

"Did you?"

He emptied the pockets of his pants with sharp, jerky movements, slamming his cell phone and a handful of change onto his dresser. Something white fluttered to the floor. A business card. Amy stooped and got it before Chris. She turned it over and read: TEMPO WHITLEY, VICE-PRESIDENT OF MARKETING, MILANO COSMETICS.

She was stunned. It hadn't occurred to her that the breathy-voiced girl on the line could be someone so successful. Chris snatched the card from her hand, but not before she'd seen the words sprawled in blue ink: "Call me."

"How many times, Chris?"

"She's just a girl, Amy. It doesn't matter."

"How many times did you fuck her?"

"Oh, for God's sake—"

"Why won't you tell me? Is it where you did it? Oh, my God, did you do it here?"

"No!"

"Well, where then? A back room at Longfellow's? A hotel?"

Chris sighed again and didn't answer for a long moment, carefully lining up the creases in his pants before putting them on a hanger. "Her place," he said, very low.

"What?"

"We went to her place. Her apartment. Okay? Are you satisfied?"

He actually sounded angry, as if he'd been the one violated. She retreated back onto the bed, drawing her knees as far up as her belly would allow.

"Amy, baby, she doesn't matter." His voice was soft again, his eyes pleading. "It's just a guy thing."

His own particular version of boys will be boys. How many times had she heard that from him over the last five years? Amy turned again, trying to find a comfortable position so she could fall back to sleep.

She'd had trouble sleeping those last weeks of her pregnancy with Emma. Chris had been so kind, rubbing her back and stroking her head and tucking her against him so that, despite her massive size, she felt held and secure. And he'd been great during labor, too, helping her breathe just like they'd practiced in Lamaze, coaching her through it like a pro. So what if he'd had more late nights two weeks after she'd given birth to Emma?

"Do you really want to know where he is?" her mother said, gently burping Emma after Amy had nursed her. "Why not just be happy that he's not demanding that attention of you right now?"

"He's cheating on me!"

"He's a man, Amy. Men have different needs than we do. If he's giving you everything you need, why not just be happy?"

Why hadn't she been happy? Was it just the knowledge that he was having sex with other women? Was it the fact that she'd begun unconsciously counting her own failings, checking herself obsessively in the mirror for flaws and working out compulsively to shed the baby fat. Even sex, which had always relaxed her, became work. She'd wonder if he'd tried that same position with someone else, or whether he was comparing her to a string of other women, not to mention the fears that she'd contract a disease. He'd agreed to get tested with her, even though he informed her that he always wore condoms, and seemed to expect an apology when the results were negative. She didn't offer one.

For a time, she became obsessed with exactly how many women he'd slept with, pestering him to get a number that he refused to divulge. Then she reached the shocking conclusion that it wasn't so much a stubborn refusal to say it, as it was an inability to recall, which was an answer in itself.

In the midst of this stress was Emma. A perfect baby. That's what they'd said at the hospital. Lovely proportions, healthy color, ten fingers, ten toes and a high Apgar score. At three weeks old, she started wheezing. A faint snuffle, nothing to be concerned about, maybe she'd caught a cold, the pediatrician said. Her lungs seemed a little full. Only the cold didn't go away and the wheezing increased.

Maybe she's allergic to your breast milk. Feed her soy formula and see what happens. She hated the soy and it didn't stop the wheezing. Amy went back to breast-feeding, listening intently to every labored breath, and watching the tiny rib cage quivering in its thin layer of skin.

"Asthma," the specialist declared at eight months. A regimen of medication and breathing treatments started that had to be followed precisely. Amy did it all, while Chris seemed fixed on figuring out how it had happened.

"There's no asthma on my side," he said. "I checked with my mother and she can go back three generations. Nobody. So have you asked your mother?"

Amy had been fixing a tiny oxygen mask to their daughter's sweet little face. "Yes. None of us had it and she can't remember anybody with asthma."

"How far back?"

"For heaven's sake, Chris, what difference does it make?"

"I just want to know."

Another day he'd asked if she'd remembered to take all her prenatal vitamins. "Sometimes vitamin deficiency can lead to asthma."

He seemed afraid to touch Emma and he wanted her to do all the treatments. "You're better at it," he'd said.

"But what if she has an attack when she's out with you? You need to be able to give her the inhaler."

"You should always be with her. She responds better to you and we can't risk it."

At night, Amy was the one who monitored Emma, waking up abruptly if there was a change in her breathing. There was an eight-month period when she was so exhausted that everything was a blur and she barely noticed the change from day to night. In that time, Chris's nights got later and later and then one night he didn't come home at all.

She didn't even realize it until the following afternoon when Emma slept long enough for Amy to get a load of laundry done and she couldn't find the shirt he'd worn the day before. He came home late that night as if nothing had happened and at that moment she made a deliberate choice to feign sleep and say nothing.

Her days fell into a routine. In the mornings, she took Emma to the playground around the corner and there they'd meet other mothers and babies. On cold mornings, they'd gather at a local coffee shop instead, strollers clustered around the small tables, the babies bundled in festive winter hats and snowsuits. Often Emma cooed and laughed and her breathing wasn't a problem all day. Amy began to look at her photos again and thought about pulling together enough of them to have a show.

Chris encouraged her to take Emma out to the country, to his aunt's home in Steerforth. There would be other mothers and babies in the suburb and there would be green grass and acres of trees giving off oxygen so there was plenty of clean air. She loved the city, but Steerforth had its charms. It was a Norman Rockwell place, with its pretty frame houses and window boxes overflowing with flowers. The town was an eclectic and charming mixture of old and new. There was an old-fashioned station with trains running hourly into the city. Off she'd go to Grand Central, hauling Emma, the stroller, and a bag packed full with baby things and her photography equipment.

Chris was barely home anymore, blaming his desire to make partner for his later and later nights. He reacted angrily when Amy told him he wasn't seeing enough of Emma. One day she overheard him telling his mother that the air in Steerforth hadn't cleared up Emma's asthma as expected.

"Did you think she was going to be cured?" Amy said. "That fresh air was all she needed?"

"I never saw myself as the parent of a sick child."

She'd misunderstood him. "I guess nobody expects it, but it's the hand we've been dealt."

"It doesn't have to be! You should take her to another specialist—I don't think this one's doing enough."

She'd been astounded. Dr. Rez Mohammed was an expert in children's pulmonary problems. She'd been lucky to get Emma seen by him. They argued, speaking in angry whispers so that Emma wouldn't hear and that night, for the second time, Chris didn't return home.

The next evening, he brought her flowers and said he was sorry "we fought." He didn't mention the other woman that she could smell on his clothes. When she wondered out loud if he should get another HIV test, he reacted angrily, blaming her for not meeting his needs.

"Men need sex like women need water," her mother counseled when she'd pried the information out of Amy. "If you can't meet his needs, he's going to find it elsewhere. It would help if you fixed yourself up a little. When was the last time you got your hair styled?"

She thought about that, thought about the women she'd seen who became totally consumed by parenting and forgot they were independent people with passions, including sexual ones, of their own. She threw herself back into her photography and hired babysitters to help with Emma's care. She spent less time in Steerforth and more at the gallery in SoHo. She integrated some sexy, non-nursing clothes back into her wardrobe. She even had her hair done.

Chris seemed to notice. He came home early a few nights. One night they even made love in their small kitchen, her with her dress up, sitting on a countertop, him with his pants around his ankles, the stir-fry turned low on the stove, the lights of the city glittering across the river outside their window.

When she got her first solo show, he promised he'd be there, only to call her late that afternoon to inform her that he wouldn't be there on time, if at all.

"I'm so sorry, babe, but it's this case. I'll try to make it. I'll do everything I can to get out of here."

The crowd at the gallery hummed and glittered under the lights. They clustered around the black-and-white photographs—her photographs—on the walls and Amy watched them, nursing a glass of good champagne.

Every corner of the tiny spot in SoHo was filled with people. Evening clothes in various shades and textures of black were relieved by occasional splashes of color—the white of a French cuff, the vibrant blue of a silk tie.

She was in red, a rich red velvet dress that hugged every curve. It was a loaner from Perry, who said that she absolutely must wear it to her first solo show because everyone would want to spot the artist.

They found her, admirers of her work coming one after the other, making their way through the crowd with drinks and small canapé plates held aloft. She smiled, she laughed, she tried to keep her eyes from straying to the door every time she heard it swish open and felt wisps of cold air filter through the gallery.

It was the end of February. Winter was holding on in New York, one dreary day after another, the holidays so far in the past that everyone had forgotten that the sight of perfect snowflakes like those now falling once evoked sighs of pleasure not pain.

"We're going to get another two inches," the cabdriver had bitched to Amy as he'd raced through the maze of Manhattan traffic two hours before. "The slop's barely been cleared from the last one!"

At the sixth-hour mark, the last of the gallery emptied. Almost every photograph was marked with a sold sticker. The gallery owner, Sebastian, was finishing the last bottle of champagne, leaning against a pillar and extolling the quality of the caviar while the caterer's crew moved silently around him, softly clinking lipstick-stained glasses as they loaded them onto trays.

"Do you want a ride back, sweetheart?" he offered. "I'm heading to Williamsburg."

"No, no thanks. I'll just grab a cab."

The depression hit once she was in the taxi. The driver this time was foreign. He barely understood her and she had to repeat the address of her apartment building.

The taxi made good time, the driver having yet to learn

the art of extending his fares. She paid him, tipped him and tottered into the building, thinking that she wouldn't wear heels again for at least a month.

Lying in bed now, she thought back to that night, realizing that if the cab had taken longer, if she'd lingered in the lobby, or the elevator had been broken, things might have been different.

A man called out to hold the door just as she pushed the button and he stepped on with a bichon frise. His nose was red, his dog was shivering in its little embroidered sweater. He eyed her cleavage and Amy pulled her coat tight around her.

Seventh floor and the man got out. Up again, an almost silent climb. A faint whir of the silver box rising and the *ping* as it landed on each floor. Amy thought of how Emma loved to count the numbers up to fifteen. She hoped Emma was having fun sleeping over at her grandmother's house. The apartment would feel empty without her.

Only it wasn't empty. Lights were on in the hallway. Chris's dress coat was tossed over the back of the sofa. Another coat lay next to it. Soft music was coming from the bedroom. Soft voices. A sudden squeal.

Afterward, Amy would not remember walking down the hall, but she must have, because all at once she was at the doorway to the bedroom. Her bedroom. The one she shared with her husband—his and her sides of the bed, his and her mismatched nightstands, his and her books and glasses and mugs of forgotten tea.

It was this moment, so many months later, that she remembered most clearly as if she'd captured the image on film: Chris's naked back to her, the light tan of the shoulders that she'd kissed, the long line of the spine that she'd traced, the whiter flesh of the backside she'd gripped, all in the tight embrace of another woman.

Chapter 11

The manila envelope was tucked under the windshield wiper of Meredith's Mercedes SUV when she came out of Whole Foods. She pulled it out, careful not to scratch the black paint, and carried it into the car with her, tossing it on the passenger seat as she roared out of the parking lot.

She drove one-handed, punching a number into her cell phone and glancing from the road to the envelope. There was no return address.

"Hi, Carla, it's Meredith. I'm running a little late, okay? Let Maurice know that I'll be there in ten and he'd better dare not complain because I've had the day from hell." She listened for a moment. "Great. Thanks, Carla. You're a doll. Ciao."

She closed the phone and tossed it on the seat, picking up the envelope and looking at it more closely. Suddenly she had to brake hard as the Camry in front of her stopped short at a light. Meredith laid on the horn and flicked the driver a manicured middle finger before sliding the nail under the flap and ripping open the envelope. The light changed and she let the envelope drop on the seat as she hit the gas.

It wasn't until she'd pulled into the spa parking lot that she saw the photos that had slid out onto the leather seat.

They were all of her. Naked. Meredith flicked through them once, then again, hands shaking with rage. "You bastard, Henry!"

She thrust the photos back in the envelope and slid it under the seat so no one else could see her ex's latest attempt at shaming her. Well, it was going to backfire on him.

Cell phone in hand, she stormed into the spa as she dialed Chomsky Cellular Technology. "I want to speak to Henry," she said, handing over her purse and accepting the white robe the receptionist offered her. Walking back toward the massage rooms, she listened to the terrible elevator music Henry's company played for waiting customers before his simpering assistant told her that Henry "wasn't available."

"Yeah, I'll just bet he isn't," Meredith said, stalking into a dressing room and stripping off her clothes while she balanced the phone on her ear. She slipped on the robe and mouthed "one minute" at Maurice, who was leaning against the wall flipping through *Vanity Fair* magazine. Then she said out loud, "Listen, you tell that little rat bastard that my lawyer's seen the pictures and he's talking compensation for emotional distress."

She listened for a second. "Oh, he'll know what pictures. Just tell him!" She slammed the phone shut and climbed onto the padded table on her stomach, letting her head fall into the groove in front. "Okay, Maurice. Do me."

Marriages ruined by death, adultery, divorce—all of the sad stories had been told at one time or another by members of the single-parent support group while the others listened, hands clutching Styrofoam cups of cheap coffee.

Wednesday night's meeting was little different, except

that even longtime members were wearing the shell-shocked expression typically reserved for newcomers.

"We're all saddened by the untimely death of Sheila Sylvester," Father Michael said in an announcement. He'd made his way down to the basement early, instead of waiting to pop in and say hello at a later point in the meeting.

There were several new members who weren't sure who Sheila was and other members relayed the information in whispers. Amy could feel their eyes finding her, and she knew that she'd become the "one who found the body."

It was something Sheila would have laughed at, but Amy couldn't manage it. Instead, she found herself looking around at the members of the group. Could one of them have killed her? Sheila's brashness, her bold laughter, her frank talk had managed to offend virtually every member at one time or another, but they'd all forgiven her because she was just as likely to laugh at herself.

If someone mentioned being afraid to confront their ex in court about custody, Sheila would show up at the hearing for moral support. Once a member had mentioned how exhausting it was to single-handedly care for both her dying father and her young son and Sheila paid for a local restaurant to provide a month's worth of free dinners.

Maybe she hadn't been universally liked, but surely no one had hated her enough to kill her. Yet Amy couldn't help viewing the group with suspicion, probably because the police hadn't made any arrest and because she'd been back to the station at the behest of Detectives Black and Juarez to answer pointed questions about Sheila's relationships with others.

"Did she have any disagreements with anybody recently?" Detective Juarez said. "Did she ever mention an altercation with anybody?"

Put on the spot, she'd been unable to think of any. But sitting here, looking surreptitiously at the other members, she recalled an argument Sheila had three weeks earlier with Richard.

What had started it was never quite clear to Amy. People were milling about in small groups toward the end of the regular meeting and she'd wandered over to fetch more coffee. One minute there'd been a conversation going on about kids and the next minute Richard was red faced and yelling at Sheila.

"You don't know what you're talking about!"

"Just because you yell louder, doesn't make you smarter!" Sheila said back. "My opinions are fact based, unlike yours, which are based solely on emotion!"

What had they been fighting about? Amy didn't know. She'd pulled Sheila away from the fight, never an easy thing to do, but she hadn't gotten her to explain why Richard had been so angry. Sheila claimed not to know.

"He's overly sensitive," she'd said when Amy pressed. "He thinks his good looks are enough to carry him through everything, but he needs to learn some manners."

Richard was sitting, as he usually did, on the edge of the circle, leaning back in the metal folding chair with his eyes half-shut, as if he couldn't be bothered to stay fully awake for the conversation. Amy looked at him, trying to picture him hurting Sheila, but it was hard to get past the physical. Despite a day's worth of beard, ratty jeans, and a ragged fisherman's sweater, Richard still looked like he'd just gotten done with a photo shoot for *GQ*. He caught Amy looking and winked. She turned quickly away, trying to pretend she was looking for something or someone else, but she could feel his eyes on her and knew that he wasn't fooled.

They were introducing new members and Amy tried to concentrate on that. She listened as a teary-eyed woman named Elaine, with nails bitten to the quick, described her husband leaving her and their four children.

When Elaine was finished, Father Michael introduced another new member, a boyish-looking man with short-cropped blond hair and wire-rimmed glasses. Paul told them about his wife's death from cancer, fiddling with his glasses as he spoke in a soft voice. Most of the women and a few of the men were crying when he described holding their infant son at his mother's deathbed.

After those stories, everyone needed a break, and Amy wandered over to the refreshment table to get more coffee. Jackson made a point of walking away when she came near and she wondered if the police had interviewed him yet.

The new member, Paul, joined her by the coffee urn. He smiled at her and she said, "I'm so sorry for your loss."

"Thank you, but I'm coming to terms with it. It's been five months, but I feel as if Beth's still with me. I mean, I know she'll always be with me in spirit, but sometimes I feel as if she's really with me."

"How are you managing with your son?"

"Beth's sister watches him while I'm at work and then we have our evenings and weekends together. He's too young to remember Beth, of course, but I keep showing him her picture."

"You are so brave." Audrey joined them at the coffee urn, gripping Paul's forearm and giving it a little shake for emphasis. "I don't know many men who could manage as well as you are."

"I'm sure everyone has different methods of coping," he said, gently detaching her.

"That's a polite way to put it," she said with a bitter laugh. "When my first husband's mother died, he coped by blowing his inheritance on coke."

"You've been married more than once?" Paul said and Amy knew he was wondering why she was in a single-parent group. Having heard it all before, she hid a smile.

"I've been married three times and they were all big, big disappointments," Audrey said. "But I'm very positive and I just know that my perfect man is out there, ready to be a family with me and my little girl. I just have to trust that he'll find me." She beamed at Paul and he smiled faintly, fiddling with his glasses.

Amy excused herself and walked over to Father Michael, who was making his goodbyes. "Thank you for the nice things you said about Sheila at her funeral," she said. "I really appreciated it and I know her family did, too."

"Very kind of you to say, my dear," the elfin priest said, patting her hand. "Though you know as well as I do that Sheila would have hated it."

Amy laughed, the first genuine laugh she'd given in days. At the same time, tears sprang to her eyes. "At least you didn't call her the finest person who ever walked the earth."

Father Michael smiled. "I know she'd be haunting me if I did that." He looked distracted. "I just hope her death doesn't hurt other people."

"How do you mean?"

"The police are asking around, trying to find her killer. Innocent people could get caught under their prying eyes."

What did he mean by that? Before she could ask, Bridget pulled him away, urging him to take some cookies home. Were other members complaining about the fact that their names had been given to the police? Father Michael had seemed to support her in that earlier, but something, or somebody, had changed his mind. But what had her option been? Refuse to tell the police? Play dumb?

All at once Amy felt like she needed a break. She didn't want to hear any more sad stories or talk about what it had been like finding Sheila's body. It suddenly seemed as if the whole group existed only as a meeting place for complaints and tales of woe and she didn't want to be part of that.

Making an excuse about needing to get home to Emma, she said goodbye to their unofficial leader, Penelope, and waved to the other members of the group before escaping up the steps, through the basement doors and out into the crisp night air.

She stopped short when she saw that Richard was standing just outside the doors. His back was to her as he spoke quietly but rapidly into a cell phone.

"No fucking way. I'm not taking the fall on this. That is not the way it's going down."

She stood still, but he whirled around obviously having heard her.

"I've got to go," he said into the phone while scowling at Amy. He snapped it closed. "Why are you eavesdropping?"

"I wasn't," Amy said, scowling right back. "You're blocking the exit." She stepped around him and hurried toward her car, trying to listen without looking back to see if he was following her.

Only once she was past did the implications of what he'd said on the phone fully hit her. She turned around, sure she could hear his footsteps racing after her, but he was gone and there were only a few leaves scuttling along the empty sidewalk.

Chapter 12

The all-points bulletin that failed to produce Trevor Sylvester for almost two weeks finally worked on Friday afternoon. Black and Juarez got a call from the Blacksburg police department that their suspect was in custody and the UPS van he'd stolen had been impounded.

"Our boy did an O.J. and led staties on a high-speed chase after they tried to pull him over for speeding," Black said as they drove north to pick him up.

"So why's he in custody with them and not the staties?" Mark asked, wincing as Black came close to scraping the side of a pickup truck as he veered around it. The sun seemed to be shining directly into his eyes. He retreated behind his sunglasses and popped two more aspirin into his mouth.

"You're going to get an ulcer, you keep taking those things," Black said. "Blacksburg got him in custody because it was one of their patrol cars that he hit."

"I guess we know what Brown can do for you," Juarez muttered and Black laughed.

The shrill ring of Black's cell phone interrupted his reply

and he drove one-handed, fishing it out of his pocket and practically fishtailing the car. Juarez pressed a hand to his head and tried unsuccessfully to ignore the conversation his partner had with his wife.

"Okay, Maureen, I'll try. . . . No, I can't promise to do more than that, I told you I'm working on a case. . . . Well, then maybe you should send Jimmy. . . . Don't send Jimmy then, just wait for me to pick it up. . . . Yeah, well, it's the best I can do. . . . Really nice, Maureen, really nice. . . . I don't have time for this now. I gotta go. See you tonight."

He hung up and shoved the phone back into his jacket pocket, casting a grumpy glance over at Juarez as if daring him to say something. Mark kept his eyes on the road.

"You dating anyone?"

The question caught Mark by surprise. "Not right now."

"Left someone in the city?"

"Yeah." He felt Black's gaze, but wouldn't look at him.

"Were you serious with her?"

The image that came to him was the delicate feet that always kicked free from the sheets at night and ended up inching over to his side of the bed, tucking, like two small ice packs, against his own larger ones. "Yeah, I guess," he said.

"Did you live together?"

A simple question, but it thrust him back into that argument: "Why not share my place? If you're worried about what your parents think, then we don't have to tell them."

"It won't work," he'd said, but it was hard to hold that ground when those large eyes implored him and that smile begged him to reconsider.

He'd delayed ending the relationship as long as he could, knowing he was making excuses, and then a real one came along.

"We were going to, but my dad had his stroke."

"You got lucky," Black said. "You think dating's a bitch, try living with one!" He laughed loudly at his own humor and Juarez tried to laugh along. One of the guys. All of the other single guys on the shift had girlfriends. Even the rookie, pimply-faced and jug-eared twenty-year-old Feeney. She was one of those chubby girls who wore too-tight midriff tops and about whom everybody said, "She has such a pretty face." They were looking for an apartment together and Feeney was bemoaning the cost of the Vegas wedding they both wanted.

What would it be like to live like that? To be married, to have kids? He tried to picture himself coming home at the end of his shift, walking in and being grabbed around the knees by a toddler calling him "Dad." His wife he pictured as a pretty, black-haired Latina. She'd speak to his children in both Spanish and English. This was the life his parents wanted for him.

"You going to ask that chick out?"

"Who?"

Black stared at him. "Who? The witness, you moron."

"Oh. No. I think she's married."

"So?" Black grinned. "Seriously, you should call her."

"You sound like my mother."

"And you look like a guy who needs to get laid."

"You would know."

The older man guffawed and then slugged Juarez on the bicep. "Ain't that the truth."

They brought Trevor out wearing a prison-quality jumpsuit, "special order from the state," with flip-flops on his feet and nothing else. He stank to high heaven, having refused to bathe since they'd had him in custody, the guard informed them, his own personal protest against his "unjust imprisonment."

"We don't have the equipment like they do up at a supermax," the guard said, "otherwise, we could just strap him down and hose him off."

"That's what you think," Trevor said, straddling the chair in the interrogation room as if he were in some old-time

Western. The guard rolled his eyes and grinned at Juarez and Black.

"Whatdya want?" Trevor said, stretching his tall and lanky frame. His arms were sinewy ropes of muscle that Juarez could easily picture wielding a nail gun. His head was shaved and he had a small blond goatee that looked carefully trimmed.

"When was the last time you saw Sheila?" Black said, sitting down across from him.

"Sheila who?"

"Sheila, your ex-wife," Juarez said, taking the other seat.

Trevor made a hacking noise and Juarez thought he'd actually spit on the floor, but he seemed to think better of it. "I haven't seen that bitch in months."

He had a meanness to him that was evident in the coldness of his muddy brown eyes and the stubborn set of his small mouth. Juarez thought of what his ex must have endured and about the sad bloated woman and her vacant-eyed child at the town house.

"That's not what Mandi told us," Black said. "Mandi told us you talked to Sheila a few weeks ago. She said you were mad about not getting to attend the graduation of your son."

"What the fuck business is it of yours?" Trevor said. "Mandi's a stupid bitch if she's talking to you."

"Were you upset about Sheila refusing to allow you to attend your boy's graduation?" Juarez said.

Trevor looked away for a minute, then stared back at them and Juarez was surprised to see a shine in his eyes. Trevor crying? It didn't fit with his image.

"I've got a right to see my sons," he said. "A father should be allowed to see his sons. That's basic, man, a basic right."

Not if he's beating the crap out of the boy's mother, Juarez thought, unmoved. It was one of the first things you learned as a cop, to stay immune to the self-pity of perps. He'd interviewed a perp who'd sliced open his own mother without showing any emotion while she begged for her life, yet cried like a little boy remembering the loss of his favorite dog. It wasn't his job to understand that madness. Leave it to the defense attorneys and the psychologists to unravel and explain what made someone that way.

"Wow, that sucks. Must have really pissed you off," he said, faking sympathy he didn't begin to feel. "Women like that, makes you wonder why someone hasn't shown them."

"They need to be taken down a peg," Black added. "They need a real man to show them who's in charge."

"Got that right," Trevor said with a smirk, leaning back in his chair. He looked unconcerned and that wasn't where they wanted him, Mark thought.

"Do you own a nail gun?" he said, abruptly changing the subject.

The smirk left Trevor's face. "Yeah," he said slowly.

"Where is it?"

"Who knows? My house, my garage? I'm not doing construction now."

"When was the last time you used it?" Black said.

"How the hell should I remember?" Trevor said. "Why are you asking about my nail gun?"

"You hated Sheila, didn't you, Trevor?"

"Fuck, yeah."

"You wanted to make sure she couldn't keep you from your boys."

"Yeah."

"You wanted her to hurt, the way you were hurt. You didn't mean to kill her—"

"Kill her?" Trevor sat upright. "What the fuck are you talking about?"

"You took your nail gun, maybe just to threaten her, but then she was arguing with you and you put it to her head—"

"No!"

"—and you pressed that trigger. Pop! Pop! Two shots—"

"No fucking way, man!"

"—and she was gone."

"I did not kill Sheila! I didn't even know she was dead!"

Black slammed the table with his fist and Sylvester jumped. "Don't lie to us, Trevor!"

"I'm not lying!"

Mark stood up and leaned over Trevor. "You shot her and you took off in your van because you knew what you'd done, you'd killed your ex. And that's why you ran from the police, too."

Trevor's mouth hung open and he whipped his head from Black to Juarez before turning to look at the guard who was leaning casually against the wall closest to the door. "They're trying to frame me, man!"

"Just tell them the truth, Sylvester."

"This is bullshit. I didn't kill her. I didn't kill anybody!"

"If you didn't kill anybody, then why did you run from the police?" Black said.

"I was drunk!"

Black hesitated and Juarez felt the truth of that resonating in his gut.

"You got drunk after you killed Sheila," Black said slowly, making it more of a statement than a question, but Trevor shook his head hard.

"I had a fight with Mandi and I got drunk and didn't go to work on Monday morning. I just took off in the van."

"Monday?" Juarez said. "You disappeared on Tuesday."

"No, Monday. I called off sick and then I just took off. Didn't want to deal with no shit from nobody. Rolled over the line into another lane and bang. Just like that I've got some cop on my tail. I can't get another DUI conviction. That'll mean jail time. I left on Monday and they picked me up Tuesday morning."

"Jesus Christ," Black said under his breath. Sweating and scowling, he went to confer with the desk sergeant who'd placed the call. He was back looking just as annoyed a few minutes later.

"He was arrested early Tuesday morning," he confirmed. "He can't be the perp."

"Told you I didn't do it," Trevor said with satisfaction.

"Shut up!" Black turned on Sylvester and grabbed him by the front of the jumpsuit, yanking him out of his chair. "We've wasted more than a week looking for your sorry ass! I'm going to personally see to it that you lose your license."

"Hey! It's not my fault you wasted time! You can't pin that on me. I wasn't even that drunk."

"Yeah, and Mandi isn't even that fat."

"You can't talk about my wife!"

"I think I just did." Black stalked out of the room and Juarez followed. He'd known it in his gut, but having the proof made it easier to accept. Trevor Sylvester might have hated his ex, but he didn't have the sophistication or the know-how to have killed her.

"Maybe he hired someone and went off on a bender so suspicion would turn elsewhere," Black said as Juarez pulled the sedan back onto the highway. The sunglasses helped, but the glare was still making his head pound.

"Maybe," he said, noncommittally. "Or maybe it wasn't Trevor at all."

"So what's your theory, genius? And please don't tell me that cock-and-bull story about a serial killer."

"It fits. That's all I'm saying. Look at the evidence."

"Like I haven't been doing just that."

"But you were looking with an eye toward Trevor. Now we know it isn't Trevor—"

"We're not sure of that. Who knows? Maybe the coroner's wrong with the time of death."

"You can't be serious—"

"Why not? Who has the best motivation here? Trevor. And who has the means? Trevor." Black ticked off each point on his pasty fingers. "You've got Mandi lying to us, witnesses to a fight that Trevor and Sheila had before he vanished. It all points to Trevor."

"Except it doesn't. The real evidence points to it being someone with a lot more finesse than Trevor. Here's a guy who's so out of control that when he fights with his wife he gets drunk and steals the company truck."

"Or maybe he's so smart that he's using wife number two to help him cover up the killing of wife number one."

"Do either of them strike you as having the sophistication necessary to pull off that crime scene?" Juarez merged back onto the highway, feeling his head throbbing as he accelerated. "No blood, no weapon—seems awfully clean for those two."

"It's possible, though."

"Sure. And maybe we'll find out that Trevor's got a Harvard degree."

The surgeon didn't want the house. Meredith could tell that just from the brief glimpse she'd gotten of him as she pulled into the driveway at the same time that he was backing out in a brand-new black BMW. The realtor scrambled into her own little car, probably hoping to avoid conversation, but Meredith wouldn't let her get away. She slid down the passenger window of her SUV and called Amy's name.

"I think it went well," Amy said in a too-bright voice that just pissed off Meredith.

"Did he make an offer?"

"Not yet, but—"

"He's not going to, so you're going to need to drum up some more buyers. The house is immaculate and there are fresh flowers. You need to show it again. Tonight." She zipped up the window and sped past the drop-jawed woman into the garage. Stepping out of the car with a small bag in her hand, she pressed the intercom and called for Gloria to fetch the larger shopping bags from the rear.

There was no answer and no appearance of the small woman. "Gloria!" she shouted as she walked into the mud-room. The sight of the housekeeper's thin, cheaply knit blue sweater hanging on a hook reminded Meredith that she'd given Gloria the rest of the day off so that all showings could be private.

Cursing under her breath, Meredith schlepped back into the garage and hefted the Saks and Bloomie bags into the kitchen. Let that snippy realtor move them. She pulled a bottle of rum out of the cupboard and searched the enormous fridge for some diet Coke.

The light on her answering machine was blinking and she hit the play button as she sipped her drink.

"Meredith, it's Henry. What pictures? I have no idea what you're talking about."

Meredith snorted. "Like hell you don't."

"Talk to my lawyer if you've got some proof. And don't call me at the office!"

There was also a call from her own attorney saying that he'd gotten a call from Henry's attorney about Meredith violating the no-communication rule they'd agreed to.

Meredith laughed at that and erased both messages with a single push of her finger. She picked up the small cosmetics bag in one hand and carried it, along with her drink, up to the master bedroom. Tossing the bag on her mammoth bed, she stripped down to her panties and examined herself critically in the full-length walnut mirror that stood in a corner of the room. This was what she did every night, turning to the right, then the left, looking for dimpling flesh, for distended veins, for anything marring the commodity that she was and would be, plastic surgeons and God willing, for a long time to come.

She was examining her breasts, wondering if those babies

needed a little lift, when she froze, remembering the photos. She pivoted slowly, looking around the room for the camera. How had he managed it? She looked toward the tall windows flanking the far side of the room, but Gloria had drawn the curtains, just as she did every afternoon to prevent sun damage.

Maybe Gloria had hidden a camera, conspiring with Henry to take those shots. Was he going to sell them? Post them on the Internet? She hastily pulled a silk robe from the walk-in closet and covered herself.

She caught a glimpse of her worried expression in the mirror as she retrieved her drink and hastily wiped all expression off her face. Worry caused wrinkles and she couldn't afford wrinkles, not competing in this marriage market. Botox, definitely, before she relocated to Aspen. Or Palm Beach. She knew it was going to be one of those two places, but which one was still a mystery. She needed to figure out just how many men were available. With statistics in hand, she'd be able to make a clear, rational decision about where to go to meet her future husband.

It was important to stay stress free and toward that end she'd take a long soak in the whirlpool tub.

If Gloria had been there, Meredith would have asked her to run the bath and add the papaya salt, but Gloria was out relaxing somewhere so she had to do the work herself. She had one foot in the water when she realized that she'd left the facial mask she'd just purchased on her bed. Knotting the robe tightly about her again, she walked out to fetch it.

She thought she heard the stairs creak as if someone were climbing them and she listened for a moment, holding the robe around her. What if Henry had decided to pay a little visit? He damn well better not. "Henry? Is that you?" No one answered. She crept to the door of the bedroom and looked out, but the hallway was empty. She was hearing things now, she thought, closing the door with a decisive click. That bastard's photos had made her paranoid.

Going back in the bathroom, she smeared the avocado spread in a thin layer on her face and climbed into the tub. She sank back and reached for the remote for the TV mounted on the wall. It should have been in its little gold stand and wasn't.

"I really don't need this shit today," she said out loud, splashing water over the side as she stood up and attempted to find the remote and her drink.

Again she heard a noise, a slight thud, but she'd found the remote on top of the vanity and she wasn't about to pull on her robe again and check for ghosts that weren't there. God, she needed to get out of this town.

The water felt good. She switched on the jets and they bubbled against her back and legs, the avocado mask tingling pleasantly on her face. There was some celebrity news show on and she watched it for a while, wondering what it would be like to have sex with a man who looked like George Clooney.

It would be nice if she could meet someone like that, but the men she tended to date were older and had spent more time devoted to business than to grooming. It usually took a long time to rise that high in business—Henry had been positively lizardlike—but there were exceptions. Maybe she could enjoy a little R&R with a younger man before settling down again.

She closed her eyes, listening to the news about a celebrity wedding and letting her body relax. It felt so good to lie here and the only thing that would make it better was a sale.

Chapter 13

He could smell her. Guy paused in the doorway to the massive kitchen and sniffed the air. An aroma of Beautiful and underneath it, a faint musky and unmistakable scent of fresh cunt.

It took very little time to get into the Chomsky house. Security systems only worked if they were switched on and luckily for Guy, that stupid bitch rarely remembered to do that. He returned the lock pick to his pack and closed the back door behind him.

Unzipping the top compartment of his backpack, he pulled out disposable paper pants and a shirt in anemic blue from a medical supply company. He stuffed his black hooded jacket into the backpack and slipped the paper outfit on over his dark, long-sleeved T-shirt and sweatpants. Paper booties fit easily over his no-name sneakers and a plastic cap tucked tightly around his head. Last, he exchanged his leather gloves for latex. When he was fully dressed he pulled out the nail gun.

She'd just come home. The Diet Coke can on the counter was cold to his touch. He left the kitchen and moved toward the front of the house, careful to stay away from the windows and go softly on the tiled floor in the hall.

His footsteps were silent on the carpeted stairs. He could hear movement somewhere on the floor above him and he climbed toward the sound, pausing when he heard the door open and Meredith's voice calling out for Henry.

Was she expecting her ex? He'd have to move faster. When he heard water running he took the stairs two at a time. He swung his arm too fast and the nail gun slammed against a step. He dropped to the floor, fully expecting to hear the door open and her footsteps coming to investigate, but nothing happened.

After a moment, he got to his feet and tucked the gun under his arm so it wouldn't hit anything else. He knew the location of the master bedroom and he crept toward it, aware of his pulse quickening. He had to be careful not to let the excitement get to him, make him lose focus. Mistakes happened when you lost focus. He didn't make mistakes.

He turned the knob slowly on the bedroom door and then pushed it open in one fast flurry, but the room was empty. The noise coming from the master bath explained why. That door was ajar. He skulked over to it and peered through the crack. Steam partially fogged the long mirror above the vanity, but he could just see the reflection of slim pale legs floating in the water.

A sudden creak made Meredith's eyes fly open. She swung her head toward the noise and saw the door slowly opening.

"Who's there?" she demanded, scrambling up from the water and hitting the mute button on the TV. A strange looking man stepped inside the room. He looked like he'd stepped out of surgery.

"What the hell are you doing?" she shrieked, grabbing for a towel. "Get out!"

Instead of responding, he moved closer. His face was a pale oval and his eyes had an intensity in them that unnerved her. He held something in his right hand, it wasn't a gun, was it? He aimed it at her.

She screamed and jumped over the side of the tub, scrambling to get away from him, but slipping on the tile floor. He calmly moved toward her, the weapon held aloft. She backed against the double vanity. "What the fuck is that?" she cried. "Who are you?"

In answer he grabbed her by the arm and pushed her back to the tub. She fell in with a splash, clunking her head on the wall behind. Water cascaded onto the floor and the towel she'd been clutching fell with it, instantly soggy and forgotten.

Meredith's head hurt and she'd jarred her tailbone against one of the jets, but adrenaline pushed the pain to the background. She struggled up from the water a second time, but he grabbed her again, this time by the throat.

"Aaagh!" Her screams were choked off. She couldn't breathe. His hand crushed her windpipe with incredible force. She felt her wet back rubbing against the plaster wall. He'd stepped into the tub to hold her and she watched the water soaking through the paper pants, revealing darkness underneath.

"Don't be afraid," he whispered, loosening his hold ever so slightly. She looked up into impassive, sharklike eyes. "Ssh," he warned, "I don't want to hurt you, but you have to be quiet."

She tried to nod, to show her compliance, but shifted her legs, trying to get into position to knee him in the groin.

He let go of her neck, but only to move his arm to her chest. He was so close that she could smell his acrid, sweaty odor.

"Let me go," she said, her voice hoarse and high, not her voice at all. "I'll give you what you want, but just let me go."

He didn't seem to hear her. She had the feeling that anything she said was like the noise of a mosquito buzzing and he'd take no notice. When he shifted, trying to grab her arm, she kneed him hard in the groin.

It knocked him off balance and he fell backwards, cracking his head as he thudded onto the wet tile floor.

For a few precious seconds she was free. Meredith scrambled out of the tub, but as she stepped over him, he grabbed her ankle.

"Stupid bitch!" The rage made his voice completely different. Demonic. He climbed her like a ladder, pulling her down as he rose to his feet. Then he hauled her back in the tub and slammed her head hard against the back wall.

Silver sparks killed her vision and she tasted blood. His hand grabbed hers and she fought him, struggling to pull free, hitting him with her other hand until a blinding pain shot through her right arm.

"You bastard!" she screamed, blood spilling from her mouth. He'd let go of her arm and she tried to bring her hurt hand to her face, but it wouldn't move. It was stuck to the wall.

"What the fuck did you do to me?" she cried as he reached for her other hand. This time she saw him press the gunlike weapon against her palm before the pain shot through her.

When he pressed the gun against the back of her neck she realized she wasn't going to live. The unfairness of it struck her. She shouldn't die. Young, beautiful people don't die. She tried to say this, but couldn't form more than one little word, uttered in a plaintive voice completely unlike her own: "Why?"

Chapter 14

Emma was adamant: Mommy had promised, *promised*, that they would play a game tonight. The fact that Amy couldn't recall making that promise, and that she'd told her that afternoon that a babysitter would be coming over, were apparently not part of a five-year-old's logic.

"No! Don't go, Mommy!" Emma wailed, screaming and thrashing at the door while Chloe Newman, the college student that babysat for Emma regularly, held her around the waist and tried to soothe her.

"She'll be okay, Mrs. Moran," Chloe said. "Don't worry."

"Just call me if she doesn't settle down. And it's Amy, okay?"

"Sure," Chloe said, but they'd been over this before and Amy knew that nineteen-year-old Chloe wouldn't call a thirty-one-year-old by her first name. Somehow, without realizing it, Amy had become one of the grown-ups. Freaky.

"Okay, the numbers are on the fridge, just like always, and all the meds are on the counter. I shouldn't be more than two hours, but if something comes up I'll call you. Emma's had dinner, but she still needs to use the nebulizer. Do you remember how to do that?"

"Sure, Mrs.—" Chloe caught herself. "Sure, no problem. And I'm sure Emma will help me."

Amy could still hear Emma screaming as she got in the car. She turned the key in the ignition and nothing happened. She tried again. Still nothing.

Emma's wails died away as Amy raced back up the walk. "You're staying, Mommy?"

"No, Em, Mommy's not staying," she said, adding to Chloe, "the car's dead."

She called AAA to tow the car to the garage and then she called a taxi. Fifteen minutes later, she was waving good-bye again to her wailing daughter.

"Your kid must really love you," the cabbie said with a grin.

It was hard leaving at night. Emma seemed to have more attacks at night than at any other time and Amy couldn't shake the feeling that if she were there in person an attack wouldn't happen. She knew it was irrational, just as she knew that Chloe was perfectly capable of calling for help if an attack should occur. It was just that the worst-case scenarios tended to play in Amy's mind when she worked at night.

She didn't want to go back to Meredith Chomsky's, not after spending the day there. Not ever, truth be told, but she wanted this house sold, not least because it was the only way to get rid of that damn woman. Luckily, the lawyer and her husband sounded interested. She hoped they made an offer that would pass muster with the queen.

The sale of the enormous Chomsky house would bring an equally enormous commission and Amy needed the money.

At first, she'd felt grateful to get this commission, albeit under horrible circumstances, but now she wished she'd never heard of Meredith Chomsky. How had Sheila put up with this bitch? If Amy didn't arrange a sale soon, this property would be reassigned to another agent or Braxton Realty would lose it altogether. Amy wasn't sure which humiliation would be worse. She urged the cabdriver to go faster, anxious to get there before the potential buyers.

It was good form to arrive before them. This way they'd see a well-lit, inviting home as they pulled in the drive. Subtle things like that could really make or break a deal.

The Chomsky estate sat on a pristine acre of prime Connecticut real estate, the house at the end of a short, curving drive. There were large stone lanterns marking the entrance, but then the lane was dark except for a few, ground-level lights along the sides of the drive. Amy paid the driver and arranged for a return ride two hours later.

Elation at arriving twenty minutes early gave way to despair when she saw the lights on all over the house and spotted Meredith's mammoth SUV through the garage windows. Meredith was not the kind of seller that helped close a deal.

She rang the doorbell instead of using the key in the lockbox. No point in angering Meredith before the buyers arrived. While she waited, Amy nervously checked her hair in the shiny brass knocker. A long minute passed. She rang the bell again, hearing the faint chime echoing through the house.

Maybe Meredith wasn't home after all. Amy let herself in and called out a loud "hello" just in case. She got no response. She saw car keys and a leather purse dumped on the elegant console table in the hall and called louder, "Hello? Meredith?"

She tucked the keys in the purse and hung it out of sight in the hall closet.

Moving swiftly, Amy straightened couch cushions in the family room, regretting that there wasn't enough time to start a fire in the huge stone hearth. She entered the expansive kitchen, where she found overflowing shopping bags, an empty Diet Coke can and an open bottle of rum.

"Great, just great," Amy muttered. She screwed the cap back on the rum bottle and whisked it and the Diet Coke can into the fridge. Then she looked around for a place to stash the shopping bags. She dragged them into the front hall closet and arranged them in a neat row. It took a precious six minutes, but the place was spotless when she was finished and everybody knew that kitchens were one of the biggest factors in home sales.

She ran up the stairs to check the second floor, her heels sinking into the plush carpeting. She moved quickly through the bedrooms, each empty and pristine. They were carefully and tastefully decorated. It was like being in a museum, Amy thought, running a hand over a Chippendale highboy. Everything was exquisite, but there was something sterile about it.

The master bedroom was at the opposite end of the hall. The door was closed but a thin crack of light peeked out from underneath the frame. She knocked twice in rapid succession and waited. Nothing, but she definitely heard voices. She knocked harder. Again, nothing. She pressed her ear against the door and heard canned laughter.

She had a sudden vision of a drunken Meredith sprawled in front of the TV and held back a nervous giggle as she imagined explaining *that* to the potential buyers.

Slowly, she turned the knob, wondering what Meredith's reaction would be if she wasn't drunk and Amy walked in on her. Braced for an explosion, she was surprised to see the large empty bed. Well, empty except for a small shopping bag from an overpriced skin care boutique. Picking up after Meredith was never Meredith's job.

The entertainment center opposite the bed was closed. The TV dialogue was coming from the bathroom. Fantastic, Amy thought. The lawyer and her husband would arrive just in time to join the home's owner in the master bath.

"Meredith?" she called, expecting the woman to step out

the door, screaming about invasion of privacy. Only she didn't. "Meredith," she called loudly, one last time before pushing open the bathroom door.

RED. This was the first thing she registered followed immediately by *BODY*, then *BLOOD*. The words screamed through her head as she stared at what had been Meredith Chomsky. She was hanging by her hands and her hair from the back wall. Her lower body was sprawled, legs akimbo, in the water, which was red.

It looked as if nails had been driven through her palms, which were shredding from the weight of her body. Her long blond hair had been yanked up and also nailed, holding her head forward so that Amy could see the sightless red sockets where her eyes had been.

She bolted from the room, gagging and struggling to find her cell phone. Clutching the banister with one hand, she stumbled down the steps as she dialed 911.

"What's your emergency?" The female voice was nasally and disinterested.

"I need the police."

"What's your emergency?" the voice repeated more loudly.

"A woman's dead. She's in her tub. There's a lot of blood."

"How do you know she's dead?"

"There's blood . . . eyes gone . . . she's dead." Amy struggled to find the words.

"What's your address?"

"Oh, God, um, something Brindle Lane." She tried to think straight. "Two-fifty Brindle Lane!"

"Ma'am, I'm dispatching someone right now. You need to calm down."

"I'm in a client's home and she's dead in a tub full of blood!" Amy cried. "Why in the hell should I calm down?"

"Don't yell at me, ma'am, I'm just doing my job."

"Oh, God. Just get the detectives. Juarez. Detective Juarez.

And his partner. The other guy. Pale, short, bad glasses? Do you know who I mean?"

"The police are coming, ma'am, just try to calm down."

That was a ludicrous suggestion, but Amy was far too stressed out to complain.

She made it to the bottom of the stairs when she realized that she couldn't escape. Not without a car. Amy panicked, running for the front door as if she could flee on foot, but as she passed the hall closet, she remembered Meredith's keys.

Yanking open the closet door, she ripped the purse from its hook and held it upside down so the keys spilled out on the floor, along with everything else. Scooping them up, she ran through the kitchen for the garage. She pushed a button on the key ring. The gleaming black Mercedes SUV opened. Amy slid onto the smooth leather of the driver's seat and slammed the door shut, hitting the lock button. Only then did she realize that she hadn't opened the garage door.

There had to be a button on the key ring, but none of the ones she pushed did more than turn on the lights or unlock the door. Terrified, she hit the lock button again and searched the car for a garage opener. There was a manila envelope addressed to Meredith Chomsky on the toffee-colored leather passenger seat. The print looked familiar and there was no return address, but Amy didn't really know what it was until she found a second envelope within the first. Only the word written on the outside of the envelope was different: SLUT.

Inside were six photos, just like the packet sent to Sheila, and also just like Sheila's the pictures were of Meredith naked, lounging in her bedroom or getting undressed. Amy sifted through them rapidly.

"Put your hands in the air and step out of the vehicle!"

A cop stood in the doorway, gun drawn. Amy dropped the photos and held up her hands.

"It's okay," she said. "I'm the one who—"

"Get out of the vehicle! Now!"

Chapter 14

Acutely aware of the gun pointing at her, Amy scooted across the leather seat with her hands in the air. She dropped them to push open the car door.

"Hands up! Keep them where I can see them!"

She shot them back up and nudged the door open with her knee. It was a long drop from the SUV. She slipped out of the car, landing on the garage floor with her arms wobbling from the effort to keep her balance in heels.

Without taking his eyes or his gun off her, the cop reached back a hand and pushed a button on the wall. The garage door rose with a whir, folding into the ceiling and there stood another cop with his gun aimed straight at her.

"Turn and face the car," cop number one ordered.

"Listen, I'm the one—"

"Face the car!"

Angry, as well as afraid, Amy did as he said, turning slowly, her hands still up in the air. "Please listen—"

"Put your hands on the car, palms down!"

Amy smacked her palms down on the cold metal. "I'm the one who called the police, damn it!"

Cop number two moved closer and then Amy flinched as the first cop's hands touched her waist and then moved quickly over her body, patting her down.

She blinked back tears and held still, resisting the urge to kick the guy. He stepped back after a few seconds.

"Okay, you can turn around."

Suddenly, they wanted the information she'd been trying to give them all along. Who was she? What was she doing in the car? What was she doing with the photos?

She explained as quickly and coherently as she could, realizing that they hadn't found Meredith yet. Cop number one stepped back into the house. Cop number two led her outside to the patrol car she hadn't heard pull up, just as another police car, siren loudly blaring, came up the drive, followed by an ambulance.

Amy sat in the backseat of the patrol car, under some hybrid of house arrest. Car arrest? They hadn't actually said she was being arrested, but they had, very pointedly, advised her to stay.

More patrol cars screamed up the drive, followed by plain cars and a coroner's van. Soon the quiet neighborhood was filled with the squeal of sirens and the static rasp of police radios.

Amy saw Detective Juarez arrive with his partner and hurry into the house. Then she was interviewed by a seemingly endless stream of police officers, all of them quizzing her about the same things: What time did she find the body? Where was she before that? Did she know the victim?

She had no idea how much time passed, only that it seemed to go on forever. It was like Sheila all over again, only this time the detectives wanted her to stay.

At some point, she began to shake all over. The paramedics said it was shock. She didn't even register who they were until the man handing her a blanket addressed her by name. Then she realized that he was the same emergency response worker who'd done such a great job with Emma. She saw his dangling ID, Ryan something. She tried to focus, trying to tell him that this death was the same as Sheila's, but he didn't seem to know what she meant.

"It's okay, Ms. Moran, you just need to sit here and let us take care of it." He guided her from the patrol car to the back of their truck and she waited there, the rough blanket around her shoulders.

She'd forgotten all about the lawyer and her husband until they pulled up with their son. They'd gotten lost and had clearly been bickering until they saw all the police. Amy briefly explained the situation.

"Cool!" the young boy declared when he saw the cops and the ambulance, but his parents looked horrified.

"I'm so sorry this didn't work out," Amy said, striving to sound professional and knowing how absurd it was to even care under the circumstances. "We'll try and reschedule at the earliest possible time," she said, as if it were something as innocuous as bad weather preventing them from viewing the property.

Ryan appeared with a bottle of water, holding it for her because she couldn't manage, water slopping over the sides as she choked down a mouthful.

"Easy," he said. "It's okay. Just slow down and drink it."

When she was finished, she thanked him, apologizing for her nerves. "Just a little shaky," she said.

"Totally understandable," Ryan said. "Was she a friend?"

"No. Just a client. I'm a realtor." Amy indicated the Braxton Realty sign that had finally been posted in the yard. "I'm selling her home. Or I was. I don't know what's going to happen now."

"Are you sure there isn't someone I can call to be with you? Your husband?"

"I'm not married," she said, then realized that he was looking at the wedding band she still hadn't taken off. "Well,

I'm separated. Divorce in the works. So no, I don't have a husband to call."

"Maybe a friend?"

"My closest friend in this town is dead," Amy said, the tears she'd held back suddenly spilling over. "She was killed just like this woman."

"Jesus! That's terrible!" He reached past her and found some tissues for her in the ambulance. "Here."

"Thanks."

"I wish there was more I could do."

His partner came around to the back of the truck. "We got another call we got to take."

He frowned and walked around the side of the vehicle with her while Amy mopped her face and blew her nose, trying to regain some sort of control. Ryan reappeared.

"Look, I'm sorry, but we've got to go. Another emergency. But we could drop you off at the hospital on our way."

Amy shook her head. "No, I'm okay. I don't need the hospital. I just need to get home. Emma needs me."

He frowned again, clearly ambivalent about leaving.

"Then at least let's get you somewhere warm," he said, ushering her up to the house. They were stopped in the hall by the young cop. She was to wait outside, he apologetically told her, and the detectives would come to talk to her soon.

"She's not waiting outside, it's too cold," Ryan said. "If you want her here, then she needs to sit inside."

So she was ushered into the living room and offered one of the vast club chairs near the fireplace. Twenty minutes of feet tramping up and down the stairs and loud voices followed, but every officer who passed by the room ignored her.

She suddenly thought to call Chloe, pulling out her cell phone and trying to steady her voice while she explained, without detail, what had happened.

Emma was asleep and breathing fine, Chloe said. She'd just checked on her. That relieved some of Amy's anxiety, but she kept thinking of the photos she'd found and the similarities between this death and Sheila's.

She glanced at her watch and realized that the cab she'd taken to Meredith's house would be arriving any minute to take her back home. As she got up to check on it, Detectives Juarez and Black finally came downstairs and over to talk to her. They looked grim and Juarez jotted down details of what she said while Black kept giving her searching looks that she found disconcerting.

"What time did you say you made it back here, Mrs. Moran?" he said.

"I'm not sure. Seven? Seven-fifteen? I went home after the last showing and made my daughter dinner. I came here as soon as the babysitter arrived."

"And Mrs. Chomsky was expecting you?"

"Yes."

"But you let yourself into the house?"

"I wasn't expecting Meredith—Mrs. Chomsky—to be home. She knew there was a showing and usually that's done without the owner on the property."

Detective Black gave a grunt that might have been acknowledgment or dissent and he produced the manila envelope that he had tucked under one arm.

"What were you doing with these photos, Mrs. Moran?"

Amy sighed. Not this again. "As I explained to the other officer, they were in the car. I found them."

"Weren't you putting them in the car?"

"No!"

"You're a photographer, Mrs. Moran. Isn't that right?"

"Yes." She should have seen this coming, but she hadn't. Now going into the car seemed like the stupidest thing she'd ever done.

"Didn't you take these photos, Mrs. Moran?"

"No!"

"And the photos of Sheila Sylvester?"

"Absolutely not!"

He simply stared at her, a slight smile—or was it a smirk?—hovering around his lips. Detective Juarez didn't say a word, but he'd taken the mailer from his partner and was examining the photos.

"You could have taken these photos, though. Isn't that right, Mrs. Moran?" Black said.

"I could have, but I didn't."

"Where were these photos developed?"

"I have no idea," Amy said.

"You can't tell from the photos?"

"Sometimes there's a serial number," Amy said, holding out her hand for a photo. Juarez passed one to her and Amy caught a brief glimpse of a naked Meredith gazing at herself in a mirror before flipping the photo over to examine the back.

It was clean and she flipped back to the front, looking less at the photo itself than at the quality of the photo, reducing Meredith's black-and-white image to so many pixels.

"I think these are digital prints," she said after a minute. "They're probably produced from a computer printer."

Black simply nodded, but Juarez was staring intently at the other photos.

"How can you tell that?" he asked.

"This is high-quality paper," Amy said, "but the resolution is ever so slightly different from regular film."

"So these could be done on a home computer? Not a photo lab?"

Amy nodded. "You have to have a little expertise, but you don't have to be a professional photographer to do this."

"But you could be, right?" Detective Black said. It was definitely a smirk.

"I didn't take the photos, detective," Amy said, tersely. "Either set. I think I've given you as much information as I can and I really need to get home to my daughter. Now."

She didn't wait for their permission to leave, just turned and headed for the door.

"Do you have any trips planned, Mrs. Moran?" Detective Black called after her, surprising Amy. She turned to shake her head at him.

"Good," he said and gave her a sinister smile. "Don't leave town."

Chapter 15

Guy stretched out on his couch and switched on the TV, wondering if there was any coverage yet. Surely at least one young, intrepid reporter had listened to a police scanner and arrived in time to pick up an exclusive.

Not that the police would have much to say. There wasn't any danger of leaving incriminating evidence behind. He'd taken care of that immediately, just as he always did.

It was simple, really, a matter of making sure that everything that came into proximity with the body was disposable, and slipping off those paper clothes and the latex gloves, bagging them and sending the bag down an incinerator chute of a neighboring apartment building.

Underneath the medical supply store paper pants and smock, he always wore regular clothes: cheap, dark denim jeans and a Hanes T-shirt, clothes for the masses and sold in masses at low-cost warehouse stores, which was exactly where he'd bought them. Generic sneakers were covered in paper hospital booties, easy to slip on and off and also easy to burn. He'd taken to covering his hair with the plastic shower caps found in most major hotel chains.

By far the hardest thing about the whole operation was getting the paper bag containing the paper clothing safely down the incinerator. A resident stopped him once, eyed him suspiciously and informed him that strangers weren't allowed to dispose of their garbage in that building. He pretended to be a visiting family member and that had been the end of it. But now he was much more careful, scanning the halls for busybodies before making the drop-off.

He took another sip of his vodka tonic, feeling the effect on an empty stomach, but without the energy to make a meal. Maybe he'd order a pizza later.

It was always like this after a kill. The energy that buzzed through his body in the days or weeks before was gone. He was like an artist or a showman. Everything went into his creation and then he was spent. Once or twice he'd actually slept twenty-four hours straight through after a kill.

Flipping idly through the channels, he came to rest on one of the so-called reality shows. Bunch of whiny people forced to compete against each other in some luxurious house, but he couldn't figure out what they were competing for. Such a bunch of complainers, all of them. A little hardship and all they could do was whine and cry about the unfairness of it all. As if life came with some guarantee of fairness.

There was no equity in life; there never had been. You had to make your own fairness. They should stop whining and get to work, Guy thought, just as he had. He hadn't sat about bitching that his mom hadn't loved him. No, he'd worked hard, gotten his education, attended a good college on a scholarship and graduated at the top of his class.

Had his mom said she was proud of him then? No, but you didn't see him going on some talk show to complain about it. Stiff upper lip. That's all you had in life, that, and your determination to get ahead.

He took another sip of his drink, enjoying the icy shock against his throat. He didn't mind icy drinks in icy weather or hot drinks in the sweltering heat. He was impervious to things like weather. He'd trained himself to be that way, to be stronger than the elements.

In college, he'd taken advanced psychology courses and seen experiments researchers did with hypnosis, submerging the arms of hypnotized test subjects in icy water and recording their reactions. Though their brains registered the pain, the test subjects were able to withstand it under hypnosis.

Intrigued by this phenomenon, he'd studied hypnosis, transcendentalism, spiritual ecstasy and even drug-induced euphoria, learning about separating the body and the brain and harnessing them both. He practiced self-deprivation, fasting to extremes and working the muscles of his body until he felt his joints humming like a machine.

He could have been a contestant on one of these reality shows, maybe best suited to the one in which participants had to forage on deserted islands. Only it would be stronger if they weren't content with foraging for coconuts, bananas and little bits of fish. No stupid games, just one: the hunt. He'd have hunted down the weaker contestants, picking off the plump ones first, roasting the juicy bits over a campfire.

He chuckled, thinking of pitching that concept to network executives: *Lord of the Flies* meets *Survivor*. He took the last few swallows of his drink, sucking the ice cubes free of any lingering vodka, and forced himself off the sofa and into the kitchen. Into the dishwasher with the glass. Into the liquor cabinet with the vodka. Into the fridge with the tonic. He carefully wrapped the lime he'd cut a wedge from and re-frigerated that as well.

Only after everything was in its place did he leave the kitchen and head to the bathroom for his shower. Standing under the dual-head spray in the glass-enclosed shower cubicle, he allowed the events of that evening to replay in his mind. It was his treat to relive it, his reward for a job well done.

He'd liked killing this woman almost as much as Sheila. Maybe more. She so clearly needed to be taken down, this bitch who thought she was better than everybody else, who had claimed so much more than she deserved with that little plastic doll's body.

The look on her face when she'd noticed him. He rubbed soap slowly over his body, closing his eyes and remembering the fear in her eyes. He'd run the gun along her body just for fun, not because he'd really needed to count the vertebrae to know where he needed to shoot. He could feel her hot breath against his gloved hand and he'd known she was pleading, begging him to spare her life. That power was such a rush.

He'd told her that she didn't have to worry, that he was going to display her at her best, and he'd shoved the statue high inside her, ramming it in her cunt, feeling the force of her screams against his hand.

The hand with the soap trailed down his body, circling his navel before dropping lower. He soaped his penis with long, languid strokes, leaning against the shower wall as he watched it rise.

Nailing that dead weight to the wall was an effort, but he'd taken his time to get it just right, standing back to admire his exhibit.

Amy had arrived soon after, just as he'd known she would. He'd waited in the bathroom linen closet this time. Chancy, that move, but he'd calculated correctly that calling for help would be her top priority. At one point, she'd stood so close to him that he could have touched her hair and he would have liked to do that, to run his hands through that long, silky mane. She had it tied back. He didn't like that. Women should wear their hair loose. He'd made Violet do that, taking out whatever holders she'd put in it, freeing her hair so that it swam around her shoulders.

Thinking of Violet made his erection flag and he pushed her out of his mind. He thought of Amy again, thinking of freeing her hair, of wrapping that mane around his hand, of pulling her to him by her hair. He pictured those frightened eyes staring at him, those lips parted for him, that whimper one of desire for him.

He came with a yell, shooting all over the glass of the shower walls.

Chapter 16

Bev looked up from *People* magazine and waved a slip of paper as Amy walked through the doors of Braxton Realty. "Poppy wants to see you. Immediately."

Amy took it from her. "She's in? On a Saturday?"

Bev nodded, her moon face solemn. She leaned across the desk to whisper, "She heard what happened to Meredith Chomsky."

So had everyone. It was the front page on the local paper, top of the news on all the local stations and had even made it as a small item in the news roundup in the metro section of the *New York Times*.

She switched off the radio coverage on the drive in to the office, unwilling to hear any more speculation. Already, reporters were asking if the two murders were connected. How much longer would it take for them to find her?

She didn't usually go to the office on Saturday, but knew that she needed to today. Chloe couldn't babysit again, but Amy had been able to trade babysitting with Audrey, whose daughter was one of Emma's friends. And Emma had been happy to go, just as soon as she'd extracted a promise from her mother that they'd go to Waldorf Park afterwards and feed the ducks.

Poppy Braxton's office really *was* an office, as opposed to the cubicles the rest of the realtors had. It was in the back corner, glass enclosed, like some sort of hothouse with Poppy, the brightly colored flower, on display. Amy had to pass all the other cubicles as she walked back, trying not to notice the stares and the whispers that followed.

Poppy had the local paper spread open on her desk, Amy saw through the glass, and her perfectly coiffed blond head was moving with lightning speed as she followed its pages. She was wearing a magenta suit that hurt Amy's eyes when she got close enough to knock.

"Come in, Amy, come in." With practiced ease, Poppy was out of her seat and ushering Amy to a chair in front of the desk. The fact that she carefully closed the door wasn't lost on Amy.

"What a shock," Poppy said. "What a truly terrible shock. I know that Meredith could be a—" She paused, searching for the word.

"Bitch," Amy supplied.

Poppy tittered. "Well, yes, but I was going to say a difficult client. I know she had her faults, but she was counting on Braxton, Amy, and I feel we've let her down."

For a brief moment, Amy thought that Poppy had been talking to the police and was about to accuse her of killing Meredith.

"We're still selling her house, aren't we?" Amy said.

Poppy opened her mouth to speak and hesitated. The phone rang in that moment. The older woman looked at the caller ID and then up at Amy. "I'm so sorry, but I really must take this. One minute, promise!" She waggled a manicured finger at Amy and then spun around in her chair, carrying the phone with her.

Amy stared at the large painting that graced the wall

above Poppy's desk. It was a field of poppies in summer, a carpet of vibrant red flowers. In the office it was privately called "After the Bloodletting."

Poppy spoke to the caller in English, then in French. Was that for her benefit? Amy wondered. She glanced at the photos on Poppy's desk. A family photo. Poppy, her handsome husband, Chuck somebody-or-other, and two beautiful blond children posed on a beach. It looked like a Ralph Lauren commercial.

"Oh, that is too funny!" Poppy switched back to English, laughing heartily. "Yes, of course. Of course. *Au revoir*, darling." She bussed the phone and swung back around. "Now, Amy, where were we?"

"Meredith's house," Amy said, trying to smile. She felt underdressed in her white blouse and navy blue skirt. The sparkly brooch on the lapel of Poppy's suit seemed to mock her.

"Oh, yes. That is a very delicate matter. Meredith's sister—that's who inherits the property—does want the house sold. When people die unexpectedly in the middle of a sale, then usually it's that realtor's job to see that sale to the end."

Amy had fixed on the word "usually." She dug her toes into the soles of her shoes and tightened her grip on the chair.

"But in this case, which I'm sure you can see is not the usual case," Poppy waited for Amy's nod. "it's going to take special handling. Expert handling."

The raw feeling in Amy's stomach was growing. "I think I can handle it," she said, forcing a smile, trying to project assuredness, competence, readiness for any challenge.

Poppy returned her smile. "You are turning into a really fine realtor, Amy. Braxton is proud to have you on the team."

"Thank you," Amy said automatically, sure there was another "but" coming.

"However, we really feel that a sale this delicate needs to be handled by one of the senior members of our team."

Who was the "we" Amy wondered, or was that the royal "we"? There was no team in real estate. Individual commissions were what counted and a big commission was being taken away from her. Her mind raced, thinking of having to sell the house because she couldn't afford to pay the mortgage, of having to move away from the place that Emma loved, the little stability she'd been able to offer her daughter.

"I can handle this sale, Poppy," Amy said. "I can handle it, just like I'm handling the first house—where Sheila was . . ." —she struggled but couldn't bring the word *murder* past her lips—"was found."

"But that's just it, Amy." Poppy leaned forward, her brow furrowing. "This is the second house of yours that's become the scene of a police investigation. That makes clients nervous." She brushed a strand of straight blond hair back into place in its perfect bob and sighed. "I know how you feel, Amy, believe me, I do."

No, she didn't. She'd been spoon-fed her entire life and inherited the company from her father. She wasn't a single mother. Her husband was in banking. They lived in an enormous home in the best part of town. The differences between them couldn't be much more stark and the ridiculousness of Poppy's statement gave Amy strength.

"Forgive me, Poppy, but you don't," she said and stood up. Poppy gaped at her for a second, then quickly stood. "I need this commission and I'm going to sell this house. That's the way Sheila wanted it and that's what I intend to do. Thanks for your offer of help, but when I need it, I'll ask for it."

She headed for the door, trying not to scuttle, more than a little nervous about turning her back on Poppy. It was easy to picture Poppy Braxton packing. Was there a little pearl-handled snub nose hidden in that desk?

"Two weeks." Poppy's voice rang out like a shot, crisp with warning. "I'll give you two weeks to get an offer. If you haven't gotten it by then, that property is being turned over to someone else."

Amy sat down behind her own desk feeling as if she'd won the battle but at a great personal cost. Poppy didn't like being crossed. From now on, Amy wouldn't be able to count on any support from the powers-that-be at Braxton.

There was a short stack of messages on her desk and something else. A small box of European chocolates wrapped in gold foil and cellophane. Amy buzzed the front desk, and when Bev answered, asked who had delivered them.

"A delivery service—FedEx or UPS? I don't remember."

"But who's it from?"

"No clue. But there was a card with it, wasn't there?"

Amy found a small card underneath the bow. It contained one line, "A token of my affection."

They had to be from Chris. Only he knew that she liked this brand of chocolate.

She was tempted to call and thank him, but she paused with her hand on the phone. Why make it so easy? He could send her a present, but what she really wanted from him was the assurance that he'd never, ever cheat on her again. She'd wait for his call, but she could still enjoy the gift.

It was the one bright spot in an otherwise hectic morning. She kept looking at the chocolates while she fielded phone calls from anxious sellers who wanted to know if there was something wrong with Braxton's security and whether they should take their homes off the market. In between reassuring them, she was also going through the trickier task of trying to reschedule a closing date for the property where Sheila was killed.

The banker's wife was hedging. "I just don't think I can be comfortable there," she said. "It's bad karma."

The sellers were furious with Amy, as if she was somehow personally responsible for the sale stalling. "Have you made it clear that we're keeping the hand money?" the man said. "Losing money is pretty bad karma—tell her that."

Some of the realtors, including Douglas, tried to ask her questions about Meredith's death, but she remained tight-lipped about it. It was not simply because she didn't want to talk to him, but also because she wasn't sure just how much it was prudent to say.

The initial shock of finding Meredith had passed and Amy could look at the murder with some degree of objectivity. If Trevor had an alibi for Sheila's death, and the same person had done both killings, then who was that person? And why? Who hated both Meredith and Sheila enough to kill them?

"What can I get for you?" The young man at the ice cream counter smiled expectantly at Penelope, metal scoop held aloft. She was torn, seriously tempted to have a double cone so she could try both the Chocolate Toffee Crunch and the Banana Road Rage, but the sight of the woman next to her virtuously eating a kiddie scoop of sherbet reined her in.

"I'll have a single scoop of the Chocolate Toffee Crunch on a sugar cone," she said, opening her change purse to count out how much money she needed. Someone bumped into her and change spilled onto the floor.

"Oh, excuse me," said a young girl's voice, giggling an apology as Penelope slowly bent over, feeling her knees protest as she shifted her weight forward. She fumbled for the change, catching a glimpse of skinny legs in red stockings, the sort of fashion that made her own legs look like sides of beef.

She handed the guy the money and took her cone, trying not to notice the two girls whispering about her as she slowly made her way through the crowd to a seat in the rear.

A woman at the next table was sharing an ice cream cone with a toddler and she kept giving Penelope disapproving looks. The fat weren't allowed to eat ice cream. She should be eating carrots or hiding in her house until she was skinny. Penelope took a consoling lick of the Chocolate Toffee Crunch, letting the smooth cream swirl around her entire mouth and melt on her tongue.

At one point she'd managed to get herself down to a size twelve, mainly by eating nothing but carrot sticks and grapefruit and religiously walking two miles a day. She'd looked good. She'd even felt good, enjoying shopping for the first time in her life, but that was before she found out the truth about Dave.

He'd always been so supportive of her—fat or skinny. "You look great!" he'd say, giving her a squeeze that made her jiggle. "I love your love handles!"

Sometimes he indulged with her, bringing home pints of her favorite flavors or one of those cheesecakes from the Italian bakery in Bayonne that she loved so much. But he was so good looking, with that frosted hair and toned body. She needed to be pretty for him and she'd done it, stopping the ice cream, stopping the cheesecake, throwing away the kids' leftovers and ending the Sunday stop at Dunkin' Donuts and the midnight runs to the 7-Eleven because she was craving a Slurpee.

She joined Slim Down and attended all the meetings religiously, enduring the public weigh-ins and the boring testimonials because she knew, she just knew that one day she was going to be the wife that Dave deserved.

The day she reached her goal weight, she went out shopping and bought the most beautiful red dress she'd ever seen. She looked so good in that dress that when she came out of the dressing room, the girl who'd helped her actually clapped her hands with delight.

"That's the one for you!" she declared and then she'd

helped Penelope find shoes that went with it, and a purse. It was the most fun—the only fun—Penelope had ever had shopping.

She confided in the young woman, told her how she was going to surprise her husband, how she'd arranged a babysitter for the kids and how she lost all that weight. The girl was so supportive, so eager to help her reach the dream that she'd worked so hard to achieve.

Her plan was to take Dave out for dinner, but when she called his office and found out he'd already left for the day, she decided to start the festivities early. She arranged for Owen and Amanda to get picked up after school and she wore the red dress home, tottering a little in black heels much higher than she usually wore. His car was in the drive and usually she'd honk or do something to catch his attention because she was always so excited to see him. But this time she wanted him to be the excited one, so she parked on the street and quietly entered through the back door.

The shoes were hard to walk in and they clicked loudly on the kitchen floor so she slipped them off, carrying them in one hand as she floated through the kitchen, pausing to peek in the living room, but no Dave, and then up the stairs. Maybe he was lying down. He'd complained lately of migraines that made him come home at lunchtime.

She could hear him moaning in the bedroom as she approached and thought she'd better plan on staying in tonight after all because he did not sound good. Then she pushed open the door and—

And there stood that detective who'd come to talk to them at the single parents' group. He was so good looking with that dark hair and toned body. He hadn't spotted her yet. All his attention was on the ice cream he was getting, but she'd never be able to slip past without his noticing and there was no place for her to hide.

He turned at that moment and spotted her. "Penelope?"

he said in a cheerful voice and he moved fluidly between the small tables until he was standing in front of her own. "I met you at the single parents' group. Detective Mark Juarez." He stuck out his hand, but it was holding a mint chocolate-chip cone. He laughed and transferred it to the other hand.

"Hi," she said, her own voice squeaky, watching her pudgy hand disappear in his. He shook it gently and let go. "Mind if I sit down?" he said and she did mind. Already she could see that they were attracting attention, that people were staring at the good-looking cop and the fat girl and wondering how the two of them paired up.

"I guess not," she said, pushing the other chair out with her toe.

"Thanks." He sat down and appraised her over his cone, licking for a moment in silence. She looked away, feigning indifference, though she could feel her face heating up.

"Have you heard about the other killing?" he said.

"Yeah." She'd seen it on TV, and read about it in the *Steerforth Herald*.

"I'm sure you were upset by the news."

"Um, yeah, I guess." She tried to savor her cone, but the detective was distracting. He wore a striped cotton shirt, button-down, with the cuffs folded back so she could see the small dark hairs around his wrists. Dave had favored shirts like that and he'd worn them the same way, those precise cuffs, that same amount of wrist showing. Of course, Dave was fair and his hands smaller than this cop's.

"You knew Meredith Chomsky, didn't you?" Juarez said.

"What?" Penelope looked up at him, trying to focus. He'd stopped licking his cone and was staring at her. "I guess," she said. "I knew her a little."

"You belonged to the same health club?"

"Yeah." Now her entire body felt hot with embarrassment. It was like some bad commercial—she and Meredith Chomsky, the before and after-diet pics.

"You even took the same aerobics class, right?"

"Yeah." It occurred to her, only now, that this was no accidental meeting. He'd wanted to talk to her, and had probably followed her from her office.

"I understand you had a run-in with her in class?"

Was he making a pun? She'd had a run-in all right. The teacher had been leading them through a series of jazz moves and Penelope lost her balance, slipping on that polished floor and taking Meredith down like a bowling pin.

"The aerobics teacher told me that Meredith yelled at you?" His voice was gentle, but the eyes were watching her intently.

Suddenly, Penelope didn't want any more ice cream. She stood up and headed for the trashcan with her dripping cone. The detective stood up as well, following behind her, tossing his cone without a backwards look.

"Meredith Chomsky humiliated you in front of a roomful of people," he said.

"I don't want to talk about it," Penelope said, pushing past him and heading for the exit. The teenage girls were huddled around a table near the door. One of them snickered as she passed and whispered something to her friends.

"She said some very hurtful things, didn't she?" the detective said as she pushed open the door. He followed her outside.

"*Hurtful?*" Was that the word she'd use? "Get off me, you fat bitch," Meredith had said, shrieking for help to extricate her from under the "elephant." She complained of back pain when both she and Penelope got to their feet, and then she demanded to know if there wasn't a weight limit for the class.

"Yes," Penelope said. "She said hurtful things."

"And you stopped going to the club, right?"

Tears prickled in Penelope's eyes, but she held them back. She hadn't held them back that day. They spilled down her cheeks as she lumbered from the class and headed straight for the locker room. "I-I couldn't face going again," she whispered.

"Until yesterday," Juarez said, his voice soft, his eyes filled with pity that was as damaging, in its own way, as the snickers and whispers from others

"I read that she'd been killed. I thought—well, I thought that it would be okay to go back."

"Where were you on Wednesday evening?"

"At home."

"Alone?"

Did he need it spelled out—nobody wanted her! She lived alone and she'd die alone, a fat old woman who'd only been loved once and then by a man who used her as a shield to hide his real interests.

"Yes, I was alone."

"And what about the week before. The morning of Tuesday, the sixth?"

"I don't know. Work, I suppose."

"So you weren't killing Sheila Sylvester on Tuesday morning?"

"No!" She knew he'd intended to shock her and it worked. "I liked Sheila!"

"Even though she told you at a meeting that you needed to lose weight?"

"It's obvious I need to lose weight, detective."

"But it isn't nice hearing it, especially from someone who's supposed to be your friend."

"She didn't mean it like that. She wasn't nasty, she wasn't like Meredith."

"She was trying to help you?"

"Yes. She said I had a pretty face and I could have a pretty body to match." Her face flamed saying the words out loud, but he didn't react.

"I didn't kill her and I didn't kill Meredith," she said. "I don't know who told you that story about Sheila, but if you want some weird coincidences you shouldn't be checking me out. Have you talked to Jackson? He's the one you should talk to if you want to know about Meredith."

He pulled out a small notebook, flipping through it rapidly and she took the opportunity to walk away. He caught up to her.

"Why should I talk to Jackson?" he said.

She didn't hesitate. Let someone else deal with this. "Because he dated her."

Chapter 17

Jackson Lapinski's restaurant, Shade Blue, was a favorite with connoisseurs of fine dining and not just in Steerforth. It was not uncommon on the weekends to find Manhattanites waiting at the bar for their table to open up, or in good weather sitting outside at the café tables, drinking one of the wines from his small but excellent cellar.

The nature of the restaurant business was to handle various food crises and handle them well. The salmon didn't arrive? Substitute marlin. The soup was too salty? Add raw potato cubes to absorb it. The custard caught on fire? Turn it into flambé.

The one crisis they weren't used to dealing with was police scrutiny. Mark Juarez could feel the eyes of every souschef and waiter on him when he arrived an hour before lunch. Jackson was wearing a white jacket with a single, dramatic red smear down the front and he could not or would not stand still, moving around the kitchen at a ferocious rate of speed, barking orders at the staff and sampling numerous dishes.

"Yes, I dated Meredith Chomsky," he freely admitted

when he learned the reason for Mark's visit. "It was years ago. We were both a lot younger and I still had hair." He laughed heartily at his own humor, running one hand over his shaved head.

"When was the last time you talked to her?"

"I don't know—a long, long time ago." He moved over to another stove and an enormous pot and took a quick taste of a yellow sauce, looking like an overgrown hummingbird hovering over a flower. "Come here," he said, waving Mark closer. "You've got to taste this."

A fresh spoon appeared out of nowhere and Mark dutifully tasted.

"It's delicious."

"Yes, yes, it should be." Jackson smiled. He said something unintelligible in cooking lingo to the short Asian man in the white chef's coat directing traffic around that station.

"Phone records indicate that you spoke to Ms. Chomsky two weeks ago," Mark pushed on, following Jackson to the next stop where several young pastry chefs were making what looked like chocolate tarts.

"Did I?" Jackson seemed unperturbed. "What's happened, is she saying that I did something?"

"Meredith Chomsky is dead," Juarez said, looking for impact and surprised when he got it from everyone else in the room. Everyone stopped to stare in his direction, but he looked only at Jackson's face, gauging his reaction.

Jackson paused, too, but that stopping was his only visible emotion. "How did she die?" he asked after a minute.

"Shot," Juarez said. They would not reveal the weapon.

"That's too bad," Jackson said. "She was a physically lovely creature." He began moving again and the rest of his staff joined suit.

"Only physically?"

Jackson smiled. "An ugly personality that could not be hidden, ultimately, by that perfect body."

"How long did you date?" Mark asked, following him to another stove. Jackson tasted something and spat it out.

"This is terrible! What are you trying to do? Close us down? I give you beautiful vegetables and you offer me this crap? I should fire your ass. Throw out this swill and do it again!"

The cook being subjected to this tirade was a young woman with purple hair and a nose ring. She nodded and went back to work as if being berated like this was all part of the job.

"We dated for about six months before she realized that it wasn't as exciting dating a chef as she'd thought," Jackson answered Juarez in a normal tone. He seemed more amused than offended by the recollection.

"Do you remember the phone conversation you had with Meredith?"

"Well, knowing Meredith, she was probably trying to score something. Ever since the review in the *Times*, we've been completely booked every night. She probably wanted me to make an exception for her."

"Did you?"

Jackson laughed, spilling some of the capers he was adding to a salad another young chef had brought for him to check. "I have no idea!" he said. "How long ago was it? You'd have to ask Holly to check the books. Holly? Where's Holly?"

"You sent her to get the wine," a tattooed young man reminded him.

"Yes, yes, of course I did." Jackson patted him beatifically on the cheek and threw up his arms for Juarez. "So, do you want to come back and talk to her?"

"Not especially. Can someone else give us this information?"

The other man sighed and stroked his goatee. "Not as easily, no. It's her system, not mine. Holly is the manager, you see, and the maitre d'. She does not interfere in my kitchen and I do not interfere with her books." He smiled as if this was completely understandable, but his smile faded a bit when Juarez asked him to account for his whereabouts on the day and night in question.

"Am I, Jackson Lapinski, really a suspect?" he asked with indignation. "What possible motive do I have?"

"You dated one of the victims and were known to have had a loud argument with the other, Sheila Sylvester."

"This is absurd. So I fought with her at a meeting. It doesn't mean that I killed her."

"Nonetheless, Mr. Lapinski, I do need to know where you were on those dates."

"Fine. Let me look." Jackson stalked to a room just off the kitchen that was equipped as a small office. A suit coat was hanging from the back of the chair and he pulled a PDA from it. Juarez looked around the office while Jackson poked at the gadget with a stylus.

The office had a bookcase so stuffed with cookbooks that it seemed in danger of collapsing and a wooden desk with an iMac and silver-framed photos of Jackson with two young boys. There was a smaller framed photo, hidden slightly behind the others, of a beautiful, red-haired woman.

Juarez picked it up to look at it more closely and Jackson looked up from his PDA and frowned. He plucked the frame from Juarez's hands and put it back in place behind the others.

"As you can see, on the evening of the sixteenth I was at the restaurant," he said, drawing Juarez's attention to the screen.

"And the morning of the sixth?"

Jackson scrolled again. "There is nothing on the sixth, so I'm sure I was at home, sleeping."

"These your kids, Mr. Lapinski?" Juarez nodded at the photos of the boys.

"Yes."

"Nice-looking boys. How old are they?"

"Eight and ten."

"It must be hard, juggling their schedules with being a chef."

Jackson's face shuttered. "I manage."

"But you're a single dad, right? That's how you knew Sheila Sylvester, from the support group?"

"My therapist recommended it."

He said "therapist" the way some people say "mother-in-law," as if this were someone to be endured.

"Is that your wife?" Juarez reached for the frame with the red-haired woman's picture and Jackson immediately put his hand on the opposite corner, stopping him.

"I don't think that's any of your business, detective," he said. He moved in front of the desk, blocking Juarez's view and gestured toward the door. "I've answered your questions, detective, so if you don't mind, I must return to my kitchen."

Emma loved the ducks at Waldorf Park, running back and forth from her mother to the edge of the small pond, joyfully flinging handfuls of stale bread into the still water. It was one of those rare fall days when the sun was high and hot in a bright blue sky and if it weren't for the carpet of red and gold leaves covering the ground, you could believe it was early summer.

Amy leaned back on the park bench, tilting her face up toward the heat, closing her eyes against the brightness and letting Emma's chatter become background music while she pondered her conversation with the detectives.

Perhaps it was the shock of finding Meredith, combined with discovering that Trevor wasn't responsible for Sheila's death, but Amy hadn't fully grasped her own connection to the murders. Two gruesome killings, both at her properties, both left for her to discover. It couldn't be coincidental.

When she thought it was Trevor, she hadn't been afraid. Horrified, yes, by the nature of Sheila's death, by the loss of her friend and the emotional support that relationship had represented, but not afraid. Now she was scared. Everyone was a suspect. She caught herself looking around, wondering if the killer was lurking nearby.

She also felt fully the impact of finding the photos at Meredith's. In trying to protect herself, she'd ended up as a suspect. Even now, the police could be watching her.

Amy turned to scan the small parking lot some twenty-five feet away. Was that someone standing near the copse of pine trees? She got up to get a better look, leaving the bench and crossing the lawn to the crushed limestone path that ran from the pond to the parking lot.

The figure she saw near the trees turned out to be a tennis player coming to take advantage of the weather at the outdoor courts, but there were other things that caught her attention. A car idled with a shadowy figure behind the wheel. A man, smoking, slouched against the slide of the large brightly colored playground opposite the parking lot, though there wasn't a child in sight.

Suspicion took hold like a virus. Amy shook herself mentally and turned back to Emma. The ducks were still circling the shore, waiting for bread, but Emma was gone.

The edge of the pond where she'd been standing was empty. Amy looked farther on, fully expecting to see the familiar dark little head bobbing, but there was nobody.

"Emma!" Amy called, trying to make her voice carry across the pond. The limestone path circled the pond and then shot off it, like spokes on a wheel, diverging into the woods or toward the picnic pavilions.

She ran along the right bank of the pond, feeling panic rising like a storm. She scanned the edges, looking along the rocks that bordered the pond, at the grasses and mums that grew among them. She'd thought they were so pretty, but now they seemed like thoughtless planning. A child could hide in those grasses, sit down behind those rocks and not be seen. A child could slip into the water on the other side of the rocks and nobody would notice at all.

"Emma!" She was screaming it now, turning in circles to see the whole of the park. An older woman had paused on the path and was staring at her, not noticing that the toddler whose hand she held had released a pink balloon and it was floating higher and higher in the sky.

Emma wasn't at the shiny new playground across the field. She wasn't at the tennis courts; she wasn't behind any of the rocks or grasses near the water's edge. If she'd slipped into the pond, there were no ripples now. Amy saw a small handful of crusts on the grass on the far side of the pond, well away from the water, and she hoped Emma had dropped them.

"Where are you, Emma?" she shouted, her voice ragged at this point. She bargained with God. *Let her be alive and I'll never complain about her illness again. Let her be safe and I'll never let her out of my sight again. Let her be alive. Let her be well.*

Just as the panic had begun to solidify into a rock-hard certainty that Emma had been snatched, Amy heard someone call her name.

"Amy! Over here!"

She turned and saw a man waving from the small walking bridge she'd just passed. It crossed a gully at the edge of the parkland and suddenly she remembered the old playground.

It seemed to take forever to stop, turn back and run across that bridge, though afterwards she realized it was really just seconds. The man looked familiar. He was carrying a baby in a backpack. She realized it was Paul, the new guy from the single parents' support group. He was smiling.

"It's okay," he said. "She's here. She's okay."

He moved aside so Amy could run ahead of him. There, on the old metal jungle gym that the town still hadn't removed, was Emma.

"Mommy! Look at me!" She was hanging upside down, swinging from a bar in the center so that she looked like an exotic bird in a cage. Amy ran toward her, vision blurred for a moment by tears of relief. She reached out to her daughter, but Emma protested, "I can do it" and pulled herself up before jumping to the ground.

Amy caught her in a bone-crushing hug and Emma allowed it for a moment before wiggling to get away. "Mommy, let go!"

Only Amy couldn't, not all the way. She let her daughter pull back far enough to see her face, but she kept Emma's arms in a firm grip. "What have I told you about wandering off?" she said, speaking sternly.

"But I didn't, Mommy. I said I was going to play." Emma's voice was plaintive.

Had she? Amy wasn't sure. She'd been distracted; maybe Emma had told her. "Okay, baby, it's okay," she said as Emma started to cry. She loosened her grip, but pulled Emma back into a hug, stroking her hair. "Just make sure Mommy hears you, okay? I don't want to lose you."

Some movement on the edge of the old playground caught her eye and she looked up to see Paul.

"Thank you so much," she said. "I was frantic."

"I can imagine." He smiled, lightly jogging the baby up and down in its carrier. The baby was a solemn little boy with a moon face and big brown eyes. The only resemblance he bore to his father was found in his small tuft of light hair.

"This is Brendan." Paul reached behind him and lifted one of the baby's chubby hands to wave. Amy laughed.

"He's cute."

"Thanks. We think so—" He stopped short, the smile fading. "I mean, I think so."

She remembered that he was a widower. "I'm sorry. It must be hard."

"He misses Beth. They say he'll be too young to remember, but I can't help think he knows he's been left with the less competent parent."

There was so much pain in his voice that Amy reached out and touched his arm.

"I'm sure you're a great dad," she said. "I think it's just the nature of parenting that you always feel inadequate for the job."

He put his hand over hers. "That's very kind. Thanks."

Emma abruptly tugged at Amy's other hand, pulling her away. "Let's swing," she said. She shot a fierce look at Paul before smiling in a winsome way at her mother. "Just you and me."

"Emma!" Amy was embarrassed. "Maybe Mr. Marsh wants to join us."

He laughed gently. "Paul, please. No, I wouldn't want to intrude in your mother-daughter time."

"Perhaps another time then," Amy said.

"That would be great." He pulled out his wallet and extracted a business card. "Call me anytime."

She left him at the old playground with his little boy and walked back with Emma, taking care to keep hold of her hand, to the new playground across from the parking lot. As they approached, she saw the strange man who'd been smoking lingering against one of the cars. When they got to the park, he was gone.

Chapter 18

Early Monday morning, Mark left his parents' house to find his car blocked by a small, wiry man with a shock of red hair and a feral grin.

"Peter Gibson," he said, sticking out his hand as if Mark was meeting him at a party and not on a quiet suburban street.

Mark shook hands, feeling the dull throbbing behind his eyes that always accompanied his hangovers. "Yeah?"

"I'm with the *Steerforth Herald*, Detective Juarez. Care to comment on how the investigation's going?"

"It's going," Mark said. "I've got work to do, Mr. Gibson, so if you'll excuse me." He looked pointedly at the man and then at his car.

"Sure, yeah, of course." Peter Gibson bobbed his head in affable agreement, but didn't move an inch. "Just one thing, detective. This is the second murder in two weeks in Steerforth—is there a connection between the two crimes?"

"It's under investigation," Mark repeated. His head was really throbbing. He thought longingly of the aspirin in the glove compartment.

"Is a serial killer loose in Steerforth?"

His eyes whipped up to Gibson's. "Where did you hear that?"

"I've got sources. They say the killer's leaving notes with the bodies—"

"Your source is wrong—there are no notes—"

"But it is the same guy, right? Is he going to kill again?"

Juarez pushed past him and opened his car door. Gibson wedged his small body between the door and the frame. "The public's got a right to know if there's a killer at large, detective."

"The police will protect the public from any killer," Mark said, prying him out of the door.

Gibson's grin got wider. "Can I quote you on that?"

"Get away or I'll arrest you for impeding a police investigation."

The reporter was still standing there when Mark sped away. Mark eyed him in the rearview mirror until that shock of red hair disappeared from view.

He drove into Manhattan, grateful that he was going to the Upper East Side. He told himself that he was only concerned about traffic, and not that he was happy to avoid passing familiar streets.

He couldn't stop his mind from counting the blocks, though, and remembering one street in particular and its prewar brownstones. He couldn't help recalling the thin maple trees spaced along the sidewalk, their branches straining upward to catch glimpses of the sun between the buildings. It had been autumn when they'd met, and he'd been plucking a gorgeous orange-red leaf from the sidewalk when he'd heard a laughing voice declaring that those leaves belonged to the building. He'd looked up to see a smiling face, the dancing eyes flirting with him.

Mark switched stations on the radio, hunting for chatter, anything to drown the memories. Things of the past were in the past. It was over and had to be over. He had a new job, a new life and he had to accept that.

The offices for Chris Moran's law firm were at a posh address. It was an old building with newer design elements, high end with wood and chrome. Juarez paced in the outer office, looking at the black-and-white photos of old Manhattan and even older partners on the walls.

The receptionist, a gazellelike creature with almond eyes and lips that looked enameled, eyed him as if she'd like to call security to have him removed. He'd dressed up, too. Nice pants, nice tie. Still, he felt out of place.

It was a long fifteen minutes and then a tall, strikingly handsome man strode through the glass doors and headed for Mark. He was wearing a suit that must have cost more than Mark made in a year. His hair was the blond of summers on the cape and his skin still bore the faint glow of a tan.

"I'm Chris Moran," he said, his voice full of the confidence born of prep schools and trust funds. His lips were turned up in a smile of welcome, but his pale blue eyes held a question. He smelled faintly of expensive aftershave. "And who might you be?"

Mark introduced himself. He flashed his detective's shield. He said his piece about a murder investigation. When he mentioned Amy, her husband, who'd been listening patiently, uncrossed his arms and ushered him through the glass doors and into his office.

"I'm not sure I'm following you, detective," Moran said once they were seated, one behind and one in front of the large mahogany desk. A silver paperweight and a leather blotter with silver trim adorned its surface, along with a mahogany inbox piled high with briefs. There were no personal photos anywhere to be found.

"Is my wife a suspect in these crimes?"

"We're questioning everyone, sir," Mark said with prac-

ticed ease. Not that Chris Moran seemed to need pacifying.
If the news upset him, he was hiding it well.

"Why are you questioning me?"

"Just routine. Your wife discovered both bodies. You're
her spouse and might be able to shed some light on your
wife's relationship to the deceased, etcetera. It's just what we
do—dotting the *i*'s and crossing the *t*'s." He smiled, doing his
best to convey that this was casual. Two guys getting together to talk. Some people were actually fooled by that.

"I don't think I can help you, detective," Moran said with
his own smile. "My wife and I are separated and have been
for over seven months." He spread his hands as if to indicate
that he had nothing to share.

"But you go to Steerforth regularly, right? To see your
daughter?"

The man's face barely changed, an almost imperceptible
tightening of the lips, but Juarez was used to looking for the
reaction and he noticed it.

"Yes, of course, detective. I visit my daughter as often as
my schedule allows."

"Were you in Steerforth on Tuesday, the sixth of September?"

"If it was a Tuesday, I'm sure I was working."

"The following Friday, the sixteenth?"

Moran's smile was strained. "Again, detective, if it was a
weekday I'm sure I was here."

"This would have been in the evening on the sixteenth."

"If you need to know precisely what I was doing, I'm sure
my secretary can pull my calendar up for you."

"That would be great," Juarez said. Moran buzzed his
secretary and had Juarez repeat the dates in question. The
secretary said she'd buzz him back.

"Did Amy send you?" the lawyer asked as they waited.
"This isn't about the murder investigation at all, is it?"

"Excuse me?" Juarez said and Moran laughed in a nasty way.

Leaning forward in the large office chair, he leveled an index finger at Juarez. "If this is about the mortgage, you can tell her to forget it. She has to sell—I'm not bailing her out this month."

Juarez kept his features blank. "I don't know anything about your mortgage, Mr. Moran. I'm a homicide detective investigating two murders. Did you know Sheila Sylvester?"

Moran settled back in his chair and picked up the silver paperweight, his face settling into a sour expression as if the detective wasn't playing his game. "I met her once," he said. "Brassy woman. Bit of a bitch."

"Do you know of anyone who might have wanted to kill her?"

Moran snorted. "I'm sure you can find a lot of people. She had a lot of opinions and she wasn't afraid to share them."

"Did you dislike her?"

"Enough to kill her, you mean?" Moran smiled, tossing the paperweight from hand to hand. "I didn't know her well enough to dislike her or to kill her."

"Yet you sent her a letter telling her that she'd better stop filling your wife's head with—what word did you use—*crap*?"

Surprise, fear and anger passed in quick succession across Moran's face like storm clouds while Juarez kept a bland smile on his own. "I think I've got a copy with me," he said, reaching into the breast pocket of his jacket. "Let's see what you wrote."

Moran dropped the paperweight back on his desk, shifting in his seat as Juarez unfolded the copy of the letter he'd found in Sheila's home.

"Aah, I was right—*crap* was the word you used. You wrote, 'Leave Amy alone and stop filling her head with all your feminist crap.'"

"There was a context for that, detective."

"Yeah?"

"She was telling my wife to demand all sorts of things from me, that she should screw me in the divorce."

"So you wrote her this letter to put a stop to that?"

"Yes. I wanted her to mind her own business."

"What did you mean when you wrote—" Juarez looked down at the letter again. " 'If you don't stop, I'll be on you like flies on shit and you'll be sorry you ever heard my name.' "

Moran laughed weakly. "A little poetic license, detective."

"So you weren't threatening her?"

"Not in the way you're thinking!" The lawyer sounded genuinely shocked. "With legal action, sure. I wanted her to know that I would sue her interfering ass, that's all."

The secretary buzzed back in with the calendar information. The lawyer had been having dinner with a client on the sixteenth and then drinks with a friend. She had minimal information for the sixth. A meeting in Hoboken at nine A.M., but nothing before then.

"Plenty of time to get back and forth from Steerforth, wouldn't you say?" Juarez looked expectantly at the other man.

"In this traffic? That's difficult at the best of times, detective."

"But not impossible."

Moran actually looked nonplussed for a moment. That was satisfying. "Look, if my meeting wasn't until nine, I'm sure I was here. Someone will have seen me. I certainly wasn't in Connecticut, detective."

"Still, it would help me out if you had someone to vouch for that. Also, I need the name of the friend you were having drinks with on Friday night."

"I hardly think that's necessary." Moran managed a look of outrage that probably worked in a courtroom, but didn't affect Mark. He simply waited.

After a moment, Moran opened a drawer in the mahogany desk. He pulled out a small leather notebook and flipped through its pages. A black book, Mark realized, and understood that something more than this man's sense of entitlement had driven the marriage to ground.

"Christina Rawson," Chris Moran said after a moment. Without being asked, he took a note off a pad engraved with his initials and scribbled a number on it.

"Here." He handed it to Mark, who glanced at the exchange before pocketing it. Then he stood up.

"Thank you for your time, Mr. Moran."

Moran walked Juarez as far as the receptionist, convivial since he believed he'd alibied himself for both dates. As Juarez headed toward the elevators, Moran stopped him with a final question.

"This Meredith Chomsky—was she a ballbuster, too?"

Chief Tom Warburton presented the picture-perfect image of the small town head-of-police. He was in his mid-sixties, tall, broad-shouldered, with a thick, white head of hair, a rugged face with a chiseled chin and a stomach that hinted at the rock-hard man he'd once been. He had just enough paunch to convey maturity without suggesting too many Krispy Kremes.

He had the gift of a reassuring smile that conveyed order, moral righteousness and problems solved that had gotten him re-elected to his office more than fifteen times. He'd run unopposed for years, but still used the campaign slogan some ad agency had developed for him in the 1970s: All crime solved before its prime.

He was smiling now, greeting the phalanx of reporters that had gathered for the press conference he'd organized in the brand-new conference room he'd managed to get state funding for after 9/11.

Standing behind him and off to the sides were the deputy chief, a couple of captains, and Lieutenant Martin Farley, head of homicide's detective bureau and Mark's immediate boss. Tall, thin, and freckled, with a long face and eyes perpetually red-rimmed, he looked like a giraffe coming off a crack habit. He had none of the chief's charisma but all of the crap.

"Nice of you to show up," he growled as Mark slipped into the room.

"Didn't want to steal your thunder, boss," he said, giving him a shit-eating grin. He sat down next to Black at the end of a long table that had a podium for the chief at its center. Several microphones were distributed along its length.

"I hate this kind of thing," Black said, pulling nervously at his collar. He looked more pasty than usual and there were little bits of red-tinged tissue paper stuck to the side of his neck where he'd cut himself shaving.

"Detective Juarez, how nice of you to join us." The chief's voice made both Mark and Black flinch.

"Sorry, sir, I was interviewing a suspect," Mark said.

The chief leaned in to the two men, cupping a giant calloused hand around the microphone closest to them. "Sit up straight and follow the script, boys, and we'll give these jackals what they want to hear so we can get back to work. Got it?" His smile never wavered, but his eyes were piercing steel.

He didn't wait for their reply, but Black nodded his head anyway, nervously patting down his thinning blond hair. Mark pulled his chair closer to the table and looked, for the first time, at the audience before him.

Reporters were still filing in, but more than seventy-five percent of the seats had been filled. Television cameramen, with their massive cameras, had taken up strategic positions in the rear and on the sides. TV and print reporters, some with microcassette recorders, others with small notebooks, were chatting with one another or talking into cell phones. A few were typing away on laptops.

Mark tried to still the anxiety that he felt on seeing them. It wasn't as if any of them were the same reporters that he'd faced after the shooting. Stories about out-of-control cops had been popular in New York and they were eager to paint him as the trigger-happy cop who had it in for poor street hustlers. His face, glowering and stunned, had greeted him from the front pages of tabloids for a few weeks running, opposite a photo of the boy, which had probably been taken in the eighth grade because he'd looked so young and angelic. Then some crazy had shot up a subway train and they'd forgotten all about him.

"Thank you all for coming, ladies and gentlemen," the chief began, standing behind a wooden podium with the Steerforth crest displayed prominently in gold. He'd placed the American and the Connecticut flags strategically near him so that they framed him in the photos. In his full uniform, he looked like a military general. All that was missing were rows of ribbons on his chest.

He reviewed what they already knew—the body of Meredith Chomsky had been found in a house on Brindle Lane. Police were investigating. Evidence found at the scene indicated that this killing and that of realtor Sheila Sylvester might—he stressed the *might*—be related.

Mark could see that the media had already considered that option. They had the strained quality of dogs being held back by an invisible leash. They waited, though, for the chief to introduce the "two lead detectives on the case" before springing.

"Do you have any suspects in custody?"

"Not at this time."

"How were the women killed?"

"They were shot with a nail gun."

The buzz in the room increased with this news. Mark

overheard one reporter mutter, "Holy shit!" The questions flew faster. They wanted particulars about the nail gun, which the chief had decreed would not be released. Ditto with crime scene details, leaving the detectives to deflect all those questions to the best of their ability.

Out of the sea of waving hands, Mark picked one, only to stare, aghast, as up stood a wiry man with a shock of red hair. Peter Gibson grinned at him.

"Hello again, detective. Can you tell us what methods the police are using to protect Steerforth from this serial killer?"

Black grabbed the microphone. "No one said anything about a serial killer."

Gibson looked confused. "Detective Juarez did. When I spoke to you this morning, detective, didn't you mention that the police would protect the public from this killer?"

Pandemonium erupted. The frenzy of questions increased and the chief stepped back from the podium and let Lieutenant Farley in to try to restore order. "If I could speak," he said several times into his microphone, face turning an unattractive shade of red. Reduced to shouting, "Settle down!" his voice was hoarse when he finally got the floor.

"Detective Juarez is new to our department," he said with a strained smile that matched the chief's. "He's used to big-city crime and he's looking with big-city eyes at this." The chief was nodding behind him and shot Mark a look that told him very clearly that he'd better agree and now.

"The lieutenant is right," Mark said, "I am new to the department." The chief's smile relaxed and Black gave an audible sigh of relief. For one long moment Mark considered leaving it there, not saying anything else. But what the hell—no one else in this investigation would take the lead with this, he might as well. "However," he continued, "serial killers have been urban, suburban and rural. There is no one demographic."

"You are so dead," Black muttered beside him, looking down at the tabletop.

"The killer of both Sheila Sylvester and Meredith Chomsky knew his victims. It is clear from some evidence that he'd been watching them for some time. He had gained access to their homes."

The reporters were scribbling furiously, the cameras were focused on Mark's face and he didn't dare look in the chief's direction.

"This doesn't mean it is a serial killer. Just that it's a possibility," he added.

"When do you think the killer will strike again?" a TV reporter asked Mark.

"We have no way of knowing if or when that will happen," the chief said. "We certainly hope it doesn't."

"Have you had any communication with the killer?"

"No," the chief said.

"What does the killer call himself?"

"He doesn't," Mark said.

"Does the Toolman take any trophies?" It was Gibson again and that was it. The reporters erupted again, competing with each other to ask questions, all of them using the now unofficial name of the killer.

The chief ended it, stepping back from the podium and conferring with Lieutenant Farley for a moment before exiting.

"That's all, thank you for coming." Farley repeated this over and over until the room was empty. Then his smile disappeared and he focused his steely gaze on Juarez.

"You," he said. "Chief's office. Now!"

Black hummed an executioner's song and Mark flipped him the bird.

The chief had taken off his jacket and cap and was sitting behind his massive walnut desk with his arms crossed when Mark entered.

"Sit!"

Mark sat. Was it his imagination or were the chairs in front of the chief's desk shorter than the one behind it?

Lieutenant Farley was perched like a vulture on the edge of a small filing cabinet behind the chief.

"Well?" the chief boomed. "What the hell do you have to say for yourself?"

"I didn't tell him anything, but they can guess the truth—"

The chief's voice blasted him. "I'm the truth in this department!"

"There is clear evidence that this could be the work of a serial killer."

"Could be! Emphasis on *could*! It is our job to keep the peace in this community, detective. How do you propose we do that when you go around riling up everyone?"

"I didn't mean to do that—"

"What did you mean to do? Other than disobey a direct order. I told you to follow my script in there, didn't I?"

"Yes, sir."

"And you didn't do that, did you?"

"No, sir."

The chief nodded. "Damn right you didn't. Before you opened your big mouth all we had the press clamoring about was two separate killings—"

"They're connected. Gibson knew it. So does everyone else in there."

"Shut up!" The chief's shout stunned Mark. "You've done enough talking for one day! I'm putting an official reprimand in your file, detective, and if we weren't so understaffed, you'd be reassigned to desk duty for the rest of your youth. Got something to say about that, wiseass?"

It took all of Mark's self-restraint to keep from replying, but he tightened his lips and shook his head.

"Good." The chief bit the word off and sat back for a moment, staring hard at Juarez. He picked up a piece of paper and waved it at him. "Any idea what this is?"

Mark shook his head and the chief slammed it down on

the desk in front of him. It appeared to be a phone number, but before he could read it, the chief snatched it away.

"This is a message from the mayor," he said, holding it up like a flag. "He wants to talk to me. You know why he wants to talk to me?"

Again, Mark shook his head, though he could have hazarded a guess. He winced as the chief crumpled the message into his fist and pounded it on the desk.

"You! You are the reason he wants to talk to me! The media didn't know these killings were related until you volunteered that information. Thanks to you, we've got them believing in 'the Toolman.' They are now clamoring for more information. And when they clamor, the whole town clamors. So instead of looking for a killer, I have to spend my time fielding phone calls from the mayor's office and other bigwigs in this town who want to know why the hell they weren't informed that Steerforth had a serial killer on the loose."

"I'm sorry, sir."

At those words a nasty smile spread across the chief's face. "No, son, you're not sorry, not yet, but you're going to be. Since you're so convinced that this is the work of a serial killer, you can pull extra shifts until the perp is apprehended."

Juarez stifled a groan, but he couldn't hide his dismay entirely. It seemed to please the chief, who actually chuckled.

"Don't worry, detective, I'm sure you'll manage to squeeze in some sleep somewhere," he said cheerily. Then the smile vanished. "Now get out."

Mark stood up, feeling shaken and pissed. All he'd done was try to do his job; he didn't deserve this shit.

"I hope your father wasn't watching TV," Farley called as Mark walked out the door. "What an embarrassment."

Chapter 19

They'd dubbed him the Toolman. There was the headline across the front page of the local paper. Guy was so surprised when he saw it he felt light-headed.

He'd never had a nickname before Guy, but of course this was different. More like a professional title, really, and he decided he should celebrate. He dialed the office and told them he wouldn't be in, offering no excuses and ignoring the cold voice of the receptionist. Then he called Braxton Realty.

Getting the information he needed was simple. He pretended he was a client with an appointment and that he suddenly had another property he wanted to visit as well. Could she squeeze him in? The receptionist at Braxton was very helpful, happily filling him in on Amy's schedule without asking any difficult questions. He jotted it down and then read the newspaper while eating breakfast.

He read all the accounts of the killings, though he was disappointed by how little information was included. Next he watched the morning news shows while sipping his cup of tea. He waited to make sure he caught all the coverage, getting a little frisson of pleasure every time he heard the anchors say "Toolman."

It was over all too soon. He cleared his breakfast dishes, loading them carefully into the dishwasher, wiped down the table's surface and washed the nonstick frying pan that he hated to leave in the dishwasher. Then he fetched his scissors and the file box and painstakingly cut out every article in the newspaper.

He slipped them into acid-free sleeves and put them in the correct order in the file box and carried the box back into his home office, putting it back in the closet. There was the small freezer and he was tempted, so tempted to take it out and play with its contents, but that would have to wait. He had other things to do.

The camera was in his desk drawer and he took it out and hooked it up to his computer. Downloading his latest photos took ten minutes at the most and he enjoyed watching them appear on the screen.

He felt himself growing hard as he rearranged them, enjoying the way shadows enhanced the hollows and light highlighted the texture of bare skin. When he was done, he stored them all in a file marked with just one word: AMY.

Chapter 20

Every real estate agent knew there were different kinds of customers. Those who were just looking. Call them the "D" group. Those that were just looking, but if something they liked came along they might make an offer. Call them the "C" group. Those that were seriously looking, but very particular about what house they'd buy: the "B" group. And those that were seriously looking and seriously needed a house: the "A" group.

Every realtor wanted "A's," but most realtors ended up with lots of people in the "B" and "C" group. The trick of successful realtors, Sheila had taught Amy, was to try to mainly get "A's" and "B's", transform the "B's" to "A's", the "C's" to "B's" and avoid the "D's" like the plague.

There were different categories for the houses, too, of course. The crappy little house that would take a miracle to unload; the nice-size, nice-lot house that showed well until you opened the door and the prospective buyer stepped on the rust orange shag carpeting and realized the place hadn't been updated since 1975; the house that would sell in a minute if the owner didn't insist on overpricing it; and the quirky house with the strange layout that lingered on the market long after everything else had sold.

Now Amy had a new category to add to that list: The house that no one wants because a terrible crime has been committed there and it's carrying bad karma. It was amazing how superstitious some people were. They didn't want to look at the homes of divorcing couples, or houses with the number 13 in them. They wouldn't set foot near a home where murder had been committed.

There were others, though, for whom it was the main attraction. They were definitely in the "D" category and Amy had come to think of *them* as ghouls.

"How soon can we see the inside? Will there still be crime scene tape in the bedroom?" The portly man shifted his gaze from the front of Meredith's house to look at Amy, excitement apparent in his voice and face.

"Another few days. Maybe by the end of the week. I think it definitely has the space you need, Mr. Hanover."

"Were you the one that found the body?"

Amy schooled her features to hide her repulsion. She needed this sale, she reminded herself. It didn't matter if what it took was some investment banker cum creepy mystery writer's interest in buying a home where a crime had actually taken place.

"Yes," she said. "Is your family going to be arriving this week, Mr. Hanover?"

"What? Oh, yeah, my wife's flying in with them on Thursday. Listen, I'd really like to interview you about what you saw. Great research for my novel. What do you say?"

Not now, not ever, Amy felt like saying but didn't. She managed a regretful smile. "Unfortunately I can't talk about it. I'm part of the police investigation and am really not free to say anything at all."

"Oh, right," Mr. Hanover smacked his own head. "Of course you can't." He reached one small, manicured hand inside his suit jacket and pulled out a gold business card case. "Let me give you my card," he said, extracting one. In black ink on a card bordered in what looked like blood, Robert Hanover was printed in big letters. Below it was one word: Writer.

"This is my favorite card," he said. "Someday I hope to only have to use that one. Once the novel gets optioned then it's bye-bye banking."

For a moment, Amy felt sorry for him. She knew all about putting aside your passion to work a job you didn't really want in order to support a family. On the other hand, she'd worked hard as an artist, not dreaming about being one by visiting museums, but really working at it. And she needed to work at this job, too, and make this sale or she wasn't going to be able to provide for Emma.

"So why don't I see if I can get you and your wife in the house on Thursday afternoon. Will that work for you, Mr. Hanover?"

"I'm not sure," he said, suddenly vague. "Maybe it's better if I just see it."

"I realize your wife has seen the pictures, but wouldn't she like to see the house in person?"

"Well, the truth is, I don't think Mary Alice will go for this house. Not after what happened."

Amy bit her lip to prevent the scream from escaping. "But you like the house, right, Mr. Hanover?"

"Oh, please call me Robert."

"Robert." She smiled and tried to make it intimate. "You like this house. This house has the atmosphere you need to write your novel. What can we do to make it work for your wife?"

Twenty minutes later she'd managed to talk Mr. Hanover into taking his wife through the house even if he had to pretend it was another property to get her there. She waved after the cab that was taking him back to the hotel and entered

Braxton's offices feeling the sudden urge to do recreational drugs. An urge that increased when she saw Vikram Padwardan sitting on the couch in reception. He leapt up when he saw her and extended a copy of the local paper in her direction.

"This is not what you promised us, Mrs. Moran," he said, his pleasant singsong accent at odds with the scowl on his face. "This is not the relaxing country estate of the advertisement. This is scandal."

The banker and his wife had backed out of the deal on the house where Sheila had died, wealthy enough not to care about the loss of their hand money. Amy's renewed advertising effort had hit pay dirt with a chemical engineer and his pediatrician wife. They had two children and enough money saved for a down payment to take them out of Newark. It had all seemed golden.

"It will all blow over soon, Mr. Padwardan," she said in a soothing voice, but he was shaking his head before she was finished.

"No, no it will not. This Toolman label will hang over this house forever. My wife does not want our children to be living in the house of the murder."

"This will not be known as the house of the murder once you move in, Mr. Padwardan. Believe me, then it will be known as the Padwardan house. This is just a strange coincidence that it happened to be at your house. The murder has no connection to the house itself and the poor victim didn't live in the house, so it will not stay on in the house."

He looked skeptical, but he didn't speak, obviously considering what she had to say. Amy tried to sell it then, working as hard as she'd ever worked to convince him that this wouldn't taint his house and that there had been many good memories in the house and all he needed to add to this was a few good memories of his own to make it feel like home.

He left pacified, at least, if not 100 percent convinced. Amy felt so exhausted she thought she could probably sleep standing up, but she needed to show another house and not, thank God, either of the crime scene homes. She'd stopped by the office just to grab a few comps and pull the official information on the 1940s-era two-bedroom bungalow that was selling for close to a million because it was just two blocks off the sound.

"You got a call from Detective Black," the receptionist said, handing over some messages. "Also, Paul called and said Emma's breathing's a little ragged."

"Okay, thanks," Amy gathered the slips of paper and walked toward her cubicle, mentally planning the rest of her day. She had to show the house—she couldn't afford not to—but maybe she had enough time to swing by Paul's house first. He'd been generous enough to offer to watch Emma because Chloe was sick and Amy was without a babysitter.

She'd been reluctant to leave Emma with anyone else, but she'd been desperate and Paul just happened to call when she was trying to decide whether to cancel the showings or take Emma with her. He'd immediately suggested that he babysit and even offered to pick Emma up, but Amy definitely didn't feel comfortable with that. She drove Emma to his house, which was on the other side of town, a nice, quiet, residential street.

Paul came to the door with Brendan in his arms, and the baby immediately smiled and gurgled at Emma. Amy stayed for twenty minutes, long enough to see that his place was safe and that Emma was happy. Paul explained that he did a lot of telecommuting since his wife's death so he could be with Brendan. She'd secretly hoped to see a photo of his wife, but the only picture in the living room was a framed, studio shot of an infant Brendan.

Paul walked her to the door when she left, but Emma barely waved, completely preoccupied with rolling a ball to the gurgling, happy baby. For a moment, Amy fantasized that this was her house and her family with her handsome and supportive husband saying goodbye as she headed out to work.

The chaste peck on the cheek he gave her dispelled that notion, but she wondered. He was a nice, attractive man, a good father and had a good job. She wished she felt something more for him.

There was a bottle of wine tied in a red silk bag sitting on her desk. The attached note said simply, "A glass of good wine with a good friend. These are the things you never want to end." It was signed just as the note with the chocolates, "An Admirer."

Amy slipped the bottle out of the gift bag, smiling as she saw the Quinta Do Crasso label. She'd shared a bottle of this rich red wine with Chris the night she graduated from art school. Only he knew how special this was to her. She thought again about calling him, but as her hand touched the phone the intercom buzzed. Bev's voice told her that someone was up front to see her.

For a moment Amy didn't recognize the dark-haired man sifting through magazines in the reception area. He stood up and smiled when he saw her and then she knew him.

"Ryan Grogan," he said, sticking out a hand. "I'm the paramedic who helped your daughter?"

"Of course!" She shook. "I didn't recognize you without your uniform."

He was wearing a short leather jacket over a black Henley shirt and blue jeans and this casual look suited him. Very well.

She didn't realize he'd said something until she saw him grin. Amy blushed and stopped staring.

"I'm sorry, what was that?"

"I said I needed to talk to someone about selling a house, can you help?"

"Absolutely."

Amy could see Bev listening and making no pretense about it, leaning her head on one hand and gawking at them.

"Why don't we go back to my desk," Amy said, leading the way through the door. Ryan followed.

"It's my mom's house," he said, taking a seat next to her desk. "She's getting older and she can't take care of things like she used to."

"So she's ready to sell?"

Ryan made a face. "That's just it—she isn't. She thinks she's fine and she wants to stay there. But she's getting weaker and I'm afraid she's going to fall."

"Are you a co-owner of the house?" Amy said.

Ryan shook his head. "No. It's all hers. And I know that means I can't sell it out from under her, but I was wondering if you could talk to her. See if she'll change her mind."

Amy was skeptical. "I'll try, but chances are she'll refuse to talk with me. What's her name?"

"Louisa." He wrote it down on a notepad along with the number. "Thank you. I really appreciate it."

"No problem. I can't promise anything, but I'll try."

"That's all I'm asking." He smiled, but made no move to leave.

"Was there anything else you wanted to talk about?" she said. "Another property?"

"No, nothing like that." He gave a nervous laugh and slapped his hands against his knees. "I'm trying to think of some clever way to do this, but I don't have one, so I'll just ask you straight out. Would you like to have lunch some time?"

Amy's jaw dropped. A man was asking her out on a date. She hadn't been asked out since she was in college. She pulled herself together. "Okay, I mean, yes, that would be fun."

He beamed at her. "Great. Great. Well, how about tomorrow?"

It was her turn to laugh. "Let me check my schedule."

She felt lighter then she had in days when he left, humming to herself as she gathered her papers. A feeling that lasted all the way to the parking lot, only to fade abruptly when she saw the short figure of Detective Black leaning against her car.

"How you doing, Mrs. Moran?" Detective Black straightened up as Amy approached, smiling in a predatory way, the air around him tangy with the smell of the yellow mustard staining his tie.

"Busy," Amy said, walking around him to open the car door. He moved a hand against hers.

"Wait."

Amy jerked her hand away. "What do you want?"

"To talk to you."

"I've told you everything I know—"

"You didn't tell me that you hated Meredith Chomsky."

"Find me someone who liked her and that'll be news."

"She was hassling you about selling her house."

"So I killed her to make the house sell faster?" Amy laughed.

"You killed her to make sure you held onto the commission."

Amy hesitated and Black smiled with satisfaction. "That's ridiculous," she said, but it sounded weak and Black leapt on it.

"Your colleagues don't seem to think so."

"Who would that be?"

Black ignored her. He pulled out a notebook and flipped through it. "According to some of them you've been desperate for a big sale since you arrived at Braxton."

"I'm a real estate agent, detective—we're all desperate for the big sale."

"Are all agents photographers?"

"I'm sure you know they aren't," Amy said, but her heart quickened, knowing where this was leading.

"You took those pictures, didn't you, Ms. Moran?"

"No."

"And you were planting them in Meredith Chomsky's car when that officer stopped you."

"No!"

"Do you have a darkroom in your house?"

"Yes."

"And you develop all your own work?"

"Yes, mostly."

"Mind if I take a look?"

"Yes."

"I'm going to get a search warrant."

"You do that."

Black frowned and stepped closer to Amy. "You don't want to piss me off, Ms. Moran, you really don't."

Amy's eyes tingled from the smell of mustard. "I need to pick up my daughter," she said, trying to keep her voice steady. "So if you'll excuse me."

She stepped around him and this time he didn't try to stop her when she opened the car door.

As she pulled out of the parking lot she saw Douglas sitting in his white BMW, watching her. He smiled triumphantly as she roared past.

Chapter 21

The motel room was sterile: a bed with a thin aqua spread, two cheap wood-grain nightstands, threadbare carpet and a TV bolted to a stand. The woman, Cathy, with a last name he'd forgotten, was flipping through the channels. "Don't they have any porn?" she said, winking at Mark.

He was very drunk and yet he raised the beer bottle and took another deep swallow. He was sitting back against the headboard and Cathy was near his feet. So far, he'd shed only his shoes, jacket and tie. She was in a lilac bra and panties. He tried to remember what she'd been wearing when he met her in the bar, but he couldn't get beyond a fuzzy sweater.

The initial surprise of his dad rejoining them at the supper table had quickly been overcome by the purgatory of watching this once strong, hulking man dribbling food out of the slack side of his mouth.

His mother attempted to wipe it clean with a napkin, only to have Oscar Juarez swipe at her, with the scythelike claw that had been his left hand. During pauses in the laboriously long meal, he'd scribbled questions with his good hand on the white board he'd brought downstairs with him, demanding to know "what the hell" the press conference had been about and "what were you thinking?"

Mark answered with nonanswers, trying to assure his parents that all was well, that he wasn't in any trouble, that he wasn't the only one in the department to believe in his theory. In other words, he lied.

His mother had accepted this, the wrinkles in her forehead caused by concern for his well-being, but there was skepticism in his father's eyes, the only part of his face that could show much expression. He'd kept those steady, dark eyes on his son throughout the rest of the meal.

That was why Mark had gone to the bar. He needed to escape and he kept telling himself this as the second beer became a third, then a fourth. He'd become a fixture at the counter, settling onto a favorite stool, the red vinyl faded and cracked from years of use but pleasingly close to the door and a fast exit if he wanted it.

He convinced himself that the fact that he could feel the sudden burst of cold air whenever the bar door opened meant he wasn't drinking too much. He convinced himself that you couldn't be an alcoholic on beer alone. He listened to the women who managed to find him, their eyelids glittery with powder, their lips frosted with sweet-smelling gel, and he pushed out of his mind the feel of that soft hair between his fingers, the weight of another's skin against his, the sweet, almost shy smile that had made it easy to wake in the morning.

Cathy had a full head of tousled blond hair, a harsh color in the motel room. It had looked different in the soft light of the bar.

"Aren't you going to get undressed?" she said, faking a pout.

"Yeah, okay." He put the bottle down on the nightstand and started on his shirt.

"Let me," she said, crawling up the bed to him, her breasts dangling in the bra. He put his hand out to feel one and she let him, placing her hand over his and applying pressure so he was massaging her. "That's it, baby, don't be afraid," she whispered, leaning close to his ear. Her breath was smoke and whiskey laden. She pressed soft kisses on his cheeks and then he felt her small hands unbuttoning his shirt.

He tried to relax, tried to enjoy the sensation of her soft skin, of her soft hands. She pushed the shirt from his shoulders and pulled it off his arms one at a time. Then she started on his pants, pushing his hands away when he went to help her.

"Let me," she said again, caressing the crotch of his slacks. He closed his eyes and let her work, feeling himself harden as hands brushed against him, once, then again. His pants came off and when he sat up to help, she pushed him back on the bed. So he lay down and kept his eyes closed, even when he felt his boxers sliding off his hips, even when he felt hands on his cock and balls. All the stroking, tickling, sucking—his eyes flew open.

She'd taken him in her mouth and the sudden wet stunned him, such a wonderful sensation. Then he made the mistake of looking and there she was, kneeling between his legs, smiling up at him as much as she could with his cock filling her mouth.

Mark squeezed his eyes shut, willing himself just to feel, but the feelings were flagging and so was his erection. He shifted, reaching blindly for her, taking her in his arms so that she released him and returned his embrace.

He crushed her breasts against his chest and kissed her hard, searching her mouth with his tongue, willing himself to enjoy the sensation of skin against skin. But then he ran her hair through his fingers and it felt sticky, not soft.

She knew the impossibility of it before he did, pulling away, eyeing his penis, which was shrinking.

"You're drunk," she said and then she laughed, just a little laugh, but he hated her for it. Suddenly he didn't know what he was doing there at all and he reached for his boxers, pants, shirt, scrambling to get his clothes on and get out.

"Don't go," she said. "Please. It's okay. We can still have fun. We can do other things." She dipped her voice on the last two words, but he didn't want to know what that meant. He buttoned his shirt wrong and tucked it into his pants anyway. Zip, button, and buckle the belt. He searched for his shoes and she threw them at him from the other side of the bed.

"Here, asshole!"

One of them hit him on the shoulder and he blocked the other with his hand.

"I'm sorry," he mumbled, stooping to pull them on, his fingers fumbling with the shoestrings.

"Yeah. Whatever." She had her back to him, dressing with a jerky rapidity that reminded him of a bird.

"Well, um, take care," he said, stepping past her to the door, trying to avoid making eye contact.

"Go to hell."

He was too drunk to drive, he knew that, but he couldn't stay here. He drove his car only as far as the parking lot to the strip mall next door, doused the lights, locked the doors and curled up in the backseat to sleep.

High-pitched whining woke him at dawn. He struggled upright, head throbbing, neck aching, and peeled his eyes open only to close them immediately against the harsh, gray light. The whining stopped, then started again. He realized it was his cell phone.

Two rings to extricate it from his pocket. One ring to get it to his ear. "Juarez," he croaked.

"Where the fuck are you?" It was Black and he sounded like he'd passed pissed-off an hour ago. "Boss has been by every ten minutes looking for you, so you'd better get your ass in here or he's going to eat your balls for breakfast!"

The phone slammed down before Mark had a chance to respond. He rubbed his eyes and peered at the clock on the dash. It was after eight.

"Shit!" Mark climbed into the front seat, groaning as all his joints protested. His head hit the rearview mirror and he caught a glimpse of himself as he adjusted it, barely recognizing the man with the bloodshot eyes and puffy gray skin.

Peeling out of the empty parking lot, he burned rubber all the way home, making it to his parents' house in ten minutes. His mother was in the kitchen fixing breakfast for his father and still dressed for work. Her uniform still looked pressed, and there wasn't a hair out of place on her graying head. She gave him a hard look, lips tightly compressed, but didn't comment as he ran upstairs, undressing as he went, and jumped in the shower.

The water felt like an assault, but he kept the spray turned up and washed as fast as he could, shaving at the same speed, then getting into the least wrinkled clothes he could find. He took his damp towel and ran it down any visible creases.

Lacing his shoes reminded him of the night before and he had to fight hard to drive those unpleasant images out of his mind.

He clattered down the steps and collided with his mother, who was coming up.

"Whoa!" she said, quickly lifting his father's tray out of danger.

"Sorry." He gave her a quick peck on the cheek. "I'm late for work. Thanks for taking care of Dad this morning."

"Late night again?" she called after him, sarcasm evident in her voice.

"Yeah," he said, ignoring her tone. "I'll see you tonight."

He was seconds from leaving, had his hand on the front door, when her voice stopped him. "Mark. Wait."

Crap. He turned, watched her hustling down the steps in

waffle-weave nursing shoes. She called them her "ugly shoes." "I'm running late, Mom."

"Did you have breakfast?"

"I'll grab something on the way."

"Come in the kitchen, I can make something for you quick."

"Mom, I don't have time," he said, but she gave him a look that silenced him.

He salvaged his pride by standing in the doorway of the small kitchen, refusing to sit down at the chrome-legged table they'd had since before he was born. He watched as she whipped out a frying pan, eggs, cheese. The smell of frying eggs was nauseating, but he couldn't tell her that.

"I want to know what's going on."

He considered pretending he didn't know what she was talking about, but the looks she was shooting from the stove made it clear she wasn't buying. "I've just been working a lot."

"And?"

"And?" he repeated stupidly, shifting his gaze ever so slightly so it looked like he was meeting her eye when he was really looking at the refrigerator. There were pictures on the fridge. His two older sisters. Their husbands. His nieces and nephews. *When are you going to get married, Mark? You need some nice woman to come home to. Got to have someone to carry on the Juarez name.*

"And is that why you're drinking so much," his mother's voice interrupted his thoughts, "or is it because you quit the NYPD and came home?"

"No, well, not exactly."

"Because you didn't have to come home. Your father and I are managing just fine."

"I know, Mom, I know. I wanted to come home. I wanted to help."

She stared at him for a long moment, then deftly assembled a fried-egg-and-cheese toasted sandwich, wrapped it in aluminum foil and ushered him to the door. She stopped him there, her hand on his arm.

"Mark, I know you're unhappy."

"I'm not—"

"Ssh." She put a finger to his lips. "Don't lie to me. Please. I'm your mother. A mother always knows about her children." She tightened her grip, looking into his eyes as if she were trying to look inside his soul. "A mother always supports her children. No matter what choices they make."

At the station at last, fresh cup of coffee in hand, Mark parked himself at his desk and made dozens of phone calls, scribbling notes on white steno pads as he went, his investigation becoming a diagram of concentric circles and little spokes.

"I've already talked to Poppy Braxton and Douglas Martin," Black said in early afternoon, his phone balanced against his ear while he pried open another can of Diet Coke. "You want my notes or my theory first?"

"I know your theory," Juarez said, holding out a hand for Black's notes. He skimmed them and handed them back without comment.

Black took a swig of Coke and smiled. "C'mon, I know you've got something to say."

"I'm too polite to say it," Juarez replied with a grin, stretching his arms over his head until his back cracked. He tossed over his own notepad. "Any names look familiar?"

Black took his time reading, fiddling with the godawful-shade-of-green tie he'd chosen, no doubt, for how it clashed with his pale skin.

"Well?" Juarez prompted him.

"You don't seriously think these are real possibilities, do you?" he said at last.

"No more far-fetched than your theory."

"Christ, Juarez," Black said, drawing out the name like he always did, "I know you're attracted to this woman, but c'mon."

"What?" He gave Black a half smile, waiting for the punch line. His partner shrugged.

"I know you like her."

Mark laughed, astonished. "I don't like her!"

"Okay, you've got the hots for her. Big difference."

"I don't like her," Mark repeated, speaking slowly. "Not in that way."

Black scoffed. "You're telling me you don't feel anything for a chick like that? She's beautiful."

"Sounds like you're the one who's got the hots for her."

Black shot him a look of mock outrage. "I'm a married man!" Then he laughed. "Hey, I'm allowed to look. I didn't sign away my eyes."

"Well, look all you want. She's not my type."

Black assessed him for a moment and then smiled broadly. "Ooh, I got it. You go for blonds, right? You'd rather be with a blond than a brunette?"

Honey-blond. A color somewhere between brown and blond and finer than his own dark hair. Juarez could remember the soft feel of it running through his fingers, the way it was always unkempt seconds after being styled, the way it felt brushing it out of laughing brown eyes.

"She's a blond, right? The one you left in the city?" Black's words jarred him back to the present.

"Let's stick to the case, okay." Juarez said, looking back out the window. He felt Black's eyes on him, but then the older man shrugged.

"Sure. Just trying to look out for you."

"I don't need you playing matchmaker for me."

Black slammed his Coke can down. "What's your problem, Juarez?"

Drawing out the name again, just like he always did. Mark felt the anger churning right below the surface, struggling to pull him down. "No problem. Just stay out of my personal life."

"Fine, fucker," Black said. He got out of his chair and slammed it against the desk before stomping out of the room. Juarez watched him go, trying not to give a shit that he'd hurt the guy's feelings.

The photos were in Amy's dream. There was Sheila naked, splayed on her bed, and *click, click, click*, there were the photos. It was as if Amy were the photographer. Sheila smiling. *Click*. Sheila cupping her breasts. *Click*. Sheila crucified on the floor.

The scene changed. Had she made it change? Another bed, another room. Chris now. Naked except for his boxers, his hair sleep tousled the way she remembered it. Holding the bottle of wine he'd sent to her in one hand, two glasses in the other. Smiling and beckoning to her. Come out from behind the camera and take a drink. He fills the glasses deftly, hands one to her. She lifts it to her lips and sees that it's blood not wine.

She woke up in a cold sweat, sitting up in the bed. The clock radio glowing five A.M. Alone, on her side of the bed. No Chris, no Sheila. But she could hear something in the dark, some guttural sound. A moment's panic before she realized what it was and raced down the dark hallway to Emma's room.

The smiling moon night-light cast a yellowish glow. Emma was lying on her back, eyes wide and panicked, in the middle of an attack. She sounded like someone in the throes of dying. The sound from her throat was a death rattle, not a breath. She looked like a fish stranded on land, the small rib cage heaving in and out with each attempt to suck air into the damaged lungs.

"Emma! Sit up, baby." Amy slipped an arm under her, and lifted her into a sitting position. The little girl's eyes swiveled to her mother. *Jesus, no. No, baby*. Amy propped pillows behind her, a large stuffed unicorn bracing her in an upright position, afraid to let go but needing to, *just for a moment, baby*, while she got her medicine.

With fumbling hands she found the nebulizer and set it up. Slipped the mask over Emma's small face.

"It's okay, just breathe in, baby."

The medicine looked greenish through the mask. Emma breathed in and out, the sound labored. Amy sat behind her, propping her up and holding the mask in place, regulating the amount of medicine flowing. They sat like that for a long time, till the light in the room was daylight coming through the curtains and Amy could feel Emma breathing normally, sleeping comfortably against her chest.

At nine, Emma woke again and Amy carried her into the kitchen wrapped in a blanket. The bottle of wine that Chris had sent was sitting on the counter and she put it out of sight because it reminded her of the dream. She thought about the dream while she fixed them breakfast, watching Emma carefully while she made pancakes, pouring the batter into a Mickey Mouse head on the griddle, trying to coax a smile onto that pale face.

How had those photographs been taken? All of them in the bedroom, but there was no evidence that anyone had been in the houses. No reports of break-ins from Sheila or Meredith. So how had they been taken?

She flipped the pancake onto a plate and presented it to Emma, thinking about the tiny cameras she'd seen in stores, more like spy equipment than a photographer's.

"Mommy, syrup."

Emma liked the bottle shaped like a woman. She never mentioned the maple-leaf-shaped bottle they used to have because that was the only kind of syrup her daddy would eat.

Real stuff, not that flavored corn syrup "commercial crap." That's what he'd called it, Emma mimicking him sometimes. He probably still bought it, but Amy couldn't afford to.

She drizzled syrup over Emma's pancakes and some over her own and ate them mechanically, thinking of the dream again and pushing the creepiness aside, clearing her mind to think only of the photos. If she'd been the photographer, really, how would she have taken those shots?

It gave her an idea and after Emma was done eating and she'd bundled her into the living room to watch *Sesame Street*, Amy went into her home office. She took down various cameras from shelves, hauling them into her own bedroom to do a little experimenting.

At 10:45, Chloe arrived, cheeks ruddy with the cold, her long blond hair stuck under an ugly knit hat that was fashionable if not pretty. Emma ran to greet her, pushing past her mother to throw her arms around the young woman's jean-clad legs so hard that she almost knocked her over.

"Chloe Bloey!"

"Emmy Memmy!"

Their own silly names for each other and Amy smiled at the laughter that always accompanied them. Here was something to be grateful for, she thought, that this college student actually cared for her daughter and didn't just care about the money.

"I'll only be gone for a few hours," she said. She waited until Emma had run to her room to get some toy to tell Chloe about the attack she'd had. "She seems fine now, but call me if that changes."

"Okay, will do."

"And the emergency number's right by the phone, like always, along with my cell phone number and number for Braxton, but try my cell first."

She hadn't realized until that moment that she wasn't planning to go into the office at all.

Chapter 22

Fighting the influx of big discount chains, the local camera store offered specialty services—one-hour developing, specialized prints, discounts on enlargements, unique Christmas card and baby announcements—with the ambience of an old-time shop.

Hung on the walls near the latest equipment, which was neatly displayed in glass cabinets, were cameras of yesteryear. Detective Black identified the small Kodak he'd owned as a young man, as well as the Brownie his father had owned. It didn't fill him with nostalgia; it just made him feel old.

The twenty-something behind the counter was what was referred to now as metrosexual. He wore skintight black jeans, a tight white T-shirt that highlighted his thin chest and a Kanji tattoo on one bicep. His blond-tipped hair was carefully mussed, and he looked like he was wearing eyeliner and had small silver hoops in both ears.

Things had been a lot simpler when guys like this could be written off as pansies, Black thought, watching as Mr.

Silver Hoops openly flirted with the very hot and very hotly dressed young woman who'd walked in just ahead of him.

"I love those Nikons, don't you?" the girl was saying as Black moved closer, trying to catch the guy's attention. She was leaning against the counter so that the navel ring visible above her jeans clicked against the glass.

"Yeah, they're bad," the clerk said, leaning forward so that he could check out her cleavage.

"Excuse me," Black interrupted. They both turned to look at him, giving him the universal teenage expression of boredom mixed with anger, like he was dog shit they were being forced to scrape off their designer shoes.

He pulled out his badge and the expressions changed. Miss Naval Ring's eyes got big and she thanked Mr. Silver Hoops and took off. Probably packing some meth in that tiny little purse, Black thought, following her hot ass out the door along with Silver Hoops.

"I want to know what kind of film this is," the detective said once she was gone, laying the least salacious of photos of Meredith Chomsky on the counter. In it, she was staring at something, probably a mirror, one hand raised to the spaghetti strap of a dark silk teddy.

Silver Hoops whistled. "Hot chick," he said before fixing his eyes on Black with a knowing look. "I can't do this kind of developing for you, man," he said. "It's illegal."

"Yeah, nimrod, I know—I'm a cop, remember?" Black lost his patience sooner than he expected. "Is this standard paper? I don't see any mark on it."

Holding the photo by the edges, Silver Hoops examined it carefully. "This is printed out on a computer," he said at last. "There's lots of different paper that can be used, but I think this stock is done by Xerox."

"So this wasn't done at a lab or in a darkroom?"

"No, man, this was done on a personal printer."

"Any sense which one?"

Silver Hoops shrugged. "Could be done on any number of printers," he said, moving over to a display case filled with them. "Like this Epson model." He pointed to one. "Or this Fuji." He moved down the case, launching into jargon about pixels and acid-free quality and matte versus glossy. It was all too much for Black, who finally interrupted him.

"Do you keep a list of which models are stocked and sold?"

"Yeah, man, but I can't give that out to you. That's like, private data."

"I could get a subpoena," Black said, "but if I do, I'm going to have a really good look around and who knows what I'll find?"

He let his gaze fall on the edge of the *Penthouse* he'd noticed lurking below the counter and sniffed the air just a bit. Was that pot he smelled?

"Let me just find the file," Silver Hoops said. Five minutes later, he'd pulled it up on the computer and swung the screen around so that Black could scroll through it. In addition to the lists of printers stocked, there were also names and phone numbers of people who'd purchased the printers in the last year.

Halfway down the list, Black hit pay dirt.

When Detective Juarez saw Amy waiting for him beyond the front desk, he got a funny look on his face and glanced quickly around as if there was someone behind him. The desk sergeant grinned.

"She's been waiting for you," he said to the detective, giving a nod to Amy, who'd been looking through the wanted posters hanging from a bulletin board, but turned in time to catch it. An incomprehensible statement, but it made the detective blush.

He took her by the upper arm, a little too firmly for her liking, and led her down a hall into a small, bare room, closing the door behind them. "What are you doing here?"

"I had an idea about the photos. How they might have been taken. But I need you to test it out with me."

"Why would I want to do that?"

He'd seemed friendlier before, not treating her the way the other detective did. She wondered if she'd made a mistake. Maybe he suspected her, too. But no, she'd seen the clips of the press conference on the nightly news. He thought it was a serial killer. Surely he didn't think she fit that profile.

"Because you want to find out who killed Sheila Sylvester and Meredith Chomsky."

"And how does that involve you?"

"I'll show you. At least I'll try to. But we have to go to one of the houses. And I need the photos. I have an idea."

Juarez stared at her for a long moment, arms crossed, and then he nodded. "Okay. We can take my car."

He put a hand on her arm again as they left the room. "Just wait for me outside, though, okay? I'll pull the car around."

She waited for him across the street, feeding the meter where she'd parked her Toyota, checking her watch because she didn't want to stay away from the office too long.

Detective Juarez finally pulled around front in a brown sedan and got out to open the passenger door for her.

"We can go to Sheila's house," he said, "but not the Chomsky place. Not right now. Okay?"

She nodded, feeling for the camera she'd stuck in her purse. For the first few minutes of driving, there was an awkward silence. A newer manila envelope was stuck on the seat between them and she knew it contained the photos, but she didn't want to see them again. Not yet. She shifted in her seat, rubbing her hands surreptitiously down the front legs of her jeans, wondering if this had been a good idea after all. What if she was wrong?

The detective stared straight ahead, both hands on the wheel, his face solemn. He looked tired, she thought, noticing the smoky blue circles under his eyes and the way his mouth dragged down at the corners.

When they stopped in a traffic backup, Juarez put a flashing blue light up on his dash and turned on a siren. Cars parted like the Red Sea and they sailed past.

"Nice," Amy said. "I've always wondered if you guys were really running to emergencies."

Juarez grinned. "Job perk."

It wasn't until he turned onto Sheila's street that Amy felt any sadness. She didn't say anything, but just the sight of her friend's house was enough to bring tears to her eyes. Juarez stopped the car in front of 1730 Roland Street.

Amy stared up at the two-story, pale yellow house with the periwinkle blue shutters. Sheila had been so proud of her home; her very own house that she'd worked so hard for. Amy could still remember the faint perfume of the purple mums Sheila had planted in the big stoneware urns that flanked her walkway. The flowers were still there, shriveled stalks and heads hardened by frost.

"I just realized—I don't have a key," she said to Juarez, blinking hard to keep the tears at bay, determined that she wasn't going to cry in front of him. She tried to hold on to the toughness that Sheila had taught her, but just thinking of Sheila made her ache so badly that she wanted to fall to her knees right there on the walkway and sob.

If Juarez noticed, he didn't say. Instead he fished in his pocket and held up a key. "Let's go in the front," he said.

It wasn't a crime scene, so the house wasn't circled with yellow tape, but there was a small strip across the front door and a sign stating that the entrance was barred because this residence was part of an ongoing police investigation.

Juarez removed the tape without any hesitation and he knew where the light switch was in the front hall. It was dim inside and it took Amy a second to realize that curtains were drawn in every window of the house. That was unlike Sheila. She'd loved light. She loved the fact that her house had so many windows. "Not like so many of these crap construction new jobs," she'd said to Amy.

"You've been here before, right?" Juarez said, his voice almost jarring in the stillness of the front hall. Amy nodded.

"Many times," she said. It seemed odd to see the front hall devoid of a tangle of boys' shoes and backpacks or to not hear the sound of rock music blaring. The boys were gone, too, of course. She'd seen them drive away with Sheila's sister after the funeral, and it struck her that the murder of one person wasn't simply a single, grotesque act of violence, but the wiping out of an entire family.

Sheila had struggled and succeeded to build a good life for her and her sons and in an instant it had all been erased.

"Are you okay?" Juarez said, looking at her. "I guess this must be hard."

She nodded again, unable to speak. She led the way up the carpeted stairs to the second floor, trying not to think of the sound of the boys' feet clambering down them and of Sheila yelling to "stop running like a herd of elephants inside the house."

Family photos had been removed from the upstairs hall, whiter spots against the wallpaper looking like ghosts of the life that had once been. She stopped at the door to Sheila's room and turned to the detective.

"He was in this room," she said in a hushed tone as if he could hear the ghosts, too. "Or his camera was. Some of the photos were taken from here. I've been trying to figure out how."

He nodded and she walked ahead of him into the room that had been Sheila's sanctuary. It was a large master bedroom, much larger than the original home's, but the combination of two smaller rooms into one large suite had been done with such skill that it was easy to believe that some colonial-era couple had enjoyed this spot.

The place of honor went to the king-sized bed with carved pilasters and a pink net canopy. On the bed itself was the hot pink satin spread that Sheila adored. "White trash," she'd joked when she showed Amy the room. "I dreamed of a bed like this when I was a child and when I could finally afford one, I figured why not?"

She'd had the satin mules and the negligee to go with it. They were probably still hanging in the walk-in closet.

She'd tried them on for Amy once. The boys were away, Emma had gone to her grandmother's and Sheila and Amy had a girls' night out, laughing like teenagers and watching a movie cuddled up on this huge bed with its dozens of ridiculous pillows.

Juarez walked to one of the curtained windows and drew the shades up. Light filled the room and highlighted the layer of dust covering everything. Sheila hated cleaning. She thought the best thing about having made a good living was being able to afford a cleaning woman.

Without saying a word, Juarez took the photos of Sheila out of the envelope he'd carried in and laid them one by one on the bed. For a minute, they both looked at them in silence and then he asked, "Do you think he took these outside or inside?"

Amy walked slowly around the room, considering the angles. Then she walked to one of the windows and looked out. There was a tall maple tree in the yard, but it was hard to believe that someone had actually climbed into its branches to take pictures.

"We actually sent a guy up the tree," he said, following her gaze. "Nothing. No prints, no evidence, and no sign that anyone was even up there."

"I don't think he climbed the tree," Amy said. "That would have attracted attention." She looked at the base of the tree and contemplated the height of the long windows in the room.

At least one of the photos could have been taken from ground level with a telephoto lens. If Sheila had been standing close to one of the windows, it was probable that at least one photo had been taken that way. But what about the others? The ones of her on the bed?

"I think it must have been someone she knew," Juarez said, as if he could read her mind. He held up the photo where Sheila was lounging naked in bed, knees bent so her crotch was jutting at the viewer, a cordless phone to one ear.

"These could be posed," the detective said. "Maybe she was being blackmailed."

Amy shook her head. "I don't think so. This isn't a flattering pose—I can't imagine Sheila allowing herself to be shot looking like that."

"Then how did he get it? That shot had to come from inside."

"Maybe." Amy looked at the photos again and then back at the windows. She'd had to see the room first, had to see the bed relative to the windows, but the angle was right.

"I think I know how," she said, stepping to the window farthest from the bed. The windows were casement that opened out with a crank and the screens were on the inside. Amy took out the screen and cranked open the window as far as it could go, leaning forward over the sill and running her hands along the outside of the aluminum sash. Her fingers grazed over something and stopped. She turned sideways in the tight space so she could look up. What she saw made her smile.

"What is it?" Juarez said. "What did you find?"

"Take a look." She exchanged places with Juarez so that he could see it, too.

Attached to the sash at the roofline was a small metal tripod with a swing arm. A camera could be screwed on and moved into position.

Juarez whistled appreciatively at the work. "Clever—it's so small and tight I never noticed it."

"All he had to do was screw in the camera—"

"And he had clear pictures of the bed."

Something sounded behind them and Amy jumped. Juarez whirled around, hand up and on the holster under his jacket. Detective Black was standing in the bedroom doorway, with a tight smile on his face, clapping.

"Brilliant detective work, Juarez," he said and then the smile vanished. "And quite a coincidence. It gives us something more to talk about down at the station. Let's go, Ms. Moran. I'm taking you in for questioning."

Chapter 23

Black stepped forward and took Amy by the bicep. Mark put his hand out to stop him, but the older man shook him off without pausing.

"This is stupid," Mark said, following them from the room. He saw the woman's shoulders twitching and realized she was shaking. Black probably saw this as evidence of her guilt, but even innocent people were freaked out by the prospect of police interrogation.

"No, Juarez, stupid is taking a suspect back to a crime scene—"

"This isn't a crime scene—"

"And letting her lead you around by the dick."

"Jesus, Emmett, I brought her here to help us figure out how the pictures were taken—and she's done that. You should be thanking her, not treating her like a criminal."

Black didn't respond, but he tightened his grip on Amy's arm and picked up the pace.

"I have to call my babysitter," she said, sounding panicked and looking from Mark to Black and back again.

"You can make a call when we get to the station," Black

said. Mark followed them from the room, still trying to make his point with his partner.

"She isn't the perp," he said. "If you'd stop and look at the evidence, you'd see that this has all the hallmarks of a sexual crime."

Black hit his head like he was on one of the old V-8 commercials. "Oh, yeah, I forgot about the evidence of sexual assault we found at the scenes."

"There doesn't have to be assault for it to be sexual—"

"And it doesn't have to be a serial killer just because there are two killings close together."

Amy stumbled on the steps, but Black jerked her arm up to keep her from falling.

"What real evidence could you possibly have?"

Instead of answering him, Black addressed Amy. "What kind of printer do you have?"

"Printer?" She tried pulling her arm free without success.

"Computer printer. What kind do you have?"

"I don't know, I think it's an Epson."

"Do you know the model number?"

"No."

"Are you going somewhere with this?" Mark said. They'd reached the front hall and he saw a uniformed cop standing in the doorway, obviously waiting for them. Mark stepped in front of Black and caught the uniformed cop's forward movement out of the corner of his eye. Black waved him to a stop.

"You have an Epson R2400 printer," Black said, addressing Amy, but including Mark in his glare. "The same make and model used to print off the photos found with both victims."

Mark opened his mouth to speak, but Amy beat him to it.

"Lots of photographers use this model."

"Not lots of photographers who specialize in naked photos. Isn't that your specialty, Ms. Moran?" He stepped forward again and this time Mark moved aside. The uniformed cop ran ahead of them and opened the door to a patrol car. Black ushered Amy inside, pushing his hand hard on the top of her head so she wouldn't hit the frame. She grimaced, but got in the car without a word.

"Circumstantial evidence," Juarez tried as Black slammed the car door shut.

Black laughed. "You sound like a defense attorney, Juarez. Maybe you should consider that, because after the boss gets done reaming your ass, you're going to want a new job."

"I need to call my babysitter," Amy repeated in the patrol car as they sped in the direction of town. The uniformed cop, who was driving, didn't respond, but Amy could see the corner of Black's lips curve upward into a Grinchlike smile before he gave her a three-word reply, "At the station."

It was like something out of one of those cop dramas that she and Chris used to watch on TV. They used to snuggle up together on the couch to watch them. It was funny she should think of that now, think of him now, except that Detective Black had mentioned her right to an attorney and what other attorney could she call?

She was grateful the car was going fast because the siren certainly called attention to them. She could feel the stares of pedestrians and motorists forced to pull onto the shoulder to let them pass. She ducked her head, letting her hair fall forward like a veil, and examined her feet.

The car smelled like sweat with a hint of vomit, as if someone had been sick in the backseat and the car had been scrubbed repeatedly to try to get rid of the scent. There was one of those small pine tree deodorizers hanging from the metal grille and the fact that it was dangling there, and not from the rearview mirror, seemed to signify the status of anyone traveling in the backseat: Animals. Zoo creatures. Human offal.

Black looked back at her once, that evil grin in place and he actually winked at her, the bastard, before turning his attention back to the road.

"Pull in the back," he directed the uniformed cop, and the car turned off Selden Street and the front of the station, and pulled into the rear parking lot. Amy was relieved to be back here, anxious about being seen being taken into the station, though she was sure that wasn't Black's motive.

"Can't let the press get wind of you before we've got this wrapped up," Black said in a pleasant voice as he pulled her roughly from the backseat. She banged her knee against the doorframe, but he didn't pause.

Amy had been in the station just that morning as well as two weeks ago, the morning of Sheila's death. Then she'd been treated with a great deal of kindness. What followed her entry this time was anything but kind.

She was searched with far too much efficiency by a female cop who looked like a plus-size model and acted like she was playing a guard in a concentration camp film. Her purse was searched, too, before being returned to her.

To say it was humiliating was an understatement. Amy felt raw, not just embarrassed, but stripped of her dignity. Black pulled a chair next to the desk and urged her to sit down. He moved a phone in front of her.

"C'mon, Ms. Moran, you got a call to make, you'd better make it."

She dialed her own home number, hands trembling over the buttons. "It's busy," she said, holding out the receiver so Black could listen.

"Tough luck." He reached for the phone.

Amy put her hand over it. "I get a phone call, not a busy signal."

Black sighed. "Look, you can try one more time, but that's it."

Chloe was probably online. Who else could she call?

She thought of Ryan, but he was probably working and she didn't have his number with her anyway. Her mother never stayed home during the day—she had a hundred different charitable organizations and clubs. Desperate, Amy suddenly thought of something.

"I need a number."

"Do I look like the Yellow Pages?"

"I've got it in my coat. It's in my car." She held out her keys.

Black sighed again and pushed up from the desk. "All right, where in your coat?"

"One of the pockets. It's a business card. It says Paul Marsh."

A young, pudgy policeman was left to watch her and when she offered him a polite smile, he blushed and then glowered as if she'd crossed some line. Amy felt like she was in some Lifetime movie of the week, the one in which the innocent mother is locked up and changed by her prison experience, like a low-budget *Shawshank Redemption*.

"Here." Black slapped the business card down on the edge of the desk along with her keys. "Make it quick."

Paul answered on the third ring.

She explained what had happened with as few details as possible and at his insistence gave him a list of things to do: call Chloe and ask her to stay with Emma until she got home, call Braxton and ask Bev to cancel the two showings she had this afternoon and call Chris and explain the need for his help.

"I know it's a lot to ask," she said when she finished explaining. "If you don't think you can do it, I'll understand—"

"Amy, stop," Paul said. "Of course I'll do it. I'm going to make the calls now. Try not to worry."

Detective Black made no pretense of doing something else and allowing her privacy. He stared at her openly, taking large bites out of a meatball sub that another cop brought to him. All over the place, police officers were eating lunch. The pungent aroma of fried meat and tomato sauce mixed poorly with the sauerkraut from another cop's reuben. Amy felt her stomach churning.

"Thanks," she said to Paul. "I'll be okay if I know Emma's all right and Chris comes. Thank you so much."

As soon as she hung up the phone, Black put down the sub. "All right, Ms. Moran, we're going to have a talk," he said, making a production out of wiping his hands on a napkin. He missed his mouth, where a trace amount of tomato sauce clung to the faint bristles of his mustache.

"I want a lawyer present," Amy said quickly. There were some benefits to being married to an attorney. When they'd watched those cop dramas, Chris had always laughed when people allowed themselves to be questioned without a lawyer present.

"They're just looking for someone to pin the crime on," he'd said, "and you don't want to be that person. No one should ever talk to cops without a lawyer in the room."

Black didn't seemed fazed by this request, nor did he seem particularly inclined to wait. "When did you meet Sheila Sylvester?" he said.

"I'd prefer to wait until my lawyer's present," Amy said.

"Well, your lawyer's not going to be here for a while, so why don't we get some stuff cleared up right now? That way we don't have to waste time on it later." He smiled in a way that was probably supposed to look sincere, but looked creepy instead, the tomato sauce coating the corners of his mustache like blood.

"I'd prefer to wait," Amy repeated politely.

"Were you jealous of Sheila Sylvester's success?"

Amy looked away, trying to appear unconcerned, though her pulse was doing double-time and she was clutching the sides of the chair tightly to hide her trembling hands.

"Meredith Chomsky was a bitch, wasn't she?"

She looked down at the patterns in the polished tile floor, then over at another desk. The young, pudgy policeman was talking on the phone and sipping a can of Slim-Fast.

"It's just you and your daughter, isn't it, Ms. Moran? You're separated from your husband?"

Anger crept into the fear, and Amy welcomed the distraction, but still she said nothing. She listened to his attempts to draw her out, mouthing silent prayers for Chris to make an appearance.

"If you didn't make that sale, then someone else would get the money and you need that money, right? Because you've got to support your daughter and that medication she takes is expensive, right?"

Amy felt the anger rise beyond endurance, pushing her to speak. "Detective Black," she said and he stopped immediately, looking attentive. "I am not going to tell you anything without a lawyer present—"

"I'm just talking—"

"And if you dare to mention my daughter or her health in my presence again, I will not speak to you at all."

Five minutes later, she was being escorted to an interrogation room by the concentration camp guard, whose name, according to her badge, was Peaches LaRue.

Always ready for an audience, Lieutenant Farley cornered Mark in the entrance to the building. He gave Mark a public dressing-down about his "complete lack of judgment" and "piss-poor investigative techniques" for a full two minutes, allowing no interruption, before he collected himself enough to realize that such a public display was really beneath his dignity.

He ordered Juarez to his office like a child being summoned to see the principal and stalked off to that grand place, fully expecting Mark to follow. Which he did. Just not right away. Mark thought if he walked into the boss's office at that moment he'd probably hit him. Instead he took the time to check for messages, faking a calm he didn't feel, letting his fellow officers stare all they wanted. Then he got a bottle of water from the vending machine and took a few swallows before carrying it with him up the steps.

"You are completely out of line," the lieutenant began the minute Mark entered. "And completely out of control. Perhaps your big-city experience has gone to your head, detective, or maybe you've forgotten all your academy training, but you do not take a crime suspect to a crime scene."

"Excuse me, boss, but Sheila Sylvester's house is not a crime scene and this isn't a standard case."

"You're absolutely right, detective. This isn't a standard case. This is a double homicide—"

"I know that, but I really think—"

"That is precisely the problem, detective. *You* think. Everything is not about what *you* think. There are rules."

"Lieutenant, did you hear what Amy Moran found in the house?"

Farley shook his head as if that didn't matter. "I think your partner's right and you're letting your dick rule your brain here. Did it even occur to you that she could have put that tripod on the roof?"

"That's ridiculous!"

"Is it? Why? Because you don't want to think of her as a killer?"

"If she's lying about this, she's the best damn liar I've ever encountered."

"Did you glove her before she touched things?"

Mark hesitated. Shit. "The house was already dusted and her prints weren't found."

"So the answer is no?"

"She isn't the killer, boss."

"Answer my question, detective!" It came out as a roar. Mark took a deep breath.

"No, sir."

"You're acting on instinct, Juarez, and instinct alone does not solve cases!"

Mark didn't say anything. There was nothing to say. The implications of what he'd done hit him like a massive weight. By touching the tripod, Amy Moran would eliminate herself as a suspect. What if her prints were already on that tripod from when she'd installed it? He thought he'd been so smart taking her to the house, but instead he'd nullified the importance of that evidence. He'd fucked up and fucked up royally.

"You're reassigned to desk duty, detective." The lieutenant's voice was coolly matter-of-fact. "Please hand over your weapon."

An hour and a half passed before a lawyer showed up. During the wait, which felt three times as long, Amy tried not to worry about Emma as she got to know every inch of the sparsely furnished room. It was just like on television, complete with bare industrial table and chairs, caged clock loudly ticking high on the wall, and an opaque window that Amy knew had to be two-way glass.

The door banged open. "Your lawyer's here," Peaches LaRue announced with a little smirk on her face. She moved aside and instead of Chris, there was a skinny young man with wiry hair and small eyeglasses.

"I'm Nathan Feldman," he said. He shook her hand earnestly. His was damp. "Chris Moran asked me to come." He looked like he'd just graduated from law school.

"First, I need you to tell me what you've been charged with," he said, looking very earnest as he pulled a legal pad out of his briefcase.

"Didn't you talk to Chris?" Of course he hadn't come himself. It was the middle of the workday. He was probably involved in an important case. He couldn't take time off just because his wife had been arrested. She understood that, so why was there a lump in her throat?

Feldman had a sympathetic look on his long face. "I'm sure you can bring me up to speed quickly and we can decide on a good approach. The first thing to know is that you shouldn't answer any of the detectives' questions without checking with me first."

She tried to explain the facts to him, but it sounded nuts even to her. She just happened to stumble upon not one, but two murders. She just happened to own the same computer printer from which the killer was printing pictures.

Amy could see the growing skepticism in Nathan Feldman's face. She wasn't sure she believed herself anymore.

She hadn't seen Detective Juarez since they got to the station and any hope that she'd had of his interceding was long gone by the time Detective Black entered the room.

"We're taping this," Black said, fiddling with a small microphone that was affixed to the desk. "Please state your complete name for the record."

"Amy Elizabeth Moran."

"And her attorney—" Black looked at the other man.

The young lawyer cleared his throat loudly before offering a tremulous, "Nathan Feldman."

It wasn't going to go well, Amy thought, and for a moment she jumped ahead in her mind to the courtroom where the prosecutor would hold up the photos and claim that it was obvious that she was the photographer and make a jury believe it. Then she'd be sent to prison and what would happen to Emma?

She shook her head, chasing the images away. This wasn't a movie and she wasn't *The Fugitive*. There was no one-armed man to chase.

"How long have you worked at Braxton Realty?" Black began.

Amy glanced at Feldman, who nodded. "Six months."

"Is that where you met Sheila Sylvester?"

"No."

Black paused, waiting for her to elaborate, but Amy didn't.

"Where did you meet?" he said at last, his eyes narrowing. Feldman gave her the nod, so Amy elaborated.

"The Single Parent Support Group, which meets at St. Andrew's Church."

There were more and more questions: about their relationship, about her relationship with Meredith, about her marriage. It went on and on and Amy couldn't follow the pattern, if there was one, which was probably the point. She was exhausted by the time Black lifted the folder resting on the table under his right elbow and opened it.

Inside were photos of naked women, but not Sheila and not Meredith. Suddenly Amy knew why she'd been brought here.

Chapter 24

"Did you take this picture, Ms. Moran?"

"You know I did."

"Just answer the question, please."

"Yes."

Black addressed the microphone: "The photo in question is of a naked woman lying on a bed near an open window." He turned back to Amy, holding the photo out so both Feldman and Amy could see it. "Who's the woman in this photo?"

Feldman cleared his throat, but when Amy looked at him he looked startled and she realized he'd been reacting to the naked model and not signaling her.

"Who's the woman in the photo?"

"A model named Lisa Kenen. Where did you get this?"

Black reached over and shut off the recorder. "We searched your house, Ms. Moran. All legal," he added hastily, forestalling Feldman. "We got a warrant."

"You searched my house? While my daughter was there?"

Amy stood up, desperate at that thought of how Emma had reacted.

"Sit down, Ms. Moran!" Black ordered. "Nothing was damaged."

"Where's my daughter? Is she okay?"

Feldman put a hand on Amy's arm. "She's alright. I spoke to the babysitter."

Amy sank slowly back into her chair. Black turned back on the microphone and pulled out one of the photos of Sheila and laid it next to the picture she'd taken.

"This photo is remarkably similar, isn't it?"

"If you mean that this is also a black-and-white photo of a naked white woman, than yes, I guess it's similar," Amy said.

"Where was the first photo taken?"

"At a loft in Brooklyn."

"Not in Steerforth?"

"No, that's why I said Brooklyn."

Black grimaced. "Isn't it true, Ms. Moran, that you're an experienced photographer and that you're quite well known for your pictures of naked ladies?"

He made it sound like brothel work. "Yes, I'm experienced, but as to quite well known—"

"You've had more than one private show based entirely on photos like these, correct?"

"No."

The detective paused. "What part of what I said is incorrect?"

"I haven't had more than one show—I've had one solo show and it wasn't strictly nudes."

"Why didn't you tell police about these photos when you were originally questioned?"

"It didn't seem relevant."

"How could it not seem relevant when you claimed to have found a similar series of photos?"

"Because I didn't take them."

Black slammed a fist on the table. Feldman jumped. "Ms. Moran, this is not a game—"

"I didn't think it was, detective," Amy said, anger making her voice shake. She steadied it and went on. "If I had any doubts, the last few hours that I've spent sitting here have certainly dispelled them."

Black held up the photos of Sheila. "Did you take these photos of Sheila Sylvester?"

"No."

Slam with one set of photos, up with the ones of Meredith. "Did you take these?"

"No."

"So how do you explain that all of these photos were printed off the same type of printer?" Black jabbed a stubby finger at her photos and the ones sent by whoever had killed Sheila and Meredith.

"I can't explain it."

"On the morning of Tuesday, September 6, did you drive to 120 Lambert Lane?"

"Yes."

And so it went on. Question upon question that she'd answered already and now had to answer again. Minutiae about the morning, minutiae about the house, even minutiae about finding Sheila. How exactly had she been positioned? Was her head pointing toward the wall or away? Were her legs spread? How wide? Amy assumed all of this was designed to entrap her and so did Feldman, who interrupted frequently.

"How do you explain that there was no sign of forced entry, yet Sheila Sylvester was killed inside that house."

"I can't explain it."

"You and Sheila were the only ones with the code to the lockbox, correct?"

"Yes."

"And the lockbox was intact."

"Yes."

"So how did the killer get in?"

Feldman held up a hand to interrupt, but Amy answered anyway: "That is the million dollar question, isn't it?"

Juarez was grateful that he didn't see Black for the rest of the day. Given the mood he was in when he left the lieutenant's office, if he'd run into that asshole he might have clocked him.

He left behind the unmarked car and pulled out on the Harley he'd taken to work, heading out of town along the strip of highway that was the demarcation line between rich and poor in Steerforth. He needed a place to be alone, a place where nobody knew he was a cop, a place where he could forget that himself because he wasn't sure that he wanted to be—hell, had the talent to be—a cop anymore.

He pulled out on the straightaway, going full throttle, smart enough to wear a helmet, but stupid enough to wish he could feel that wind through his hair. His mother had given him shit when he bought a motorcycle, his father a grudging admiration. Like he resented the fact that his son could have something he couldn't and all the freedom that motorcycles represented.

A red neon sign with a flickering *T* advertised Tony's bar, the fanciest thing about the gray concrete cubicle sitting alone in a gravel parking lot. The huge skid mark he dug in the lot gave him satisfaction. There were only a few other cars and that gave him more. He didn't need company to drink.

"Sam Adams draft," he said and took a stool at a dark corner of the bar to dissuade anyone from joining him.

There were peanut shells on the floor and a bowl on the counter and he dug into them, downing the first beer in two large swallows because he needed to.

There was a pot-bellied man with lots of tattoos at the

next table with an anorexic blond girl who attracted Mark's attention with her high-pitched giggle. She looked barely legal, but she was wriggling around on him like some sort of lap dancer and then she leaned forward and licked beer off the man's mustache.

What would his mother think if he brought home someone like that? Imagining her horror made him laugh. He waved the bottle at the bartender and the guy slid down another one.

There was some bad country twang playing on the jukebox, apparently picked by the toothless old geezer sitting near the machine. He had an expression of disdain that might have been caused by his need for dentures.

A third man was apparently asleep over his whiskey or he was just crying. Mark tried to feel pity for him, but he couldn't summon any. The only pity he had left was for his own sorry life.

He finished beer number three without realizing it and by the start of beer five he was feeling the buzz, that pleasant sensation that would lead to the oblivion he so desperately needed.

"Hey." The voice was soft, seductive. The woman had appeared at his elbow without his noticing. She was older, definitely legal. A too-tight sweater accentuated her breasts, which were squeezed together to form a V of cleavage.

"Does that hurt?" Mark asked, giggling a little after he said it.

"This, sweetie? No. You wanna touch?" She took a seat next to him. Leaned closer offering him access. He shook his head, laughing.

She laughed, too, a throaty chuckle, and her brown eyes were sparkling at him. If he looked at them through the glass he could almost imagine they were someone else's.

"C'mon, sweetie," she said, tugging him up from the seat. "You come with me now. You've had enough."

He had to count the empties. How come there were nine of them? Had she added hers? He must have said that out loud because she laughed at that as well.

The room swayed gently, a rocking motion that reminded him of his parents' porch swing. On summer nights as a boy he'd come home from running around with the neighborhood kids and find his parents sitting together, holding hands on the swing, rocking back and forth, laughing and talking quietly together.

Was that kind of love something he'd ever have? He must have said that aloud, too, because the woman reassured him, her hand a warm pressure on his arm, her voice a tickly, whiskey-scented whisper. "Don't worry, sweetheart, you'll get love."

Somehow they were in a bedroom. He couldn't remember getting here and where was here?

"Is this your place?" he asked and his voice sounded like it was coming from far away.

She said it was. "Why don't you get comfortable and take that shirt off." There was a lamp on the bedside table covered with a red silk scarf and it made the room look like rose. The bed was a wide sea, it wobbled when he lay down on it, guided by her hand.

The comforter was a deep blue and he thought of the Jersey shore and hot summers in the sand and the feel of a hand reaching for his in the darkness of a city night, the streetlamp leaving wisps of light across the bed, and then he felt the warmth of blood pouring from a young boy's chest.

"It's okay, it's okay," the voice crooned and he was holding the woman or she was holding him and tears were welling in his eyes, distorting the room. Her hands were on his body, stroking, soothing, feathering across his skin and he needed the touch, could imagine it was someone else's and when her hand traveled from his chest, down and down again, he closed his eyes.

"Okay," she murmured again, once she'd guided him into her and then they were rocking together, holding onto each other and he willed her to be someone else and wondered once who she was willing him to be. Then he gave himself over to it and nothing mattered, not the job, not the death, not his failures as a man. Nothing mattered but that need for release.

Emma kept asking for her mother. "She'll be home soon." Chloe Newman repeated the same thing she'd said all afternoon. It was evening now, after six already, and she hadn't heard from anybody since talking to the lawyer who'd called to check in with her.

She was trying to study, but it was kind of hard with Emma looking up from the TV every five minutes to ask when her mother was coming home.

What if she didn't make it home tonight? Chloe got up from the comfy armchair and pretended to stretch, hoping Emma wouldn't notice that she was really checking for headlights from the living room window. The street was dark.

There was still a pile of toys sitting outside their bin in a corner. The police had emptied it, searching for what she didn't know, but neglected to refill it. There was junk all over the place, neat stacks of it, but they'd emptied every cupboard, all the bookcases, and all the drawers. Amy's office and darkroom were in disarray, all file drawers opened, photos everywhere. Everything in the house had been gone through and though most of it had been put back, it was wildly disorganized.

Understandably, this had upset Emma. When she saw the mess the first two fingers of her right hand crept into her mouth and stayed there. She wouldn't play, sitting on the sofa and clutching her stuffed unicorn with her free hand, eyes staring blankly at the TV. Chloe took her outside to get her away from it, but Emma had been very quiet.

She'd made up for it since then. For the last half-hour she'd been reciting a mantra that began with, "When's Mommy coming?" and cycled through "I want Mommy!" and "I miss Mommy," before starting back at the beginning. Chloe had taken two Advil and her head was still pounding. She had a major exam tomorrow in her political science class and she'd resorted to sticking in a DVD for Emma so she could try and study, but Emma didn't have any interest in Pooh and the Hufflelump, she wanted her mother and she wanted her now.

"Would you like mac and cheese for dinner?" Chloe offered, hoping there were boxes in the cupboard as she offered the bribe. It was Emma's favorite meal and one that her mother saved for special occasions because it wasn't particularly nutritious. This occasion was special enough, Chloe decided.

" 'Kay," Emma said. "Is Mommy coming home for dinner?"

"Probably," Chloe said. "But she might be late. We'll save her some."

"Can I help make it?" Emma got up from the carpet where she'd been lounging and came to Chloe with a hopeful expression. Chloe hid her groan. That was the sure way to make any job take twice as long, but she smiled and nodded.

"Sure. Go wash your hands."

Emma scurried off to the bathroom and Chloe listened to her breathing. It was wheezier than usual, but she seemed okay. She'd have her do a nebulizer after dinner. The phone rang, startling her.

Chloe picked up the cordless handset and carried it with her to the stove. "Hello?"

No one spoke, but she could sense someone on the line.

"Hello? Hello? Who's calling?"

Silence, but now she could definitely hear breathing. A heavy sound. Then the phone quietly disconnected.

That was creepy. Chloe put the phone down and grabbed the milk from the fridge, but her eyes strayed to the darkness outside the kitchen door. She could barely see the outline of the swing set in the yard, but she could hear the creaking of the empty swings.

"What are you doing?" A guttural whisper behind her.

Chloe spun around, but it was only Emma, her voice deeper because her breathing was constricted.

"Oh, you scared me!" Chloe laughed. "Nothing's wrong, I was just closing the curtains. Let's make mac and cheese!"

"Yeah!"

Chloe glanced out the window one more time, then pulled the curtain across, closing out the dark. She helped Emma measure the milk and let her pour it into a saucepan while she checked the water for the noodles. The phone rang again as she was draining the pasta.

"I'll get it." Emma jumped down from her stool.

"No, Emma!" Chloe shouted to stop her. "Let me!"

In her haste, she splashed boiling water over her hand and cried out.

"You're hurt!" Emma cried, rushing to help.

"Stay back, Emma, it's boiling water!" Chloe pushed the pot farther back in the sink.

The phone kept ringing and ringing. Chloe grabbed it. "Hello."

Again there was silence. Someone on the other end listening, waiting.

"What do you want?" Chloe tried.

"Are you home alone?" The voice was high, guttural, and inhuman.

Chloe slammed the phone down.

"Who was it, Chloe? Was it Mommy?"

"No. Just a wrong number."

"What's a wrong number?"

Chloe's hand was throbbing as well as her head. She ran ice water over it and while she was doing that the milk she'd forgotten about boiled over on the stove.

"Shit!" Chloe leaped and pulled Emma away from the stove. The little girl started crying, her wheezing increasing with every sob.

"It's okay, sweetie." Chloe tried calming her, but then she noticed that Emma's lips were blue.

"We need to do the inhaler right now, Em." Chloe ran for the bedroom, grabbing the rescue inhaler and the spacer from a box on the shelf painted with little fairies and frogs and took it back to Emma, who'd sunk down onto the kitchen floor.

"Oh, God." Chloe dropped next to her, fumbling with the spacer. "Here, Em, let's get this in you."

Emma's eyes rolled back in her head and Chloe screamed and jumped up for the phone.

Amy rode to the hospital in the back of a police cruiser, sitting forward on the seat, her hands clenched in fists on her knees, as if her posture could make the car move faster.

Detective Black had immediately offered to drive her to the hospital when a younger officer delivered the message about Emma. She might have appreciated the offer more, given that he was running every red light and taking corners at seventy miles an hour, but all she could think was that he was responsible for Emma's attack.

She was out of the car the moment he pulled into the emergency drive, passing through the automatic doors and slamming, breathless, against the reception desk.

"My daughter was rushed here with an asthma attack. Emma Moran."

The nurse behind the desk moved with agonizing slowness. She probably wasn't even a nurse, just some clerk who'd been given a penny-ante power position and enjoyed using it. "What's the name again?" she said, stepping over to the computer screen.

"Emma Moran. She's five."

"Five?"

"Yes!"

"I don't see it here—" the woman started, then, "oh, here it is. She's in the ICU."

Amy took off running for the elevators, the woman calling after her. "You can't go there! I need you to fill out some paperwork."

An elevator slid open and Amy stepped in and slammed the close door button.

Chloe was in the hall outside Emma's room. She looked up when Amy called her name, eyes bloodshot, and nose red.

"I'm so sorry," she said and she kept repeating that while Amy stood in the room with Emma, who was unconscious and in an oxygen tent. Her skin looked waxy and it was as if Amy could see straight through her, all the veins standing out like a blue road map, her rib cage wholly visible, a fragile shell covering her poor damaged lungs. The little heart seemed visible, too, pulsating at the top of her chest, the constant, steady movement the only thing that gave Amy hope.

She hadn't cried when Black hauled her in for questioning. She hadn't cried during the long, horrible afternoon in the station, but now she wept, breaking down into the loud, strangled sobs that choked and hurt in their effort to get out of her body. Chloe held her for a moment, crying too, but she was looking for forgiveness, and in the end Amy was comforting her, trying to reassure her that it wasn't her fault and that she didn't blame her.

Chapter 25

"Hey, get up, you've got to leave." The voice was matter-of-fact and way too loud.

Mark swam out of the dream he'd been having in which the boy in the hall had soft brown eyes and was holding a nail gun. A woman wearing a uniform was standing above him and she looked impatient.

"Look, I hate to have to kick you out so early, but I've got to get my kid to school and me to the diner. You've got to take off."

She took a drag on a cigarette and exhaled the smoke in his direction. Mark coughed and rolled to a sitting position. The bedroom that had looked soft and romantic at night was far less so by day. The rose-colored cloth that covered the lamp turned out to be a blouse that had been tossed onto it. Other clothes were on the floor and on an old armchair. The sheets on the bed looked like they needed to be washed and the room itself smelled, of cigarette smoke and cat urine. There was a bong on the dresser sitting below the cracked mirror and among dozens of bottles of perfume, nail polish and pills.

"Here're your clothes," the woman said, tossing them onto his lap. She took another puff of her cigarette and washed it down with a swig of Diet Coke. Her voice seemed harsh in the morning, not smoky but old. She was probably in her thirties, but she looked haggard in the morning light, as if she were a dozen years older. Maybe she was.

Mark dressed hurriedly while she primped in front of the mirror, applying all sorts of makeup and teasing her limp blonde hair.

"Mom, I can't find my math book." A blonde-haired boy stood in the doorway and Mark froze in the middle of buttoning his shirt, his pants open around his hips. The boy's gaze fell on him, but his expression didn't alter, as if he were looking at something he'd seen a million times before.

"Hi," Mark said, tucking his shirt rapidly into his pants.

"Hey," the kid responded without any interest.

"I don't know where it is, Chad, you probably left it on the couch." The woman's spoke from under her hair. She was bent in, half brushing it rapidly.

The kid disappeared without a backward glance.

"That your son?"

The woman pulled her hair back into a ponytail and began pinning loose strands to her head with bobby pins. She managed to keep her cigarette in her mouth the whole time. "Yeah."

"Where's his father?"

"What are you? A social worker?"

"No. Just think it must be hard to be a single parent."

The woman regarded him for a moment and then snorted. "Listen, sweetie, what we had was a fuck. Nothing more. You are just one in a series."

She must have read it in his face because she laughed and it sounded harsh and cold. "Don't worry, you wore a rubber." She pointed and Mark saw an overflowing wastebasket with a used condom on top. Relief mixed in equal parts with nausea.

"I don't want another kid," she said. "And I manage just fine. He doesn't need some man fucking him up, so don't get any ideas about creating your own happy little family with us. I don't need no man fucking me up, either."

She drove him back to the bar parking lot and his bike, pausing just long enough for him to get out of the car before speeding off in her Cavalier, blue smoke shooting out the exhaust pipe, the engine pinging like it had never known a drop of oil.

He reeked of cigarette smoke, perfume, and stale beer, and what he wanted more than anything else in the world was a long, hot shower, but Mark didn't head toward home. He couldn't face his mother's censure, not after yesterday. She'd probably be worried about him, but she'd been married to a cop for almost forty years and she knew how to temper that with the reality of the job.

There was a Holiday Inn near the parkway. It was clean, it was anonymous, it would do. He checked in for one night and if the kid behind the counter thought anything of the fact that Mark had no luggage he was careful not to show it.

Mark took a forty-five-minute shower, shampooing his hair three times, washing his body twice. He simply stood under the spray once he was clean, trying not to think of anything. He put all his clothes in the plastic bag for laundry service, left it outside the door and hung the Do Not Disturb sign and then he folded back the covers of the vast king-size bed and fell into it.

When he woke up, he was clear-headed and ravenous and shocked to discover that it was almost four P.M. He'd slept almost the entire day. He ordered room service and shaved, pleased to discover that his clothes had been returned and were waiting outside his door along with his shoes, buffed to a high shine, and the newspaper. He read it over a meal of a salad, turkey burger and water. It was time to cleanse his system.

They were still talking about Meredith Chomsky's killing. Speculation about who stood to benefit from her death ranged from her ex-husband to his adult children. All of them super-wealthy, of course, which made them even easier targets.

There was no mention of any arrests, so clearly Black hadn't weaseled a confession out of Amy Moran. Had he detained her? Was he out searching for something more so he could make the collar?

Mark thought about calling the desk sergeant, but not yet. Not until he'd figured out what he was going to do. His own impatience with this case had led him to act foolishly and if he didn't rectify this with some real evidence, he was probably going to be fired. If he hadn't been fired already.

Jesus, it was hard to imagine sinking lower than being fired by the Steerforth police force. What had happened here? How had he gone from the guy who graduated at the top of his class at the academy, the guy who made detective after only a year, the guy who had a reputation for clean, smart police work to the guy stupid enough to contaminate a crime scene?

It was tempting to give into self-pity, but he'd already wasted enough time on that. He shuddered as he thought of the woman at the bar. He needed to get tested after that encounter, condom or not. What the hell had he been thinking? Clearly he wasn't thinking at all, he'd been doing nothing but drinking, trying to obliterate all thought.

Now was the time for clear thinking and Mark tried to recapture the elation he'd felt yesterday, the sense that he was making real progress with the case. Yes, it had been a mistake not to glove Amy Moran, but bringing her to the house had been a smart move. Up to that point, they hadn't known how the killer was taking pictures. Now here was a crucial piece of evidence that he—or she—had been stalking these women.

The problem was that he couldn't prove that Amy Moran hadn't planted that tripod. Or could he? All at once it occurred to Mark that there *was* a way to get proof.

Twenty-five minutes later he'd checked out of the hotel and was walking the aisles of the Buy-and-Fly with a basket on his arm. He picked up Ziploc baggies in two sizes, large and small, a manicure set that included tweezers, magnification card, a flashlight, a box of disposable latex gloves, a disposable camera and after some searching, a small set of screwdrivers.

Ten minutes later he turned his bike onto a street lined with large houses and started up the long driveway toward one of them, feeling very conspicuous.

Without his gun he felt naked and he had no right, given that he'd been remanded to desk duty, to enter the Chomsky house. If he were very lucky there'd be no cops guarding the crime scene. If he were a little bit lucky, the cop guarding would be a rookie who wouldn't know about his demotion.

He got very lucky. There was no one around. The yellow tape blocking the front door billowed in the wind. He stepped under it and tried the door but it was locked. So were the windows at ground level. He wandered around to the side of the house and there was another door, also locked. A large terra-cotta urn sat next to it, a white flowering plant overflowing its edges. On impulse, Mark shifted the urn and there, underneath, was a key.

If he did this, he was breaking and entering. If he got caught he'd undoubtedly lose his job. If he didn't do this, he didn't know if he had a job to go back to. Mark put the key in the lock.

The door opened with a soft click and Mark was afraid an alarm might sound, but there was silence. He closed and locked the door behind him, pocketing the key. His footsteps

seemed loud on the tile floor. He walked through the mud-
room and saw that he was in the kitchen. A clock in the
shape of a rooster was ticking loudly on the wall. It seemed
to be telling him to hurry. He pulled the latex gloves out of
his pocket and donned a pair. Then he took a paper towel off
a roll near the sink and wiped down the doorknob and the
key.

It took him a couple of minutes to navigate his way
through the huge house, but at last he found his way upstairs
and to the master bedroom. This time, he didn't have the
benefit of the photographs and had to try and remember
what they'd looked like. Hadn't Meredith Chomsky been on
the bed in several of them? He tried what Amy Moran had
and went to every window, removing the screen so he could
see and feel his way outside. There was nothing.

There had to be something more. Amy had said that the
killer had taken the pictures from inside the house, but where?
He combed the room, looking for equipment on the bedside
tables, on the faux antique vanity crowded with silver-backed
hairbrushes and bottles of every body lotion on the market,
and in and around the entertainment center hidden in a massive wardrobe. There was nothing.

What if he was wrong and there was nothing to be found
here? Mark felt more and more anxious. He slipped off his
shoes and climbed on the vanity bench to check within the
overhead light fixtures. Nothing. He used one of the small
screwdrivers he'd bought to painstakingly remove the forced
air vent in the floor, but there was nothing in there.

He'd just finished screwing the cover back on when there
was a loud crash from a room nearby. Mark went for his gun,
but it wasn't there. He jumped to his feet and ran to the door,
staying close to the wall before darting a foot and then his
body into the open. There was no one in the hall and no one
in the other bedrooms.

A large, framed picture was facedown on the floor in a

guest room two doors down. The glass had cracked when it landed on the hardwood, but he couldn't figure out how it had gotten knocked off the dresser. He checked the closet and under the bed, but there was no opportunistic thief lurking.

He was walking toward the door when something darted in his peripheral vision and he whirled around. A large, black cat with a white diamond on his head landed on the bed and looked at him with a satisfied expression before loudly meowing.

Mark laughed, relieved. He'd have to tell someone at the station about the animal. Had it been fed since its mistress's death? He walked back to the master bedroom, wondering where on earth the cat had been hiding not to have been spotted by all the cops and crime scene workers combing this home. Maybe he'd made a home for himself in the walls.

And just like that, it hit him. Mark surveyed the salmon-colored walls up and down, running his hands over the surface and then he started knocking. He rapped his fist on one section, then another, listening for a hollow sound. But no wall was completely hollow and the walls in these newer homes were made of drywall not plaster, so nothing sounded solid or empty. He was just about to give up when he hit a section where the thud of his fist against the wall seemed different, softer.

It was at the edge of a wall, where it opened up for the walk-in closet. Mark turned on the lights in there and shifted the clothes on that end of the wall and then it was clear. There was an access panel at floor level that had probably been installed when the house was built. It was probably to get access to the wires for all the elaborate wiring, but it had clearly been put to other uses. The panel had been expanded, made taller, but still shorter than the height of the clothing rack so it wasn't visible behind the clothes. And the clothes in this section of the closet were things that remained in storage bags and appeared to be mainly men's suits. Apparently Henry Chomsky hadn't cleared out all his belongings and Meredith had never touched this section of the closet.

Mark carefully removed the access panel, aimed the flashlight into the dark space and there it was. A tripod just like the one Amy Moran had found on Sheila Sylvester's roof was attached to the wall at eye level with a small hole where a beam of light was shining through. Mark went back into the bedroom to see it from that angle and it still took him a minute to spot it. It gave a perfect view of the bed but was small enough and low enough that no one would spot it.

Excitement at his find mixed with nausea. Just because he was a cop didn't mean he was immune to feelings about the crimes he uncovered. It was impossible to stay completely detached, though the successful cops, the ones who managed to stay married and made it to retirement without eating their own weapons, had somehow learned to compartmentalize the despair.

He stepped back into the access panel and examined it minutely, sweeping the flashlight up and down its surface. He wished he had the klieg lights that the crime scene investigators used, but he had to make do with a five-buck cheapie. What he needed was some evidence that someone other than Amy Moran had used this space. The size was one indicator. Amy was tall, but not this tall, and it had been cut for a six-foot person to fit. There might be prints on the tripod, it was hard to tell, but Mark didn't think so. If the guy was this careful, he was going to take the time to wear gloves. Still, he'd have to have it checked out.

There was a small scrap of paper stuck in the tripod's shaft. Mark pulled it out and unwrapped it. It was about the size of a fortune and had one word written on it: Peek-a-boo!

Mark was so pissed off he almost ripped it to shreds. This sick fuck was toying with him. There wouldn't be prints on the tripod. They wouldn't find his prints because this was a game and he was hoping they'd find his secret little cubby. The disappointment was so strong that Mark wanted to give up, but the realization that he'd gone this far and that he had the choice between continuing to search for some hard evidence or giving up and returning defeated with this new transgression on his record spurred him forward.

He examined the tripod again, carefully going over every surface with the light in one hand and the magnifying lens in the other. Then he checked the floors, the ceilings and then the hole. He moved the light closer to the small hole, leaning in to try and see what it had looked like from this vantage point. Had the guy been sitting here every time he took a picture? Had he put his own eye up to the hole to watch her getting undressed?

The lens caught something, a thin dark line. Was it a shadow? Mark ran the flashlight over the hole again, very slowly. It must have been a trick of the light, but no, there it was again. Something very thin. Feeling excitement building Mark pulled out the tweezers and carefully plucked it from the hole. It was an eyelash.

Chapter 26

Amy looked so pretty when she was watching her daughter. Totally unselfconscious, her hair pulled back in a soft ponytail. He wanted to kiss the small tendrils that escaped onto the back of her neck. He wanted to put his hands on that slim white column and watch the marks of his own fingers spread like blossoms on her flesh.

She didn't know he was watching. No one ever knew. He was so good at this that he could write a book about it, but of course that wouldn't be nearly as much fun as watching. Maybe years from now, when he retired. He could be like those former snitches and make some movie or television deal along with the book and people would come and appreciate how smart he was. They'd know it was a talent. They wouldn't be like Violet and call him a Peeping Tom, a filthy stalker, a pervert.

Thinking of Violet made him angry. It made his throat tighten and his hands burn and he didn't want to feel this pain, not today. He had someone else now. Violet had been an error.

Amy hadn't left her little girl's bedside, sleeping in a

chair pulled up next to it. She was sitting there still, holding one tiny hand in both of hers, looking so tired and so desperate that he longed to make it better for her, but of course he couldn't. Not yet.

He needed to get things ready first. That had been another mistake with Violet. He hadn't been able to get their home prepared, hadn't been able to present it to her the way he would have liked. That was why she'd gotten into things she shouldn't have. It was his fault, really, as much as hers, but some things couldn't be made right.

Now he could start again and this time he'd do it correctly. He'd take care of Amy because she needed him. And she'd understand about his needs. She'd be open to it, he could tell. Sometimes he sketched pictures of what she'd look like cuffed to a bed or hanging from a pole, suspended in space, her bare toes searching for the floor, and these images were enough to get him through a sleepless night.

He was going to make a special room. Sometimes he drew sketches of this space and what it should have. He wandered the aisles of home improvement stores considering different weights of insulation and various thicknesses of sheetrock. He bought a stud finder because it was going to be necessary to insert the hooks into a solid piece of lumber. The hooks were steel, round and solid, because they had to be big, heavy enough to support chains and the weight of a person. The chains took longer to find because he needed them coated for easy clean up.

Looking at everything he had amassed gave him a sense of security, of connection. It would take a while, but eventually he'd have the life he dreamed of and the woman to share it with.

It was clear that meeting her had been fate. It could have been anyone else on that morning, there were many realtors, but it was Amy. It was as if God was saying to him that while Violet had been a mistake, this one wasn't.

Killing Meredith had been a gift for her. She'd hated that woman and he'd made her go away. He hadn't meant to get her in trouble with the police, but he enjoyed watching her handle them. The police were no match for her, just as they'd never been a match for him. That pleased him, that she was smart. Only a smart woman would understand him.

Lately, she'd come to him in his dreams, a cool figure in white, her long, dark hair flowing. She'd lie next to him on the bed with that same enigmatic smile that had been Violet's. Sometimes the smile changed, was someone else's, and then the face would change, too, and he'd see other women that he'd known. Then their bodies would change, too, and he'd see them as they'd looked in those last, precious moments with their bodies. He'd wake up with a scream, but with the evidence of his arousal slick on his legs and the sheets.

He needed Amy and it had to be soon. What he would do about the daughter, he wasn't sure. It seemed to him that there had to be something done with her, because when he pictured the house and the life he'd have with Amy it didn't include the child.

The girl was frail. Perhaps she would die from this attack. If not, well, then her death was just another gift he would give Amy, the gift of freedom to devote herself to her lover's wishes and needs. Sometimes sacrifices were necessary.

Chapter 27

Each labored breath that Emma took was matched by one from Amy. She sat by her daughter's bedside, holding onto her hand, trying not to notice all the tubes and the oxygen mask, and the medicine that was keeping Emma alive. She was alive, that was the important factor. Nothing else mattered.

"You need to take a break," her mother said, wrapping an arm around Amy from behind. There was a faint smell of wool and Chanel No. 5.

"I can't," Amy said, reaching up to grip Dorothy Busby's hand.

"You haven't taken a break in hours."

Amy didn't respond, just kept looking at her daughter. She was afraid to look away, afraid to leave, afraid to sleep. She knew it was irrational but she couldn't help thinking that her own vigilance was all that was keeping her daughter alive.

"I need to be here when she wakes up."

"I'll be here. If she wakes up, I can call you."

Amy blanched. "She's going to wake up, Mom."

"I know."

"Don't say if, it's just when."

"Go, Amy." Her mother tugged on her arm, trying to pry her from the armchair that she'd pulled up next to the wide hospital bed. "Go home and get some sleep."

"I can't go home. I can't leave."

"You'll be no good to Emma if you're exhausted."

The truth of that made Amy hesitate. It was after midnight. Fatigue was hammering behind her eyes, beating a tattoo along her spine. Her muscles felt strained from the stress of staying alert, as if she were poised to run the mile and was just waiting for the starter's pistol. The thought of sleep, of her own bed, swam into her vision like a mirage.

"But what if she needs me and I'm not here?" she said.

"I'll call you. You can come right back."

"You'll call if anything changes?" Amy stood up slowly.

"Yes."

"Promise me, Mother. Any change at all and you call me." She stretched her arms over her head, every part of her aching from so many tense hours in that chair.

"I said I would—"

"Promise!"

"All right, I promise," her mother said. "There now. Are you satisfied?"

Amy nodded. She picked up her purse from under the chair and checked that her cell phone was on. Dorothy settled into the chair that Amy had vacated. She pulled a paperback out of her own purse.

"How are you going to keep an eye on her if you're reading?"

"I'm watching," her mother said, "I'm just doing a little reading, too. Go. Don't worry."

Amy's hand shook as she turned the key in the ignition. The police had brought her repaired car to the hospital parking lot, but she didn't feel appreciative.

She could feel despair taking hold and she was too tired to fight it, letting the depression sink in and with it the self-pity. Everything she'd fought for was gone or just about gone. She had no marriage, she barely had a home, her job was in jeopardy and so was her freedom. She'd lost her best friend and stood accused of murdering her and another woman and the stress of all this had given her daughter a profound asthma attack.

In the hospital room she hadn't been able to bear it, but driving home alone in the car, Amy made herself face the possibility that Emma could die. Looking at that squarely was like standing on the edge of a gaping dark hole. She didn't know what would happen if she fell over the edge of that hole, but she had a feeling she'd never come out of it.

Memories flooded her. She recalled the year that Emma was one and how she'd bundle her into a stroller in the mornings and take her out for a two-mile cruise around the neighborhood, sometimes with other moms, sometimes alone, and it had always ended the same way, with a stop at the small coffee shop down the block from their apartment.

The early exhaustion of motherhood had passed, Emma was sleeping most nights, and while she had asthma and Chris had been unfaithful, Amy was blissfully unaware of just how bad life could get. She'd been so happy then. What had it been like to have nothing more to worry about than how she'd lose the last five pounds of pregnancy weight?

For the last fifteen hours, while she sat at her daughter's bedside, Amy had relived every moment of Emma's young life, trying to hold onto the best moments. She savored the memories of Emma's laugh, her smile, her first words. She remembered what it felt like to have Emma's hand slip into hers and grab hold, to hear Emma's small voice saying, "I love you, Mommy."

The thought of not hearing that again filled Amy with such sorrow that she couldn't contain it. The sobs burst forth in machine-gun bursts of noise that filled the silence of the car. It was a relief not to have to muffle them. She was almost cried out when she turned the car onto her dark street.

The house was eerily still. It was the first time that Amy had ever been here alone. She hung her coat in the hall closet, uncomfortably aware that she could hear the pinging of wire hangers even after she closed the door. The floorboards creaked under her feet as she walked toward the kitchen. She flipped the light switch and saw the mess left behind when Chloe called the ambulance.

A strong smell of something burnt permeated the room. Abandoned on the counter were a saucepan with a thin foam of curdled milk and a pot half-filled with water. Next to them was an open box of macaroni and cheese. A rescue inhaler and spacer were on the floor against the wall. Amy picked them up and set them on the table next to a vase of white roses she hadn't noticed before. The creamy petals seemed to glow under the fluorescent light. Even their beauty couldn't make her summon a smile.

It occurred to her that she hadn't eaten in—how long? She couldn't remember, but any hunger she'd felt had passed long ago into emptiness. All she wanted was sleep and as she slowly climbed the steps to the second floor, she was grateful for the fatigue. She wasn't sure she could sleep alone in this house, otherwise.

Emma's room was as it had been before Amy left what seemed like years, but was only really a morning ago. She stood in the doorway for a moment, looking at the empty bed and the scattered stuffed animals. The room smelled like Emma, a sweet mixture of baby shampoo and the soft skin at the back of her neck. Amy drank it in, resisting the urge to bury her face in the pink floral sheets because if she did that she might never get back up.

Her own bedroom was at the end of the hall. She kicked

off her shoes as she reached for the light switch. Something moved in the corner.

"Amy?"

It was a man's voice. She screamed and kept screaming even as her hand scrabbled blindly for the light.

"Amy, it's me! It's me! Chris!"

Her fingers found the switch, flipped it and the room blazed with light. She could see a tall figure blinking in the corner and her scream died away as her brain registered that it was—yes, really—Chris.

"What are you doing here?" she cried. "You scared me to death!"

"I'm sorry, I fell asleep." He rubbed his eyes. "Where have you been? What's wrong? Your mother left a message at the office to call you ASAP. She said it was an emergency."

"Emma had a bad attack."

His eyes widened. "Where is she? Is she okay? I've been trying to reach you for hours. I tried calling the hospital, but they won't give out information. Finally I just came here."

His must be the messages she hadn't collected off her cell phone. She saw his suit jacket draped on the armchair in the corner and realized that he must have fallen asleep while waiting for her.

"How did you get in?"

"I still have a key, Amy," he said, "though I did wonder if you'd changed the locks."

There was no accusation in his voice, just regret. He rubbed his eyes again, ran a tired hand over his face. She could see the faintest shadow along his jaw. His yellow silk tie was pulled loose and he'd unbuttoned the collar of his dress shirt and turned back the sleeves.

"How is she?" he repeated, reaching back to grab his suit jacket. "Why are you home?"

"She's only semiconscious. They gave her the oral steroids and she's on oxygen, but it could be a while before she fully comes to." She struggled to keep her voice steady. "I didn't want to leave, but my mother's with her. I came home to get some sleep, then I'm going back."

"I'll go back with you," he said as he reached out a hand and gently tucked a loose strand of hair behind her ear. "You must be exhausted."

She nodded. "It's been a long day." She sank down on the bed and he took a seat next to her.

"I'm sorry, Amy," he said. "For everything."

These were the words she'd secretly longed to hear him say, but never under these circumstances. Would she gain her husband back only to lose her daughter? No! No, she must not think that. Emma was going to be okay.

"I've missed you," Chris said in a husky voice. He stroked her face, lightly tracing her features with her fingertips, and she closed her eyes, afraid she might cry again.

Then his lips found her face and when they reached her mouth it felt like the most natural thing in the world to return his kiss, despite everything that had passed between them and what had happened since. And when his kiss progressed, she let it happen, letting what had always worked between them work again, blocking out Emma's illness and Sheila's murder and the way Meredith's body had looked hanging in that tub and the dreadful *tick, tick, tick* of the industrial clock in the interrogation room.

Afterwards they fell asleep together on top of the comforter on the bed, tangled in their clothes and a blanket. When Amy slept, it was blessedly deep and dreamless.

Mark trapped the eyelash carefully in a Ziploc bag and sealed it. He scoured the hidden space for anything else, but there was nothing. Not that he needed anything else. This was enough to get DNA and when the test proved that the DNA was not Amy Moran's, he'd clear not just her name but his own record.

He took out the disposable camera and took shots of the inside and the outside of the hidden space, knowing they weren't professional quality, but trying to make sure that they showed up on film.

When he was finished, he closed everything up, hiding the space again, moving the clothes back in place, leaving the house as untouched as it was when he arrived. He put the key back under the planter and jogged down the driveway, hoping that if some nosy neighbor spotted him they wouldn't be able to give a good enough description to ID him.

As a civilian, it took him the full hour and twenty to get to Meridien and the crime lab.

Being inside the crime lab was a little like being in a hospital. The floors had the dull shine of frequent polishing and depending on the time of year, there was a lemon or pine smell in the air. This time it was pine, a strong enough disinfectant scent, but not quite strong enough to mask the other scent that hovered in the air at all times. It was a vaguely familiar, metallic smell and the casual visitor would sometimes comment on it, but the lab workers and the cops knew what it was without asking. Blood.

Loud rap music was coming from a door standing ajar. Luis Pinero was standing in front of a large, high-powered microscope and he held up a hand without looking up when Mark entered the lab.

"Don't move please. It's taken me five fucking tries to get this baby in focus and I'm not going for six."

Mark watched him peering at something and muttering under his breath and smiled. Luis always talked to himself when he worked. Every once in a while he would chant the lyrics along with whatever singer was belting from the boom box set up on a shelf.

The lab was filled with high-tech equipment that Mark didn't know the name or function of and some that he did. He'd known Luis, a forensic scientist, for eight years, introduced to him when he was visiting his father years ago on the job. A picture of Luis's wife and two small sons had place of honor on his desk next to a New York Mets signed baseball.

"Your crap team doesn't have the cojones to make it to the playoffs this year."

Pinero's head shot up and he grinned at seeing his visitor. "You badmouthing my team, burro? Everyone knows your team is like some boy band, buying the talent not cultivating it."

He hopped off the stool and embraced Mark, both of them laughing. "Long time no see, bro," Luis said, "are you applying for work?"

"News travels fast, I see."

Luis laughed, but he looked concerned. "It does when you've pissed off Chief Photo-Op himself. Is it true that you've been reassigned?"

Mark nodded and explained it, ending with pulling the baggie with the eyelash out of his pocket.

"This is the evidence you want me to examine?"

"Yeah, you don't have to thank me for keeping it so small."

"Good, 'cause I won't." Luis took the bag and peered at the eyelash. "DNA screens take time, man, and on the side it'll take longer."

"I don't have longer. How fast can you do it?"

"This isn't like the laundry, you know. I'm dealing with a backlog of work and there's only so much that can get done every day and you're not the only one with an asshole for a boss."

"How long, Luis?"

"Usually, it would take at least a month—"

"A month!"

Luis waved his hand. "Settle down, I said usually. I'll try to put a rush on it. Maybe two weeks."

"How about two days?"

"Christ, Juarez, I'm not a miracle worker. Let's try dealing with reality, here, okay?"

"The reality is that someone is killing people and that someone's going to do it again if we don't catch him."

A distant ringing woke Amy. She sat up, momentarily, disoriented at finding herself entwined with Chris on her bed, and realized the noise was the phone.

It wasn't in its cradle on her nightstand. She reached to the floor, falling out of bed onto her knees, searching through the heap of clothing they'd left there. It had somehow slipped into one of Chris's shoes.

Her mother didn't bother to say hello. "Emma's awake! She's talking!"

"We'll be right there!"

Chris was already pulling on his clothes. They dressed in a breathless silence and Amy took the upstairs bathroom while Chris raced down to use the one on the first floor.

He was on his cell phone in the kitchen when she came down. She heard him before he saw her.

"Of course, baby. I promised, didn't I? We'll do that, too, but I can't get away for at least another week."

A wave of nausea washed over Amy and she stopped in the kitchen doorway, gripping the frame. Chris pivoted around the linoleum floor, stopping short when he saw her. The perfect O of surprise on his face might have been funny under different circumstances.

"I gotta go," he said into the phone and snapped it shut. He gave Amy a big, fake smile. "Ready to go?"

She nodded. "Just need a glass of water." She passed him to get a glass and filled it at the sink.

It could have been his secretary on the phone. He used "baby" a lot, it didn't mean anything. It was gray outside the kitchen window, fog hovering above the dead grass. The clock chimed half-past six.

"Who did these come from?" He was fingering the roses on the table. He had a quirky half smile.

"Yes, I wonder who," she said, playing along.

"No, really Amy, who sent them? Do you have an admirer?"

He wasn't joking. "I guess I do," she said slowly. "Actually, I thought you were my admirer."

She said it lightly—keep it light, don't let him see the hurt— but when he laughed she felt it like a blow in her stomach.

He must have seen it on her face, she'd never been good at hiding her reactions, because he stopped laughing. "I wish I had," he said quickly, but the damage was done.

They took two cars to the hospital by unspoken agreement. She parked first, ran ahead of him into the hospital, but he caught up with her in the corridor. Took her hand. They entered the room that way and Dorothy Busby's smile was bigger than Emma's.

"I want to go home, Mommy." Emma's voice was listless and muffled by the oxygen mask, but it was her voice. Amy blinked back tears.

"I know, sweetie, I know." She kissed Emma's hand and then her face, being careful not to crush her, but needing to feel the life in her.

"Where were you, Mommy? I wanted you."

"I'm so sorry, honey. Mommy wanted you, too."

Then Emma noticed her father and her eyes lit up. "Daddy!"

Amy moved so Chris could sit next to their daughter. She watched as Emma lifted her thin arms to wind around her father's neck. She had an IV in her left hand and the veins stood out against her pale skin.

Dorothy Busby was at her side. "Did you call him?" she whispered excitedly.

"No, you did."

Amy's mother didn't look in the least abashed. "He has a right to know if his daughter's ill," she said. "Look how happy Emma is to see him!"

Emma *was* happy. Chris had lowered the railing and was perched on the bed facing her, holding her hands in his while they chatted in low voices. Whatever he said made Emma giggle, and the sound tore at Amy.

"I'm going to get some coffee," she said. "Do you want anything?"

Chris and Emma ignored her, but her mother stood up. "You just got here," she said. "Stay with Chris and Emma. I'll get the coffee."

"No, Mom, I'll do it. You must be tired from sleeping here."

The reality of everything she'd been through in the past few days was starting to take its toll. Her hands shook as she counted out the money for the coffee and she sank into a booth in the cafeteria, unable to handle the trip back up to the ICU.

"Here, take this." Something soft was pressed in her hands. A man's handkerchief.

She looked up through her tears and saw Ryan dressed in his paramedic's uniform. She hadn't seen him since they'd shared a brief lunch together in what seemed a lifetime ago. He slid into the seat across from her and clutched her hand. "I heard about Emma, how's she doing?"

"Better," she said, trying to swallow her tears, but the look of sympathy on his face only made them flow faster.

"I know it doesn't seem like it right now, but Emma's tough. She's going to get better."

She nodded, gulping. "I know she will. I know." How

could she tell him that she was crying because she'd been foolish enough to believe that her husband had changed?

"It's just—it's been a stressful time."

"I heard about the police. I can't believe they think you could have done those things."

The scorn in his voice buoyed her spirits slightly.

"But they do," she said. "And if I get arrested, I'll lose my job and what will happen to Emma?"

"Don't go there."

"I don't know if I can handle it—"

"You don't have to handle that now, so don't." His voice was firm, but his eyes radiated compassion.

She wiped her eyes, sniffling and trying to contain it. "I should go. My mother's with Emma." And my husband.

She hesitantly offered him the handkerchief, but he smiled and shook his head.

"Keep it." He stood up. "I've got to go, too, but I'm glad I got a chance to see you. My timing really sucks, but I wanted to know if you'd like to go out again. I really enjoyed our lunch."

"I did too."

"I've wanted to call you, but your life seemed, well, pretty complicated."

She laughed weakly. "There's an understatement."

He took a napkin from the metal dispenser on the table and scribbled a number on it. "If you want to grab a bite, or you just want someone to talk to, call me." He handed it to her. "That's my cell—so you can always find me." He squeezed her hand again. "Hang in there."

She stopped in a bathroom to splash cold water on her face before going back up to the ICU, but her mother gave her a penetrating look as she accepted the coffee Amy handed to her.

Chris was preparing to depart. He had his coat on and had

raised the bedrail. "I don't want you to go, Daddy," Emma said in her raspy voice, weakly clutching one of his hands.

"I know, baby, and Daddy doesn't want to go. But I have to."

He peppered her forehead and cheeks with kisses and ended by kissing both of her hands. Emma's lower lip trembled.

"I've got to talk to Mommy for a minute before I leave," he said. "I'll be right outside and then I'm going to wave to you. So you get ready to wave back, okay?"

The hallway was empty except for a rolling cart piled high with hospital bed linens. The nurses' station was just around the corner. Amy could hear the hum of activity and voices. Someone laughed, a high twinkling sound.

"I want you to come back to New York," Chris said. "As soon as Emma's given a clean bill of health."

Amy tried to speak but couldn't around the lump in her throat. She shook her head.

"No?" Chris looked puzzled. "Why? I've missed you, you've missed me—you said as much last night—and Emma needs us together. I told you I'm sorry. Let's move on."

"Who were you on the phone with?" she said.

"This morning?" He looked hunted. "Nobody important."

"A female nobody?"

He sighed, a long, drawn-out whistle of exasperation. "C'mon, Amy, I'm only human. I don't know what more you want from me!"

Amy answered him, knowing she was saying goodbye to her marriage. "Fidelity."

Chapter 28

Desk duty involved a whole lot of paperwork. Farley carried a cardboard box full of old case files into the squad room and dumped them on Mark's desk with a terse "This should keep you busy," and the expectation that he'd be spending his morning doing nothing but scutwork.

"That guy has you in his sights and he just keeps pulling the trigger," Black said with a grin as he eyed the towering stack. He cocked a finger at Mark. "Bam, bam, bam!"

Detective Dickson passed by with a cup of coffee and laughed at Black's remark. Mark picked up half the stack and held it out to them. "I'll be happy to share the love."

"No way, man." Detective Dickson raised his free hand and fled, laughing.

Black smirked. "No can do. Gotta go interview a potential witness."

"Who?"

"Neighbor of Amy Moran's. Old lady. She's got a clear view of their house from hers. Figured she might have seen something."

"What? Amy Moran wielding a nail gun?" Mark laughed.

"You're not going to be laughing when I get the arrest warrant."

"No, I'm going to be looking at the sky," Mark said, "'cause on that day pigs will fly."

"Yeah, keep up that shit," Black said, straining to get on his worn blue blazer. "But don't come complaining to me when you don't get the collar."

"Ditto, partner."

Black snorted. "What? You're going to find the crucial information while you're a desk jockey?"

"They have this new invention," he said speaking slowly, "it's called the in-ter-net."

Black flipped him the bird and offered his parting advice, "Better not let the boss catch you surfing."

It had occurred to Mark that being desk-bound gave him one advantage—time to access VICAP, the Violent Criminal Apprehension Program, the FBI's comprehensive on-line dragnet.

In this database were the records of hundreds of crimes and hundreds of offenders. If his killer was a serial offender, it was possible to track down similar crimes elsewhere.

He made a cursory attempt to get through the paperwork, doing enough to appear engaged whenever Farley happened to pass by, but he spent most of his time on-line.

He smiled as he successfully connected with the database. The faces on the screen didn't smile back. They were hard, stone-cold killers and baby-face teenagers trying to look tough for the camera. In some eyes you could see fear and that fear was the only glimpse into their humanity. In some he saw joy, but these weren't the photos that frightened him. The ones that scared him were the faces with nothing in their eyes.

He'd never agreed when people referred to violent felons

as "animals." Most of the animals he'd known had more compassion than these men. He'd been a cop for eight years, but he still wasn't inured to the litany of crimes.

Bodies slashed and burned. People tortured. Children lured away with false promises. Reading crime databases was like taking all that was evil on the earth and reflecting on it all at once. No wonder there were so many cops who became alcoholics.

Thinking about that brought him perilously close to the events after the bar the other night and he really, really didn't want to think about that.

He forced the thought of that awful encounter out of his mind and focused on his search. Serial killers was much too large a subset. Even serial killers in the Northeast garnered too many names and cases. He expanded the search to include realtors and serial killers, but didn't find any matches.

He tried missing fingers and that brought all sorts of hits, but unfortunately once he'd delve a little deeper, none of them was a good match. Either no names or faces matched or the person could be eliminated due to location or other facts about the case.

After an hour the only thing Mark knew was that there were far too many unsolved homicides in the United States. He tried dozens of different searches, but the cases they yielded didn't jump out at him. It occurred to him that maybe he wouldn't recognize a case similar to this and that all of the cases seemed similar after a while.

He'd been at it for over four hours before he hit a possible connection. A series of unsolved murders in Elizabeth, New Jersey. Five killings, all of them female, spaced over a relatively short period of time — three months — with a few common denominators. They'd all been in houses either for sale or going on the market, they were all single women, and there was evidence that the killer had stalked them prior to the killings.

This perp had strangled his victims. That was a big difference, but it could be that Mark's guy had just changed killing methods. And there was nothing about missing fingers or any other trophies. Maybe just an oversight or maybe it wasn't the same guy at all.

Juarez looked away from the screen for a moment and rubbed his eyes. They were aching from staring at the screen so long and so was his neck. He stood up and stretched as hard as he could, hearing his back crack, before sitting back down. He'd take street work any day over this job.

"C'mon, give me something solid," he muttered, scrolling through the information. Then he saw it. A single line at the bottom of a page: "One witness."

Mary Deerborn was seventy-eight years old, a tiny frail-looking woman with a heart-shaped face and eyes still haunted by the loss of her husband. Stephen Deerborn had died the year before, she informed Detective Black when she saw him eyeing a picture of the two of them in the hallway of her two-story frame colonial.

"I was all of twenty-five when we moved here," she said as she ushered Detective Black into a pleasantly furnished living room. She offered him one of the wing chairs that flanked the fireplace and took her own seat on a floral sofa. "An old married lady of three years and a new mother. Of course, I was hardly more than a baby myself!" She gave a sweet little laugh.

He saw that a tray with a teapot and two china cups with saucers rested on the coffee table between them and resigned himself to the social call that Mrs. Deerborn clearly expected as the cost for getting any information.

There were pictures from the couple's long marriage on the end tables and the mantel. Smiling children grew up to have children of their own and brought them back to the house where they'd posed for countless Christmases and Easters. It made Black nostalgic for his grandmother and the look and feel of the tiny Cape Cod where she'd lived and died.

"We have seven grandchildren," she said, handing over a cup of tea with a steady hand. "It's just a shame that Stephen went so soon."

"How old was Mr. Deerborn?" Black asked, accepting her offer of sugar. They were in little cubes in a silver bowl. He hadn't seen sugar cubes in years.

"Only eighty-three," she said, sighing with regret. "He was perfectly healthy, too. Well, except for the cancer at the end."

Black hid a smile behind his cup. "Thank you for agreeing to see me, ma'am." He put the teacup carefully down and pulled out his notebook. "As I told you on the phone, I just wanted to follow up with you about what you told Officer Feeney about your neighbor across the street."

"Mrs. Moran is such a nice young woman and her daughter is a very sweet little girl." Mrs. Deerborn sighed again. "It makes me miss my own grandchildren. I wish they lived as close. But that's not the way things are nowadays. Children scatter to the ends of the earth."

"That's certainly true, ma'am," Black said. He couldn't agree more. Not that there weren't some mornings when he wouldn't like to see the back of Emmett Junior and his snot-nosed friends. The delicate chiming of Mrs. Deerborn's mantel clock pulled him from thoughts of his own family and back to work.

"As Officer Feeney mentioned when he spoke with you on the phone, we're trying to track Mrs. Moran's whereabouts for the morning of September 6 and the evening of September 14."

"Those are the days on which the murders occurred, detective?"

"Yes, ma'am."

"Oh dear." Mrs. Deerborn set down her own teacup and clasped her hands in the lap of her lavender wool skirt. "I never dreamed we'd have such crimes in Steerforth, did you?"

Black didn't point out that he was a homicide detective so yes, he'd done more than dream it. His toes were tapping against the Oriental rug and he wished she'd get to something useful.

"Well, I know that Mrs. Moran had nothing to do with those crimes," the elderly lady said stoutly.

"You have some proof of this?" Black tried to keep any testiness out of his voice.

"Well, not precisely, not what you'd call proof," she said, drawing the words out. Then she thrust out her chin. "I'm a good judge of character, detective, and I always have been. Mrs. Moran is not the type of person who'd do such an awful thing."

Black itched to tell her about the cherubic looking twenty-year-old who'd attended church every Sunday and burned down his house with his mother locked inside so he could collect on an insurance policy, but he restrained himself.

"But the morning of the sixth, Mrs. Deerborn. You saw something then?"

"No, dear, not on the sixth. It was the eighth I mentioned. That's when I saw him."

"Him?" he said. "Who's him?"

"Why, the man I told Officer Feeney about."

Black took his glasses off and pinched the bridge of his nose. He was going to personally hang Feeney out the second floor window by his toes.

"I thought you told Officer Feeney that you'd seen Mrs. Moran leave her house on the sixth?"

"Oh, yes, that's true."

"And what time was that?"

Mrs. Deerborn brushed that question away with a small hand. "Oh, the usual time. But that isn't important, detective."

"No?"

"What's important is the man."

Pudgy Feeney would be crying for help, but none would be forthcoming. He'd strip him to his undershorts first.

"Tell me about the man."

Mrs. Deerborn smiled. "Okay. As I told Officer Feeney, I didn't think anything of it at first—I'm not a suspicious person, you know."

"Of course you're not." Black scribbled Feeney's name on his notepad and drew a little skull and crossbones next to it.

"And I might not have noticed anything if it hadn't been for Sammy."

"Sammy?"

"My terrier. Didn't I mention that I had a dog?"

"No, I don't think you did."

"Oh. Well, he's out back now. On a lead, of course."

"Of course."

"I don't believe in letting dogs run loose, tearing up other people's gardens. That's happened to me before and I've lost all my tulips—"

Black had a sudden taste for whiskey. Was there a polite way to ask for her to doctor his tea?

"But you were talking about Sammy," he interrupted her.

"Oh, yes, where was I?" Mrs. Deerborn looked confused for a moment and then she smiled. "So I might not have seen anything if it weren't for Sammy's barking."

"You saw a man?"

"He's a good dog, you see, and he doesn't bark at people he knows. So I knew it wasn't the postman or any of our neighbors—"

Get to the fucking point! Black screamed in his head. He thought he could probably crush the bone china cup in one hand. He imagined how it would feel to do that, or to crush it to a fine powder under his heel. Better yet, he could hurl the damn thing into the recesses of the fireplace and listen to it smash against the stone.

"—and I saw him walking up the side of the yard and then disappear around the back of the house. If he were a deliveryman, wouldn't he just go up the walkway? So I thought it was very, very strange. I watched for a while, but then I didn't see him anymore."

"And Mrs. Moran never spoke of anything missing?"

"Oh, no. At least not to me." Mrs. Moran put a hand to her mouth. "I do hope it wasn't a burglar. Nothing was taken, was it?"

"Not that I know of." Black pocketed his notebook and stood up. "Thank you so much, Mrs. Deerborn. That's been very helpful."

She stood hastily. "But don't you want to know what he looked like, detective?"

Feeney was a dead man. "Sure," Black said, digging back out his book. "Did you get a good look at him?"

Chapter 29

"I'm concerned about Emma." Dr. Sirisha Reddy, the pulmonolgist, spoke to Amy in the hospital corridor outside Emma's room. "The attacks are increasing in frequency and intensity. Her levels are all over the board."

Amy nodded, her arms folded tightly over her chest. She was so nervous she couldn't speak.

"We've talked about her triggers," Dr. Reddy said. She was a tiny woman and made up for that fact by wearing three-inch high heels, which still left her four inches below Amy. "What do think could be causing it now? Is Emma under any particular stress at the moment?"

"Yes, quite a bit." Amy struggled to explain what had happened in the last few weeks while Dr. Reddy listened quietly, hands deep in the pockets of her white lab coat.

"I know that Emma wants to go home, and perhaps being here will not help lower her stress," Dr. Reddy said when Amy had finished. "But I want to see those levels at the same place for at least forty-eight hours before we consider a discharge."

She patted Amy's arm in a maternal fashion that was reassuring. "You're not to blame yourself," she said kindly but firmly.

"I've talked to Mommy," she said to Emma once the grown-ups were done conversing in the hall. "And you're going to stay here another night."

"I want to go home," Emma said, pulling fretfully at the oxygen mask.

"I know, sweetie, and you'll be going home very soon, but you need to get all better first," Amy said.

"Guess what I have for you because you've been so brave?" Dr. Reddy slipped a hand into the pocket of her lab coat and Emma's eyes widened with anticipation. Dr. Reddy produced a sparkly pink pencil with a fluffy pink topper. "Surprise!"

Emma reached out and the doctor gave it to her. "What do you say?" Amy reminded her in a low voice.

"Thank you," Emma chirped.

"You've very welcome."

Dorothy Busby admired the pencil, too, and promised to find a pencil sharpener for Emma. Now that Emma was feeling better, she'd gotten fretful.

"This mask is itchy." She tried to pull it off, but Amy restrained her.

"Leave it on for now, okay? Let's wait for Dr. Reddy to say it's okay to take it off because it's helping you to breathe."

Emma looked tearful, but she listened. Her voice was hoarse, like it always was after an attack, and she had bruises from the IV.

"I'm thirsty."

Amy poured ice water from the plastic pitcher into a cup and reached for the bed's remote control.

"No, me! Me!" Emma grabbed it from her mother and moved the bed up. Amy smiled, happy that something about these hospitalizations pleased her. She held the mask away and helped Emma take several sips from the cup. The little girl fell back against the pillows and stared at her mother for several minutes.

"The police are bad, Mommy. They messed up our house."

Dorothy started to say something, but Amy shook her head. "Did that scare you, Em?" she said in a casual voice.

Emma nodded. She was quiet for a few more minutes, and then she shifted the mask to ask, "Are you a criminal, Mommy?"

The question took Amy by surprise and her mother answered for her. "Emma! Of course not!"

"Why do you ask?" Amy said.

"Because the police took you," Emma said as if it was the most reasonable thing in the world, but Amy could see the fear deep in her eyes.

"It wasn't like that, Em," she said, trying to explain but her daughter cut her off.

"Are you going to leave me, like you left Daddy?"

Amy's breath caught in her throat. For a second she couldn't speak. "No, sweetie," she said when she was able to talk. She tried to sound as calm as she didn't feel. "I am not going to leave you. Not now. Not ever."

And as quickly as she'd brought it up, Emma dropped the subject, seemingly reassured for the moment and her interests darting to the bed again. She giggled as she used the remote to raise it up and then down.

Dorothy Busby admonished her to be careful that she didn't break it and gestured to her daughter. She waited for Amy to step to the doorway and then she launched. "Do you hear what that child is saying?"

"My hearing's just as good as yours, Mom."

"Don't get smart with me. She's frightened. She misses her father."

"I know—"

"Did you talk to Chris about going back to New York?"

"No."

"Don't you think it's time you got over this?"

"Don't you think he could change his behavior?"

"He's a man, Amy—"

"So what? Being a man means he can't be honest or trust-worthy?"

"Your daughter needs a father, Amy."

"She has a father."

"She needs the security of a man in the house. You need that security. Look at what's happened."

"Believe me, Mom, I'm well aware of what's going on."

"Do you really mean to tell me that you think any of this would have happened if you hadn't left Chris and moved here?"

It was exactly this sort of statement by her mother that took Amy's breath away. "Do you think that my leaving Chris is responsible for my friend getting murdered?"

"Of course not. But if you hadn't left Chris you wouldn't be dealing with any of this, would you?"

Emma called to them from the bed. "Mommy? Nana? I'm hungry."

Dorothy returned to Emma's side and patted her arm. "I'll go ask the nurses when you can eat. How about a popsicle, sweetie?"

"Cherry!"

"Okay, a cherry popsicle if the nurses say it's okay."

Emma was kneeling on the bed, playing with the remote for the TV.

"Careful of your IV," Amy said, gently moving her back to a sitting position. She picked up the oxygen mask that her daughter had abandoned on the bed and put it back on over Emma's protests. "You've got to wear it for now. Just a while longer, I promise."

They found a children's show on PBS. Amy sat next to

Emma on the bed, her arm wrapped protectively around her daughter's shoulder. She stared at the bright, flickering images on the screen without really seeing them.

Maybe her mother was right and none of this would have happened if she hadn't left Chris. But what other self-respecting option did she have?

She was bitterly ashamed of having fallen for his charm again. She'd believed him—really believed him—when he said he was sorry. In the cold light of day she could see how much she'd wanted to believe that he'd changed his behavior.

Suddenly Amy thought of something that this second betrayal had completely pushed from her mind. If the flowers and other gifts hadn't come from Chris, then who on earth had sent them?

Detective Jimmy Shuster of the Elizabeth, New Jersey, police department sounded like a two-pack-a-day smoker.

"I got all the files," he said to Mark, sounding like he'd just that moment climbed up from the dim environs of the department's basement with a boxful of information. "What do you want to know?"

"Mainly about the woman your perp didn't manage to kill. What happened there?"

"Well, we're not even sure it's the same perp, but there were a lot of similarities. She answered an ad to see an apartment in a newer high-rise. She calls and leaves a message and a man calls her back. Tells her to show up at two P.M. on a Thursday. She shows up. Man attacks her, tries to strangle her, but she manages to get loose, break a window and scream for help. Perp took off."

Mark held the phone with one hand and took notes with the other. He was sitting at his parents' kitchen table after returning home, ostensibly for a late lunch. He couldn't let Farley hear him making this call. He thought his parents knew about his reassignment—there was something in his mother's face—but they didn't say anything so neither did he. His mother had run to the grocery store and his father was working with a speech therapist upstairs.

"What made you think it was the same perp?" he asked Shuster.

"Well, the weapon for one. All of the victims were killed using a pair of stockings. Then there were the doors. There was no sign of forced entry in any of these cases. Either the guy knew these women or he had some way of getting in the house. The vic who survived said she'd never seen him before and his description didn't ring any bells for the condo owner, but somehow the guy managed to get into a unit."

"Anything else?"

"He'd watched the women. Probably stalked them for some time before killing them. This is one careful motherfucker. He knew when these women would be alone."

"Any trophies?"

"Oh, yeah." Jimmy laughed, a harsh, cackling noise. "Fingers. Fucker's obsessed with 'em."

Mark punched a fist in the air in triumph. This was the same guy!

"Always the ring finger," Shuster said. "At first we thought it was the rings he wanted, but one of the vics didn't even have a ring, so it had to be the fingers themselves. Sick bastard."

"I want to talk to the survivor. Do you have a name and address for her?"

"Sure. Patty Bulowski." He spelled it for Mark and gave him the address. "But good luck with trying to talk to her."

"Not receptive?"

"A whack job. Don't know if it was just the attack or she was always like that."

* * *

Chloe didn't recall who'd brought the flowers. "I don't remember them being delivered," she said when Amy caught up with her on the university campus. "Are you sure they arrived while I was at your house?"

"I thought so because they were there when I got home."

Chloe shifted her messenger bag to the opposite shoulder and played thoughtfully with a piece of her long, blonde hair. They'd paused on a walkway that crossed the middle of campus and a continuous stream of students flowed around them like a river around rocks.

"I just don't remember them being delivered—wait! They were there when we got back from the park. So they must have been delivered while the police were searching the house."

She looked pleased, but Amy felt far from it. "The *police* signed for the flowers?" She found that hard to envision. She thanked Chloe and watched her walk off toward one of the ivy-covered brick buildings. It took five minutes to walk briskly back across campus, only to discover that she'd been ticketed for parking too close to a fire hydrant.

She drove to the office next and was happy to find Bev dozing behind a copy of *People* magazine at the front desk.

"Do you remember the delivery of wine I got?" she said.

"Sure," Bev said. "Your secret admirer!" She grinned and winked.

"Do you keep a record of deliveries? Is there any way to tell who delivered it?"

Bev held up one manicured finger. She opened a drawer, pulled out a notebook and plopped it on the desk. "Let's see," she said, opening it and flipping through the pages. "Do you remember what day it was?"

Amy tried to remember the possible day or days in question. Bev traced down a long line of signatures. "Here you go. Bob from Minuteman Delivery Service. That's who brought it."

"Minuteman? I've never heard of them before," Amy said.

"They're local. Here, you can look them up." Bev produced a hefty Yellow Pages. Amy was writing down their number when Poppy Braxton and Hope Chiswell breezed through the front doors, wafting a heavy floral scent ahead of them.

"Amy!" Poppy exclaimed in a falsely enthusiastic voice. She was wearing a full-length mink coat. Her blonde page-boy glowed against the gleaming fur. "Congratulations on the sale! You must be thrilled."

The house where Sheila had died had finally sold, below value and not to the original buyers. The sellers had complained through the entire process, finishing by berating Amy at the closing. The only people thrilled were the Patwardan family who'd bought the place.

"Thanks," Amy said, returning a terse smile. She was not in the mood for Poppy and Hope, not that she was ever in the mood for the bitch duo, as she'd come to think of them.

"Is that a new coat, Amy?" Hope said, rubbing the sleeve of the red wool jacket that Amy had dug out of mothballs that morning. Hope's entire ensemble was in creamy, winter white, all the better to show off her auburn hair. "No? Well it suits you. Red must be your color."

It fell like middle school all over again, when Amy wasn't one of the popular girls and didn't understand the games they played.

"Now if you can just manage to sell the Chomsky house," Poppy said.

"Without another killing," Hope added.

They both laughed. Ha, ha, yes, murder was so funny. Bev was smiling in a dopey sort of way, looking as if she didn't understand the joke, but was happy to be included. Amy flipped the Yellow Pages closed and handed it back to her with a quiet thanks.

"Maybe you'll be the one to sell the new construction at the Bellamy Estates," Hope added over her shoulder as the duo continued on into the main of the office. Their laughter floated behind them.

Amy pulled up in front of Minuteman Delivery Service, inconveniently hidden in a small storefront a block off main, a bare five minutes before they were set to close.

"You just made it!" the young woman behind the desk said with a level of enthusiasm that hardly seemed warranted by the job. "What do you need to send? A manuscript? Tax form? Love letter?" She began pulling padded mailers out from below the counter. "How big is it?"

Amy shook her head. "Actually, I'm looking for some information."

The smile wavered on the woman's face. "Oh. So you've got nothing to deliver?"

"I'm afraid not."

The young woman gave a genuine sigh of disappointment. She slipped the mailers back under the counter and leaned on her elbows, playing with the multiple silver bangles dangling from one thin wrist. The small room smelled like patchouli and envelope paste. "What do you need to know?"

Amy explained about the delivery and the date. The young woman nodded in time. "Sure, we've got a record," she said. "There wasn't something wrong with the delivery, was there?"

"No, not at all."

"Good." She straightened up and went to the monitor at the end of the wooden counter. "We're trying to compete with UPS and FedEx, you know," she said, tapping rapidly on the keys. "Not to mention U.S. Mail. There's a lot of competition in this business. And I mean a lot of competition."

She scanned the screen intently, scrolling up and down

with a mouse incongruously shaped like a cat. "Yep, here it is. Bob took it. Delivery of a bottle of wine."

"That's it. Who ordered the delivery?"

The woman looked puzzled. "You mean you don't know?"

"No, it was an anonymous gift. And I wanted to thank them."

"Okay, let's see." She tapped a few more keys and searched the screen. "Here you go. No first name, just the initials I.M. Last name is an odd one: Nemo." She looked up at Amy. "Is that someone you know?"

"I.M. Nemo?" Amy clarified, feeling a creeping sensation along her spine.

"Yeah. Weird name. Only time I've heard of a Nemo, except for the movie, of course. I love that movie."

"And Captain Nemo," Amy said.

"Is that a sequel? I didn't see that."

She shook her head, aware of the prickling of the tiny hairs along the back of her scalp. "It's a character in a Jules Verne novel. *Twenty Thousand Leagues Under the Sea.*"

"Never read it," the woman said cheerfully. "Of course, I'm not much of a reader. I like TV better."

When Amy left the business a few minutes later it was with very little additional information. I.M. Nemo was a man. He'd paid cash. She couldn't remember what he looked like or anything at all about him other than the name.

Amy felt dazed. I.M. Nemo wasn't real, that she knew. But why would the giver wish to remain anonymous? And why that particular pseudonym? She'd had a year of Latin in high school and recognized this word, if little else. *Nemo* meant "no one."

Chapter 30

The house where Patty Bulowski lived had seen better days. It was a small saltbox with white aluminun siding that had turned gray over the years from traffic and smog.

Mark had trouble finding her street, driving around Elizabeth and passing hundreds of other urban houses that looked similar to hers. Some were older, some bigger, all of them looking like the owners had stopped caring a long time ago about what their neighbors thought.

The house next to Bulowski's was a large Victorian that had been split up into rentals. A hand-lettered sign advertising apartments for let was stuck crookedly in the crabgrass that passed for a front lawn.

There was a chain-link fence surrounding the Bulowski house that looked newer than the home itself and a large sign posted next to the gate that said BEWARE OF THE DOG.

A Ford Taurus with a dent in its right fender sat in the driveway. There was a plastic doghouse in the postage stamp back yard, with leaves from a maple tree spread around it, half burying the chain extending from it and the large dog dish sitting in front.

Juarez swung open the gate and started up the walk. He rang the bell and there was an immediate sound of loud barking. A constant bark and growl, bark and growl.

A woman's voice said, "Quiet, Ranger, quiet, boy," and then the barking abruptly ceased. "What do you want?"

"I'm Mark Juarez, Ms. Bulowski, I'm a homicide detective from Connecticut. I wanted to talk to you about what happened five years ago in the condo." Mark held up his badge to the peephole. He could feel her looking at him. His skin was crawling.

"That happened around here, not Connecticut."

"There have been some killings in Steerforth that look like the work of the same guy that killed here. That almost killed you. It would really help us if I could talk to you."

"I don't want to talk about it," the woman said, but this time her voice was so low he could barely hear it. "It was a long time ago."

"We have some new evidence, Ms. Bulowski."

"Go away!"

"I need your help. Please. At least two more women have been killed."

"If you don't leave, I'm going to sic my dog on you!"

"You don't have a dog, Ms. Bulowski," Mark said.

Immediate silence. Then the door cracked open with a security chain in place. A woman's face appeared, white with frightened pale eyes and mousy brown hair pulled severely back.

"How did you know that?" she said. The hand holding the door in place was shaking.

"There are leaves all over the chain and the bowl and the barking dog is a recording," Mark said.

She looked even more frightened for a moment. "I can't have a real dog, I'm allergic."

He nodded. "They're a good decoy. Most people are fooled."

"I had to do something after—after what happened."

He nodded again, feeling the panic emanating in waves off her. "I've got two sisters—I know what it's like."

"Have they been attacked?" she immediately demanded, the tremulous voice becoming rigid and hard and then just as quickly fading away.

"No," he said. "No, they haven't."

"Then you can't know."

He nodded. It had been a misstep. "I just meant that I know women are vulnerable."

"I never felt vulnerable before." There was a hint of pride in her voice. He remembered the police report that Shuster had read to him. That she'd been strong enough to slip his grip and smash a window. His gaze fell involuntarily to the hands clutching the doorframe and he could see shiny white scars.

"I told everything I know to Detective Shuster. Talk to him."

"I have," Mark said, "but it's better if we can hear it from you. I'm sorry, Ms. Bulowski, I'm not trying to bring you pain, but it's really, really important."

She stared at him for a long moment and Mark held his breath and met her gaze, hoping that he looked sincere, non-threatening.

"Empty your pockets," she said at last.

"What?"

"Empty your pockets. I want to see everything in your pockets."

It was her version of a pat-down, Mark realized, and he readily removed his wallet and keys and pulled all of his pants pockets inside out, circling slowly so she could check him. He emptied his jacket pockets, too, and took it off, offering it to her to check, but she shook her head. He patted his own shirt down, showing her that nothing was hidden there or at the waistband of his pants and then he lifted the legs of his pants one at a time so that she could see that he didn't have an ankle holster.

The door closed and then he heard the scrape of the chain being removed. When the door reopened it was only marginally wider. She waited for Mark to slip past and then carefully locked and bolted the door behind him.

"The living room's on the right," she said, being careful, Mark noticed, to stay behind him. Every hair on his body was alert and he remembered what Shuster had said about her mental state and tried to move sideways to keep her in his peripheral vision.

The house was small and immaculate. The carpet under their feet was pale, the couch and matching loveseat a watery shade of blue that matched her eyes. There were photos on an end table. A laughing young woman was in all of them: Hair highlighted blond, long strands blowing in the breeze while she held onto the mast of a sailboat and a handsome man held onto her; a white tennis outfit and a dark tan, clutching a racket; shorts and T-shirt revealing a toned, trim body while she clung to the side of a rock in a harness.

The woman sitting across from him had to be the same, but it was as if she'd had all the energy and vitality sucked out of her. Her face had lost its healthy glow. She looked sallow and her hair seemed to have thinned. A worry line creased the space between her eyes. Her body was thinner than it had been, but he could tell this only from the bones visible in her wrists and her neck for she was swaddled in a capacious tracksuit at least a size too large.

"What do you want to know?" she said, taking a seat across from him on the loveseat. Her hands were tightly clenched in her lap and she sat forward, posture rigid.

"Tell me about what happened that day."

"I went to look at a condo. I thought it would be nice. Maintenance free."

"How did you find out it was available?"

"An ad in the Sunday paper. A man said that if I came on a Thursday he could show me the place."

"How did you get there?"

"Car."

"So you parked outside the building . . ."

"Yes. I parked. I went in. He answered the door. He was smiling."

She shivered and her hands moved to opposite elbows, clutching.

Mark glanced at his notebook, at the description she'd given Shuster. "You said he was tall, six-foot-something?"

"Yes."

"Unusually tall? Six-four or above?"

She shook her head. "Just tall."

"Hair color?"

"Brown. But I thought it might not have been his. I thought it was a toupee." She rocked forward and back, a minute movement, but she kept at it.

"Why did you think that?"

"It sat too far forward." She quickly tapped the center of her forehead and grabbed her elbow again. "He had glasses on, too. Thick ones in black frames."

"You said he was smiling. Did you see his teeth?"

"I don't know, I don't remember."

Mark heard the rise in her voice, so he pulled back. "So he let you in and then what happened?"

"He told me to go ahead and look around, so I did." She met Mark's eyes for a moment. "He seemed nice. That was my first impression. He seemed nice."

"Where were you when he attacked you?"

Her eyes dropped. "In the bedroom."

"Did he surprise you?"

"I was looking in the closet." Her rocking intensified. "I heard his footsteps. I started to say something, just to make conversation. Something about the storage."

"And that's when he hit you?"

She nodded.

"From behind?"

She started to cry. One hand loosened its grip on her elbow and swiped at the tears rolling down her face. "It was so stupid. But he'd been so friendly. I didn't get any creepy vibes, you know?"

"You thought you could trust him," Mark said.

Patty Bulowski nodded, the tears still streaming down her face. Mark spotted a box of Kleenex on a nearby table and brought it to her. She smiled her thanks, blotting her face.

"What did he hit you with?"

"I don't know. Something hard. On my neck. Maybe just his fist."

"You fell to the floor?"

She nodded. The rocking had picked up a bit.

"And he landed on top of you?"

The woman covered her face with her hands and sobbed. Mark glanced away and then back. These were the moments he hated being a cop.

"What did he do next, Ms. Bulowski?"

"He tied my wrists. L-like this." She raised shaking arms above her head. "Then he wrapped something around my neck. He pulled it tight. I was choking." She put her hands to her throat. "I couldn't breathe. I thought I was going to die."

"But you fought back?"

She nodded, one hand straying to her mouth. She didn't speak for a moment, just kept rocking, and Mark waited, careful not to push, trying to judge how much he could ask without her clamming up.

"He hadn't tied my ankles," she said at last. "I don't think he thought I could do anything with my feet. Not like that. Not when I was lying on my stomach."

"But you did?"

Another nod. "I kicked him. I could reach his back—I'm pretty flexible—and I had on high-heeled boots."

"You cut him with the boot?"

"I must have, because he cried out and the rope—it was really a stocking—around my neck went slack."

"How did you get to the window?" he asked, picturing the description that Shuster had supplied of the woman breaking free and kicking out the glass to scream for help. It was hard to reconcile that image with this defeated figure.

"I managed to get turned around and I grabbed him—down there," she pointed to her crotch. "One hand on each and I twisted as hard as I could."

Mark winced. "I'm betting that was successful."

For a split second an actual smile blossomed on Patty Bulowski's face, like sun appearing through gray clouds, and then it vanished. "I broke away and there was the glass. It was a big window. I didn't know if it opened. I couldn't have gotten it open anyway. I could hear him behind me and I knew he was going to kill me. I smashed the glass with my tied hands and then kicked the rest with my boots."

"Did he leave then?" Mark asked.

"He couldn't pull me away from the glass." Her voice got higher. "He tried. His breath was on my neck, his arm was around my neck. But I kicked him again. He let go then and I screamed. I just kept screaming."

"And someone heard the noise?"

"Yes. They called the police."

She stood up abruptly, swiping at her eyes with jerky movements. "That's all I know. I don't want to talk about it anymore. I've told you everything. Please leave."

Mark scrambled to his feet.

"Please, Ms. Bulowski, just a few more questions."

"I don't want to talk about it anymore," she repeated, wringing her hands and stepping slowly toward the hall. "Please. Just go. Please." She directed him with a shaking hand.

They moved into the hall and seeing the pictures on the

wall prompted Juarez to ask, "Did you receive any photos before the attack? Naked photos of you?"

The woman's already pale face turned chalky before suddenly flooding with color. She nodded.

"I gave them to the police," she said. "I took them in right away, but they couldn't do anything. There was no address on the mailer, no fingerprints on anything. They asked me if I had an ex-lover who might have taken them."

The bitterness in her voice didn't surprise Mark. She must have felt completely alone.

"How long after the photos were you attacked?"

"Two weeks."

He pulled a card from his pocket and handed it to her. "If you think of anything else, anything at all, please call me. I want to catch this guy, Ms. Bulowski."

She nodded and he heard the locks turning as the door closed behind him. He had his hand on the gate when he heard the door reopen.

He came back up the walk. "You thought of something else?"

"It's probably nothing," she said, holding on to the door-frame. "But it's one of the reasons I wanted to move."

He waited, wondering what Shuster could have missed.

"Someone had been in my house."

After she'd been back to the hospital and had dinner with Emma and her mother, Amy read her daughter a bedtime story, kissed Dorothy Busby good-bye and returned home alone. This time the house was really and truly empty. No Chris lurking in the bedroom. So why was her fear greater than the night before? Because the night before she hadn't realized that the gifts weren't coming from her husband.

Flowers that seemingly just appeared, a bottle of wine sent by an anonymous stranger. The chocolates she'd tracked to a store in New York, which had no record of the purchaser beyond the fact that he'd paid in cash. Neither of the local florists had filled orders for a dozen white roses.

The first thing she did in the house was to check every door and window and make sure that all of them were locked. Then she drew the curtains, anxious to keep the darkness out. She noticed that the downstairs lights were on at Mrs. Deerborn's across the street and just that glow in the darkness offered some reassurance that she wasn't alone.

The words she'd said to Chris and her mother seemed foolish now. Maybe she was hanging on to stubborn pride in refusing to return to him. Certainly at this moment she desperately wanted the security of someone bigger and stronger.

She turned on as many lights in the house as she could. Her electric bill would skyrocket, but she needed the comfort and security. That done, she poured a glass of wine—not from the bottle that had been sent—and took it with her into the living room.

She curled up in an armchair and called Perry back, relieved when she answered with her usual, strident "Greetings!" Someone like Perry would understand how Amy was feeling. She had the imagination necessary to feel real empathy.

"You should pack your things and come stay with me," she said when Amy had finished detailing the last few days. "Do it now. Right this minute."

"I can't."

"Of course you can. Your job's flexible enough—"

"Emma's in the hospital."

"When she's recovered then. You said she'd be out in a few days. That gives you time to pack."

"It's not just that. This **is** our home. Emma's in school."

"For heaven's sake, Amy, she's in kindergarten, not Harvard."

"I know, but it's the continuity. She doesn't need any more disruption. We don't need that."

What she didn't say was that it was also about fulfilling a promise, albeit unspoken, that she'd made to Sheila. She owed it to Sheila to stay, to fight this through and not give in because of fear.

Like Sheila before her, Amy had worked damn hard to get her real estate license, to build the life she'd managed to make for her and Emma in Steerforth. To establish the community they'd managed to establish. If she left now, it would be an insult to Sheila's memory and what would she have to show for all her hard work? Nothing.

"It's a very generous offer," she said to Perry, "but I just can't accept it."

"Don't give a definite no," Perry said. "The offer's always good. We can all squeeze into the studio. I'd welcome the company. Anything to take my mind off this dreadful painting."

"I'm sure it's not dreadful."

"The honorable judge looks like a cross between Herman Munster and Bozo the Clown. I have no idea why they gave me this commission, I have no talent whatsoever."

Amy smiled, taking a sip of wine. This was familiar territory and comforting in its sameness.

"I'm sure it's lovely."

"Just wait till you see it."

Amy hung up the phone feeling better and more relaxed than she had in a while, and resolute enough to attack her dilemma with new vigor.

She'd left a message for Detective Juarez. She wondered if he'd call back at night. Probably not. She could always take the wine and the roses down to the station, but what if that awful Detective Black was there? He'd find some way of turning it around and making it look as if Amy had sent them to herself.

Leaving the comfort of her chair, she fetched a notepad and pen from her office, stepping over piles of photos disrupted by the police to get to them. She settled back in the living room, feet curled under her, and set to work making a list.

The gifts were recorded first and a list of possible givers. Ryan? Paul? She knew that both of them liked her. Perhaps one of the other men from the single parents' group. Richard? He didn't seem like the type to send presents, though she could easily picture him trying to mess with her mind by using a creepy pseudonym.

Only how would any of these men know that she liked these things? She couldn't recall ever talking about her preferences at the single parents' group and she hadn't entertained anyone in Steerforth beyond Sheila.

Her brain was fuzzy from the combined effects of stress, fatigue and alcohol, but as she stared idly at the wall, wondering how someone might have found out about her favorites, it suddenly became clear. The truth had been staring her in the face.

She got up from the chair and approached the arrangement of photos hanging on the wall. She'd hung them with Chris some years ago and they'd been gathering dust ever since. Only they weren't dusty anymore. The glass looked suspiciously bright and when she ran her finger slowly along the top of one of the black frames it came away clean.

There in the center of the arrangement was a photo taken the night she'd graduated from art school. A younger version of herself sitting at a table with Chris, both of them clinking glasses of deep red wine, the bottle clearly visible on the table in the foreground. The same bottle of wine that she'd received as a gift.

Feeling light-headed, she moved slowly toward her bedroom, knowing what she'd find before she got there, but needing to see it, needing to see clearly what she'd missed.

They were where they'd always been on her dresser. A series of her own photos mounted in silver frames of varying shapes and sizes. Different angles, different lighting, but the subject was the same in each. White roses.

Chapter 31

The locksmith arrived at Amy Moran's house just as the fingerprint guys were finishing. The house was coated in fine black powder and the locksmith, an older man with *Herb* embroidered over his work shirt pocket, complained about it as he unloaded his tools.

"This stuff wash out?" he asked Detective Juarez as he knelt beside the back door. "The wife's not going to be happy if it doesn't."

Mark ignored him, having greater concerns than laundry. He'd arrived at the station early, not hungover for the first time in a long while, shirt neatly pressed, tie picked with care, and determined to present a clean and sober image to Lieutenant Farley along with the evidence.

His boss had been quiet for a long time after hearing him out before suddenly demanding, "You got the number for this Detective Shuster?"

From there things had moved so quickly that Mark hadn't had time to enjoy being vindicated. The lieutenant was talking about forming a serial killer task force when Amy Moran arrived at the station, asking for help because someone had broken into her house.

Only there was no break-in. No visible way that a perp could have gotten access. Juarez and Black had been through every inch of the house and the windows and doors were locked. So how had the perp managed to leave the flowers?

"She must have given someone the key," Black said in a low voice as he came into the kitchen. He'd sulked when he first learned of the official switch in theories, but after about an hour he'd managed to convince himself that he'd always known it was a serial killer, but just needed hard evidence to prove it and thank God Juarez had finally buckled down and found it.

"I've checked every possible way in," he said, wiping a hand across his forehead and smearing charcoal dust across him in the process. "There's not so much as a tear in a screen. The perp—if it's the perp—has got a key."

"Maybe," Mark said. He was both nervous and agitated, feeling like a racehorse held at the starting gate and waiting for the bell. He had proof that it wasn't Amy Moran. He had proof that the same killer had struck before. He only had instinct that the gifts left in Amy's home and delivered to her office were the work of the killer. He needed something more.

"Feeney's back to the neighbor's getting a better description of the man she saw up here," Black said. For some reason he seemed embarrassed by this, the tips of his ears coloring.

Mark turned his attention to the door where Herb was wrestling to dismantle the existing lock. Beyond the door was the backyard. He stepped out onto the porch, shivering. They were predicting the first frost for the end of the week. It was supposed to be a long winter. He stepped down onto the dry grass and walked toward the swing set. Amy said she'd found something out here—a doll of Emma's that wasn't for outside play. She'd blamed Emma for it, but given everything else that she'd discovered, now she wasn't sure.

It was easy to see how someone could have lurked back here, Mark thought, looking at the relative isolation of the house. It was the smallest house on the block, and while it wasn't separated by much acreage from its neighbors, the high box hedges and old trees provided a degree of privacy that made it possible to get in and out with little risk of being seen. Unless you had nosy or lonely neighbors. Thank God for the Mrs. Deerborns of the world. They made police work a lot easier.

He walked around the house, trying to put himself in the mind of the killer, imagining what he would do if he wanted to get into the house. There was, as Black had observed, no conceivable way.

Amy glanced out her office window and saw Detective Juarez standing in her backyard with his arms crossed, staring into space. She'd had enough of police. Less than a week ago they'd trashed her house in search of evidence to arrest her and now they were back trashing her house again in search of evidence to arrest someone else.

Not that she wasn't glad they'd finally decided she wasn't the killer, but her nerves were shot. After last night's scary discovery, she couldn't sleep in the house. She'd left immediately, driving back to the hospital and sleeping fitfully in a chair next to Emma's bed.

Before moving to Steerforth her dealings with police were limited to the occasional reprimand from a traffic cop and lifting Emma up to pet the noses of the horses ridden by mounted police in Central Park. *So move back to New York.* She could hear her mother's voice in her head. With a sigh of frustration, she bent back over the list she was making.

The police wanted a list of every single person that she and Emma knew in Steerforth. Some of those people were on the list she'd given them of Sheila's friends and acquaintances. This was a list about her. For it was clear that someone was interested in her and that someone was very likely the person who had killed Sheila and Meredith.

She'd been told that the murders in Steerforth were similar to another series of killings in New Jersey, but she didn't know how. She didn't want to know, to tell the truth. She was scared and tired and beginning to wonder if sticking this out was really the best course of action.

Just thinking about leaving made her feel defeated, though, and she tried to concentrate on the list. Every single person was quite some list. Emma's teacher, the school nurse, Father Michael, Ryan, Audrey, Penelope, Paul, Richard, Douglas—it just went on and on. She couldn't forget Dr. Reddy or the pediatrician. How about the name of the mechanic who'd done the oil change for the Toyota?

In the end, she covered four sheets of lined paper and presented it to Detective Juarez with a wry smile. "I don't know how useful it will be, but I've done my best."

"Thank you." He looked it over quickly before folding it and sticking it in his pocket. "It's more about making connections between both places," he said. "I'll try and find out if any of the people you know were in anyway connected to New Jersey at the time of the murders there."

He said it matter-of-factly, but it made her shiver.

"What else can I do?" she said. "You saw the locksmith, but I can't get a security system estimate until the middle of next week. And I'm not even sure I'll be able to afford it."

"I'd suggest you get a dog, but I guess you can't because of Emma's asthma?"

She nodded. "That's definitely out. Too bad, because she'd love one and I'd definitely feel safer with a dog."

"The security system's really your next best option."

She hesitated. "I've considered getting a gun permit."

"Do you know how to shoot?"

She was gratified he hadn't laughed. "No, not really. I've done it once. But they have classes. I could learn."

"I wouldn't recommend it even if you knew how," he said. "It's an illusion of safety, but it could easily be used against you."

"So what else can I do?"

Now it was his turn to hesitate. "Look, Ms. Moran, I don't want to scare you, but I think there's only one real option."

Of course the minute someone said not to feel scared, she felt exactly that. "What is it?"

"You should leave. Go stay with family or friends."

"I can't do that," she said. "Emma's in the hospital and besides, this is our home, I've got to work. I can't just leave."

He nodded. "I understand, but you should seriously think about it. We can't guarantee your safety here."

Amy nodded, her hands clammy. She couldn't leave. She'd worked so hard to make this a home. There had to be another way.

"What if we lured the bastard here by using me as the bait?"

"No way," he said, shaking his head to emphasize it. "It's too risky. I wouldn't even consider that at this point."

"But you would consider it?"

He sighed and rubbed his eyes. "Look, Ms. Moran, I've given you my professional opinion. I think you should leave. We'll do everything we can to keep you safe here, but I don't want to see you or your daughter hurt."

They both knew that in this case *hurt* was a euphemism for *killed*. Amy felt nauseous.

"It's great to change the locks," Detective Juarez said,

"and it might slow down this bastard. But whoever is doing this killing has fixated on you and that isn't going to stop."

The police were gone by mid-afternoon. The locksmith paid and gone by four. Gray dust and metal shavings covered the rooms and she spent the next hour absorbed in cleaning. She couldn't bring Emma back to a house this dusty. *You shouldn't bring Emma back here at all.* The voice in her head sounded a warning, but she pushed against it. Fear could not get the upper hand here. She couldn't let it.

She'd spend the night at the hospital, that was safer, and then tomorrow she'd think about leaving. With any luck Emma would be discharged and she'd do that one open house and then they'd go. Where? She couldn't go back to Chris. She couldn't possibly move in to Perry's, no matter what she said. The studio wasn't big enough. Maybe her mother's. There was definitely room at her childhood home. But just for a short time. Just until they caught the bastard.

That was how she'd come to think of him—a cold, ruthless bastard. The police had taken the roses as evidence, but if they hadn't she would have shredded them. She felt sick at the thought of how happy she'd been to receive them.

When she'd finished vacuuming it was dusk. The dark came early these days and she shivered at the shadows outside. She hadn't wanted to be here at night. She hurried to the bedroom and put together a small overnight bag.

She hummed under her breath as she packed, a nervous little tune to fill the silence. She was just about finished when the doorbell rang.

She flinched at the noise. *Bing, bong.* Two tones, high then low, that echoed through the house. Stock-still and terrified, it wasn't until the noise repeated that she had the courage to move. She ran for the kitchen on shaking legs and jerked open the utensils drawer, pulling out the biggest knife she owned.

She crept to the front door, knife clutched and faintly trembling in her right hand. The outside light was off. She switched it on and pressed her eye to the peephole.

It was Ryan. He was wearing his uniform and carrying a large brown bag. Relief made her feel weak. She swung open the door, hanging onto the frame, and smiled weakly at him.

"Hi."

"Sorry to drop by unannounced," he said with a wide smile of his own. "But I thought we could do dinner if you haven't eaten. Do you like Chinese food?" He held up the bag.

"I was just about to go to the hospital, but dinner first sounds great," she said, smiling back, so glad to have his company—any company—that she forgot all about holding the knife until she ushered him in with it and he blanched.

"I thought maybe you were—someone else," she said sheepishly.

"Like who? Norman Bates?" His laugh was nervous.

She explained what had happened while leading the way to the kitchen, where he unpacked the cartons of food and listened to her, really listened, interrupting only to ask relevant questions.

"What are you going to do?" he said when she'd finished and they were sitting across from each other at her kitchen table.

"I going to leave, just for a while, but it's hard."

"This is your life—you've built it here."

"Exactly." She picked at the sesame chicken. "I need stability for Emma and neither choice offers that, but it's safer to go."

He nodded. "I think Emma can handle it. She's tough."

"I hope so. I don't know how the school will handle her absence."

"Kindergarten dropout." Ryan grinned.

"Do you think it will go on her permanent record?"

They laughed. It felt good to laugh. Amy felt the knot in her stomach ease and then, all at once, she was crying.

"Oh, hey, it's okay." Ryan was out of his chair at once. He put his arm around her, while she sniffled and swiped at the tears.

"Sorry, it's just been a long day."

"Don't apologize. You're under a lot of stress."

His hand was warm against her shoulders, his voice comfortingly matter-of-fact, and she smiled at him through her tears. He leaned closer and thumbed a tear off her nose and they laughed and then he kissed her.

It was a slight brush against her lips, but it still made her gasp. He pulled back and they looked at each other soberly and then she leaned forward and returned the kiss.

As if by unspoken agreement they moved frantically and without words, kissing harder and harder, pressing their mouths into each other, pressing their bodies together, and then reaching to undress each other with frantic, fumbling hands.

Afterwards, she had no sense of how they got from the kitchen to the bedroom, just that they made it there half-dressed, stripping each other the rest of the way, his hands struggling with her bra, hers fumbling with his belt. He was whispering things to her that she couldn't comprehend, though she caught snatches of words about her flesh, her smell, her being and knew that he was pleased with her.

They learned each other's bodies quickly, a frenetic coupling, the pleasant shock of flesh against flesh. It was fast and hard, but then he waited, holding out for her to come before he finished, and when he did, his body falling into hers, his sigh of contentment soothed a place in her that had been scarred.

Chapter 32

The most surprising thing about the Harrigans' house was that they had one of her photos hanging in the master bedroom. It was a female nude reclining, soft shades of gray and white. Amy recognized it as one in a series of portraits she'd done about five years ago, shortly before she'd given birth to Emma.

"That's my work," she said to Poppy Braxton, pausing to admire where they'd hung it in place on the wall behind the massive king-sized bed, covered in a caramel-colored satin quilt and dozens of matching pillows.

"I advised them to take it down," Poppy said, glancing at it as she swept nonexistent wrinkles out of the comforter. "People can get touchy about nudity. Not good for sales."

The house was in a newer plan in what had once been part of a woodland estate. Amy thought of it as fantasy housing. Every house had some touches of original housing from the area, but bulked up, like the builders had gone on steroids. Large windows in the master bedroom looked out on a kidney-shaped pool built to resemble a pond, complete with a natural rock fountain.

A pool house stood beside it on the edge of a small emerald square of lawn and on the other side of the pool was a portico separating the main house from a two-car garage.

"Like all homeowners, they want the house sold for asking price yesterday," Poppy complained as they finished their inspection of the second floor and made their way down a back set of stairs into the mammoth kitchen.

"I think they're asking too much," Amy said, "but they wouldn't come down." She coveted the six-burner Viking stove and granite countertops. A Lean Cuisine box had been left out like an affront to the cooking potential of the space. Poppy clicked her tongue and whisked it into the trash compacter.

"Of course they are. They've been here barely two years and think because of the housing bubble they're going to make a fortune. Please. This isn't Westport, not yet. I've told lots of sellers that, of course, but do they listen to me?"

Amy wasn't listening to her. She was looking out the window at the front of the house, down the sloping lawn to the street where the unmarked cop car was parked. A Ford Taurus. It stuck out like a sore thumb in this neighborhood. The Harrigans, for instance, owned a Mercedes SUV, a BMW convertible and a Hummer. The teenage son drove the Hummer.

She could see Officer Feeney standing next to the car. He'd been assigned to watch the house and had walked through it first, checking all rooms, all closets, while Poppy complimented him on his thoroughness, at the same time lamenting the necessity of doing it.

She was here as overseer of the open house, making no secret of the fact that she thought Amy needed to be shown how it was done. "Let's just make sure nothing happens," she said, as if her presence could deflect crime.

As Amy watched, Detective Juarez arrived to sit with

Feeney. They would monitor the open house while Detective Black joined a contingent of other officers watching Amy's house.

"The likelihood of him trying anything is slim," Juarez had said. "You'll be in a house in broad daylight in a plan with other houses and nosy neighbors."

Amy couldn't imagine trying anything when it was so obvious that police were on the scene. The second unmarked car was another Taurus. Feeney's ill-fitting suit and the way he was scanning the neighborhood while Juarez talked to him all made it pretty obvious.

Poppy had insisted the police stay outside the house, informing them with as little subtlety as possible in typical Poppy Braxton fashion. "We're trying to sell homes," she'd explained to Feeney. "To do that, we have to create a certain kind of ambience. You are not part of that ambience."

Rolling the cover off the pool and pulling out two deck chairs and cushions created ambience. Poppy coerced Officer Feeney into doing this work, commenting shamelessly on how strong he was as she stood back and directed. The weather was cooperating—an unseasonably warm fall day, not warm enough to swim, but warm enough to remember how good it felt. Satisfied with the house inside and out, Poppy gave it her finishing touch by lighting cinnamon candles throughout.

"The weather's almost too nice," she said to Amy, fussing with the flowers in a vase on the dining room table where Amy had displayed packets giving potential buyers information on room sizes and taxes. "I hope this isn't a total waste of time."

The first visitors were neighbors, most of who confessed to being just curious, but still took plenty of time meandering through the house. Amy asked every visitor to sign a visitors' log, but some people were reluctant to do so. They didn't want to be hectored by real estate agents and Amy certainly couldn't tell them that she was trying to keep track of potential suspects.

The first hour passed and Amy started to relax. There were no strange people, nothing out of the ordinary. She described the features of the home to older couples, young families, a single woman and a father house-hunting for his son. She pointed out exceptional features, suggested different uses of the five bedrooms depending on the audience, and trooped up and down stairs and in and out doors until her feet hurt.

She checked her cell phone when there was a lull, sitting down at the kitchen table and kicking off her shoes. She'd already checked for messages twice, but there could be a call from the hospital. That was her justification and not that she was looking for a message from Ryan. He hadn't called, but it was possible he'd left a message on her home machine. She let her other messages play while thinking about him.

She wanted to believe he'd called because she didn't want to believe that he might be regretting what happened. Perhaps he was afraid that he'd saddled himself with a mother and her kid and she didn't want him to think that. She'd had sex without any expectation beyond that of satisfying a primal need to be held and loved.

Sudden footsteps on the stairs startled her. An older, bearded man in a full-length wool coat stepped into the kitchen and stopped short, blinking at Amy through small tortoiseshell glasses.

"Excuse me," he said in a gruff voice. "I didn't mean to disturb you."

"No, that is, you didn't," Amy said, slipping back into her heels and pocketing her phone. "I didn't realize anyone was still here. Have you seen the kitchen?"

He nodded. "The other woman told me there was a door through here to the garage?"

Amy showed him to it. "Would you like me to show you the rest of the property?"

"That isn't necessary. I'll just look around."

"Of course."

As soon as he'd exited, her cell phone rang. Detective Juarez sounded breathless. "They've spotted a strange car near your house and I'm heading over there. Don't be concerned, it's probably nothing, but we've got to check it out. Officer Feeney will remain outside."

She looked out a front window on her way upstairs and could see Officer Feeney sitting in his car. He looked like he was eating something.

She could hear a couple in the master bedroom and knew they'd been fooling around on the bed by the sudden scrambling noise and red faces as she walked in.

"Can I answer any questions?"

"Does any of the furniture come with the place?" the man asked with apparent casualness but his eyes strayed to the bed.

When they'd headed down to see the kitchen, Amy lingered, looking out the window and seeing the older man walking along the side of the pool. He looked as if he might topple in.

In all, close to fifty people came through the home, which was almost an unheard of number, according to Poppy. "If you're lucky that young couple I was talking to will make an offer. He's an investment banker and she's a broker. I'm sure their financing will be a snap."

Late-afternoon sun streaked the dining room with light while they gathered the materials. "If you'll get the lights and windows upstairs," Poppy said, "I'll shut up the pool and the garage and then I've got to get going. Jack's made reservations for us at Shade Blue."

Amy didn't know where she and Emma would be eating. Probably a rest stop McDonald's.

The Harrigans weren't returning until Monday, so the home had to be completely secured. Amy checked the windows in every room on the first floor and drew the blinds. The light was fading fast and the streetlights had switched on. She was a little annoyed that Feeney hadn't made it back in the house yet to check things. She'd called him five minutes ago. At least he was out there; she could just see his form in the car.

"Wait. Let's not take him yet. We've got to wait until he approaches the house."

Juarez spoke tersely into the mike and got a grunt of acknowledgement from Detective Dickson in the other unmarked. The dingy white car circled the block again, cruising slowly past Amy's house. This time Juarez caught a glimpse of a white man wearing a knit hat behind the wheel.

He could feel the adrenaline coursing through him, giving him power. This was what he liked about police work, the hunt, the chase, the moment when all the hours of boring work paid off.

The white car circled for the fifth time and this time it idled near Amy's house. They could see the guy looking up at the porch and then around him. Juarez slid farther down in his seat. The motor stopped and the door opened. A lanky white guy stepped out wearing dark blue jeans, worn white at the knees and the seat, and a brown corduroy jacket patched at the elbows. A blue knit hat was pulled low on his head.

"Let's see what he does," Juarez said into the mike, and then crooned, "C'mon, man, head for the house. You know you want to."

Instead the man ducked back into the car, but he emerged just as suddenly holding something wrapped in cellophane. A bouquet of flowers.

* * *

Poppy headed out the back door as fast as she could in her Manolo Blahniks. She loved these shoes and the way they made her legs look and Jack certainly responded to them, but they were a bitch on cement.

She groaned when she saw the lounge chairs. They had to go back in the pool house. Well, she wasn't hauling these herself. Young officer pizza face could help—he certainly hadn't done much else. So much for tax dollars at work.

Of course she'd have to traipse down the driveway to get to him. That would just make her later. Sighing, Poppy headed for the chairs.

The door to the pool house had been left ajar. All the better. She began dragging one of the lounge chairs toward the open door. It was loud and very heavy. She looked toward the house, hoping Amy would see her and come out to help, but no such luck.

Chair number one got stowed in the space specially created for all the pool junk the family had acquired. Then she had to work on chair number two. She was securing it in the locker designed for them when she heard footsteps in the doorway.

"Nice timing," she said, irritably without turning around.

Amy hurried up the wide carpeted steps to the second floor, trying to quell the sense of fear that came from being in the house alone. The Harrigans' faces smiled out at her from photos hanging on the walls and she hurried past them, checking the windows in two of the children's bedrooms before heading into the bathroom next door.

A candle flickered in the darkness, catching the face of a clown-shaped soap dispenser and throwing its shadow high against the brightly painted wall. Amy blew it out and hurried out of the darkness into the next room. She glanced out the window at the pool as she passed through the master bedroom and was surprised to see that it was still uncovered. Wind was rippling the water and a few leaves had blown across the surface. Poppy must have forgotten it.

She checked that the windows were locked and drew the curtains and did the same in two more bedrooms before hurrying down the back stairs to the first floor and the kitchen.

Her heels clicked on the tiled floor, echoing in the vast room. The stainless-steel appliances mirrored a blurred reflection of her as she checked to make sure things were off and the windows were locked. She walked through the mudroom to the back door that opened out to the portico and the pool.

The minute she got the door open she could hear banging. The door to the pool house was open and slamming into the wall behind it as a strong wind blew against it. Focused on the door and irritated that it had been left open, it wasn't until Amy was almost level with the pool that she noticed the dark form floating in the center.

Poppy's body was nailed to a board and floating faceup.

"It's him!" Dickson's voice hissed over the mike. "He's got the flowers! Let's nail him."

"Wait!" Juarez commanded. "Let's see what he does. Just wait."

The guy avoided the walkway at the front of the house, coming in from the side, climbing up the small hill quickly, his sneakers slipping in the leaf-covered lawn. He passed the swing set and disappeared from view around the back of the house.

"Now!" Juarez shouted. He dropped the mike and sprinted from the car, hand reaching for his piece. He saw Dickson and Black coming from the other side and they converged on the house, pieces drawn.

"Freeze, motherfucker!" Juarez shouted so loud that the guy actually dropped the flowers.

"Hey, man, no problem," the man said, holding his hands up without being asked, his head whipping back and forth from Juarez to Black and Dickson. Black slammed him hard against the side of the house, smashing his face up against the frame and the guy cried out and blood spilled from his mouth in a thin stream.

"What were you doing with the flowers?" Juarez demanded, holstering his piece as Dickson expertly cuffed the man and pulled him around to face them.

"Nothing. J-just delivering them." He was young and he didn't look familiar. His eyes were a watery blue. Vacant. He reeked of pot.

"What's your name?" Juarez demanded, patting him down, searching his pockets for a wallet that he extracted as the guy answered.

"Brian. Brian Keesey."

There was no Brian Keesey on their list of suspects. Amy had never mentioned a Brian. Something wasn't right. He looked in Brian's wallet. Up-to-date license. Same guy, same name. A community college ID. Fifty bucks. A red foil-wrapped condom that had probably been in there since the first Clinton administration.

"How do you know Amy Moran?"

"Who?"

"Amy Moran," Black shouted. "This is her house, you moron."

"I don't know who she is."

"So why are you delivering"—Juarez looked at the bundle on the ground and noticed the hard, black buds wrapped in black tissue paper—"dead flowers to her."

"Some guy paid me to."

"Who? Who paid you to deliver them?"

"I don't know. Some guy."

"You didn't get his name?"

"He didn't tell me. I didn't ask. He said he'd give me fifty bucks if I took these flowers to a woman's house and left them by the back door."

"And you didn't think there was anything strange about that?" Black demanded, shoving the guy's shoulder against the wall.

"Ow!" The guy shrank from him. "It wasn't like it was drugs, man. They were just flowers. I figured it was for an ex. I asked him that and he said the woman had screwed with him."

"What did he look like?" Juarez demanded.

"I don't know. Just an average guy."

"White? Black?"

"White."

"Hair color?"

"Dark brown. Curly."

"Eyes?"

"He wore glasses."

"Build?"

Brian shrugged again. "I don't know. Average. Maybe a little big in the shoulders."

His description wasn't great, but Juarez thought he'd do better with a police artist. When he said as much, Brian protested.

"No way, man, I don't want to be involved."

"You're already involved, ass wipe," Black said. "The minute you took that fifty bucks you got involved."

"I didn't do anything wrong."

"Listen, Brian, this guy you took the money from probably killed two women. So you're going to do exactly as you're told or I'm going to charge you with possession for the nickel bag you've got stowed in your car."

Juarez could have laughed at Brian's mouth hanging open

like a fish, but something was niggling him. That feeling again, the instinct that something wasn't right.

"Have you done this before?" he said.

"No. Never." Brian shook his head repeatedly, as if that made his denial more sincere. Black obviously didn't believe him, taking the opportunity to give him another shove against the wall. Juarez knew it was the truth. Why? Why had the killer given this job to this kid?

It hit him at that same moment that the radios in both cars started bleeping like mad.

"Fuck! We've been played!" He bolted for his car, leaving Black shouting behind him.

The key almost snapped in the ignition and the transmission protested as he jackknifed in the road and floored the accelerator in the opposite direction. The voice of the dispatcher, "We've got a homicide reported at 225 Oakhurst Lane. All available cars report immediately."

That it was Poppy there was no doubt. The same hot pink suit, the same blond hair, though it was plastered to her face in long wet strands. Her shoes were still on her feet, though the heel of one had snapped right off. Her eyes were gone, pools of blood in their place. The three-carat diamond wedding set she'd sported on her left hand was missing, as was the finger. She'd been nailed to a surfboard, her arms positioned above her head, her legs crossed at the ankles, the fiberglass shattered in spots.

Amy stumbled backward, falling on the cement and scraping her knee before rising and running. She moved with self-preservation. She couldn't go back to the house; she couldn't go in the garage. She pushed her way through the manicured hedges that bordered the portico and tore through the flowerbeds beyond it, heading down the front lawn toward the unmarked police car. She could see Feeney sitting there, but she couldn't make her voice loud enough to alert him. She pounded on the car as she came abreast, but he didn't move. He'd fallen asleep over his newspaper. She ran to the driver's side and yanked open the door.

"He's here!" she shouted, shaking Officer Feeney by the shoulder. He slumped to the side and that's when she saw the blood spilling in a wide arc from his throat.

Chapter 33

Blood was hard to get rid of it, which was why Guy generally preferred swift, sweet measures, but it was satisfying. Like finger painting. He'd longed to leave a message in blood—a little Hitchcock edge—but he hadn't had the time.

As it was, he'd gotten a little spatter on his heavy cotton shirt and that had to go into the incinerator. Pity. He'd liked that shirt.

He was sitting on the couch with his right arm encased in a warm bath of Epsom salts that he'd rigged up in a large crystal bowl. All that nailing at one time had just about done him in. Thank God it was fairly quiet. He'd thought the surfboard might not work, the fiberglass split so easily, but he'd managed it. It was a much nicer touch than leaving her floating in the pool. Besides, her body fat count was so low she probably would have sunk like a stone.

He took another sip of his vodka tonic and thought again of the look on that woman's face when she'd seen him in the pool house. Sometimes he wished he had a partner so that he could capture that image on film! What he wouldn't give for a wall of those photos. That wasn't a good idea, though.

Those sorts of partnerships always soured. It was a good way to get caught and it was always the other guy who sold you down the river.

He clicked through the numerous cable stations until he found a nice serial killer drama. They were fun to laugh at usually. Either the killers were bumbling fools or the detectives or both. Tonight he couldn't get into it. He was feeling restless.

He'd had this feeling before. He knew what it was. He was getting tired of the game. It was time to wrap this up. He was angry, too. Angry that Amy didn't understand what he was trying to do.

He crunched his way through the ice cubes in the glass and then slowly got up, careful to keep his right arm immobile, and carried the glass back into the kitchen.

Violet stared at him from the refrigerator. She was naked in the picture. She'd agreed to that. Stretching on the faux mink blanket because he told her that Marilyn Monroe had done something similar, and you could say this about Vi, she wanted to be a star.

He selected a knife from the butcher block with his left hand and fiddled with the photo, thinking of Amy and her betrayal. He'd been a fool to believe in her. He could see that now. She'd never been Violet, not really. She was a whore, just like the rest of them. They were all whores. Stupid bitches in heat. Not worthy of a decent man. Not worthy of living.

He flicked the knife back and forth as he thought about what he would do to Amy. Little pieces of the photo dropped to the floor.

After a few minutes he stepped back and surveyed his work. Now Violet was missing her left breast as well as her right. He couldn't shove something up her cunt, so he'd taken it right out. A neat little square, removing the center of her whoredom.

Soon he would remove the new whore. The imposter. That's how he thought of Amy. She had to be punished for that. She had to be taught her place. He would bring her to see it before he released her soul. He would help her acknowledge her sinful nature, her whore self. She would be absolved.

Chapter 34

The coroner made two trips to Oakhurst Lane. Officer Feeney's body was carried out first, because there were fewer photographs needed and because he was one of their own. By the time they'd made it back to the station, the whole town knew there'd been two more murders committed because reporters had joined the crowd that gathered beyond the crime scene tape at the Harrigans' house.

The chief personally visited Mrs. Feeney, the officer's sixty-two-year-old mother, who doted on the son who'd still lived with her. Unfortunately, nobody realized that Mrs. Feeney loathed her son's fiancé, so no one thought to tell her. She showed up at the department, plump face puffy from hours of crying, nails bitten to the quick from worrying because she hadn't heard from him.

She'd been hysterical when they told her. They had to call an ambulance to have her taken to the hospital in shock.

Juarez drove straight from the station to the bar. He shook his head at the draft that the bartender offered him and ordered a shot of Jack Daniel's instead. It went down smooth, so he ordered another.

A hand came forward and anchored it to the bar just as he was about to lift it to his lips.

"Mark, son, good to see you."

Father Michael was on the stool next to him. Mark didn't know when he'd landed there, but he did know he wasn't in any mood to talk to the priest or anybody else.

"I heard you had a rough day," the priest said. "Rough day for the whole force."

"Rough day for Feeney." Mark tried to pull up the glass, but Father Michael's grip on it remained the same. The priest was surprisingly strong.

"Rough day for everyone who worked with him," he said. "This isn't going to help make it better."

"No offense, Father, but that isn't any of your business."

"I've known you how long, Mark?"

He shrugged. "I don't know. Fifteen years?"

"In fifteen years when have I ever told you how to run your life?"

"Never."

"Exactly. Never. Not once. Not when you stopped going to Mass. Not when you moved to the city. Not even when you came back to Steerforth and began drinking."

"What's your point?"

"My point is that since I've made it a point not to interfere in your business, you could do me the courtesy of listening the one and only time that I do."

Mark started to say something but the implacable look on the elderly priest's face stopped him.

"You're hurting," Father Michael said. "I can see that. Your parents can see that. But you won't let anyone in. You're trying to bury the pain and it just won't work, son."

"You've been talking to my parents?"

"Your mother still attends Mass regularly. She's concerned about you."

"She doesn't have to be. I'm fine."

"But she is. And you and I both know that you're far from fine."

The shot had mysteriously vanished to be replaced by seltzer. Mark cast the bartender a dark look, but the man was oblivious, drying glasses down at the other end of the bar.

"Look, I know you mean well, Father, but—"

"It's not your fault that Officer Feeney got hurt."

"He was a rookie. I shouldn't have left him there. The bastard played us. He set it up, but I shouldn't have let it happen. I should have known."

"You had no way of knowing. Just as you had no way of knowing what would happen with that other young man."

Juarez glared at him. "What do you know about that?"

The priest held out his hands. "Little to nothing. Because that's how much you've shared with the people who love you. But we're not blind. We read the papers."

"Yeah, well, maybe I don't want to talk about it. Maybe I don't want to think about how I've fucked up."

"You can't hide from your mistakes because they're part of who you are."

"Shit, Father, why don't you get your own show? You could be the Vatican's answer to Dr. Phil."

The priest didn't respond, but he dug in his pocket.

"No, Father, let me," Mark said, patting his arm. "I'll gladly pick up the tab if you'll leave me in peace. What's that you're drinking?"

"Cranberry juice," Father Michael said. He pulled something out of his pocket and dropped it with a clink in front of Juarez. It was a small metal disk with a numeral 10 on it.

"What's this?" Mark picked it up and tossed it in his hand.

"Ten years of hard work. Ten years of being honest about who I am and what I am. Ten years of accepting the mistakes I've made and struggling not to make the same ones again."

Mark stared at the disk and handed it back to him. "Alcoholics Anonymous?"

"Yep."

"I wouldn't have pegged you for an alcoholic, Father."

"I wouldn't have pegged you for one, either."

Mark winced. He stared at the seltzer and took a sip, wincing again at the taste.

"At one time I hid from myself in a bottle, too," Father Michael said. "But you can't hide from God."

"I'm not sure there is a God," Mark muttered, feeling sure his mother would have slapped him for that pronouncement.

"That's okay. He's sure about you."

"Yeah," Mark said. "And how do you know that, Father? You think you know me? You don't know anything about me!" He slammed the glass of seltzer down and water splashed across the bar.

The bartender paused, looking over at them. Father Michael simply stared at Mark. He sighed and put his head in his hands.

"Look, Father, I'm sorry, but this isn't a good time."

He felt the priest's hand on his arm and then Father Michael spoke in a low, hard voice. "Thirty-five years ago I tried to hide who I was because I didn't like that person and thought that God must not like him either."

There was a pause and Mark raised his head and looked at Father Michael. The priest's eyes were glassy and he coughed, once, before continuing. "Don't make the same mistake I did. Don't run away from the truth."

It was dark when Mark left the bar, the night air crisp in that particular way that happens only in autumn, and he remembered the smell of bonfires and apple cider and the warm feeling he'd had seeing his mother cutting his father a slice of pumpkin pie at the end of a long shift.

He didn't know he was driving to Manhattan, not consciously, until he hit the outskirts of the city. Even then, he didn't acknowledge where he was going or why, just driving and thinking, remembering Feeney with his stupid grin and his raw excitement over being a cop and the way that Tyson had laughed when he told a joke and the way his father had looked at the end of a shift, coming into the house in that uniform and hanging his cap on a hook by the kitchen door.

The smells in the city were different in the fall. The hot, smoky scent of chestnut stands and ash can fires. The wafts of Italian and Chinese and Syrian and Mexican and Ethiopian cuisines spilling out from restaurants as steam-covered doors swung open for diners. The advertisements for the Thanksgiving Day parade.

He drove into the bowels of the city, into the places where people had triple locks on their doors and mean dogs. He didn't acknowledge where he was going until he arrived in front of the building and then he pulled across the street from it and parked.

At first all he could do was sit there and stare up at the building, his mind reliving that night. Then he heard kids gathering around the car and someone hit the window with something and a voice yelled, "Hey, spic! What you doing?"

So he stepped out of the car and he flashed his badge and they scattered. It was the sort of neighborhood where everyone feared the police.

The only thing that held Amy together was the need to get Emma. Staying focused on Emma helped her manage the fear. She was so frightened that if she gave into it she would huddle on the ground in a fetal position and never get up.

She'd been foolhardy to think that she could brave this, that she was being strong by not fleeing in the face of a killer. She thought she'd been tough enough to outwit him, but he'd just been toying with her. He'd killed Poppy to toy with her.

She kept seeing Poppy's body in the pool and she didn't

want to see it, or the line of blood appearing around Officer Feeney's neck when his head lolled.

She accepted the police escort to the hospital, but she wouldn't let them drive her. Emma didn't need that additional stress and holding on to what Emma needed was the only thing holding Amy together.

Emma was waiting to go. There was color in her face and a small bandage covered the spot where the IV had been.

"Mommy!" She threw herself at her mother, landing hard against Amy's shins and knees, wrapping her small arms tightly around her mother's waist. Amy swung her up into her arms and held her tight until Emma started to squirm.

"Are we going home, Mommy?" Emma said as Amy signed the papers at the nurses' desk. "Are we, Mommy?"

"How would you like to go on a trip?" Amy said. She clutched Emma's hand tightly and led her out to the car. As they pulled out of the lot, the patrol car fell in behind them.

Juarez entered the apartment building easily. The lock was broken and the foyer was littered with empty soda bottles and cigarette butts. He didn't remember this trash, but he remembered the stairs. He mounted them slowly, hearing Tyson's complaining and static from their radios, feeling the cold metal of the gun butt under his right hand, smelling the grease from years of poorly ventilated cooking.

Five flights up. Tyson's cursing echoed in his ears. *"Probably some faggots!"* He took the steps slowly but in his mind they were racing up them again. Then he was in the hallway and the light was dim, a single bulb hanging in the middle. He stared at the linoleum floor, searching it as he walked without realizing that he was looking for blood. He stopped outside 513.

The whispered voices, Tyson grinning over his shoulder.

The door swings open and there's that unmistakable pop, Mark swears he hears that pop, and Tyson clutches his chest and drops, all in one motion. Mark shouts his name and then the figure in the doorway swings his way, arm rising in his direction, something dark in the hand and it's automatic response time. Mark fires his own gun once, single, accurate hit, and the figure falls back, landing against Tyson.

Everything moves into triple speed. There's screaming from the open doorway. A man moves toward the figure on the floor and Mark shouts at him to get down, get the fuck down, asshole, and put your hands where I can see them!

And the man's shouting, "Why did you shoot him? Why did you shoot him?"

Mark gets him cuffed and then he's checking the boy, for he can see now that he's a boy, late teens or early twenties at most, and he's reaching for the boy's gun, but there isn't a gun. There's only a cell phone in the kid's hand and there's blood everywhere: on the boy, on Tyson, pouring onto the cracked and dusty linoleum. He radios for back up, for an ambulance, and he's pressing his hands against the wound in the boy's side, trying to slow down that blood. The boy's skinny and he's wearing a thin shirt that won't staunch the blood and Mark knows that it's too much blood and where the fuck is the ambulance?

Tyson's not breathing and he's got to do CPR on him fast, and he takes the boy's hands and places them over the wound. "Hold on, okay, kid? Ambulance is coming, just keep your hands there!"

He's performing the second round of CPR on Tyson and he can hear the whine of sirens when he sees the life fading from the kid's eyes like a dimmer switch being turned down.

Mark slid down the wall opposite the door, feeling again the blood on the boy's side, the boy's hands cold and trembling in his. He could see the fear in the boy's eyes and hear the man moaning, "Why did you shoot him? Why did you shoot him?"

There'd been an investigation and he'd had to turn over his weapon for a while, but he'd been lucky. Luckier than Tyson, who recovered from the massive heart attack that had felled him at the apartment door, but who had to retire. Luckier than the boy, who was a prostitute and who lay in the morgue for two weeks without any family coming to claim him. A throwaway kid, one of hundreds, maybe even thousands, rejected by their families for numerous reasons: The way they looked, the way they acted, who they chose to love.

He was sorry. He was so sorry. He wanted to take back that moment of firing. He wanted a rewind button, he wanted to spin back to the moment they got the call and tell Tyson they weren't going to respond.

He heard shuffling footsteps. The door to number 513 slowly opened. "What you want? You okay?"

A small Chinese woman was looking down at him, clutching the door to her like she was afraid he was going to attack her. He shook his head, trying to speak, to explain that he was sorry, that he didn't mean to shoot anybody.

The door closed and he heard the pop in his head again and watched Tyson fall to the floor. The pop had been a car backfiring. The heart attack felled Tyson microseconds after the pop. The boy held his cell phone out like a weapon. A tragic combination of events.

The door swung open again and the woman thrust a box of tissues out. "Here."

Mark touched his face and realized for the first time that he was crying.

At the house the uniformed officers combed the house and the yard before letting Amy and Emma out of the car.

"We'll be here all night, ma'am," one of the officers said to her. Emma's fingers slipped into her mouth and she stared wide-eyed at them.

"It's okay, baby," Amy murmured, reassuring herself as much as she was hoping to reassure her daughter.

"I'm not a baby," Emma protested.

"No, you're not, are you? You're a big girl." She stopped Emma from running ahead. "Walk with Mommy, big girl."

She looked up at the house, the place she'd worked so hard to make a home, and she felt nothing but fear. The cops were leaning against the patrol car a short distance away. One of them was smoking a cigarette and they were talking quietly.

This killer. This great, amorphous creature—that's how she thought of him—had managed to get into the house that the cops had searched. He'd killed Poppy, he'd killed Officer Feeney.

She couldn't stay. It had made sense at one point, but it didn't anymore. She didn't want to leave, to leave was to concede defeat, but it was also to save their lives.

"What do you want for dinner, sweetie?"

"I dunno." Emma dragged her coat along the ground, humming a little song.

"Pick up your coat, Em."

"Can we have ice cream?"

"Maybe for dessert. Not for dinner."

"Why?"

Her hands fumbled with the doorknob. She knew the police had just been inside, but still she opened hesitantly, half expecting someone to jump out at her. She felt like the Jamie Lee Curtis character in *Halloween*.

"Why, Mommy?"

"Why what?"

"Why can't we have ice cream for dinner."

"Because it's not a dinner food, it's a dessert food."

"Why?"

"Get your suitcase out of the closet, Em."

She saw Emma's hand reaching for the closet door and suddenly called, "No! I'll do it."

Emma jumped. "I can do it."

"I know you can, but Mommy's going to do it. You can get your crayons packed, okay?"

They would have checked the closet, right? She had to steel herself to turn the knob. A mental count of three and then she did a fast twist and pull, jumping back as she did so and—nothing. The closet was empty. The metal hangers pinged quietly against one another.

Amy let out her breath and grabbed Emma's suitcase and her own.

"Mommy, did you make these pictures?"

"Hmm?" She closed the closet door and turned to see Emma holding up photographs.

"What are those, Em?"

The little hands were clutching the photos, Emma's eyes very wide. Amy knew then. She knew as the small hands turned them slowly around. She knew before she saw her naked body lying on her bed. She snatched the photos from Emma's hand.

"Where did you get these?" she cried, her voice loud and scary. Emma shrank from her, but she couldn't help repeating it. "Where, Emma?"

"Here!" her daughter shrieked, pointing at the coffee table. A manila envelope sat alone at its center with a single word scrawled across the cover in red: WHORE.

Mark mopped at his face with the Kleenex, taking deep breaths to calm down.

It wasn't your fault. He heard Father Michael's voice in his head. *Sometimes things happen and there is no reason for them. There are tragic accidents. It's part of the mystery of life.*

He touched his hand to the floor. He thought of the boy's eyes dimming and he sobbed some more and prayed for the boy and for Tyson and for the man who'd used the boy. And then he prayed for himself. When he was done, he stood up and knocked on the door and handed over the tissues with a thank you and a twenty-dollar bill. The woman took the tissues, but pushed back the money.

"You go now," she said, eyeing him suspiciously. "You go home."

He took the five flights faster on the way out. Each level down seemed to lighten something inside him.

You go home. He was in the car and driving in a few minutes. Someone had stolen his hubcaps while he'd been inside, but at least the stereo was intact. He swiped at his eyes and started the car. *You go home.* He turned the car up 14th Street. The streets got cleaner in the West Village, the houses nicer. Working streetlamps. Less graffiti. Painted trim on old brownstones and lights above the front doors. It had been a fall day when he'd first come down here. Taking a break from the mean streets on his day off.

He found a parking spot next to a hydrant and put his light on the roof. He was only a few feet from the apartment. *You go home.*

There were six steps up to the front door. The light above the door cast a glow on the stoop. The bell was a series of chimes. He listened to it ring and suddenly realized that he looked like shit. He brushed at the dust on his pants and ran his hands through his hair. There was movement at the door and he knew he'd been spotted. He held his breath, feeling faint for a moment, and then the door swung open.

A slender man stood in the doorway wearing blue jeans and a T-shirt, his feet bare. His eyes were large and brown.

His hair was honey-colored and it needed to be cut. He brushed it impatiently out of his eyes. He was shivering.

"Ash." Mark's voice croaked on the name. It was the first time in months that he'd said it out loud. "I'm sorry."

He couldn't stop the tears that fell from his eyes and then the other man lifted one slender hand and brushed at his cheek.

"Welcome home."

Chapter 35

Amy dropped the photos back onto the table as if they burned.

"What's wrong, Mommy?"

"Nothing, baby. Nothing's wrong."

"I'm not a baby, Mom, remember?" Emma said with the exasperation of a five-year-old.

"You're right, sweetie, you're not a baby." Amy knelt next to her daughter. "You're a big girl now and I need your help. I need you to pack your pink suitcase, Em. Do you think you can do that?"

"Where are we going?"

"We're going to Nana's house."

"We are?" Emma sounded delighted. "Right now?"

"Yes, right now. We need to go really fast. So you pack all your stuffed animals. I'll get your clothes."

"Even my big unicorn?"

The largest of her stuffed animals, the giant unicorn that her father had indulged her with, the toy that Amy wouldn't let her take on trips because it was too large.

"Yep. Even your big unicorn."

Amy whipped clothes from her dresser, shoving them into her own suitcase. She grabbed clothes from the closet and added them with their hangers still on. Her hands shook as she yanked open the desk drawers in her office and removed all their important documents: Emma's birth certificate, her birth certificate, their Social Security numbers. She grabbed her two best cameras, the extra telephoto lens, and then she took the photo of Emma as a newborn off her wall and added it as well.

The cops were surprised when they stepped outside, each of them pulling a bag behind them, Amy tightly gripping Emma's free hand.

"Ma'am, you don't have to leave. We'll be watching the house all night," one of the officers said. He was a tall man with graying hair and gray-blue eyes. He looked like someone's grandfather, but Amy didn't trust him. She didn't trust anyone.

"He's been here," she said. "There's a manila envelope with some photos on the coffee table. It's from him. I don't know how he put them there, I don't know how he got in, but they're from him. It needs to go to Detective Juarez. He'll understand." She loaded the bags and Emma into the car.

"Detective Juarez requested round-the-clock protection for you," the other officer said. "You'll be safe here."

Amy shook her head. "No, we won't. It's not safe to stay. I wanted to stay. I really, really wanted to make it work—" She stopped, choked up. "We're going," she said after a minute. "I'll call Detective Juarez tomorrow to explain."

Emma hummed a little song in the backseat and Amy watched the house receding in the rearview mirror feeling as if she was watching her dreams for an independent life slipping away. She blinked back tears and locked the car doors before pressing her foot harder on the accelerator. It was only an hour-and-a-half drive to her mother's house. If they made good time she could be there before midnight.

*   *   *

Morning and consciousness came together. Mark didn't know where he was for a moment and then he recognized the midnight blue comforter and saw the Pride flag hanging on the wall and he knew.

He rolled over and saw Ash asleep next to him, curled up like always, one hand softly cupped near his face. Mark stroked the soft, fine hair, running strands between his fingers, and Ash's eyes opened and he smiled at him.

"Hey."

"Hey yourself."

Ash let him continue stroking, saying nothing and just looking at him. The room was the same as when Mark had last been here, more than six months before. The large, carved four-poster that Ash inherited from an aunt, the shelves filled with books, the numerous pictures on the wall of Ash and his family and friends. The Pride flag from some long-ago parade. The empty cast from a teenage skiing accident. The program signed by Placido Domingo. The Yankees pennant that had hung over his bed as a child.

Mark saw that the photos had been carefully rearranged to cover the hole left by the removal of one. Soon after they met a friend of Ash's took their picture at a party. The two of them, side by side, arms loosely wrapped around each other's waists. Ash beamed at the camera, leaning back slightly against Mark's shoulder while Mark sat very straight with a more reserved smile.

Ash had hung it in the center, the place of honor on his wall, and it was gone.

"I still have it," he said, seeing Mark's gaze. "When you first left, I used to study it."

Mark waited, not saying anything, his stomach hurting because he wanted to ask why but was afraid of the answer.

"I couldn't understand why you'd left. We were happy. We were going to share this place. I couldn't understand what went wrong. But then I looked at the picture and I saw it in your face. In your eyes. You didn't want that picture or this life with me. I was your secret—that was all."

Mark kept stroking his hair, letting him talk, feeling the pain of that separation spilling from both of them.

"I'm sorry," he said at last. "I was afraid. I'd barely come out to myself. When you said 'move in together,' it was just too much. I wanted it, but I couldn't handle it."

"And now you can?"

There was a bitter note in his voice. Mark didn't blame him. "Yes."

"Why? What's changed?"

He wanted to say "everything." He was not the same person he'd been six months ago. Going home had changed him. The case had changed him. Trying to hide who he was had changed him.

"I miss you," he said instead. "I've missed you every day that I've been gone. I need you. I need us. I'm tired of hiding this part of my life."

Ash didn't say anything, but he sat up in bed and reached for the T-shirt that had been left in a ball on the floor last night. He pulled it on and stepped over to a large plush armchair to get his jeans.

Dressed, he crossed his arms across his chest and looked at Mark. "What about your family?"

"What about them?"

"Have you told them?"

"No."

Ash sighed and headed out of the room. Mark scrambled out of bed and went after him, leaving his own clothes behind. Ash was in the small kitchen making coffee, slamming open the fridge to get the beans, grinding them with a set look to his face, pouring them in the expensive Italian coffee machine that he'd bought at an overpriced cooking store around the corner.

They'd argued about it, but in a teasing, happy way, conscious that they were sounding like an established couple to argue about a purchase. Mark had told him that he could have gotten a better deal somewhere else, Ash arguing that the best coffee comes from the best preparation.

"Can I have a cup, too?" Mark asked. He was shivering in nothing but his boxer shorts. Ash snarled something unintelligible in response, but he got another mug out of the cupboard.

"I'm going to tell them," Mark said. "I just haven't yet."

"I've heard that before."

"Well, I was lying before—to myself as well as to you."

Ash watched the coffee brewing with his back to Mark. "Why should I believe you this time?" he said. He sounded angry, but there was a plaintiveness in his voice that moved Mark to cross the room to him. Ash stiffened when he touched his back, but didn't pull away.

"I'm sorry," Mark said. He let his arm drop and wrap around the smaller man's waist and he pulled Ash back against his chest. The other man didn't resist him, but he was stiff in his arms.

"I will tell them," he said. "But I need to know what to say."

Ash pulled free and turned around, leaning against the counter with his arms crossed. "How about, 'I'm gay.' "

Mark smiled, relieved to be able to find some humor in this. His stomach unknotted a little. "Yeah, I'd planned on that. But I was talking about whether I could tell them about us."

There was a long silence except for the drip of the coffee maker. When it stopped, Ash poured two mugs and added cream to one. He handed it to Mark.

"Is there an us?" he said, looking from his mug into Mark's eyes.

"I want there to be," Mark said. "I don't want to be with anyone else."

"I slept with someone else," Ash said, aiming for casual but his voice climbed higher, betraying him. He gave Mark a wide berth and headed into the living room and the large, brown sofa, curling up on one end.

Mark followed, allowing the pain of that statement to hurt him the way he knew that Ash wanted it to. He sat down on the opposite end.

"And?"

"And what?"

"Are you with him?"

Ash laughed then, the light sound that Mark had missed. "You're so old-fashioned," he said. "No, I'm not with him. I'm not having his baby so we decided to forego the shotgun wedding."

"Okay, smartass. I meant are you still seeing him?"

Ash shook his head, still smiling. "It was just one night. I was missing you and he looked like you."

The pleasure this gave Mark was so immediate and so sweet that he felt for a moment like his heart might stop just from the feeling. They sipped their coffee for a few moments in silence. Ash gradually let his feet slide over until they were resting against Mark's side. It was something else they'd shared. He was always nudging Mark to rub his feet, trying to manipulate him into giving foot rubs, and being a general pain in the ass about it.

For a moment, Mark wished that he could go back and that nothing else had taken place. That he could choose again, to stay here, to stay within this apartment, within this love, and never have to have experienced all the pain of the last six months.

All at once he remembered something. "I slept with someone, too."

Ash gaped at him. "Really?"

"Yeah, really. You don't have to sound so shocked."

"I can't help it. I thought you were trying to go straight."

Mark didn't say anything, but he could feel his face turning red.

Ash started to laugh. "No!"

"Yes."

"Oh my God. Well, I guess I have to ask. Are you still with her?"

"Shut up."

But Ash had given in to a fit of giggles. "Is she carrying your love child?"

Mark picked up a velvet throw pillow and tossed it at him. Ash deflected it, laughing so hard he was snorting. "I can see the tabloid piece, 'My Gay Love-Child.'"

Mark pounced on him and wrestled him onto his back. "Shut. Up," he said, punctuating the words with kisses.

"Hmm . . . what will you give me?"

"This." And Mark kissed him once. "And this." And then over again.

Chapter 36

Say what you would about Dorothy Busby, and Amy had said plenty, her mother didn't bat an eyelash when she showed up at ten minutes to twelve carrying Emma in her arms. She just opened the door to her immaculate colonial home and stepped aside.

For the first day, Amy did little but sleep. She stayed in the guest room at the end of the hall on the second floor while Emma had her old room. She was dimly aware of the two of them laughing together when she woke sometime late that morning, but she barely had the strength to use the bathroom and drink some water before returning to the soft comfort of the queen-sized bed and falling back into a deep, but troubled sleep.

She woke for the second time late in the afternoon. Her mother seemed to realize that what she needed was nurturing, for she quietly offered her a dinner of soup and bread and didn't press her for any information beyond asking if she'd spoken to the police.

She spent the next morning reconnecting with her childhood home, examining the photos that lined the hallways

and revisiting the memories each of them held. Here she was
with her brother Michael at the beach. Here they were huddled together around a campfire. Here was a formal portrait
that her mother had insisted on the summer she turned
twelve and was pudgy with impending adolescence.

She wandered into her parents' bedroom and remembered the security of crawling between her parents when
she'd had a bad dream. Amy's father had been dead for more
than five years, but this was another room that Dorothy
Busby kept the same. His highboy still stood against one
wall with his gold cufflinks on the surface next to a photo of
a young Dorothy.

Amy fingered the cufflinks and lifted the lid of the old
cigar box next to them. There were no cigars left inside, just
the faint odor of tobacco lingered, but there was something.
A key.

Small, silver—not a house key, Amy decided. What then?
She searched his drawers and saw nothing that had a lock.
Then she looked high on the closet shelves and found a
metal box.

The key turned smoothly in its lock. Inside was a pale
blue hand towel folded into thirds. She drew back a corner
and recoiled from what lay inside. A shiny, charcoal gray
handgun.

She'd actually fired a handgun once. Long ago as part of
a personal safety class for high school girls that went a little
too far in most of the parents' opinions. It had been dropped
the following semester and so had the teacher, a heavyset
mannish woman who'd talked a lot about taking back the
world from men. She'd been the sort of woman her father
had disparagingly labeled "butch."

Amy never knew her father owned a gun. She ran a finger
lightly down the muzzle, wondering what her mother had
thought of this purchase.

It was strange that she hadn't thought of it before, but

until Sheila's murder, Amy lived in a world virtually insulated from crime. She'd heard about things, of course. The robbery over in Norwalk in which an elderly couple had been tied up and badly frightened. The stick-up at the convenience store. There had been rumors of the date rape of a senior when she was a freshman in high school and she remembered watching the girl in the hallways at the school and how everyone had whispered about her as if what had happened to her was shameful.

Had her father purchased this gun because he felt threatened in some way? She vaguely remembered some discussion about a hostile employee. Or was it just something he thought a man should have? She wouldn't be surprised to discover that her brother knew about it, but she hadn't been told.

She lifted it up, felt the power in the heft in her hand. Checked, just like she'd been taught all those years ago, and sure enough the safety was on, but she popped out the clip and saw that it was fully loaded.

Slow footsteps sounded on the stairs and Amy hurriedly tucked the towel back around the gun, locked the box and shoved it back in the closet. She'd just returned the key to the cigar box when her mother entered the bedroom, carrying a basket of laundry.

"Oh!" She put a hand to her chest and let the laundry basket drop with a plop. "What are you doing in here?"

"Just remembering Daddy."

Her mother smiled and came to the dresser Amy leaned against. She opened the top drawer. "Do you know that I still keep his handkerchiefs here," she said, lifting one of the snow white squares monogrammed with his initials. "I just couldn't bear to part with them. Silly."

"It's sweet."

"Why don't you go downstairs and settle in on the couch. I'll make you something to eat."

Emma was sitting at the kitchen table in her pajamas watching cartoons when her mother came down for breakfast, a bowl of some sugary, artificially colored cereal in front of her.

"Hmm . . . that looks nutritious," Amy said, kissing her daughter's cheek before heading for the coffeemaker.

"It won't hurt her," Dorothy Busby said. She was mixing something with her hands in a large ceramic bowl. Amy poured a mug of coffee and doctored it with skim milk and sugar, leaning against the granite countertop to watch her mother. Despite the early hour, the older woman was already neatly dressed in slacks and a light sweater, her short, iron-gray hair pulled back and fastened with a tortoiseshell barrette at the nape of her neck. Little pearl studs in her ears, matinee-length pearls around her neck and the faint scent of Chanel No. 5 completed her look.

A flowered apron covered her clothes and she'd carefully folded back the sleeves of her sweater to do her work. Her platinum wedding set was sitting in a small silver dish above the sink, the same spot where she always put them when she was working. It was the only time she ever had them off.

"What's that?" Amy said.

"Stuffing. Can you get me the whole chicken in the fridge?" Amy brought it to her. "What's the occasion?"

"Just a family dinner. I'm celebrating having my girls with me."

"Nana's taking me shopping," Emma announced.

"Go get dressed, then we'll decide what we're going to do."

"She's going to buy me a present!"

"We'll see." Amy waited until Emma ran upstairs before talking to her mother. "It's not a good idea. She just got out of the hospital. It's bad enough that she's playing with Riley. If she gets around all the scents in the stores, she could have another attack."

"Oh for heaven's sake, Amy. The dog's outside, poor thing, and all I'm talking about is a simple shopping trip."

"Let's stay here, okay. We could take Emma to the park."

Her mother seemed slightly mollified. "Do you have any other outfits for her? Those jeans are pretty worn at the knee."

"She likes it and that's the style, Mom. Besides, it's comfortable."

Dorothy sighed. "How is she going to learn to act like a lady if you won't teach her?"

Amy had a sudden vision of herself as a young girl, tearing down the hill on her bike, shrieking at the top of her lungs. "The whole neighborhood could hear you!" her mother had scolded when she came home. "That's not ladylike behavior."

"I don't want her to be a lady," she said to her mother. "I want her to be a little girl."

"You know what I mean, Amy."

"I know exactly what you mean, but some things are more important than others."

Dorothy didn't say more, but she turned her back on her daughter, cleaning the kitchen with short, sharp movements.

Amy left her there and did a nebulizer with Emma, watching her daughter sucking in the green air behind the mask, looking, as she always did with this treatment, so much more frail than she acted.

"I'm going shopping with Nana!" she announced as soon as Amy removed the mask.

"We'll go to the park today."

"I want to go shopping! Nana wants to buy me a present."

"Maybe another day. But today we're going to stay here."

"Why?"

"Because I said so." Because it's safe here, she felt like saying, but couldn't. She didn't want to scare Emma any more than she'd already been scared. It was great that her daughter seemed completely unaffected by what had been happening at home. It was as if she'd left all that stress behind in Steerforth.

Amy wished that was true for her, but coming here had just brought different stress. What was she going to do? She didn't know how to answer that yet, but she could endure Emma's cold shoulder while she figured it out. Let her daughter think that she'd spoiled her fun day with her grandmother. It was better than telling her the truth.

She watched Emma playing with the porcelain music box that Amy's father had given her when she was about her daughter's age. He'd brought it back from one of his conference trips, the hinged lid opening to reveal a tiny fairy, also made of porcelain, with a real tulle tutu and translucent wings. She held a tiny wand aloft and spun around and around while the tinny sound of "When You Wish Upon a Star" played over and over again.

Amy felt a sudden yearning to be a child again, to return to a time when she believed in the power of wishes.

"Make a wish, Mommy," Emma said, holding the box aloft.

Amy closed her eyes and wished to go back in time, to when things were easy. She remembered the moments early in her relationship with Chris, when she was nothing but excited that other women looked at him, thinking that they couldn't have him, that he was hers. She remembered sitting in the hospital bed with Chris sitting next to her, warm against her hip and day-old Emma in her arms, thinking that now her life was complete.

Before the asthma, before the cheating, before the world she thought she was building splintered then shattered.

Late in the afternoon they took their walk, three generations of Busby women, but not at the park as originally planned because Emma chose the beach instead.

Dorothy came out of the house buttoning a red barn coat

and locked the door. "There. We've got at least an hour before the chicken's done. As long as we make it back to the
house by then we should be fine."

It was a brisk fall day and the leaves were falling faster.
The maple trees that bordered the road along the beach were
in high color, a swath of rosy, orange-red splendor. The wind
came faster along the water, blowing across the small pebbles and coarse sand and muting the noise of the traffic a few
feet away.

Emma ran along the beach in front of them, pausing to
examine empty crab casings and mussel shells. Amy remembered doing this when she was a girl, running along with
Michael while their parents walked sedately behind them.

She remembered walking along this beach as an adult,
too, the week after her father died. The funeral had come and
gone along with the steady stream of visitors. The thank-you
notes for all the flowers and food had been written and Amy
remembered how they'd been waiting, a tidy stack of small
ivory cards bordered in black, on the table near the front
door.

Then, as now, Dorothy Busby had walked along in silence, hugging her jacket around her as if to contain the
grief. She'd seemed to slip so easily from one role to the
next, wife then widow, mother than grandmother. If these
transitions caused her angst she was careful not to show it.

Emma began picking up flat pebbles, trying to skim them
along the water's surface. Amy remembered the weekend
two years ago when Chris taught her to do that. She'd always
been astonished by the patience he could exhibit when he
chose, the way he'd repeatedly wrapped her small fingers
around each pebble, guiding her arm in the motion needed to
make the stone skip across the surface of the sound.

"Have you talked to Chris?" Dorothy said, as if she could
read Amy's mind.

"No."

"You should call him."

"No, Mom, I shouldn't."

Dorothy sighed, scanning the water, as if the words she looked for were hiding in its silver ripples. "It's time to stop this, Amy."

"Stop what?"

"This notion that you're going to support Emma and yourself and do it all alone. This is just foolishness. You need a man in your life—if all this killing hasn't taught you that I don't know what will."

"I'm earning good money now—"

"Oh, I'm not talking about finances," Dorothy interrupted. "You're a smart girl and I have no doubt that you could earn enough to survive with Emma. But why make that choice?"

"He's still cheating on me, Mom."

"You need to let that go."

"He didn't just do it once. He's done it over and over again. He's going to continue doing it."

"Haven't you ever heard of forgiveness? You don't want to hold onto these hurts, Amy, it's just hurting you."

"How many times am I suppose to forgive that? And how can I forgive someone who isn't really sorry?"

"He's said he's sorry, hasn't he?"

"He keeps doing it, Mom, how sorry could he be?"

Dorothy waved her hand as if brushing away a fly. "He's a man, Amy. To men, sex is like water."

The phrase was what did it. The same words, the same intonation. Fifteen years fell away and Amy remembered the moment when she'd learned the truth about her parents' marriage.

She and her friends were Christmas shopping at the mall when she spotted a man who looked like her father. Only it couldn't be her father because he had his arm around a woman with curling red hair that draped down the back of a long, fur coat. They had their backs to Amy, the man nuzzling the woman's neck as they stood at a jewelry counter.

Then the man turned and Amy saw that it wasn't just a similar-looking man in a camel's hair coat, it was her father. At the same minute, he saw her, too, and they stared at each other for what felt like an eternity. The smile slipped from her father's face. She turned away, running to catch up with her friends.

She remembered the noise of the mall, the tinny sound of Christmas carols and the greasy smells of the food court. She remembered the sour taste her Diet Coke left in her mouth, the way she smiled and laughed with her friends as if nothing was wrong, the way she took the bus home, struggling to hold back tears.

Deciding on the bus that she couldn't hurt her mother, she'd said nothing, using a headache as her excuse for going to bed early, beating her father's return home. She lay awake in bed until she heard his car pull in the drive and then she'd feigned sleep when she heard his footsteps on the stairs.

The door creaked open, she'd felt the light from the hall across her face, but she wouldn't open her eyes to see him standing in the doorway. After a moment he shut the door.

She waited until he left in the morning, which wasn't hard because he took the early train into Manhattan. When she came down for breakfast her mother fussed over her, but waited until Michael had gobbled up his meal and left before sitting across from her daughter.

"Daddy told me that he saw you at the mall yesterday," her mother began and Amy looked up at her, unable to hide her surprise.

"He said you seemed upset," Dorothy Busby continued. "I don't want you to be upset, Amy."

"Did he say *who* he was with?"

Her mother nodded. Took a sip of tea. "I know who he was with, Amy. That was Daddy's special friend."

"But she and Daddy, they were—"

Her mother held up a hand. "I don't want to talk about what she and Daddy were doing, Amy. That's not important. What's important is that you know that your daddy loves all of us very, very much and wouldn't want to hurt us."

"But, Mom, he was with another wo—"

"I know, Amy!" The words barked, shutting her up. It was the only time her mother expressed any emotion about it. "What Daddy does with his special friend doesn't matter because he still loves us."

"How can you say that?"

"Because it's true. You're not a little girl anymore. I know you've had sex ed. It's time you learned one of the fundamental differences between men and women. To men sex is like water."

And here Dorothy Busby was, fifteen years later, saying the same thing. She'd never let on that her husband's cheating bothered her. Appearances mattered. This was what Amy had been taught from an early age.

It was important to dress nicely when you went into the city. It was important to comb your hair even if you were sick with the flu. It was important that the neighbors not hear you shrieking even if you'd been stung by a bee. And it was important that you never, ever acknowledged your husband's infidelity.

Throughout the family's house were photos of her mother and father. The loving couple on their wedding day, smiling on an anniversary cruise, standing on the front lawn of the Episcopal church on Easter Sunday with their two children, all of them looking like they'd stepped out of a Talbots catalog.

Nowhere was there a picture of Dorothy Busby in her nightgown sitting at the kitchen table with a bottle of bourbon open in front of her, drinking alone because her husband was spending the night with someone else.

When she was eighteen, Amy rebelled. She went to school in Rhode Island and left her hometown far behind. She adopted black as her favorite color and took up photography in earnest, focusing on nudes because it shocked her mother.

She hadn't realized until this moment that while she'd put so much energy into ridding herself of the external markers of her parents' lives, she'd continued to carry around the same internal messages and had re-created, unwittingly, the exact same life with Chris.

"You didn't like it that Daddy cheated on you, Mom."

Dorothy Busby flinched. "I don't know why you're bringing that up. That has nothing to do with this."

"You didn't like it, but you pretended it was okay. You taught me that it was okay if my husband cheated. You taught me that I couldn't expect fidelity from a man. You and Daddy taught us that this was the model of marriage and look what it's done to me and to Michael."

"I don't know what you're talking about. Michael is perfectly happy in his marriage."

"He cheats on Bonnie!"

"Oh, Amy, I wish you wouldn't use that word."

"Why? Because it's the truth?"

"Because it's vulgar."

"Well, it's a pretty vulgar thing to do, to break your wedding vows and have sex with another person."

"Men and women have different needs."

"I don't believe that, Mom. I believe that some people are selfish and they lack self-control. I believe that Daddy played around because he wanted to."

"Your father was a good man."

"And because he knew you wouldn't do anything about it, no matter how much you hated it."

The slap came so fast and as such a surprise that Amy had no time to duck. Her cheek blazed with pain and she raised her own hand to it, staring at her mother with wonder.

"Don't you talk about your father that way," Dorothy said, two spots of color high on her own cheeks, her eyes hard and shiny. "He was a good husband and a good father. Did you ever want for anything? Who do you suppose paid for all your riding lessons and your art school and your trip to Europe your junior year?"

"He hurt you, Mom. He hurt all of us. Not all men cheat."

Emma ran up to them. "Did you see? Did you see?"

"No, sweetheart, what?" her grandmother said, grateful, Amy could see, for the interruption.

"It skipped seven times!"

"Wow! That must be a record!"

Dorothy took Emma's hand and they stood together, talking about the pebbles and looking out at the sound toward the sea. Amy didn't know if her mother had really heard her, but she realized it didn't really matter. She'd faced the truth, faced her own desire to live in a fairy tale. Now she knew she could let that go.

The walk home was quiet, the two women swinging Emma by the hands. There was a small package on the front porch next to the door.

"It's addressed to you," Dorothy said, handing it to Amy so she could unlock the door. "Did you have your mail forwarded? Who on earth even knows you're here? Mmm, that chicken smells good. I'll bet it's done."

Emma ran ahead of her grandmother into the house, hurrying to go show Riley her small collection of shells. Amy slowly followed, looking at the address on the box. Her name was printed in black ink on the plain brown wrapper. No return address.

"Oh, yes, it's just perfect," she heard her mother say as she placed it on the secretary in her mother's living room and fetched a silver letter opener from one of the drawers. The paper fell away. Inside was a plain cardboard box. Her mother hummed in the kitchen and something clattered in the sink.

She sliced the tape that held the lid closed. Lifted the white tissue paper inside. And screamed.

"Jesus, Amy! What on earth is the matter?" Dorothy Busby stood in Amy's peripheral vision, hand to her chest. Amy couldn't look at her; she couldn't look away from the box. Lying on a bed of cotton was a severed white finger, complete with lacquered red nail.

Her stomach heaved and Amy held one hand to her mouth, waving her mother off with the other hand. "Don't look!" she cried. "Don't look!"

Another ear-splitting scream, this time from Emma. Amy ran for the back door, her mother ahead of her.

Emma was standing near Riley's house, the dog at her feet, screaming and screaming. There was red on her face and her hands.

"What? What is it?" Amy grabbed her by the shoulders, checking her for injuries.

"Riley's dead! Riley's dead!"

Only then did Amy notice that the dog hadn't moved, that his head was slumped at a weird angle. She knelt and carefully lifted his head by the fur on top. Blood was thickly matting his neck, dripping onto his front paws and soaking into the grass between his feet. His throat had been slit.

Chapter 37

She'd left without saying goodbye. That wasn't polite. She'd gone before Guy knew if she'd received the pictures. He'd gone to such trouble to deliver them, too. Impersonating a security system employee required careful attention to detail. He created a uniform, complete with fake ID. With a computer, color printer and a laminating machine he could become virtually anyone. That and the magnetized company logo he'd stuck on the van seemed to convince the cops.

After that, it was simply a matter of using the copy of Amy's key that he'd made. He left the envelope in a prominent spot, making sure that they'd been seen. He'd taken such great care with the photos, especially with the lighting, and he'd been pleased with the thought that a professional would be evaluating them.

Amy wouldn't be able to ignore the package. Perhaps she thought she was escaping by staying at her mother's, but it had taken only a little ingenuity to get that information out of the babysitter. After that it was more a matter of when to send her a clear message than how. The how came to him in one brilliant stroke and he enjoyed every bit of the execution, the careful wrapping of his present, the marking of the box.

All of it with gloves of course. Guy was both amused and amazed by the stories of other supposedly brilliant minds who left DNA on stamps or put their fates into the hands of local postmen. When the box was ready, he carried it in a small plastic bag out to the car. When he'd gotten close to the exit, he pulled over to the side of the road and while he pretended to be checking something under his car, actually changed license plates.

Guy wore the drab brown pants and shirt of a delivery-man, but the license plate and the uniform wouldn't stand up to much scrutiny. Killing the dog eliminated his barking, but he had to admit it was an extra little stroke that brought him pleasure.

He'd gotten the idea when he saw Emma playing with the beast, hugging its shaggy neck, lolling around on the same dirty ground. Amy should be more careful. Animals carried germs. She didn't want Emma to catch something, did she?

He befriended the dog with a little whistle and a pat, and once he'd gotten close he slipped the knife from his boot and slit it from ear to ear.

He had a talent for improvisation, for thinking on his feet, for knowing how to seize the day. Violet should have appreciated this in him, but the truth was that she was too pedestrian. She didn't understand that he was exceptional, just that he was different. And different to her was bad. Just like his mother. Another woman of limited vision.

If he had one fault, it was his inability to choose women well, for now it was clear to him that Amy was limited, too. He needed to dispatch her. It was time to move on.

Chapter 38

After Feeney's death, the mood at the station turned both grim and determined. The officers, dispatchers and even the secretaries moved at a faster pace and with resolute looks on their faces. Black ribbons were worn across the badges of uniforms and a makeshift memorial had been set up near the entryway, with an airbrushed photo of Feeney and a small votive candle and flowers.

Despite this, a calm had come over Mark that allowed him to face the longer hours and tedious work of investigation with a determination he'd previously lacked. He wasn't drinking anymore, either. Not that he didn't have a thirst for it, but he didn't need to hide anymore and so much of his drinking had been about hiding.

He stopped for his own health. And he stopped for his partner. Partner as in boyfriend. It was still a hard word for him to say. He couldn't say it at work. He hadn't said it yet to his parents, but he would just as soon as the stress of this case was behind him.

He told his parents he was moving back to the city just as soon as he helped them find a night nurse for his father. He'd said he was going to be staying with a friend, but he thought his mother might know. Once this case was behind him he would talk to her, talk to them.

Done fighting with his own feelings, he was finally free to enjoy them, to enjoy being in love, to enjoy having someone to wrap his arms around.

The hard part was going to be getting up and out of Manhattan early in the morning. He couldn't keep up this commute, he was already thinking about transferring back to the NYPD and maybe law school. He'd thought a lot about going to law school and it was something Ash was encouraging him to think about.

Sophisticated Ash, who'd come out at prep school when he was fifteen, was amused by his transformation and more than a little pleased to be the cause of it.

"You've got the most hopeful look on your face," he said when he swung open the door the next night after their reconciliation. "I feel just like the Pope about to offer a benediction."

In six months of fighting his own desires, Mark had suppressed the simple pleasures he'd shared with Ash. Watching TV together. Sharing a meal. Snuggling in that ridiculously large bed.

"You thinking about banging someone?" Black interrupted his reverie and Mark blushed.

"Yeah. You were." Black grinned, looking more than ever like an albino jack-o-lantern. "Caught you out, hound dog." He thrust a sheaf of paper at Mark. "Look at this and tell me if you notice anything."

"What is it?"

"Employment records from the Steerforth Hospital for the last three weeks for our good buddy Ryan Grogan." His grin threatened to split his face.

"No way." They'd been working their way through the list that Amy Moran had given them. Ryan Grogan's name had been low on the list. He knew the last names on the list had been added almost as an afterthought, like she didn't even remotely consider them to be possible suspects.

"Yes!"

Mark scanned the papers eagerly. "A late shift on the Sylvester murder and out sick on Feeney's.

"Bingo."

"But he was on the clock when Meredith Chomsky was murdered."

"So he swings by that house on the way in or he takes one of the vans out there."

"Yeah. It's possible. But we've still got Douglas Myers unaccounted for that first morning, plus he could have done day two and three and he has motive. What's Grogan's motive?"

Black frowned, tapping his hand on the edge of Mark's desk. "No idea, but I'll bet he's got one somewhere. Plus, how much of a motive does he need if he's serial? For all we know he's been killing them for years and hauling them around in the EMT vehicle."

"I've been trying to track down Douglas's history, see if there are any hits with New Jersey. I'll add in Grogan. See if I can find any links."

This was among the most tedious parts of police work, but the stuff that usually paid off. It was three days since the last crime scene had been cleared and the early word from the crime lab wasn't great. The partial they'd taken from the back door turned out to be Feeney's and results weren't back yet from the black fibers found in the pool house.

They were going to need some other piece of evidence, if not a positive ID, before they could nail the Toolman and who knows how many more people he would kill before they managed it.

He called the hospital to request that a copy of Ryan Grogan's resumé be faxed over and then pulled the copy of

Myers's off the fax machine. He'd had to call Braxton Realty three times to send it. The office had completely shut down since Poppy Braxton's murder.

Douglas had been working for Braxton Realty for twenty-odd years, putting him in Steerforth during the killings in New Jersey. Disappointing, but not definitive. He could have traveled the distance to troll for victims.

And this was interesting. Before getting his realtor's license, he'd worked for a small law firm in Union, New Jersey. Right next door to Elizabeth.

The thing was, though, that he didn't peg Douglas for the crimes. There was something smarmy about him, no doubt about that, but that didn't make him a killer. Still, his instincts could be wrong. It wouldn't hurt to call this other company and see if they remembered old Doug.

The fax machine was churning. The record keepers at the Steerforth Hospital were gratifyingly efficient. He scanned the sheets of paper quickly.

A single line, buried in the middle of the page, sent him running for his jacket.

Chapter 39

Blood coated Emma, but Amy scooped her up against her body, muffling her daughter's screaming against her chest, holding her shaking body as tightly as she could, but she couldn't undo what had happened.

"Oh my God," Dorothy Busby kept saying, the closest she came to cursing, literally wringing her hands. "I don't know what to do—oh my God. Riley! Oh my God! We should call the police." She turned toward the house but Amy grabbed her arm.

"No!" she said. "We can't go in the house!"

Which was how they ended up standing in neighbor Shirley Montague's kitchen while she hurriedly made coffee and tried to comfort Emma with offers of cookies, candy, cake, soda.

Emma shook her head to refuse each offer, but didn't speak. She'd submitted to Amy's handwashing, so at least the fingers stuck in her mouth were clean. Riley's blood coated the rest of her.

Amy and her mother watched from the kitchen window as five squad cars came speeding up the quiet cul-de-sac and screeched to a halt in front of the Busby home. Cops leapt out with guns drawn. Two officers waited behind the squad cars with guns drawn on the house.

Ten minutes slowly passed. Finally, one cop came out the front door and ambled down the steps to the street. Clearly, he didn't have anything substantial to report, and after a few minutes of conferring with a policewoman, she in turn strolled toward the Montagues'.

"Whoever did it isn't here now," the officer said, refusing the offer of a seat and a cup of coffee from Shirley Montague. Instead she ushered Amy and her mother outside, away from Emma.

"It doesn't look as if anyone entered the house," she said, addressing Dorothy Busby. "There are no signs of forced entry."

"There never are," Amy said.

The officer gave her a strange look. "Do you know who did this, Miss—?"

"Moran. Amy Moran. I'm her daughter."

The officer jotted this down. Amy tried to explain, succinctly, what she thought had happened. What the finger meant. Why she was staying at her mother's instead of Steerforth.

At one point the officer interrupted her to unclip the radio on her belt and relay some of this information to someone else.

A cold calm anger had taken hold of Amy. He had followed her. He knew where she was and he'd come after her. He was toying with her, hurting those close to her. She thought by leaving Steerforth that she would be safe, but she saw now that she'd been wrong.

"We can go stay with Michael," Dorothy said. "There's plenty of room since they put on that addition. We'll be safe there."

Amy shook her head. "I'm going back to Steerforth."

"What are you talking about?" Her mother looked at Amy as if she'd lost her mind. "You'll be safe at Michael's."

"I won't be safe anywhere. You take Emma, but I'm going back."

A loud wail startled them. Emma had come out of the house behind them. "No!" she cried. "Don't leave me, Mommy!"

"I'm not leaving you, sweetie. You're going to go visit your cousins. Wouldn't you like that?"

"Are you coming?"

"Not right now. You'll go with Nana."

"No! I want you, Mommy!"

Her breaths were shorter, wheezier and Amy saw the signs in the circles around her eyes and the bluish tint to her lips.

"She needs her inhaler," she said and sprinted across the street past the officers and into the house. Her purse, where in the hell was her purse? On a chair in the hall. She grabbed it and flew back outside.

"Here, Em, here." She scrabbled through the purse until her hand closed on the inhaler. She shook it and held it up to her daughter's mouth. "Here, sweetie, here."

Emma sucked in the medicine. Amy did it again. Emma's skin was pale, but her breathing seemed a little less ragged.

"Don't leave me, Mommy! Please don't leave me." Tears ran down her cheeks mixing with Riley's blood. It came away on Amy's hands as she gently wiped her daughter's eyes.

Why had he killed Riley? Wasn't it enough to send her that package? Riley wasn't a threat to anyone, if he barked at all it was in friendly greeting and he'd been chained. Why did he have to kill Emma's favorite pet?

With a sudden, horrible clarity, Amy understood. Her hands stopped moving comfortingly over Emma's cheeks and she enveloped her daughter in a fierce embrace.

"Amy? What is it?" Dorothy said.

"I'm taking Emma with me," she said. "I can't leave her."

"That's ridiculous," her mother said. "Emma will be much safer at Michael's and you know it. So would you, but you're too stubborn to realize it."

Amy shook her head. "He's found us here. He'll find us wherever we go. I'm not running anymore. I'm going to catch this son-of-a-bitch."

"Oh, Amy," her mother said with disappointment and for a second Amy thought it was because she'd done something so unladylike and actually cursed. But then tears slipped down Dorothy Busby's face and she reached for her daughter, clutching her the way that Amy had clutched Emma, and Amy realized that her mother was frightened for her safety.

While her mother talked with the police, Amy dragged out the suitcase she'd packed barely three days ago. There was no one else on the second floor when she went into her mother's room and took down the silver lock box from the closet.

She took the gun still wrapped in the towel and tucked it in her purse. With it safely hidden, she relocked the box and put it back on the shelf.

They made it back to Steerforth in record time, Emma singing along to a Wiggles CD and Amy thinking, hard, about what she was going to do once they got to town.

It was dusk when they drove down Main Street, the streetlights going on just ahead of them, giving the effect that they were bringing light back into town.

"I'm tired, Mommy. I wanna go home."

She knew she couldn't risk taking Emma back to the house, not even with police protection and she'd already made arrangements.

"We're going to see Chloe, sweetie, remember?"

Chloe was standing at the front window and waved energetically before running out of the seedy duplex to greet them.

"Hi, Em'n'm," she greeted Emma, using a nickname that usually made the little girl giggle. This time Emma could barely manage a smile.

"She's really tired," Amy apologized, hauling out Emma's blanket and the bag filled with inhalers, nebulizer and emergency information.

"Well, I've got my bed all set up for her." Chloe led the way back into the home she shared with two other college girls. The living room was full of the greasy cheese smell of the half-eaten pizza open on the trunk that served as a coffee table. A chunky girl whose name Amy never remembered was sitting at a desk, plugged into a laptop and an iPod. She acknowledged them with a wave and a smile and went back to whatever she was typing.

"Madison's out with her boyfriend," Chloe said, flipping the box lid closed. "So it's just me and Whitney."

She led the way down the hall to her bedroom, a small space that Chloe had done her best to spruce up. A double bed complete with an Indian cotton bedspread took up most of the room and she'd hung little lights along the window frame, which distracted from the fact that it looked out at a brick wall.

Amy put Emma carefully down on the bed and watched her daughter curl up with her doll and blanket. "I hope she just sleeps for you," Amy said. "I'm not sure when I'll be back, but with any luck it won't be more than a few hours."

Chloe nodded her head earnestly. It was one of the reasons that Amy liked her, that wholesome sincerity. They walked out of the bedroom and Chloe pulled the door mostly shut. "Good luck and be careful," she said in a low voice. Amy handed over the bag of equipment.

"You too," she said. "I hope it goes smoothly and you don't have a cranky little girl on your hands."

They both laughed, but Amy felt a pang of anxiety as she stepped back out of the house. "You've got my cell number, right?" she called to Chloe, who stood on the porch under the warm glow of a porch light. The young woman nodded and waved.

Amy drove straight from Chloe's to the police station. She knew what she was going to do. It was what she should have convinced them to do long ago.

The grizzled-looking sergeant's eyes widened at the sight of her, but he was on the phone. "Uh-huh," he said, "yes, ma'am, it does sound like someone should come out and look. I'll send a car." He held up one meaty finger to indicate he'd just be a minute, balancing the phone on his ear so he could scribble something onto a pad. "You bet," he said. "No problem."

He hung up and stood up. "Is everything okay, Mrs. Moran?" Too late Amy remembered the bloodstains on her clothing. "What happened?" he said, "Are you hurt?"

"It's not my blood," Amy said quickly. "I'm fine. I really need to see Detective Juarez."

But the sergeant shook his head. "I'm sorry, Mrs. Moran, but he's not in."

"But I called about an hour ago. I left a message that I was coming. He's not here?"

"No, ma'am, he's not. He probably didn't get that message because he left a couple of hours ago. Some investigative work out of town. I don't know when he's getting back."

"Out of town? Where?"

The sergeant hesitated, but then seemed to decide there was no harm in giving her the information. "He's gone to New Jersey."

"Why? Has he found something out? Does he have a suspect?"

"Look, I don't think I can tell you anything."

"This is my life at stake!" Amy cried. His eyes widened and she took a deep breath, trying to calm down. "Look, the killer found us." She explained about the blood coating Emma. She explained about the package.

He listened intently, shuddering when she described the

finger, and then he asked her to have a seat while he made some calls.

She sank down on the bench and closed her eyes, trying to relax. Fifteen minutes later the sergeant beckoned to her.

"Our detectives talked to the officers who responded to your mother's house," he said. "Detective Juarez has been alerted and he'll be back ASAP. He left something for you."

He handed over an envelope. She ripped it open. Inside was a single sheet of paper with a few words scribbled on it.

For a second she thought there'd been some mistake, that she misunderstood what he meant. She looked up at the sergeant and back down at the paper.

"Does it make sense?" he said.

"No," she said, shaking her head. She looked at the words again, struggling to accept it: "Need to confirm with witness, but it looks like Ryan Grogan."

Patty Bulowski's street seemed just as dismal the second time around, but Mark was expecting an easier reception. He saw that the dog dish had been cleared of leaves and some actual food had been left in it. Otherwise, things seemed pretty much the same, all the way down to the recorded barking that played as soon as he rang the doorbell.

He whistled as he waited for her to answer, feeling confident for the first time that he was finally, finally going to nail this bastard. Steerforth Hospital had been fairly cooperative, allowing him to take a couple of pictures he found on the bulletin board in the lounge. He didn't know what they'd say to Ryan Grogan if he noticed them missing, but by the time that happened he'd be coming back to get him with an arrest warrant.

He rang the doorbell again and the barking continued. He'd left his gun and holster hidden under the passenger seat of the car, anticipating having to endure Patty Bulowski's pat-down. Finally the barking stopped and the door opened, the security chain still in place.

"I already talked to you!" she said through the crack. He could see her eyes above the chain nervously scanning the walkway. "I don't have anything more to tell you."

"I have some pictures for you to look at."

"No."

"Don't you want to get this guy off the streets?"

"That's your job, not mine."

The door slammed. He rang the bell again and when that didn't bring a response he laid on the buzzer with his thumb and waited.

"Go away!"

"This guy has killed again and this time he killed a cop, too. I'm not leaving, Ms. Bulowski. I can't. You're the only person left alive who's seen this guy. I know you don't want another woman to suffer what you've suffered. Please, Ms. Bulowski. It will only take a minute."

The door swung open fully and there she stood, this time wearing faded jeans that made her legs look like sticks and an enormous white sweatshirt with Niagara Falls splashed in blue across the front.

She wouldn't let him in this time, but she held out her hands for the prints. "Let me see."

He hurriedly opened the manila envelope and pulled out the pictures. He'd enlarged the small color photos, which seemed to have affected the skin tone of the white people in the photo, who now looked like they all had sunburns, but their features were still visible.

Patty Bulowski looked carefully at the first photo of Ryan and the paramedic crew while Mark looked carefully at her. There was no sign of recognition, though she scanned the faces of the paramedic crew slowly.

She handed it back to Mark and shook her head. He managed to hold back the curse, but he felt anxious. The trouble he'd taken to get the photos enlarged and then to drive all the way up here—what if it was for nothing?

He handed her the second photo, bracing himself for the same lack of reaction. This photo was in better focus at least. Ryan Grogan and his partner stood grinning in front of the hospital. Patty Bulowski took one look and gasped. She thrust the picture back at Mark.

"Is he in this photo, Ms. Bulowski? Do you see him?"

She nodded, one hand clenched to her mouth, the other wrapped tightly around her waist.

"Just point to him," he said, holding the photo for her. Her hand shook as she extended it and tapped the photo once.

Chapter 40

Louisa Grogan, sixty-five years old and feeling easily a decade older, stood at the stove in the house she wouldn't leave, the house she'd bought with her very own hard-earned money, and stirred a pot of soup.

Time was, years and years ago, she would have made it from scratch, not poured this thin crap from a can. When Ryan was a baby she'd made soup from scratch. That was during her homemaker days, the few there'd been. A colicky baby, a husband whose eyes were already looking toward a future that didn't include her and the child, a cheap rental home with a landlord that ogled her even as he was demanding the rent.

She'd been something to look at back then. Not like now. She'd been what they'd used to call a "looker." So she'd tried to be a keeper, too. Tried to apologize to Frank with homemade meals for the way her body had trapped both of them with this crying, whining, demanding bundle of flesh.

So she'd made soup. And bread. And waxed the peeling linoleum floors, and lined the chipped paint cupboards with paper, and cleaned the baby's messy diapers and wiped the snot from his nose and tried to pretend that she was just an ordinary Connecticut housewife. And then Frank left.

For three days she'd lain in bed, veering between screaming fits that she hid in her pillow and crying jags that went on for so long that she burst blood vessels in her face.

On the fourth day she went out and got a job. And because she had no one to watch Ryan, she'd left him home alone. She'd be sent to prison for that today. Even then, she'd have gotten in trouble if anyone had heard him crying, but nobody paid that much attention to crying kids in those days. And Ryan learned early that he'd better not cry if he wanted to eat.

If it was a hard life for a kid, he hadn't complained. He was a good boy. Not as good looking as his father had been, but not as flighty either. Who knew what had happened to Frank. Probably gone out to California and changed his name. She'd given up looking for his face in those tabloids years ago.

The soup began to boil and she turned the burner off and poured it into a bowl. Her back was aching. Her feet were aching. She was paying for all those years of fast food and limited exercise. Walking up and down the stairs, showing off other people's homes was some exercise, but not enough.

Ryan was all for her selling the house, probably thought she'd split the profits with him, but he didn't know the first thing about real estate. This house was her biggest and best investment. Even if the real estate boom ended she could still make a killing any time she wanted to. Besides, she loved this house and they could carry her out in a box.

At one point she'd actually thought Ryan might have gone into real estate with her. She'd thought about leaving the firm in New Canaan and setting out her own shingle in Steerforth with her son as her fellow agent. But he'd always been more interested in blood and guts than money.

The soup tasted like chicken-flavored water, but she ate it along with the piece of whole-wheat toast spread ever so thinly with some soy product that pretended it came from the dairy family. She tried to imagine that all of it was what she really craved: a fat, juicy steak and a baked potato slathered in butter with a big dollop of sour cream on the side.

A knock at the back door startled her. She wasn't expecting anybody. Ryan said he had a shift tonight, and she didn't really have many friends in this town, what with working all the time.

She got to her feet and shuffled toward the door in her slippers, cursing the bad genes that had given her varicose veins. If he'd forgotten his key again she was going to kill him.

She switched on the porch light, but the bulb had burned out. It was too dark to see much, especially with the kitchen light on, but she pulled back the curtain and could just see the shadowy outline of a man.

"Ryan?"

The response was a muffled and impatient, "Yes."

It wasn't her fault he'd forgotten his key. She let the curtain drop and struggled with the lock and chain. The door opened and in walked death.

Amy stood outside the police station wondering what to do. She'd had some master plan and now it all seemed like folly. She was in shock. It couldn't be Ryan Grogan. How was that possible? Bile rose in her throat as she thought of sleeping with him.

The only thing to do was wait for Detective Juarez to return. If it was really Ryan, then maybe they'd arrest him without using her as bait. She'd been prepared to push for her plan, but now it seemed sickening. She couldn't bear the thought of seeing Ryan Grogan.

Chloe's answering machine picked up after three rings. Three girls' voices, each one identifying themselves separately, encouraged her to leave a message.

"Hey, Chloe, it's Amy. I'm on my way. See you in a few minutes."

Chapter 41

The same roommate Amy had seen earlier answered the door, this time dressed in a robe, her hair damp. She smiled.

"I've got the bag right here. C'mon in, I'll get it."

Amy stepped inside, confused. "Bag?"

"Yeah. Here it is." The roommate turned around with the bag of asthma equipment that Amy had given to Chloe. "I saw it as soon as they left and I tried to call Chloe, but she must have had her phone on vibrate or something and she didn't pick up."

"I don't understand. I'm here to pick up Emma."

It was the roommate's turn to look confused. "But she's with Chloe—they went to that guy's house."

"What guy?"

"The friend of yours who called. Sorry, but I can't think of his name. He said that you and Emma were staying at his house tonight and asked if Chloe would bring Emma over. There was some reason." She thought for a moment, brow furrowed. "Something with a P. Pete?"

Amy was surprised. "Paul?"

"Yeah! That's it!"

"Oh. Well, okay, then. I guess I'll meet them there."

She took the bag from the roommate's hand and started down the path. Suddenly she stopped and turned around. The door was about to close.

"Hey!" Amy called.

The roommate stopped, holding the door open, obviously shivering. "Yeah?

"What time did they leave?"

"Um, about thirty minutes ago?"

It was presumptuous, but Paul was like that. His friendliness didn't seem to have boundaries. He probably thought she'd be grateful, but she couldn't possibly stay overnight at his place. It sent all the wrong messages.

She felt a little uneasy when she couldn't get Chloe on her cell phone and that only increased when she didn't see Chloe's car parked outside of Paul's place.

She had to ring the doorbell twice to get any response, though she could hear what sounded like a TV drama.

When the door finally opened it was a young, pudgy woman with dirty blonde hair and a sour look on her face who answered it, jiggling Paul's son on her hip.

"Yeah?" She gave Amy a once-over that seemed to find her lacking.

"I'm here to get Emma."

"Who's Emma?"

"My daughter. I'm Paul's friend, Amy Moran."

Something changed in her face. "So where the fuck is he?"

"I don't understand," Amy said. "He's supposed to be watching my daughter, Emma, along with Brendan."

"Who's Brendan?"

There had to be something wrong with this woman. Amy pointed at the baby in her arms. "Paul's son."

The woman scowled. "This isn't Paul's son, it's his nephew, and he was supposed to be babysitting him."

"Oh." She must have mixed them up. "Well, where's Paul's son?"

The woman's laugh was a bark. "Paul doesn't have a son."

Amy stepped back, stunned. "What?"

"He doesn't have a son," the woman repeated, more slowly as if Amy was dense. "He doesn't have any children."

"I don't understand," Amy said, reeling. "His wife, who died from cancer. They had a son."

The woman laughed again. It was a nasty sound. "He had a wife all right. But she didn't die from cancer. She left him."

She started to close the door and Amy hurriedly pushed against it. "So Emma isn't here?"

"Why would she be here?"

"I told you—Paul's supposed to be watching her."

"Well, then I guess he's got her at his place."

"This is his place!"

"No, this is my house." The woman pushed against the door, but Amy had her foot inside.

"Where does he live?"

The woman sighed. "An apartment on Emerson."

"What's the number?"

"Oh, for God's sake. Wait a minute." She disappeared for a moment and returned with a slip of paper. "Forty-two twenty Emerson. Apartment 5J. Now leave me alone."

She drove as fast as she could, hoping that a cop would spot her reckless driving. Cars honked, someone swerved to avoid her and another driver swore out his window, but the police force of Steerforth was absent.

Digging in her purse for her cell phone while driving with one hand didn't make for a smooth ride. She swerved to avoid hitting a parked car as she hit the speed dial. The line was busy.

"Shit!" Amy pounded the steering wheel in frustration. She knew where Emerson was, a block of less-than-desirable housing on the fringes of town. Number 4220 turned out to be an ugly red brick building with old aluminum windows and awnings. She searched for 5J on the buzzers and pushed it. Then she pushed all of them. The door buzzed open. She skipped the elevators, taking the stairs two at a time. The fifth floor was deserted, the hallway dim from dusty overhead lamps and ancient carpeting. It smelled like mold and Indian cooking.

She pounded on Apartment 5J, but nobody came to the door. "Paul? Paul, are you in there?" she called loudly.

The apartment next door opened a crack and she saw two eyes in an old face peering out at her.

"I'm looking for Paul Marsh. Is he here?"

The eyes blinked and then there was a tiny shake of the head.

"Please. I'm looking for my daughter," Amy could hear her voice cracking. She tried to hold it together. "Paul is supposed to be watching her. I think she's inside."

"There's a super," a tremulous voice said. "First floor."

Back down the stairs, the stairwell echoing with the sound of her foot strikes. She saw a door close to the elevator with a sign next to it that read, "John Pritchard, Super."

Again, she pounded, pressing her other hand against the doorbell. This time the door opened almost immediately.

"Yes?" The man was huge and angry looking.

"I'm a friend of Paul Marsh. Nobody's answering the door and I think my daughter's in there."

He wasn't easily moved, but when she threw in "urgent" and "asthma," he relented.

He insisted on taking the elevator up. "I'm not climbing five fucking flights of stairs, lady, emergency or not."

Then he had to search the enormous key ring he'd brought along, all with identical-looking keys. "Five A, five B, five H. Here we go, Five J."

The door swung open onto an unlit hallway. John Pritchard reached for a light switch and Amy could see a living room beyond. "Paul?" the super called. "Paul, you here? You got company."

He turned to her with an accusatory look. "There's no one here, lady."

"Look, he has my daughter. I don't know where he is but I need to find him. Maybe he left me a message."

She started down the hall and Pritchard grabbed her arm.

"Whoa, miss. How do I know this isn't some kind of scam?"

"Because I'm telling you it isn't." She shook him off and thrust her purse at him. "Here. Hold this. You can check my license. I'm Amy Moran. My daughter's inhaler is in there. Her name is Emma."

The apartment was small and sterile. Meticulously neat. There was no sign of Emma having been there. Completely panicked, Amy raced through the rooms. Something seemed strange about the living room and the small dining area, but she couldn't place it until she came to the bedroom. There was an enormous, intricately carved mahogany bed taking up far too much room and she realized that all the furniture was oversized for the apartment. The large sectional sofa in the living room, the too-long table in the dining room. It had all been made for a big house, not this tiny, cramped apartment.

Positioned at the head of the vast purple comforter were two green velvet throw pillows embellished with purple rope. The center of each had a different initial embroidered in purple flowers. A large *G* and a large *V.*

The small, sliding closet held neatly arranged men's clothing. The only thing out of place in the room was the silver picture frame lying facedown on the mahogany nightstand wedged between the wall and the bed. Amy lifted it. A beautiful woman with long, black hair and deep blue eyes smiled out at her. Could this be Paul's wife?

She let it drop and hurried out of the room, heart pounding. The second bedroom had been turned into a home office. Here was another oversized piece of furniture, a burnished cherry desk crammed into the space with a large leather desk chair. The top was empty except for a computer and a framed photo of a house under construction. The house looked vaguely familiar.

She jerked open desk drawers, looking for something, anything that would tell her where he might have gone with Emma. Office supplies neatly arranged in a little sliding tray. Reams of paper. A roll of stamps. Padded envelopes. In the bottom drawer she found a locked wooden box. Amy grabbed a letter opener to try and jimmy it, but a faint humming noise caught her attention.

It was coming from the closet. She pulled back the door and the noise grew louder. A small, white freezer stood on the floor, its cord running along the closet wall and out into the room to a wall socket. It was locked, too, a silver padlock dangling from the lid. Amy tried it anyway, but it wouldn't give.

The letter opener didn't fit the padlock. She turned to the wooden box again and managed to pry the thin metal blade of the letter opener under the lid before it abruptly snapped.

Her panic became fixed on finding out what he kept locked up. She had to know what he had in the box and even more what he had in that freezer. Why were they locked? Where were the keys?

She swept through the desk again, scattering its contents in her search. At the back of one drawer she found a strange thing for a man's desk. A tin box filled with bottles of nail polish in different shades. As she shoved it back in place, pondering what on earth he wanted it for, she heard something rattle. She quickly pulled the tin back out and lifted away some bottles. Skating about on the bottom was a silver key.

It didn't fit the padlock on the freezer, but it slipped easily into the keyhole on the wooden box and turned smoothly. She lifted the lid and saw women's jewelry spread out upon a blue velvet lining. Mostly rings. Circles of gold and platinum or studded with gems. A few necklaces. A golden brooch sparkling with what looked like real emeralds. And another key.

She tried it in the freezer lock and it fit. Amy fumbled with the padlock, struggling to pull it off. The lid opened with a sucking sound and she was immediately assailed by an awful smell, like rotting fruit. She let it drop, gagging.

One hand covering her nose, she lifted the lid a second time, trying to breathe through her mouth. There were stacks of small, white cardboard boxes, all neatly labeled. They reminded her of checks boxes.

She took out the topmost box and let the lid drop back down on the noxious odor. The box felt empty. She set it down on top of the desk and lifted the lid. Then she screamed.

Lying on a bed of cotton was a human finger.

Chapter 42

The skin was pale, almost translucent, the nail painted hot pink. Amy dropped the lid, staggering back, tripping in her anxiousness to get away, falling on her knees to the carpet and vomiting until her stomach was raw with the effort.

Her mind reeled. Paul was the one who'd sent the finger to her. Paul was the killer. He'd killed Sheila, Meredith, Poppy. He would kill Emma.

She pulled herself up using a corner of the desk, her legs shaking so badly she wasn't sure she'd be able to stand. But she had to get up. She had to find her daughter.

Blinking and choking, Amy stared at the photo so her eyes wouldn't stray back to the box. The house came into focus and suddenly Amy recognized it. This was the property that Sheila couldn't unload. The Bellamy estate that all the realtors were talking about. The house that nobody wanted to purchase because the original buyers had pulled out late in the process and the home they'd chosen to build was to their specifications and new buyers at this level wanted their own tastes, not someone else's.

Amy grabbed the photo and ran past the startled Pritchard,

who was lounging on the couch, watching a big-screen TV, her purse beside him. She grabbed it, too, and took off with the man yelling after her.

"Looks like a quiet night," Mo Conway said to her fellow dispatcher.

"Now you've jinxed us," Harry Beard complained good-naturedly. He passed her the dish of M&M's they'd been sharing.

"I shouldn't be eating this junk," Mo said, shifting her weight in the chair.

"Yeah, we'll start our diet tomorrow."

They both laughed. The lights blinked on seconds before the beeping sounded. Mo immediately hit the button. "911. What's the nature of your emergency."

"I see a dead lady." It was a high-pitched voice. A kid playing a practical joke? A woman with a squeaky voice? She had to treat it as serious.

"You see a dead lady? Where?"

An address given quickly and carefully. Not a kid then. The voice was giving Mo the creeps. "Hurry. She's in the kitchen. There's a lot of blood."

The call disconnected. Mo tried to reconnect, but there was dead air. She switched to the radio. "We've got a possible homicide on 110 Lewis Street. All personnel respond immediately. Repeat, there's a possible homicide on 110 Lewis Street. All available cars respond immediately."

Detective Black got the call as he was enjoying a piece of homemade pumpkin pie in front of the TV. It was about the only thing his wife made that he liked, but she only made them in the fall and never in such great numbers that he could grow tired of it.

"Black here."

He put down the pie on the coffee table and his wife looked away from *Survivor*, the laundry she was supposedly folding abandoned in a basket at her feet. Her husband listened for a few minutes, making grunting noises.

"Okay. Yeah. I'm on my way."

He slammed the phone down and headed for the door.

"What happened?"

"Killer's struck again."

In her head, Amy was screaming Emma's name over and over again. She'd never been a great believer in women's intuition, but she felt it now. Emma was at that house. Paul had taken her to that house.

The house was in a new plan, somewhere on reclaimed farmland on the outer edges of Steerforth. It was far from town and the water, far from the very things that made living in Steerforth palatable, but then some people didn't want the small, old houses they could get closer in, they wanted these monstrosities, these McMansions.

There were several such developments, but which one was the house in? Try as she might, Amy couldn't think of it. She called the realty office, hoping to find someone in. On the sixth ring Douglas picked up.

"I need to know the address of the half-constructed house Sheila was trying to unload."

"Amy, my dear, how nice to hear from you."

"Hello, Douglas. The address please."

"My, my. Have all social niceties been abandoned? I knew that we didn't exactly get along, but I didn't think there was such overt hostility between us—"

"Douglas, I don't have time for this crap. Please just give me the address."

There was a pause, then she heard some keys tapping.

"It's off Grove Road. Bellamy Estates. Do you have a buyer coming now? You're in route?"

"What's the house number?"

"Fourteen something. It's quite obvious. It's the only one that's half-finished—"

"Great. Thanks!"

"Wait, do you have a live one—"

She hung up on him, returning the phone to her pocket. It rang immediately, but she let it go.

She drove like she was auditioning for Le Mans, taking corners tight, accelerating immediately after them. She floored the accelerator when she hit Grove Road, slowing only when she spotted the sign for Bellamy Estates, taking a hard right corner into it and braking hard to avoid slamming into a gatepost before immediately accelerating again.

The homes at the front of the development were occupied, the road paved. They were all mock colonials and tudors, houses on steroids, with pretentious sweeping driveways and Tara-like columns. There were lamps lit above several entrances, but the curving road was deserted, everyone tucked away inside their own little fantasy palaces.

There was no warning when the road changed back to dirt, her car slamming down with a screeching, grinding noise. Amy bit her tongue as her head slammed against the roof, but she kept her foot on the accelerator, peering out at the darkness surrounding her, trying to find the house she'd seen in the picture.

There was nothing being built back here. Things had been surveyed, gas lines run and the requisite half-acre divisions made, but there were just a few plots where any kind of construction was going on, and those no farther along than digging out the foundations. The same retro streetlights from the rest of the division illuminated the For Sale signs stuck in weedy plots. The listing of some of them was indicative of just how long they'd been there.

Then she saw it. Alone, up a slight elevation to the right, sat a large, two-story, framed but not finished house. She turned onto the driveway leading up to it, which was also unpaved and parked in front of the entrance, bolting from the car, gun in hand, calling out to Emma and Chloe. There was no response.

Wooden planking covered the mud where a walkway and steps would be and Amy raced up it to the front entrance, a finished, dark wooden door with a heavy brass knocker in its center. It was ajar. She pushed it open and stepped inside. The darkness became complete. She couldn't see anything and she stayed near the door, holding the gun outright, grasped firmly in both hands.

"Emma!" Her voice echoed. "Emma! Chloe!" No response, but a distant noise like paper rattling.

Her eyes were adjusting. She could see the grand, two-story entrance hall where she was standing and just make out the curving line of a stairway approximately ten feet ahead.

"Your daughter's okay, Amy."

The voice came from the darkness, a hiss in her ear. She swung left just as Paul stepped into view on her right, and as she swung back he grabbed her arm and with one short, sharp twist he had the gun.

Chapter 43

"Where's Emma?" Amy demanded, as if she was the one who still had the weapon and was not standing defenseless. She had her cell phone in her pocket and she hit the speed dial, but nothing happened.

"There's no reception out here," he said, taking it from her and tossing it away. She heard it clatter in some dark corner. She was breathing hard, stunned at how fast it had happened, afraid for her life, afraid for her daughter, wanting to tear the man in front of her from limb to limb.

"You've been a big disappointment to me, Amy," Paul said, moving slowly toward her, the gun cocked at her the entire time. "A big disappointment."

She automatically stepped back, smacking into a wall. He caught her wrists in one of his hands and pulled her arms above her head. Then he pressed the gun lightly against the hollow in her neck and she tried not to move, though she could feel her heart flailing like a trapped bird. The safety was off and she knew that the cartridge was full.

"I thought you were different," he hissed, moving the gun slowly down, lingering in the hollow between her breasts.

"People know I'm here," she said hoarsely. "They'll get the police."

"People like who?" He sounded unconcerned. His eyes were on the gun at her chest. He nudged the muzzle between the buttons on her shirt. She felt the cold like a brand against her bare skin. His eyes flicked up to hers, the pupils dark in those spookily light irises. She felt his madness most strongly in that moment, like coming face-to-face with a rabid dog or realizing the depth of coldness in a shark's eyes.

"They know you're the one," she said, trying to keep her voice from shaking.

"No they don't," he said with apparent nonchalance, but the gun was moving again, trailing down her body while his eyes stayed locked with hers, and his own breath was getting ragged. He was turned on.

The gun passed over her navel, inched its way farther down, burning her skin with its deceptively light touch. She wanted to knee him in the groin, but then the gun would go off and she wouldn't be able to find Emma. She had to stay still because Emma was here and she had to find Emma.

"They think your boyfriend did it," he said, moving the gun up and down her crotch like it was a vibrator. She thought she might throw up.

"Who?"

"Ryan," he hissed, his voice wet against her ear. "The great superhero. Paramedic man."

The last call of the afternoon had been to help an overweight man who'd somehow fallen and gotten wedged between his refrigerator and sink.

"Fat motherfucker," Anthony said, rubbing his back as they walked out of emergency at the hospital. "He should get one of those gastric bypasses. I'm going to need back surgery. Shit, it's cold out here."

Ryan was only half listening. His own back was aching and his cell phone was vibrating again. It had been vibrating all damn day. The mechanic about needing another day to finish the repairs that were going to cost twice as much as they were supposed to. His mother reminding him, like he needed reminding, that he'd promised to trim that tree in her yard.

The last one from his mother all of forty minutes ago saying she needed him to come home right away. Sounding panicked, of course, which probably meant that she couldn't figure out the VCR or that her email wasn't working.

He got back in the truck and must have slammed the door extra hard because Anthony shot him a quizzical look from the passenger side.

"Relax, man, our shift is over."

"Yeah. Not a fucking minute too soon."

Anthony laughed. "You sound happy. Me, I am happy now that it's over. I'm going over to Linda's. Did I tell you she has one of those whirlpool tubs? The ones with the jets and all? It's big enough for two, my friend, big enough for two." He thrust his groin up and down, looking like a whiter, skinnier version of Michael Jackson, and Ryan smiled despite himself.

He pulled up in front of his mother's house, feeling a little less sorry for himself, and let himself in the front door, surprised that she didn't have the porch light on for him.

"Hey, Ma, I'm here," he called, taking off his coat and dumping it over the back of an armchair in the living room. There were no lights on in there either. Weird, but maybe she was cooking something. He could see light coming from the kitchen.

"You making me dinner?" he called, walking in that direction, turning on lights as he went. One of the dining room chairs was overturned and he righted it. She still hadn't answered him, but maybe she was sulking because he hadn't called her back.

For a moment, just a moment, he thought that she'd stepped out and in a hurry. A kettle sat half-on, half-off one of the burners on the stove, as if it had been put down in a hurry, and there was a cup of tea on the table. He took this in first—the kettle, the cup of tea, the chair pushed back like she'd just been sitting there and had gotten called away. Only she hadn't.

She was on the floor between the table and the sink, lying on her back, her eyes rolled back in her head.

"Oh my God, Mom!" He sank to his knees beside her, feeling for a pulse at her neck but not finding one. Her hands were nailed palm down to the linoleum, her legs wide apart, nylons ripped down.

"Please, please," he said, not knowing whom he was asking and what he was asking for because she was dead, so obviously dead, but he couldn't stop trying. He reached his hand around her neck and his fingers came back bloody, and that and the nails in her hand were enough for him to know what he was dealing with, but he still tried CPR.

When it was clear that wasn't working he realized that he had to get help, that he had to call the police, and he stood up and saw pruning shears on the table next to his mother's teacup and on the other side, laid out as neatly as a knife in a place setting, was his mother's ring finger.

He'd put his hand on the shears, barely touched them, when the kitchen door burst in and a uniformed officer followed, gun pointing at Ryan. "Drop the weapon! Drop it, motherfucker!"

He dropped the shears. He put his hands in the air automatically. He tried to open his mouth to explain, but the officer was screaming. "Get down! Get down! Down, motherfucker, get down!"

And then he was being shoved onto his belly on the floor next to his mother's body, and he was being kicked and cuffed and read his rights, and none of it mattered except that she was dead.

"What the hell are you talking about?" Amy said. "Ryan didn't kill anyone—you did."

"He killed his mother." Paul clicked his tongue. "Such a bad boy." He rubbed the gun back and forth. "Don't worry. The police caught him. They caught the Toolman."

"Did you kill those women in New Jersey?"

"That's very blunt, Amy. Didn't your mother teach you better manners?"

The gun moved to her head. She held her breath, struggling to keep her eyes open and focused. She had to stay alert.

"I told you I'd worked at many different jobs before I became a medical researcher," he said, holding the gun cocked against her temple. "I worked as a repairman for a while when I was in school. Such a fun way to meet people."

He laughed but his eyes were cold. "I enjoy people watching. I always have. I liked watching you, Amy."

Her skin crawled. "How did you get in my house?"

The gun tapped against her skull. "Amy, Amy. I thought you were smarter than that. I picked the lock, of course."

"But how could you do that without anyone seeing you?"

"People don't pay attention to plumbers. And I came in through the back door."

"But I had the chain on."

He gave her a patronizing smile like a teacher explaining things to a slow student. "Once I had the door unlocked, I slipped my hand under the chain." The gun left her head as he used both hands to illustrate. "I slipped a thin wire over the last chain link and slowly drew the wire back while pulling the door closed. Once the door closed on the wire I simply popped the chain free."

He tapped her lightly on the nose with the gun and grinned malevolently. "You never spotted me, did you?"

She shook her head and his smile got broader. There was genuine pride in his voice as he said, "No one ever does. Sheila was completely oblivious."

Amy struggled to keep her voice neutral. "Why did you kill her?"

"She was a bitch!" he shouted and suddenly shoved the gun hard against her pubic bone.

Amy jumped and he laughed. "Are you scared?" he said conversationally. "Sheila begged me for her life, you know. She begged me. Are you going to beg me?"

"Where's Emma?" Amy said, unable to stop her voice from shaking. The gun traced the inside of her thigh.

"I told you that Emma is fine," he said in a bored voice. He leaned in closer and his voice dipped. "You know, you could have been the one." He licked a corner of her ear and she flinched. "I thought you were the one." He suckled on her earlobe. She could feel her earring clicking against his teeth, his teeth against her skin.

"I am the one," she said, trying to sound seductive. "I am the one."

He stopped abruptly and pulled back. The gun lifted off her skin. She couldn't see his expression, she didn't know what he was thinking until the gun hand rose and he slammed her in the face.

She cried out, the force of it banging her head off the drywall behind her. She could taste blood. For a moment all she saw were pinpoints of light. He took her arm while she was still blinded and jerked her along.

"You're not the one," he said and she felt the first step as her ankle slammed against it. She climbed numbly, pulled along by him. "You were never the one. It was a trick. You tricked me, Violet."

They'd gotten to the top of the stairs. She pulled against his grip. "Who's Violet?"

He ignored her if he heard her. He was pulling her down a hallway, their feet loud on the plywood subflooring. There was a dim light down the hall. It got brighter. It came from a doorway and he suddenly thrust her ahead of him into the room.

"Emma!"

Her daughter was sitting against a wall, the only other thing in the room besides a Coleman lantern across from her. Duct tape covered her mouth and wrapped around her ankles and presumably around her wrists, which were pulled behind her. Her dark hair was in disarray, her blue eyes wide and wet with tears, her whole being radiating fear. Amy forgot Paul, forgot the gun, forgot everything except her daughter and dropped next to her, kissing her face, her eyes, her covered lips. "Emma, baby, Emma!"

A savage kick against her rib cage knocked her aside and brought back reality. "Sit up!" Paul commanded, pulling her by her hair into a sitting position. He slammed her against the wall near her daughter.

"Let her go," Amy begged. "She hasn't done anything to you—"

"Shut up!" The gun was at her temple again. Amy could feel the wall vibrating with Emma's fear. She kept her mouth shut.

"Where is it?" Paul muttered, looking around. He swung around on Emma. "Where did you hide the tape, you little bitch!"

Her eyes must have flashed in that direction, because at once he turned and saw something in the corner. "Get it!" he commanded Amy.

She started to stand and he thrust her back down. "Hands and knees, bitch! Hands and knees like the bitch you are!"

She scrambled across the plywood floor, feeling splinters digging into her hands and knees, and found the roll of duct tape. She thought of using the heavy roll as a weapon, driving it into him and trying to overpower him, but when she turned back she saw that he was holding the gun to Emma's head. He had a little smirk on his face, as if he knew what she'd been thinking.

He kicked her again once she gave him the tape and made her get back into place against the wall. "You move one fucking inch and I'll kill the girl!"

He put the gun down next to him, eyeing her the whole time, and pulled a box cutter from his pocket. He cut strips of tape, never taking his eyes off her, and she thought of everything she'd ever learned in self-defense classes and tried to appear passive and nonthreatening.

"This could have been yours," he said in a conversational tone as he straddled her legs with his weight, so he could tape her wrists behind her. "This could have all been ours, but you ruined it."

"It's a nice house," she said in a low voice, desperate to say something before he taped her mouth closed and that avenue of escape was over.

"It's a dream house," he corrected her. "A palace fit for a king and queen." He moved off her legs and began taping them together at the ankle. "But it wasn't enough for you, was it, Violet? Always wanting more, more, more!"

"Violet didn't want the house?"

He stopped cutting the tape and blinked at Amy, as if he suddenly remembered who she was. "She wanted it until Sheila. It was Sheila's fault. Violet changed because Sheila told her to change. Sheila was a dangerous bitch!"

"So you killed her?"

He laughed. "Yes, I killed her. But you're like rats, you realtors. For every one I kill there are a thousand more waiting."

"Why did you kill Meredith?"

"Meredith?"

"The woman in the tub."

He laughed. "That bitch. That was for you, Amy. She was giving you such a hard time. I killed her for you and you didn't say thank you."

"Thank you."

He backhanded her again. Amy felt Emma's muffled scream and tried not to let the pain show so she wouldn't cause Emma additional stress.

"Don't be insincere, Amy. It doesn't suit you. You had such promise." He shook his head. "I warned you with that Braxton bitch, but you weren't paying attention. I worked so hard to get her on that surfboard. You wouldn't think a little whore like that would be so heavy, but then dead weight is dead weight."

He chortled suddenly, slapping his knee with glee. "Did you know she liked to watch herself fucking? She had these mirrors set up around her room. Not on the ceiling. Nothing so lowbrow for her. But I knew what they were there for. She was quite the little cunt. I enjoyed shoving the statue up her twat."

All at once there were other sounds. Crunching. A motor. A car door slamming.

"Amy?"

The voice was right outside. It sounded like Douglas. Paul hastily slapped a piece of tape over Amy's mouth and rummaged in a backpack she hadn't noticed behind the lantern.

A door creaked open below them, then slammed closed. "Amy?" This time the voice was inside.

Paul stood up, but it wasn't him anymore. He had a gray beard now, tortoiseshell glasses and a knit hat. She stared, shocked, at the old man from the open house.

Chapter 44

"Any sound and I'll kill you!" Paul who wasn't Paul hissed, tucking the gun in his pocket before running from the room. She heard his footsteps light in the hall and then the sound of him launching down the stairs.

The box cutter had been forgotten near the lantern. Amy inched her way across the floor as fast as she could. She scrambled with her fingers, cutting herself as she struggled to get the blade upright and against the tape.

It cut and she pulled and then one hand was loose. She struggled out of the tape and ripped it quickly off her ankles and face, ignoring the stinging pain. Then she turned to Emma.

As she cut her free, she could hear snatches of conversation Paul was having with Douglas. It sounded like he was claiming to be a client.

"This is going to hurt, baby," Amy whispered when she'd released Emma's arms and legs and was about to take the tape off her mouth. "Not a sound, though, okay?"

Emma nodded. Amy pulled the tape and immediately clapped her hand over Emma's mouth. Her daughter's head reared back, her eyes squeezed shut and nostrils flared with the pain but any words she said were muffled against her mother's hand.

The little girl threw her arms around her mother, tears spilling from her eyes, her body shaking, but Amy brushed them away and gently detached her. Emma's breathing was ragged.

"Do you have your inhaler, baby?" Amy said, checking her daughter's sweatshirt pocket, so incredibly grateful as her hand closed around the plastic. "Good girl. Here. Take a puff."

She gave her one shot and hoped it would help. That was all they had time for. "We're going to play hide-and-seek, baby. You're so good at that, Em. I want you to play it just like we do at home. I want you to hide and don't come out. Whatever you do, don't come out."

She brushed her daughter's hair back from her face.

"But what about you, Mommy," Emma said, whispering too, her little voice bringing tears to Amy's eyes that she quickly blinked back.

Amy put her finger to Emma's lips. "Ssh, baby. Mommy's going to hide, too. But not together, Em. Remember? It never works when you hide together." She pulled her daughter to her and kissed her forehead, taking in her smell, her feel, crushing the little body into hers for as long as she dared, which wasn't nearly enough for a good-bye.

"You go first," she whispered, letting her go. "Stay away from the stairs, Em, and find a good hiding spot. Go now."

She gave Emma a little push and her daughter gave her one more glance and then she was out the door. Gone. Amy turned off the lantern. She slid out the door with the box cutter in her hand and moved as stealthily as she could. She had to get downstairs, but she wasn't sure how. With any luck Paul wasn't on the stairs. She inched closer. Their voices were getting louder.

"I insisted she take my car to pick up Betty and the kids. The cost of gas, you know—plus, it's just safer to have one of these big cars. People don't like to hear that, but it's true. They should be back any second."

She moved closer. She could see them now. Paul had his back to her and Douglas was looking at him. She took another step. Then another. The stairs were going to be tricky. There was a little light in the hall from a streetlamp, but most of the room was in shadow. If she stayed against the wall surely she couldn't be seen. She took one step down. Then the next. The third step creaked and Douglas looked up and spotted her.

His mouth was forming her name, but before he could utter it, Paul had the gun out and shot him point-blank in the head. Douglas dropped like a stone.

"I didn't kill my own mother!" Ryan repeated for the hundredth time. "I've been out all day on calls—check with my partner, check with everybody. I just got off shift!"

The pudgy sergeant wasn't listening to him. He just moved him through the procedures—fingerprinting, mug shot, plunk him down in a room and tell him that things will go easier if he just tells them everything.

"I want a lawyer." Ryan knew that much from watching TV. At which point he was left alone in the room with two cops to watch over him.

"I've just lost my mother," he said to one of them, who stared blank-faced at him. Tears of grief and frustration threatened to spill out and he settled for punching the table, hard.

"Settle down!" the older cop said.

He let his head fall into his hands. And then there was nothing but silence and his own muffled sobs

* * *

Amy screamed and fled back up the stairs, hearing Paul running behind her. She ducked through one room and found a door that opened into another. She stood in a dark alcove and heard his heavy footsteps run past. Slipping out the other door, she listened. No sound for a moment. Then she heard his footsteps in another room and she ran as quietly as possible in the other direction.

There was room after room and in the dark it was impossible to get a sense of where she was. Some rooms had doorways blocked with plastic sheets coated in plaster dust and she fought the urge to sneeze in those rooms, wondering where Emma was, ears straining to hear not just Paul but her daughter's wheezing.

She almost fell down a flight of stairs, but caught the banister in time, and took them carefully, not sure where they led. She came to a landing and turned down another flight into some open space. Her eye was caught by plastic billowing and her foot landed heavily.

Something whizzed past her and then Paul came out through the plastic, following the bullet he'd shot at her. She ran, biting back a scream, and stomped loudly up the first few steps in the front hallway before ducking into a storage space under them.

She heard Paul pounding past and up the steps and she ran away, painfully aware of her own ragged breathing and wondering how Emma was fairing.

"Emma? Emma, where are you? Come out, come out, wherever you are."

His voice was a croon, a spooky high-pitched tone in the empty house. Amy clutched a hand to her own mouth to prevent herself from warning her daughter not to answer him. Emma was smart. Emma wouldn't do that.

"I've got ice cream, Em. It's your favorite. Chocolate chunk. C'mon, Em. I can't eat it all by myself."

Amy felt her way through a freestanding doorway into the incomplete kitchen. This wasn't a safe place to hide, there was light coming in through a corner window. She was turning to leave when she saw the coil of thick wire left by contractors on top of unfinished cabinets. A sawed-off two-by-four lay nearby.

She looked at the wire, thinking something could be done with that, and then she saw the doorframe.

Chapter 45

Moving as fast as she could, Amy wound the wire just above ground level around one plywood post and then pulled it across and secured it tautly around the other. Then she picked up the two-by-four and, summoning all her courage, slammed it as hard as she could against the floor.

In an instant there was clattering on the steps and Amy scooped up the two-by-four and crouched behind the counter, waiting. She heard Paul running in the direction of the kitchen and then a loud *whomp* and a startled exclamation as he tripped over the wire and landed flat on the floor within her reach, gun still grasped in his right hand.

Rising up, the board raised high, she whacked him across the head once and then again. He made a sound after the first blow and no sound after the second. She stepped on his right hand, keeping his other arm pinned with the board just in case, and kicked the gun clear of him. She stooped to pick it up and paused to look at him for a moment. There was blood distorting his forehead and trickling from his mouth. She looked at it and felt nothing.

* * *

Juarez got there first, his car screeching to a stop along the gravel. He got out of the car in defensive position, low and with his gun drawn, as he heard the others pull in behind him.

There was the SUV they'd been searching for. Juarez approached it, shining his flashlight. He smashed open the driver's side door and released the trunk.

"That goddamned bastard," he heard Black exclaim. He joined him and saw a girl's body folded neatly into the small space behind the seats. There was a small bit of dried blood visible around her ear and a dark matted patch in the long blond hair, but otherwise she looked quite peaceful, as if she were sleeping.

The swat team was filing around them like an army of trained robots, ignoring what they were looking at, their eyes focused only on the house. Black and Juarez joined them, their weapons drawn.

There was a silent count and then they entered the house from all sides, Juarez and Black going in the front behind one of the SWAT men. A scream from the left had them running in that direction and they found Amy Moran in the kitchen with Paul Marsh at her feet.

There was blood on her face and bruises, and her eyes were huge in the light from their flashlights, looking from one to the other, only resting when she spotted Juarez.

"It was him," she said in a shaky voice, pointing at the body on the floor. "I've got to find Emma. Emma's here. Emma's hiding."

Chapter 46

"She plays hide-and-seek," Amy said. "It's her favorite game. She's really good at hiding. Really good." She was babbling, she knew, and she could see the disbelief on their faces.

"Emma!" Detective Juarez called, but even he had a pitying look in his eyes.

"Em! It's Mommy! Come out now, baby!"

She was searching every room, every corner. They'd searched the first floor and now were on the second.

"I told her not to come out," she said, explaining it to them, wanting those looks off their faces. There was no way they would find a body. No way. "She's very good at hiding."

Her voice was shaking, her hands were shaking. She moved faster, in and out of rooms, behind doors, in closets. Every corner available. They were no longer helping, just accompanying.

They moved into a bigger room, maybe the master bedroom, and she searched the walk-in closet, but it was empty of everything.

She was desperate. This was one of the last rooms. She had to be here. "Emma! Baby!"

Juarez put a hand on her arm. "Amy," he said, his voice gentle, and she wouldn't take that voice, no, she wouldn't accept it. She shook her head, she pulled away from him. And in that moment of silence she heard it.

The faintest of sounds, it could have been mistaken for something else, the humming of an insect, the buzz of an electric saw. But Amy knew that sound for what it was and ran toward it.

There was a little door in the wall. A laundry chute. She opened it and the wheezing grew louder. Suddenly the cops were around her, using their flashlights to illuminate the space.

Emma was peering up at her, wedged like a little tree frog to the walls. "I'm not a baby," she croaked.

Amy laughed, a little hiccupping laugh that turned into a sob. She reached into the column and under her daughter's shoulders. "You're right," she said and pulled Emma out.

One of the cops had an inhaler and they used that. And then the paramedics had arrived and they gave her oxygen. Amy wouldn't leave her side while she had it, making them wait for the details she knew they would demand. It would wait. It could all wait.

When Emma was pronounced fit, Amy took her hand and led her outside.

"What about Paul? Where is he?" Emma said as they walked down the steps, away from the light and noise.

"Don't worry about him anymore," Amy said. "He's gone." She looked back at the house and then forward to the car that Juarez was leading them toward. "C'mon," she said, giving Emma's hand another squeeze. "We're going home."

Epilogue

Six Months Later

The body of Rachel Norman, aka Violet Marsh, was found on the first really warm day of spring. The man who'd bought the Toolman's house in Bellamy Estates, at a price far less than the original value, was starting over and a workman dismantling the walls found the body nailed into a crawl space. It was exactly one month to the day after her husband and killer had been sentenced to life in prison.

The story made the front page of the *Steerforth Herald* and Amy quickly folded it over, but not before Emma caught a glimpse of the headline: TOOLMAN'S WIFE FOUND DEAD.

"Was that about the bad man, Mommy?"

"Yes."

"Is he back?"

"No, Em. Absolutely not. He's in prison."

"And he's never coming back?"

"That's right."

Emma nodded and turned her attention back to her bowl

of Cheerios. For the first few weeks after their ordeal and during the month-long trauma of the trial, she'd asked Amy about Paul every day. Hearing her mother tell her that the bad man wasn't coming back had become like a mantra.

She'd only recently begun sleeping in her own bed again. Amy hoped this wasn't going to set things back.

"Go get dressed, Em," she said, pulling back her chair. "You don't want to be late for school."

"Yeah," Emma said. "Mrs. Strohmeyer is bringing her pet rabbit to show the class."

She ran for the stairs, the news apparently forgotten. Amy scanned the story quickly and buried the paper in the recycling bin.

Rachel's body was identified by a sister from a neighboring town, who'd apparently believed Paul's story that his wife had left him for another man. "She was like that," the woman said to a reporter. "No one man or one place could hold her interest for long."

If Paul Marsh had any reaction to the discovery of his wife's body, it wasn't mentioned. They wouldn't bother to prosecute him for her death. He'd recovered from the skull fracture he sustained after Amy clubbed him and was declared competent and legally sane to stand trial for the murders of Sheila Sylvester, Meredith Chomsky, Poppy Braxton, Officer Feeney, Louise Grogan, Chloe Newman and Douglas Myers. He'd also been charged with the attempted murders of Amy and Emma, who were both star witnesses for the prosecution at his trial.

Emma held up well under the pressure. The only time she broke down was in describing the death of Chloe, who'd attempted to escape from Paul's car with Emma and was battered in front of the little girl.

Outside of the courtroom was a different story. Emma barely slept at night. She woke up screaming from terrible nightmares. Sometimes Amy did, too. They slept with lights on in the house and Amy installed a top-of-the-line security system.

The day Paul was sentenced to three consecutive life terms, Amy laid flowers on Sheila and Chloe's graves.

Braxton Realty passed to Poppy's younger brother, Peter, who took down the painting of poppies in the field and replaced it with a photo of an America's Cup yacht. Another realtor took over Sheila's desk. Amy limited her showings to daytime or took Emma with her. Most evenings, once Emma was in bed, she worked on her photography. In May she was having her second show in SoHo. This time, she didn't bother to send an invitation to Chris. She did, however, invite Ryan.

The news of the discovery of Violet's body made it into the *New York Times* Metro section, but Ash spotted it before Mark. "Hey, isn't that the guy's wife? Yeah, it is, read this!"

He passed the newspaper across the breakfast table and shoveled another strip of bacon into his mouth.

"I don't know how you can eat that junk and remain so thin," Mark said, putting down his piece of whole-grain toast to take the paper.

"I'm younger," Ash said with a grin. "Faster metabolism."

"Ruder, too."

"What? You are older."

"Wiser."

"Keep telling yourself that," Ash said, rolling his eyes. Mark smiled and looked down at the paper. He'd wondered when he resigned from the force if he'd miss the job, but reading about the discovery of this poor woman's body, he realized that he felt nothing beyond a certain satisfaction that they'd caught this guy.

"You've got classes today, right?" Ash said suddenly.

Mark looked up. "Yep. All day. Why?"

"Your mom called while you were in the shower. She left a message." He got up from the table and walked into the tiny kitchen to refill his coffee.

Mark got up and hit the button on the answering machine. His mother's voice filled the room, sounding hesitant. "Hi, it's Mom, um, I mean, Elena." She cleared her throat and Mark grimaced. "I know this is last-minute notice, but I decided to hold a family dinner party tonight to celebrate your father's success—wait until you hear him, he is doing lots of talking. Anyway, I was hoping that maybe you, that is you and your . . . er . . . you and Ash would like to come."

Mark's mouth fell open and he turned to look at his partner. Ash had his arm wrapped around his own waist and his head ducked over his coffee cup.

"Did you hear that?" Mark said.

"Yeah." Ash avoided his eyes.

Mark walked over to him. "So what do you think?" he said gently. "Do you want to go?"

Ash lifted his head, his eyes now wide with surprise. "Really?"

Mark smiled. "Really."

Amy hustled Emma into her light jacket and set the security alarm before carefully closing and locking the door behind them.

"Who's going to meet me after school, Mommy?"

"I am."

"Are you sure?"

"Yep."

"But what if you have to show a house?"

"I won't."

"So I'll see you after school?"

"Yes. And I know, don't—

"—be late!" They finished together. Emma giggled. She

did this little question-and-answer every morning. It was obviously a comfort ritual and Amy would continue to offer that security as long as it was needed.

She strapped Emma into her car seat and walked around to the driver's side, pausing to admire the tulips and daffodils the warm weather had finally forced up from the flowerbeds. This was her handiwork and it bordered her small frame house beautifully. Her house. Hers and Emma's. It had taken some time, but it finally felt like home.

"We're going camping with Ryan this weekend, right?" Emma asked as Amy drove down the block.

"Right."

"Do you think he knows how to skip rocks?"

Amy smiled. "If not, I'll bet you could teach him."